THE RUBICON
PROTOCOL

KELLY GAY

BASED ON THE BESTSELLING VIDEO GAME FOR XBOX®

TITAN BOOKS

Halo: The Rubicon Protocol
Print edition ISBN: 9781803363158
E-book edition ISBN: 9781803363165

Published by Titan Books
A division of Titan Publishing Group Ltd
144 Southwark Street, London SE1 0UP
www.titanbooks.com

First Titan edition: August 2022
10 9 8 7 6 5 4 3 2 1

A CIP catalogue record for this title is available from the British Library.

Printed and bound in Great Britain by
CPI Group (UK) Ltd, Croydon, CR0 4YY.

HALO

THE RUBICON
PROTOCOL

DON'T MISS THESE OTHER THRILLING STORIES IN THE WORLDS OF

CHAPTER 1

"**S**tone, get those lifeboats deployed now!" Palmer's voice rang sharp in her ears.

"On the last load out, Commander. We've got a total of four seats open."

"*They'll never make it. I'm diverting them to Bay Ten. And watch your tail. It's a mess out there.*"

"Roger that."

A metric ton of titanium support beam pressed on Spartan Bonita Stone's armor-clad shoulders as she held up the corridor ceiling from collapsing. Her muscles burned. Pressure built in her chest, her heart working overtime to process the massive surge of adrenaline flowing through her system. Amid the smoke billowing in the passageway twenty meters ahead, a friendly was making his way to the lifeboats behind her. *Infinity* shuddered again. Power cables and plating fell and sparked and the giant beam she held aloft shifted. Her stance dropped another fifteen centimeters, putting incredible strain on her thighs and knees.

"How . . . much . . . farther?" She squeezed her eyes closed and gritted her teeth.

"Nineteen meters," Ouco, her personal AI, replied.

Stone cracked her eyes open, dialing in on the shadowy figure emerging from the haze. It was a young medic, stumbling and coughing, then suddenly falling to his knees as he gagged on the acrid white smoke of melting cables and circuitry. "Get up!" she shouted. Her muscles began to tremble from fatigue; she'd have to release the beam soon. "Get your ass up right now! If I can hold this damn beam, you can stand! One foot in front of the other!"

"I'm trying," he gasped, barely audible, as a massive fiber-optic cable fell through the broken ceiling, hitting the floor next to him. Several meters behind him, the passageway blew apart and red fragments of what looked like a Banished Seraph tore through *Infinity*'s hull.

The vacuum of space began to pull smoke and fire and debris. Horrified, the medic scrambled to his feet and ran straight for her. As soon as he slid clear under her arm, Stone ducked and pushed herself backward. The beam immediately slammed into the deck. Quickly she turned, took two steps, grabbed the kid by the arm, and raced toward the lifeboat bay, sealing the doors once they were inside.

Only two escape craft remained. Stone pushed the medic toward the lifeboat with one vacant seat left and then paused. Orders were orders and the chain of command had to be respected at all times, but there were still three empty seats in the second lifeboat and hundreds if not thousands of *Infinity*'s crew still stuck on board.

Reports continued to pour in via Spartan Channel, TEAMCOM, the battlenet . . . So many continued to fight their way throughout the massive UNSC flagship, or were already out there in fighters, hounding the Banished.

The heavy thunder of *Infinity*'s 70mm autocannons and Scythe turrets echoed relentlessly as the vessel's super-heavy magnetic accelerator cannons fired tungsten projectiles that could tear clean through an enemy warship in a single shot. Amid the weapons' constant clamor, the ship-wide PA system continued issuing evacuation directives, revising which areas to go to, and which lifesaving measures hadn't yet been destroyed by the Banished fleet. Dozens of alarms blared through the ship until everything sounded like one gigantic sustained roar.

"Spartan Stone!" A lone marine had finished ushering the medic into the first lifeboat, distress clear in her face as she met Stone's gaze. It was time to go.

Stone glanced once more down the corridors, one way now sealed and the other an impassable tangle of twisted metal and fire.

No one else was coming. No one else could.

After the first lifeboat's door sealed, Stone stepped onto the small loading platform and ducked into the second lifeboat, ignoring the sour knot in her stomach and trying to keep her focus on the now versus what she was leaving behind. She closed the hatch and strode down the aisle toward the pilot's seat. "Buckle up tight. And when I say brace, you brace. Got it?"

The response was lackluster. The five faces staring at her were pale and streaked with soot. All the passengers were dressed in standard-issue marine coveralls, a corporal among them.

"We'll be hitting the ground in a war zone. Once we land, weapons ready. I'll debark first." They continued gazing at her. "Hey!" She slammed a fist against the bulkhead, making them jump. "The Banished have taken *our* ship, *our* home, and *our* people. You gonna stand for that?"

A few heads shook and backs suddenly went a little straighter. "Well?"

"Hell, no," the corporal piped up, and then others murmured in agreement.

"That's right. *Hell. No.*"

Angry, Stone slid all four hundred kilos of her TRAILBLAZER-class GEN3 Mjolnir armor into the pilot's seat—no easy feat, but there was just enough room to maneuver.

"Link established," Ouco said. *"Ready for your input, Spartan Stone."*

It was times like these that she appreciated her choice of personal AI. Ouco's steady personality and calming baritone had a knack for setting her at ease no matter the situation. "Initiate auto escape and evasion routine."

"Initiating now."

Behind her, the cabin was eerily quiet. Five souls in her care and nine in the other lifeboat were counting on her to get them through hell in the sky and onto the surface of Zeta Halo.

She opened a channel to the companion lifeboat: "Papa Tango Delta Zero Nine, this is Echo India Bravo Zero Eight, copy?"

"Papa Nine, copy. Reading you loud and clear, Echo Eight."

Wait. She knew that easy drawl. "Murphy . . . is that you?"

The lieutenant and Pelican pilot, well-known among Spartan ranks, should have already been deployed, but should-haves didn't really apply to their current situation. The UNSC *Infinity* dropping out of slipspace smack into a Banished ambush had made navigating certain parts of the vessel impossible. She should know; she should be accelerating to the surface in a drop pod right about now.

"Yeah, lost my ride. Whole damn hangar is gone."

Another blast rocked the ship, the shockwave vibrating through the lifeboat hull as its docking clamps released.

"Roger that," she replied somberly. "Stay glued to my six. We're going to do this together. Sending landing trajectory. Once we're down, we'll be in the thick of it. Get your folks out, find cover, and then wait for me."

"Music to my ears. Will do. Murphy out."

Stone had a wealth of experience when it came to endless war and incursions into uncharted hostile territories; she'd seen her fair share of shocking, unforgettable things, but what she was feeling now was altogether new. That they were abandoning ship—and not just any ship—seemed unreal. *Infinity* was the United Nations Space Command's pride and joy, its flagship, a technologically advanced monster on every front. She wasn't supposed to falter.

And yet, she had.

Infinity had set out on a high-risk mission to stop the rogue AI, Cortana, who had taken control of Zeta Halo and was using it as a base of operations. When they arrived, however, they didn't just find the ancient ringworld—they found the Banished. The captain's steady voice still echoed in her head: *"Captain Lasky to all hands. Banished forces are present above the ring—repeat, Banished forces are between us and our target. All stations engage Banished craft. Infinity, we must reach our target."* And soon after, Commander Sarah Palmer's orders cracking over the ship-wide intercom: *"Spartans, all teams! You heard the captain. It's an ambush. Somehow the Banished beat us to the target. Your orders are simple. Eliminate hostiles with extreme prejudice!"*

"Locks released. Thrusters online," Ouco informed her as the lifeboat drifted from its docking clamps and its thrusters executed a burst to send them away from *Infinity*'s hull.

The lifeboat, an SKT-29 Bumblebee, wasn't equipped for offense or even that much defense; its sole purpose was to propel fleeing personnel down to a surface like an armor-plated bullet.

If they weren't picked off by the Banished first. . . .

Her TEAMCOM channel continued to provide live audio of Fireteam Shadow's activities. Shadow One barked through the speaker: *"Kovan, report!"*

While Stone and Kovan had orders to evac, the other two members of Fireteam Shadow stayed in the thick of things. A quick look at her display showed them hunkered down in *Infinity's* primary hangar bay, holding off the Banished incursion with Fireteam Taurus, who now appeared to be breaking off to begin their descent to the surface of the ring.

"This is Kovan," a calm voice replied. Leave it to Nina Kovan to sound as even-keeled as ever. *"Approaching drop pod now."*

"Good. Those Banished artillery guns are picking off our lifeboats and drop pods as soon as they enter lower atmosphere. Once you hit dirt, you know what to do."

"En route now, Shadow One," Stone informed him.

"See you both on the surface," he replied, and cut transmission.

"Hey, Kovan," Stone said, finally getting a good look at what they were facing as the lifeboat moved away from the ailing ship. "Remember running the HIVEMIND trials on Anvil Station?"

"How could I forget?"

"Factor it by a thousand and this is it."

A collision alert blared through the lifeboat as they cleared *Infinity's* port side, cutting off Kovan's reply. A UNSC Longsword starfighter streaked past, nearly clipping their bow as it swooped up under *Infinity's* hull and hooked a hard left, rotary cannons blazing.

"Initiating final burst," Ouco said.

The push sent the craft into open space, giving Stone an expansive look at the mayhem. Explosions, weapons fire, plasma blasts, and artillery peppered the space all around them as *Infinity* and her support ships gave everything they had. Broadswords, Pelicans, and Longswords crisscrossed space in an effort to take out Banished Seraphs, Phantoms, and Grievers and provide support to lifeboats, drop pods, and troop carriers streaming from *Infinity* while the flagship's escort frigates maneuvered to inflict maximum damage to Banished warships.

Witnessing the Banished force firsthand, the sheer number . . . she hadn't seen anything like this since the end of the Covenant War. Stone wondered what the hell the Banished were doing here. Except for those aboard *Infinity,* the UNSC's mission was—or should have been—virtually unknown. They were attempting to unseat Cortana from her place of power and eliminate the oppressive threat of her forces spread throughout the Orion Arm, something that had cost countless lives over the last year. But now a massive Banished fleet hung in the space between them and the ring, and their chances for even surviving this operation, no less completing it, were plummeting dramatically.

There was a very real risk of getting hit by friendly fire just as much as enemy fire, and while she had the advantage of faster reflexes and response times than most pilots and could use the lifeboat's thrusters to push the tiny vessel to its limits, in a war zone like this they'd be lucky to make it into the atmosphere in one piece.

Collision alerts and modifications came at Stone with lightning speed as, outside the craft, escape shuttles and drop pods exploded or took hits that sent them spinning into others or spiraling out into deep space. And while Fireteam Windfall was using their aerial expertise to provide support, it was literal pandemonium in the skies.

Spartan Vedrana Makovich lit up Stone's comms. *"Hey, Stone, you've got a Phantom coming in fast at nine o'clock!"*

"Thanks, Mako. I see it." And she also saw a way out. Four hundred meters ahead, an enemy dreadnought lay powerless with a gaping hole in its midsection, the victim of a direct hit from *Infinity*'s MAC rounds. They'd already accelerated to ninety-five meters per second and gaining. No time to apply the brakes—not that she'd use them anyway. Burning up the single-use brakes now meant they wouldn't have them later to slow down for landing.

Murphy's voice cut through the din of her comms: *"They've got a lock on us!"*

"Stay on course, Murphy."

"Wait. We're not . . . Stone, you've got to be—"

The lifeboat shot inside the dreadnought, breaking through debris and plating, its reinforced armor like a battering ram—smaller and tougher than the Phantom following them.

"Jesus," Murphy's rattled voice echoed as both lifeboats exited the damaged vessel intact, the Phantom lost somewhere behind them.

"It's not over yet," she said. "Entering upper atmosphere. Hold on."

One hundred and twenty meters per second now.

Stone glanced out the viewport. Thousands of pods and lifeboats, shuttles and ships, and damaged vessels and debris streaked on parallel trajectories toward the surface of a colossal, artificially constructed alien ring designed to both harbor life and destroy it on a galaxy-wide scale. Its inner habitable surface glowed invitingly and deceptively in the darkness of space with familiar tones of blue, green, and white.

Stone kept watch on her readouts, and listened to the channels. A cacophony of voices came through TEAMCOM, while TACCOM was constantly updating intel. As far as she could tell, Captain Lasky and the bridge crew seemed to be in good hands. And Fireteam Taurus along with the other members of Fireteam Shadow had already abandoned ship.

She counted down kilometers in her head; impact was going to be a real bitch.

Lower atmosphere now and the surface of the ring was coming up fast, that ribbon of blue and green getting wider and wider . . .

"Brace for impact!"

"Stone!" Murphy yelled. *"We've been hi—"* The audio filled with static.

She searched for the companion lifeboat through the viewport, not seeing anything. "Hang in there, Murphy!" Then she saw it, spinning out of control, coming in at her two o'clock, the back section completely gone.

"Brace—brace—brace—" the automated system warned as clouds swept past the windshield.

"Bracing positions!" she yelled over her shoulder. "Landfall on the ring in five seconds!"

Those five seconds happened in an instant.

The lifeboat slammed into the ground at a steep angle with an earsplitting *boom*. The impact threw her hard against the harness, and then immediately in the opposite direction, her head snapping back and shoulders plowing into the pilot's seat, breaking its frame. As the crashed lifeboat cut a vicious path through the earth, it shook so hard that even with her Spartan augmentations, it was difficult to focus or do anything but hold on to the harness.

"Ouco . . . speed," she managed.

"Forty meters per second."

The console in front of her suddenly spit out sparks and went black along with the cabin lights, putting them in complete darkness.

"Twenty."

The lifeboat rapidly slowed, finally coming to a stop.

The sudden absence of motion after the chaos of the past several minutes felt strangely surreal.

Stone turned in the broken seat. "Sound off, marines!"

"We're good, Spartan Stone," came a female reply. "Bumps and bruises, not much else."

"Copy that." A miracle everyone had survived. Then again, the day was still young.

With that thought, Stone disengaged her harness and pushed herself to her feet. Her muscles felt sluggish and fatigued from holding up the support beam. Diagnostics were showing some tissue damage in both shoulders, thighs, and one knee. At least she didn't feel any pain. Yet.

Her helmet light flared through the passenger cabin, beaming on the five occupants, all relatively unharmed; an incredible relief. "Soon as I blow the hatch," she said, "we fan out in pairs. The ring's already crawling with Banished. Be ready for anything."

They got up slowly, filing behind her as she disengaged the door release. Daylight flooded inside. Stone unshouldered her M395 rifle, already scanning the area for potential threats as she poked her head outside. No targets in the direct vicinity, but she knew that wouldn't last for long—the area just beyond the boulder-strewn ledge was lit up with signs of heavy fighting.

She left the lifeboat, making sure everyone was out before heading to the edge of the rocks to get a visual on their surroundings. Behind them, a wide grassy plateau led to rocky foothills and hundreds of acres of high alpine forest that stretched right up to the base of a massive snowcapped mountain range. In the sky, drop pods, evac craft, troop carriers, and burning debris rained down toward the surface like meteors, impacts shaking the ground and filling the air with constant thunder.

"Whoa," one of the marines marveled, having followed her.

She glanced down. "You all right, marine?"

"Yeah. Just . . . for all the trouble these things are supposed to cause, I guess I never thought the surface of the ring would look so . . . beautiful."

Her brow lifted.

That was certainly one way of looking at it. It was on the tip of her tongue to be sarcastic, but she let him have the moment. It wouldn't be long before he'd forget about the idyllic scene and all he'd be able to see and remember would be the brutality of war.

CHAPTER 2

M9407 SOEIV
December 12, 2559
Day 1

UNSC *Infinity* was lost.

Over seven thousand souls scattered. Who knew how many dead . . .

Communications had come in rapid-fire succession from all departments—mayhem mingled with tactical updates, orders, and team sitreps. It wasn't pretty, the things Spartan Nina Kovan heard as she entered the confines of her drop pod, the final calls for help, the shock and terror, as she strapped in and initiated deployment, going through systems check, removing safeties, and then arming the ejection tube.

The comms being fed into her helmet's heads-up display went quiet as the pod's communications suite took over. Two video screens flickered to life, one delivering relevant tactical information while the other showed a live feed of Spartan Henri Malik in the cockpit of a Sabre.

Malik, along with the rest of Fireteam Windfall, was out there picking off Banished Phantoms and fighters, clearing the space along *Infinity*'s ejection tubes to allow for the deployment of

Spartans and Orbital Drop Shock Troopers en masse.

"No time to countdown," Malik broadcast on an open channel. His head tipped sideways as the Sabre rolled, then righted. *"Path is clear. Occupied pods, fire immediately."*

Kovan bypassed the normal protocol of a thirty-second countdown and initiated ejection. The drop pod shot through the vertical ejection tube like a missile, throwing her back against the seat, and out into the blackness of space.

The view that greeted her was sobering. Hundreds just like her streamed from the burning flagship and straight into Banished-infested territory. Almost immediately, a pod at her three o'clock exploded as a Seraph streaked past. Kovan gritted her teeth as the harsh realization swept through her. Outnumbered and outgunned, she and everyone else would be damn lucky to make it into the upper atmosphere. The Banished were picking off *Infinity*'s crew with relative ease, which meant there was only one thing to do: cause as much damage as possible on the way down.

Single-occupant exoatmospheric insertion vehicles—SOEIVs—were notoriously difficult to maneuver; their job was to deliver ground forces from high orbit straight to the surface in rapid time—but all she needed was a little redirection. . . .

"Mouse, find me a target," she said, scanning the skies.

Her AI went to work, quiet as its namesake and just how she liked it, linking to the pod's targeting array and switching one of the video feeds to a grid pattern. The AI locked on to three potential targets on a similar trajectory toward the surface. Kovan made a slight course correction.

"Spartan Kovan, your drop pod's on a collision course with a deployment of Phantoms in the ring's stratosphere,"

Spartan Malik reported as his video feed materialized on-screen. *"Impact probability ninety-three percent. Adjust your course."*

"Why would I do that?" she replied as one corner of her mouth turned up. "I'm *aiming* for them."

"Somehow, I'm not surprised. Good luck, Spartan."

Once she'd made up her mind, nothing short of orders from senior command could make her back down, something Malik, along with every other Spartan, knew very well. Kovan gave him a curt nod and his form disappeared from the drop pod's viewscreen. Far beyond the tempered glass, the inner curve of the Halo ring took shape, growing increasingly larger as she torpedoed toward the stratosphere.

Approaching terminal velocity, the pod gained on the trio of Phantoms as they swept down into the ring's artificial atmosphere, firing on anything UNSC as they went.

Adrenaline coursed through Kovan's system, making her enhanced body hum with readiness. With no weapons array on the drop pod, the choice was clear: the pod itself *was* the weapon, a five-hundred-kilogram projectile aimed right at the Phantoms.

The fuselage of a Pelican whipped in front of her pod in a near-miss blur, enemy plasma still eating away at its broken edges.

As the pod broke the Halo ring's lower atmosphere, the collision alarm blared. *"Time to impact: eighteen seconds."*

She switched off the alarm.

The Phantoms broke formation, two leaving to swoop back into the upper atmosphere, while the third stayed glued to a fleeing RLT-85 shuttlepod as it dropped in front of a snowcapped mountain range, soaring over a vast alpine forest, and straight into a wide valley rife with smoke and fire as the battle raged on the surface. Another course correction kept her on the Phantom's path while Mouse calculated a midair boarding scenario. Extreme maybe, but blowing through the Banished craft like she intended was too risky with it glued so closely to the shuttle's tail.

One hundred and eighty meters per second, the pod gained on the Phantom in a flash as it fired on the fleeing shuttle.

The drop pod shuddered, and her teeth vibrated, but Kovan willed the clatter and pandemonium to fade until all she could hear was the sound of her slow, steady exhales and her beating heart. She smiled. "This is probably gonna hurt. . . ."

She came in fast, braking rockets firing moments before the pod slammed into the Phantom as it leveled off, slicing through its hull as the automatic braking chute deployed. Alarms screeched again, controls sparking as explosive bolts triggered and the drop pod's door expelled into the interior of the Phantom.

She was out in seconds, seven enemy targets appearing on her HUD as she drew her MK50 Sidekick. "Knock knock."

After being holed up in the drop pod, Kovan was ready to exact some close-quarters payback. Immediately, she fired at the two dazed enemy targets in the cockpit as the Phantom nose-dived.

"Fifty meters to impact," Mouse warned.

Out of control, the Phantom rolled. There was little time to find an anchor and the ground was coming up fast. Kovan turned and dove into the drop pod as the Phantom hit the ground like a lightning bolt. Despite the protection of her STORMFALL-class Mjolnir armor, and titanium nano-composite body suit with its shock-absorbing layer of hydrostatic gel, the sudden force rattled through her body.

A shaky groan escaped her lips as she shook off the crash effects—beyond the split-second gratitude of being alive, there wasn't time to acknowledge anything else as battlenet reports flooded through her HUD and five Sangheili targets were rousing within the crashed Phantom.

She opened her TEAMCOM channel and said, "Kovan, on the ground," and then she went to work. As soon as her feet hit the alien deck, a two-and-a-half-meter-tall Sangheili mercenary rushed her with an angry roar, mandibles wide. The collision sent her back several steps as she blocked with her forearm, ducked and spun, coming up at his side and firing a round from her MK50 into his ribcage, her combat knife already in her other hand, the blade sinking deeply into the thick cords of his muscled neck.

She was several steps ahead, knowing where her additional targets were and the directions they were moving. As the mercenary dropped, she yanked him close and used him as cover to head-shot another Sangheili that had been approaching from behind him.

Three more of his ilk took potshots at her with plasma rifles, superheated rounds peppering a stack of nearby containers as she dropped the alien body and dove for cover. In one fluid motion, she unshouldered her S7 sniper rifle and sighted, waiting for them to expose themselves. As if hiding behind consoles and supply crates was going to save them . . .

"Just a little peek. . . . Come on, don't be shy," she muttered.

"Wrap it up, Kovan," Stone said via TEAMCOM.

Oh, she'd wrap it up, all right. Neatly and with seven little bows . . .

Not even Stone could distract her now. Kovan's talent for compartmentalizing was one of her greatest strengths. Even with the relentless turmoil outside, the constant barrage of neighboring Banished AA guns vibrating through the Phantom, and debris pinging the exterior, she settled easily into her sweet spot. She had a sense for where to sight her target, an uncanny ability to determine when the smallest bit of an enemy would emerge. It felt like minutes, but in reality only a few seconds passed before the mercenary took another peek.

No hesitation. Ever.

As soon as the moment came, she took it, instantly squeezing the trigger. The impact blew out the Sangheili's throat.

Two left. One crept behind the crates, changing positions to get a shot off on her position, but as soon as he exposed a shoulder, she fired. As he fell, she delivered the head shot.

The last one had come around the bulkhead to her left in an attempt to outflank her. She stayed put, letting him do the legwork and move in close. As soon as he unsheathed his energy sword and charged, she was ready, blocking his forearm with hers, then grabbing him by his red-painted combat harness, dropping to her rear, sticking a foot in his gut, and flipping him over her head. He clumsily hit the deck and she was on top of him at once, shoving the Sidekick under his chin and firing a round.

"Fireteam Taurus is quickly approaching your location," Mouse announced.

Kovan left the dead Sangheili behind and headed toward the exit, just as her display showed Fireteam Taurus about to crest the ridge near her location. They were coming in hot, weapons drawn. "Stand down, Fireteam Taurus—friendly inside."

"Kovan . . . ?" Spartan Griffin said. *"What are you doing in there?"*

She reached the vessel's bay door and jumped to the ground. Nearby, the RLT-85 shuttlepod lay on its belly a few meters beyond against a rocky hillside. An endless barrage of drop pods, artillery fire, and crashing ships shook the ground as the air filled with explosive fallout—dirt and rocks and molten metal adding another deadly layer to the battlefield. Immediately Kovan ran for the downed shuttle. "The Phantom was in my way, so I went through it." *And then I cleaned it out.*

"Contacts incoming." Mouse fed her a wider target area, showing a number of Banished units approaching Taurus from the tail of the valley. She instinctively lifted and fired her S7 in a single motion, dropping a Jiralhanae coming over the ridge line.

"I count five Banished patrols making their way to your position," she told Griffin. "If you're going to move on those AA guns, you should do it now."

"You heard her, Taurus—let's move out. Thanks for the support, Kovan."

"Nee-yet prob-lyem."

And as soon as she saw to the shuttle, she'd join Taurus and her own fireteam to take the rest of those Banished artillery offline.

Smoke billowed from the shuttle as its hatch door blew. Personnel stumbled out, and Kovan breathed a sigh of relief.

"Banshee on approach," Mouse said.

Damn it. "I see it." Kovan put on the brakes, her heels sliding deep into the ground as she swung around, grabbed her rifle, and knelt in the dirt. She cocked her head and sighted its plasma cannon through the S7's scope as the Banshee barreled toward her position, its single fuel-rod cannon letting loose and the ground exploding in a scorching trail of radioactive red. She fired and hit the weapon, then immediately fired again, straight into the vehicle's central housing. The Banshee blew apart in a blinding explosion. Its fuselage hurtled toward her. She dove as it soared over her head and hit the side of the ridge with a deafening report.

Ignoring the rain of rocks hitting her Mjolnir, Kovan shouldered her S7 and ran to the smoking shuttle. The survivors were in pretty good shape, all things considered. Minor bumps and bruises, sooty faces, some more shocked than others. "Anyone else inside?" she asked, coming to a stop in front of them.

When no one answered, a tall, well-built man in his late twenties stepped forward. He wore a smoke-streaked navy T-shirt, torn navy slacks, combat boots, and held a rucksack over his shoulder. "The pilot is still inside," he answered. "But he didn't make it."

There were no life signs coming from the shuttle, and with the crushed bow, Kovan wasn't surprised by the unfortunate news or by the twinge of guilt that pinched her chest. The crash could have been avoided if she had intercepted the Phantom sooner. And while she knew well the price and casualties of war, it still didn't stop her from feeling the losses. Nor did it stop her from compartmentalizing and moving forward. No time to dwell, not when there were others still alive to protect.

"You must have nerves of steel to stare down a Banshee out in the open like that," the crewman marveled, eyes on the burning wreckage beyond her.

"You in charge?" she asked, ignoring the comment. The Banished were closing in on their location, her display lighting up with multiple ground targets on approach beyond the ridgeline; they needed to get moving.

"Me?" he asked, surprised. "Hell, no. I-I'm just a barber." He pulled the rucksack strap aside, revealing the retail service badge on his shirt—a crossed key and quill.

"Not anymore. You got a name and a weapon?"

"Bender. Erik Bender. And no, not yet."

"You must be pretty good with a blade, yes?" She pulled her M11 combat knife free. It was still wet with Sangheili blood. "Take it." His eyes widened, but he took the offered blade and wiped it on his pants.

The ground trembled again and a massive concussion rocked the area. "We need to go," she told the group as a unit of Broadswords streaked overhead. "Until our uplink to central command is restored, we're on our own. There are weapons, rations, and supplies in the shuttle and more firepower in my drop pod over there. I suggest you grab as much as you can, and quickly."

Evacuating an entire flagship into the middle of a war zone wasn't something Kovan or any of the other Spartans had done before—at least, not to her knowledge. *Infinity* was full of capable fighters, but she also housed scores of support staff, people who were easy pickings for the Banished.

Weapons were quickly gathered, and six out of the eight survivors took them on with a capability that told Kovan they could hold their own in battle. The other two, Bender and a shorter, pale-faced academic with dried tear-streaks on his face, were definitely not as well-versed. Bender at least had already secured a rifle. She grabbed one of the BR75s that had been gathered and held it out to the other man. "You know how to use one of these?" He had to know the basics—even support staff couldn't be assigned to the UNSC flagship without some form of training. He stared up at her, dark eyes round and mouth agape. At six feet nine inches, she towered over him and knew it could be an intimidating experience in conjunction with everything that had happened so far and the ongoing chaos around them. "What's your name and rank, soldier?"

"Jo. Gavin Jo. Petty Officer Third Class, Mortuary Specialist."

"Well, Mortuary Specialist Gavin Jo." She grabbed his hand and put the weapon in it. "Here's your new assignment. Point and shoot."

He swallowed, blinked, and stood a little straighter. "Right. Point and shoot." He checked the chamber, which gave her some hope he might come out of this alive.

With everyone armed and packed out, she opened a link to TEAMCOM. "Stone, we have a rendezvous point for *Infinity* personnel yet?"

"A few groups are heading into the mountains for cover, but it won't be easy. The Banished have patrols and scouting parties just waiting to pick off survivors. . . . If you can provide your crew with enough cover to get them into the hills, they can meet up with my group."

"Looks like that'll have to do."

"Run them to me," Stone said. *"Taurus needs your cover on those AA guns."*

"Roger that. Bringing them to your location." Kovan turned to the group. "We'll stick to the ridgeline, then head toward the mountains. I'll get you as far as I can. Keep your heads down and move when I say move, shoot when I say shoot. Understood?"

Heads nodded and several responded somewhat simultaneously, "Understood."

God, this was going to be a nightmare.

CHAPTER 3

PTD-09 SKT-29 Bumblebee
Zeta Halo
December 13, 2559
Day 2

ix hours had passed since they'd crash-landed onto Zeta Halo's surface. Six hours since the back end of the lifeboat had been shorn off. Combat medic Lucas Browning closed his eyes and swallowed down the nausea that had plagued him ever since the first threat alarm blared throughout *Infinity*'s PA.

His mind was stuck on repeat, the harrowing play-by-play of confusion, shock, loss, and fire flashing one scene after another; the massive Spartan holding up the corridor like some mythical giant, urging him forward; the horror of shooting through space, getting hit—God, that sound, he'd never forget it; the roar of wind that had swept inside as they spun, the force ripping the last two occupants from their harnesses and out into thin air.

He didn't realize his leg was bouncing until First Lieutenant TJ Murphy reached across the aisle and placed a hand on his knee. Their eyes met and Murphy gave him a slow nod that said: *You're okay.*

The silent message calmed him, and he nodded back. He was okay.

Lucas drew in a deep breath and released it, reminding himself that he'd trained for situations just like this. It was his job to remain calm, to assess and address, which he'd done the moment he'd regained consciousness, examining every occupant in the lifeboat and providing treatment. Three survivors with bumps, bruises, and concussions, one severely wounded, two dead, and two unaccounted for.

Murphy leaned his head back against the crash seat and closed his eyes. The red emergency light caught the angles of his face and shadowed the dips and depressions. It should've made him look sinister, but all Lucas saw was a strong, been-there-seen-it-all kind of face, one that made him feel safe and told him they were in capable hands.

Through the small tear in the hull's ceiling, he could see that night had fallen. Artillery fire still thundered in the distance and occasionally shook the lifeboat. They'd crashed hard and slid into some kind of ravine with such force that the vessel had become completely wedged in, leaving them with no way out.

The emergency rations provided on all lifeboats would last a week. And then what? They were trapped inside with two corpses and no working comms, and no one knew where they were. Didn't matter what rank you were, what kind of experience you had: no one here had the means or strength to peel away the lifeboat's reinforced armor plating and set them free.

Ensign Isaiah Cameron had taken apart the operations console as best he could and torn out parts to make a small, makeshift antenna, which he slipped through the rip in the hull, and then linked it up to what was left of the comms cables. Since then, they'd all taken shifts, continually trying to make contact with the UNSC, but had gotten no replies. From the sounds of the fighting,

Lucas knew they might be too far from the battle, potentially in a dead zone or deep into Banished territory.

"This is downed Bumblebee Papa Tango Delta Zero Nine, issuing Mayday, Mayday, Mayday. Does anyone copy?" Cameron's voice carried from the pilot's chair into the cabin, the low monotonous tone like a prayer issued over and over.

Lying prone in the aisle, Private Kinney let out a raspy cough.

They'd laid her at the end of the aisle to make her more comfortable. She couldn't speak, and the only thing she'd been able to do was grip Lucas's hand for a short amount of time. He only knew her name because it was stamped on her flight suit. His med kit had been sucked out of the lifeboat, and while there was another one in the supply closet, nothing in there would help heal her internal injuries. His hands were tied, and without proper aid she'd die here in the dark, flanked by the two other lost souls still strapped into their crash harnesses.

It seemed so pointless and wrong when all she needed was a standard medical bay and treatment.

Nevertheless, in a few hours her pain would be over.

He'd been so lost in thought and frustration that Murphy's hand on his shoulder gave him a start. "You're up, Browning. I'll stay with her."

Feeling defeated, Lucas pushed to his feet, every muscle sore and bruised as he shuffled up the short aisle, stepping over Robin Dimik's legs as she attempted to sleep off a nasty grade-three concussion, and then moved aside for Cameron as he left the cockpit.

Lucas settled into the pilot's seat and let out a heavy exhale as his body sank into the curve of the chair. His head fell back and his eyes closed. How the hell had this happened? He'd been stationed on the best, the biggest, the *baddest* ship the UNSC had to offer. *Infinity* wasn't supposed to lose.

He activated the comms panel, keeping his voice low when he spoke. "This is downed lifeboat Papa Tango Delta Zero Nine, Mayday, Mayday, Mayday. Does anyone copy?"

No response. He didn't expect one at this point. He waited, counting artillery thunder. Every time he got to twenty, he tried again.

Lucas wasn't sure how much he'd counted or how many calls he'd made. He was on another round of counting thunder when the comms lit briefly and a barely audible, accented voice came through.

"This is Spartan Tomas Horvath, Fireteam Intrepid, responding. Copy?"

Lucas bolted upright, heart in his throat, and hoping like hell he wasn't hearing things. He fumbled to respond. "Y-yes! Copy, copy! We copy! We're here!" *We're here.* Tears stung his eyes. "Marine Combat Medic Lucas Browning responding." Murphy suddenly appeared around the bulkhead.

"What's your sitrep, Papa Nine?" the Spartan asked.

Static resumed. Lucas exchanged a look of astonishment with Murphy as the lieutenant answered back. "Uh, situation pretty much stinks right now."

"Murphy, is that you?"

Murphy rolled his eyes and cocked a small smile. "If I had a credit for every time I've heard a Spartan say that . . . yeah, it's me. Evacuated in one of the last lifeboats with eight others. Was following Spartan Stone, but we got hit. Lost the back end. We've been trapped for the last six hours. Navigation is out. I honestly don't know where the hell we are. We lost four. One is badly injured. We're wedged in good, Spartan, and we won't make it out without help. Could sure use a hand."

"Heading to higher ground now. Will see if I can get a lock on your signal. Hang in there. I'll be there shortly."

"Roger that," Murphy said with a heavy dose of relief.

Lucas ran a hand over his head and then glanced over his shoulder to see that Dimik and Cameron had moved closer to the cockpit. In the red lighting, Dimik's nasty forehead gash looked like a black smudge and she was already sporting two black eyes along with a busted lip. She'd regained consciousness about two hours ago and never once complained.

"He's coming. He'll be here," Cam whispered, sounding as if he was trying to convince himself.

Dimik paled suddenly. "Oh God. Never mind. Getting up was a mistake." She turned and lurched toward one of the walls and dry-heaved.

Murphy reached past her and retrieved a water canister from the supply closet. "Here, take this."

Her hands trembled so badly that Murphy had to open the container for her. Carefully she returned to her crash seat, took a sip, and let her head rest gently against the side of the seat. Her eyes squeezed tightly shut, and when they opened they were shiny with tears. Dimik was in terrible pain, but she'd pushed away the painkiller that Lucas had offered her earlier. "Just make sure Kinney is comfortable," she'd said.

Lucas left the cockpit and angled past Murphy to kneel in front of Dimik. "Here, give me your hand." Once he had it, he squeezed the LI-4 point between her thumb and index finger. It wasn't much, but right now it was all he had.

"You think he'll come, the Spartan?" she asked at length.

"Never known a Spartan to not follow through," Murphy replied, "and I've worked with them a long time. If he says he'll be here, then he'll be here."

A particularly loud blast shook the hull, making them all go silent, waiting to see if another followed. When it didn't, Cam said quietly, "Time isn't exactly on our side, though. What if something happens to him?"

If Spartan Horvath didn't make it . . . the lifeboat would quickly become their tomb.

"Don't waste your worry on what-ifs, Ensign," Murphy said. "It's a circle that goes nowhere. Trust me on that one."

"How's it feel now, Dimik?" Lucas asked.

She opened her eyes to small slits and tried to feign a smile. "Hurts. Maybe a little better. I've had concussions before, too many to count actually, but this one takes the cake."

Murphy winced. "You've seen combat?"

"No. I'm a safety specialist. Glorified firefighter, really. Work in prevention and de-escalation of explosives, fire, plasma, you name it. If it explodes or burns, I know how to stop it."

"What about you, Ensign?" Lucas turned his attention to the soldier who wasn't that much older than Lucas's twenty-five years. "Assuming you work in comms."

Cam gave a halfhearted smile and echoed Dimik's response. "Yeah. If there's a button, I know how to press it."

Dimik laughed and then instantly regretted it.

Murphy took the next shift at comms and the mood inside the lifeboat drifted back into one of silent contemplation.

A few hours' worth of shift changes passed with little discourse.

Lucas must have dozed off, because the next thing he knew, Murphy was patting him on the chest. "You're up, Doc."

He rubbed the broken sleep from his eyes. "Anything? Did Horvath check back in?"

Murphy slumped wearily into one of the crash seats. "No, comms were quiet."

Artillery fire still continued from far off. It never seemed to stop for longer than twenty or thirty minutes. It was easy to sit in the pilot's seat and imagine Spartan Horvath in the thick of battle or evading Banished forces, but always in Lucas's mind, the supersoldier was making his way closer to their location. The hard part was imagining the opposite, and when his mind began to wander in that direction, he opened a channel and began another Mayday call, praying for another answer.

CHAPTER 4

Spartan Tomas Horvath paused at the top of the ridge. Below him, a wide canyon cut a path through rocky foothills dotted with thin green pines and patches of grass. Three and a half kilometers downwind, artillery fire flooded the night sky with random bursts of white, yellow, and orange, each round echoing loudly down the canyon. Across the canyon floor and up the opposite ridge to the hills and the mountains rising in the distance, the view narrowed and the landscape grew exponentially thinner as Zeta Halo curved up into the darkness.

Through his HUD, he tracked Fireteam Intrepid, its members maintaining three hundred meters of distance between them as they made their way down the ridge and into the canyon while Horvath brought up the rear.

"Pick up the pace, Horvath," Si Wheeler said, his curt tone putting a spring in Horvath's step.

His team leader was just reaching the canyon floor. They were disruptors, the lot of them. Agents of chaos and damn good at their job. They'd gotten separated from the main area of engagement where the heaviest fighting continued and had slowly been working their way back—would've been there yesterday if not for the Banished presence. The whole place was crawling with them.

Since they first touched down, Intrepid had spent the entire time fighting one skirmish after another, taking out every patrol, supply vehicle, scouting party, and support line they'd come across.

"Copy," he replied, turning off the HUD's night vision and tipping his head to the sky. It was relatively quiet now, no longer illuminated with the intense battle that had raged the day before, the sky streaked with fire and smoke.

Infinity was still out there, somewhere. Broken. Dark.

Might be survivors too, hiding, keeping a low profile, waiting for any help to arrive.

He hadn't been the only one to wonder about the flagship since they'd reached the surface. Anytime he saw one of his team members looking skyward, he knew what they were searching for and what they were feeling—the somber disbelief, the guarded hope.

Hope was great, of course, but only in moderation—too much, he'd learned, was an unnecessary drain on the psyche. Things happened when they happened; details emerged when they emerged; news broke when it broke. No reason to waste valuable time and energy in the meantime. Better to make tracks, take action, and focus on the mission at hand until such time as the Banished were wiped clean off the ring and they could go check on *Infinity* for themselves.

Horvath let out a deep exhale and continued on his downward path.

"*Picking up that lifeboat's signal again,*" Wheeler said. "*Across the canyon and up the next ridge. Horvath, double-time it to their location and see what you can do. We'll continue on and recon the artillery guns.*"

"Roger that."

As he reached the valley floor, his AI, Elfie, piped up with, *"Unknown contacts on approach."* She paused. *"Correction. Phantoms incoming."*

"Intrepid, we've got Phantoms overhead, be advised."

"We see them."

Although the desert camouflage on his ANUBIS-class GEN3 Mjolnir blended in well with the rocks, he engaged baffling sensors to hide his infrared signature as a formation of five Phantoms streaked past, heading toward the main area of engagement.

"They just keep coming," he grumbled, straightening.

"Intrepid, we need to hurry. If those Phantoms are full of re-inforcements, that's another hundred-plus head of Banished dropped on our people," Wheeler said, his tone turning darker. *"I say we take those AA guns for ourselves and start shooting these bastards out of the sky."* Horvath smiled. When Wheeler talked like that, they all knew shit was about to burn.

As Fireteam Intrepid double-timed it toward the action, Horvath ran across the canyon floor, cradling his MA5D assault rifle and dodging the short rocky formations scattered across the area. The approaching ridge was a near-vertical sheet of granite. Increasing speed, he shouldered his weapon and leapt, grabbing hold of a pocket three meters up and then climbing.

The sooner he helped out the lifeboat survivors, the sooner he could return to his team and start some trouble.

Twenty minutes later he neared the top of the ridge. "Papa Tango Delta Zero Nine, do you copy?" He paused. "Papa Nine, repeat, do you copy?"

A good fifteen seconds passed before static filled the receiver. *"Copy . . . hello? Spartan Horvath. Are you there?"*

He recognized the voice—it was the medic from before. "I'm here, Browning."

"Oh, thank God. We hadn't heard from you in hours. I thought we might've lost you."

Behind the relief in the young medic's voice, Horvath didn't miss the notes of anxiety and fear. The kid was terrified of not being found. Couldn't blame him. Trapped with no way out . . . he knew what that was like. And it could mess with the strongest of minds.

The comms went quiet again as Horvath reached the top of the ridge and began jogging across a plateau carpeted in short mounds of dry grasses and gravelly soil. A brief wave of exhaustion swept through him, but stopping even for a few minutes of rest wasn't an option.

Better to keep the medic talking. "Can you see anything outside of the lifeboat?"

"No. We're wedged into rock, a crevice or . . . I'm not sure."

"This your first engagement?"

"Yes, sir. I've been on Infinity *since she was retrofitted over Earth, but most of my training has been in the sim."*

"Hell of a time to get thrown into the deep end."

A sharp laugh came through, followed by a moment of silence before Browning spoke again. *"What's happening out there? We haven't had any news since we crashed."*

Short answer: it was a goddamn mess. Infinity *gone. Mass casualties. Ground forces scattered. Outnumbered. The Banished picking off survivors . . .* But Horvath couldn't seem to utter the words out loud, didn't want to further demoralize an already traumatized person.

"Spartan Horvath? Are you still there?"

"I'm here. Looks like we got jumped by the Banished when we arrived. . . ." But he didn't want Browning to focus on that, so he changed the conversation. "How's your injured doing?"

"Kinney is barely holding on," Browning answered, his tone becoming low and anguished. *"Her injuries can be treated. I just don't have the right tools. . . ."*

Horvath picked up the pace. If he could get there in time, get her to a med bay or bring the right equipment on-site . . . But even as the optimistic thought came, he knew it was a stretch. Reality painted a much grimmer picture.

"You see any other holes or daylight in the hull?"

"None. There's a couple of cracks in the windshield, but we can't break through it."

"Save your energy. It's made of tempered glass composite." Though they must've landed incredibly hard to cause the windshield to crack. It was a miracle any of them had survived.

Horvath finally neared the edge of the plateau. He slowed to a walk, allowing himself a breather while a transparent grid of the landscape populated through his display. "Where you from, Browning?"

"Originally Alluvion. But I was just a kid when we evacuated."

"No shit," he said in surprise, and his curse counter dinged. He ignored it, knowing he was far enough down the leaderboard not to worry about losing the bet between him and the rest of Intrepid. Their team leader had sworn up and down that he didn't curse as much as the rest of them, which was laughable—Wheeler might just have the worst potty mouth of the entire Spartan branch.

In a galaxy chock-full of habitable star systems and human civilization spread across light-years, it was always something special when you found someone from your homeworld. "That was my old stomping ground too," he told the medic. The Covenant had come through and glassed the planet when Horvath was just a teen. "Miss it like hell."

Some of the best people in the Milky Way had lived on Alluvion. Good, honest, hardworking people. Tomas Horvath was a patriot through and through, and had always felt protective of his home planet and its people. When the Covenant began glassing colonies and cleansing the galaxy of humanity, it only intensified those feelings; it led him to join the UNSC and become a soldier. And then he'd shattered his spine and thought it was all over—until he'd been selected for the SPARTAN-IV program.

"Yes, sir. Born in Vaslo, and I went to primary school in Paugary, but my experience ends there."

"Ah. I can hear the accent. Surprised you still have it. Folks from Vaslo had very little accent to begin with."

"Unlike you guys from Kuyik."

He laughed, impressed Browning was able to pinpoint his country of origin. While Horvath's speech pattern was thicker than that of most Spartans, it was tame compared to others who'd grown up in the once-vibrant city of Kuyik.

"My mom had family from there . . . So let me guess, you would have went to . . ." Browning paused. *"Arujin-Grad?"*

"Naw, never had the chance to go." All of it had been destroyed before he even reached university, though his teachers at the time swore he'd never make it through first year anyway—something about his disruptive nature getting him kicked out . . .

"The signal is increasing," Elfie said. *"I have pinpointed the lifeboat's exact location."*

"Time to rendezvous?"

"Forty-eight minutes at current speed."

Several ongoing ground battles lit up the predawn horizon, while UNSC and Banished starships launched streaks of yellow, purple, and blue across the sky. The largest engagement was in the valley to his two o'clock, which Intrepid would be closing in on soon.

"Sir? Are you still there?"

"Hang tight, Browning. I've got a solid ping on your broadcast. Looks like I'll be at your doorstep shortly."

"Thank you. Hanging tight. And . . . I know you're in the thick of it, but . . . please hurry . . . please don't forget about us."

"Not possible. You have my word."

The faint breath of relief might've been missed by others, but Horvath heard it loud and clear.

The comms signal abruptly dropped as a tremor shook the ground.

Horvath froze. Couldn't be artillery, not this close. Frowning, he scanned the horizon, not seeing anything different than what he had just moments before.

Without warning, the land beneath his feet buckled. The whole plateau dropped a half meter, as though the entire land shelf let out a tired exhale. Immediately he braced, on alert, though for what he had no idea. An eerie metallic groan issued from some point farther up the curve of the Halo. It grew until it permeated the atmosphere, the sound making his skin crawl, the depth and volume growing until his ears responded with pain.

"Talk to me, Fi. What the hell's going on?"

"Unknown energy distortion . . . Static pressure increasing at an abnormally high rate." The predawn sky began to glow purple, drawing his gaze up. *"Slipspace portal initiated."*

Shit.

The ground began shaking violently.

"Shockwave imminent."

Deep magnification showed an intense sonic wind rushing over the area, the force not merely flattening everything in its path, but ripping up the landscape in a gargantuan wave of debris. In an instant, adrenaline flared like a matchstick. He didn't think, just reacted, pivoting and bolting. But the earthen tsunami was already at his heels. Still, Horvath pushed himself and his armor to the limit until he was caught up, tumbling with earth, water, substructure, flora, and fauna. The force flung him high and off the plateau where he was battered from all sides, his heart pounding as he smacked into solid rock and tumbled. Flailing, he managed to snag a pocket on the side of the plateau wall, holding on for dear life as the supersonic wave flowed past and finally disappeared.

He hung there, breathing so heavily that it took several seconds to catch his breath. "Holy shit." Another ding echoed, and the utter absurdity of it caused laughter to bubble to his throat. "Fi . . . report?"

"Motion tracker, active camouflage, and long-range comms are offline. Armor integrity is at fifty-two percent."

He'd already taken a beating the last twenty-four hours of constant fighting. At this rate, he'd be lucky if his GEN3 lasted out the week.

Horvath pulled all six hundred kilos of body and armor up to a small ledge jutting from the side of the plateau wall, then rolled onto his back. The sky was now bright with moving streams of color as the ring and everything on it and within its protected bubble traveled through slipspace. For a long moment all he could do was marvel at the incredible scene playing out above him. But finally he sat up and tried to get his bearings, his immediate concern his fireteam. "Intrepid, do you copy?" No response.

He pushed to his feet. "I've lost contact with the team. Motion tracker's offline . . . everything is offline. That explosion—Intrepid One, *do you copy?*"

The ground shuddered once more. "Again with this?" Loose rocks tumbled down from above; the last thing he needed was to get buried under a landslide. Wasting no time, he climbed to the top of what was left of the plateau.

The ground was stark and completely barren, swept clean of topsoil, flora, and rocks.

As Horvath scanned the devastated landscape, a faint cracking sound rumbled across the ring's surface. He magnified in that direction, his jaw going slack. "Oh no. The ring . . ." It was splitting apart, the cracks spreading like lightning bolts across Zeta Halo's three-hundred-kilometer-wide surface. Dread flared white-hot through his body, momentarily holding him in place. "If you can hear me, Intrepid! Anyone! The ring is breaking apart! It's—"

In the distance, the mountains began to crumble and list, valleys and forests forced upward as kilometers of massive Forerunner substructure rose. Enormous chunks of ring began to break away. The canyon his team had traversed to the valley where the fighting continued suddenly dropped away, simply . . . *plummeted.*

No, no, no. This isn't happening.

His team was just . . . gone.

CHAPTER 5

PTD-09 SKT-29 Bumblebee
Zeta Halo
December 13, 2559
Day 2

The conversation with Spartan Horvath cut off abruptly. A second later, the lifeboat started to vibrate, and static began to buzz intermittently through comms, mixed with a faint unidentified female voice. The only intelligible words out of the garble that Lucas could identify were *copy*, *signal*, *we*, and *hell*. He swung around in the pilot's chair and met Murphy's gaze, but before he could form words to question their sit-rep, the shaking became violent and a strange synthetic echo filled the air, decibels increasing until his eardrums rang.

Murphy's eyes widened. "Strap in." He turned to the others. "Strap in now!"

The emergency lights flickered, then died, casting them in darkness.

A jolt of panic surged through Lucas, making his hands fumble the pilot's harness as he hurried to strap in. Small rocks pinged the hull and covered the hole that had given them their only source of natural light. A low roar echoed outside of the lifeboat, swelling until it sounded like the whole ring was screaming. The shuttle tipped from side to side as the stony crevice broke all around them, culminating in a massive *whoosh* overhead.

Every nerve in Lucas's body seemed frozen with fear while adrenaline made him hyperaware of his surroundings. A metal tang emerged in the back of his throat along with a peculiar sensation that pricked his skin and made the hairs on his arms rise. A succession of sharp, thunderous cracks rang out. He squeezed his eyes closed as it sounded like everything above them was coming apart.

The hull bent inward on both sides.

Oh God, they were going to be crushed. His heart raced and he sank deeper into his seat as the crack in the windshield made a spine-chilling whine. A peek revealed the glass fracture branching out into a web. The windshield began to bow.

"Lucas, get down!"

The words galvanized him. Immediately he covered his head and leaned as far as he could into the aisle, angling under the console as the window blew with a shattering *boom*. Tempered glass tore through the cabin. Dimik and Cameron screamed. Shards sliced his shoulder and hip, but Lucas barely felt the sting as quiet settled over the lifeboat.

Slowly he lifted his head.

Inhale. Exhale. Get up. Do your damn job.

In the darkness, he could just barely make out shapes in the cabin. "Is everyone okay?" He reached around the interior wall and found what he thought might be Murphy's knee. "Murphy?"

Relief washed over him at the sound of the lieutenant's voice: "Yeah, I'll live. Dimik? Cameron? Sound off."

No response.

While Lucas hurried to unbuckle his harness, a panicked "*Shit!*" whispered from the cabin. The buckle finally released and he left the cockpit, edging carefully down the dark aisle. "Cam, you okay? Answer me, buddy." Feeling his way along, his leg brushed against another. He reached out, and a soft hand suddenly gripped his. Dimik. She squeezed. "I'm okay."

He returned the squeeze and kept going. "Cam? You good?"

"No, man, not good," finally came the gruff answer. "I think Kinney's dead, and I've got a chunk of glass in my leg."

Lucas moved slowly, knowing he must be close to where they'd placed Kinney in the aisle. His foot eventually touched the top of her head and he went still. A hand hit him, palm against his stomach. "Don't move," Cam warned. Lucas knelt, reaching out to feel Cam's position. "Watch it! Don't touch me!"

"Okay, okay. I'm not moving."

"The glass is in my knee, sticking out of the side, man. It's up under the kneecap."

Oh boy. "Hang tight. I'll get an emergency light from the closet." The fact that he hadn't grabbed one right off the bat told him just how shaken he was. As he stood to head back up the aisle, a loud crash on top of the lifeboat gave him such a shock that he nearly fell forward.

Footsteps echoed overhead, heavy and armored, by the sound of them.

Lucas went stock-still, holding his breath as his thoughts turned to the Banished.

Debris rustled and the small hole in the hull once again allowed in a shaft of muted light. He remembered thinking how much he wanted to see daylight again, but now was seriously regretting that wish. He caught a shadowy movement ahead and realized Murphy was slowly reaching for his rifle.

Suddenly a hand punched through the hole in the weakened hull, making him jump. In a blink, Murphy had the weapon in his grip and aimed at the opening. Then the hand returned and began peeling back the ruined plating, creating a bigger hole. A crisp female voice filled the cabin. "Stand down, Murphy."

A Spartan helmet appeared.

In disbelief, Lucas reached for the nearest crash seat to steady himself as light from the side of her helmet flared through the cabin, causing him and everyone else to shield their eyes.

"*Stone.*" The name fell from Murphy's lips like a prayer. "My God."

Spartan Stone.

Lucas's mouth fell open. They'd been following her to the surface before getting hit. This was the super-soldier who'd kept the ceiling from collapsing back on *Infinity*. She'd saved his life. And now she was here like some giant armored angel. . . .

An intense wave of relief rolled over him. Tears thickened his throat. He'd been terrified of dying in the lifeboat, but he hadn't realized just how terrified until the moment of rescue was upon him. All the fear and despair he'd been feeling now gathered in his chest until it burned with pressure, making him rub the spot.

"Give me one sec," Stone said, retreating to peel back more of the hull, making an opening big enough to allow them to finally escape. His heart swelled. He knew Spartans were strong—he'd seen her hold up the bulkhead ceiling—but another feat of strength like this up close . . .

Once the way was clear, she poked her head back inside. It cocked as her gaze landed on Lucas. "Ah. You again," she said with a smile in her voice. "We need to stop meeting like this."

All the words in Lucas's vocabulary instantly disappeared.

Murphy's amused snort echoed through the cabin as he took charge of the situation. "Cam, you'll go first." He held out his hand to the injured ensign. "And be careful of his knee," he told Stone.

"Understood."

Stone reached inside as Murphy helped Cam step on one of the crash seats. From there Spartan Stone lifted him through the opening. Dimik was next, and once she was gone, Murphy turned his attention to Lucas. "You're up, Doc."

The lopsided grin on the lieutenant's face should've made Lucas return the smile, but instead the emotions he'd held in for the last two days spilled over. Completely mortified, he wiped at his wet eyes with an embarrassed laugh. When he looked at Murphy again, it was to find an understanding expression parked on the man's face.

"I was doubting we'd make it out of here too," he admitted. "You did good, Doc. And, hey, if it makes you feel any better, I've seen some tough old soldiers cry like babies when a Spartan swoops in to save th—"

"Spartans don't *swoop*, Murphy," Stone interrupted.

Murphy's eyes crinkled at the corners. He shrugged at Lucas and made a swooping motion with his hand, mouthing: *Yes, they do.*

"Just for that . . ." She reached inside and grabbed Murphy by the back of his uniform, hauling him out so fast that all the man could do was sputter in surprise.

The brief humor of the situation eased away. Alone, Lucas glanced around the cabin, sobering at the sight of Kinney lying in the aisle and the two marines still strapped to their chairs. It could have been any one of them, and the random nature of it made his heart heavy as he went to each fallen soldier, removed their dog tags, and placed them into his pocket.

He made his way up the aisle as Stone returned. In the dim light, his reflection stared back at him through her gold-colored visor, unrecognizable. Pale skin bruised around the left cheekbone, brow bone, and temple. Scabbed, busted lip. Shadows curved beneath eyes that appeared more haunted than he cared to acknowledge.

"Ready?" she asked.

He nodded, grabbed the med bag, and then let her lift him out of the dark cabin and into the light.

The brightness burned his eyes and it took a moment to adjust, but once done, he saw two soldiers in heavy combat gear standing on the end of the banged-up hull, reaching out to help him descend onto the rocks below. Feeling a bit weak, he accepted their help and finally reached solid ground, where a female marine was waiting.

He paused to look back, marveling at the giant Spartan decked out in faded blue armor, standing on top of the hull, scanning the surroundings. "Gets you right in the gut, doesn't it?" the marine said, also staring up at Stone before giving Lucas a smile. "Been fighting with her since landfall yesterday. Stone's a beast. Before we found you, she pulled an entire lifeboat out of the breach, saved a lot of soldiers. . . ."

Lucas cleared the thickness from his throat as the marine gestured for him to join the others. "Where are they now?" he asked, noticing that there were only five marines in all, the two on the roof, the one escorting him, and two more now tending to Cameron and Dimik while Murphy sat on a nearby rock. They had a medical bag, thank God, and supplies.

"Moved on to meet up with the rest of their squad."

Despite the heavy amount of grit and dust lingering in the air, the cool temperature was a welcome change. A dusky haze filled the overcast sky and a slight electric feel lingered in the atmosphere. And it was quiet, he realized, no artillery fire in the distance, no air traffic, nothing. . . .

While he wanted nothing more than to sit on the rocks and decompress, he went directly to check on Cam. As he passed Dimik she met his gaze and smiled. Dried blood crusted one side of her short pink-tipped hair and matted against her head wound. She'd unzipped her work overalls to the waist, revealing a white tank and tattoos up both arms. One of the marines was cleaning a fresh gash in her bicep. She gave him a thumbs-up, and he wondered if anything fazed her.

As he approached Cameron, one of the marines was obviously trying to figure out a way to remove the twenty-centimeter shard of glass stuck into the side of Cam's right knee. Lucas touched his shoulder. "I can take over."

Instant relief appeared on the guy's hardened face as he glanced over his shoulder.

"It's okay—he's a medic," Cam said. "Right, Doc?"

While medics were often referred to as "docs," Lucas definitely didn't feel like he'd earned the title just yet.

"Thank God," the marine said. "Wasn't sure what else to do except yank it out."

Cam's dark eyes flared wide and offended. "Seriously?"

Lucas hid his smile. That was exactly what he was going to do. He settled next to the ensign and sifted through the med bag, finding—hell, yes—a canister of biofoam. The glass had lodged through tendon and beneath the kneecap, cutting into the cap bone as well. The fact that Cam hadn't passed out yet from the pain was impressive. But adrenaline could do amazing things. . . .

"Okay, here's what's going to happen. I'm going to pull the glass out, but then I'm going to fill the wound with foam."

Cam's brow rose and his hands gripped the rock on either side of him. Sweat glistened on his skin. "Hold up. If there's biofoam in that bag, then there's probably a couple doses of pollysue or some other painkiller. C'mon, Doc—you gotta numb me up first."

"We're in the middle of a war zone, sir." Lucas wrapped gauze around his own hand to protect it. "Protocol dictates saving the pain meds for severe wounds."

"This isn't severe?!"

"We'll need the painkillers for injuries worse than this, trust me. Look, it'll hurt for a couple of seconds. Once the foam sinks in, it'll numb the pain."

"No, it won't. Biofoam burns like a mother—"

Lucas grabbed the shard and pulled as Cam finished the curse with a loud shout.

The glass slid out with a glob of thick blood. Quickly Lucas applied the biofoam's nozzle directly into the wound and sprayed. Instantly, nitrous oxide mixed with morphophetamine-infused liquid polyethyltriphosphate, creating a foaming effect that would encapsulate, disinfect, and numb the wound.

Cam gasped and his eyes filled with tears. "God—it *burns*."

"It'll be over in a few seconds. Hang in there."

The foam would hold for a few hours, but after that Cam would need to find treatment somewhere. And who knew what form that would take.

"Nice work, Browning."

He glanced over his shoulder and gave the approaching Spartan a nod as Murphy took a seat next to them, handed Cam some water, and then focused his attention on the super-soldier. "What the hell is happening out there, Stone?"

"Far as I can tell, some kind of explosion occurred within the ring. Huge section of it broke apart. You'll see when we get out of this ravine. We're lucky we had good cover here in the mountains and were out of the immediate fracture zones. It's quiet now, though. Dust is settling."

No one had expected *that* kind of answer. Surely Zeta Halo hadn't broken . . . had it?

Murphy rubbed a hand down his face. "Was it the Banished?"

"No, I don't think so. Whatever it was struck our forces and the Banished indiscriminately. We didn't need any more losses, but this does level the playing field a little and gives us time to regroup."

"What about the target?" Murphy asked. "Could she have a hand in what happened?"

Of course, he was talking about Cortana. The rogue human AI was the whole reason *Infinity* had made the slip to Zeta Halo to begin with, their primary mission to stop her and the forces she was marshaling not only against humanity, but the entire galaxy. Lucas had limited intel about how exactly they were going to stop her—all of that was "need-to-know" and well above his pay grade. But he did know that this Halo was apparently her base of operations and now it was also the site of the Banished ambush. Seemed too significant to be a coincidence.

"It's certainly a possibility," Stone said. "Right now, there's no sign of the target or her forces. Whatever happened, we can probably be confident that the Banished are now the dominant threat on the ring."

"Anything from central command?" Murphy asked.

"Nothing. No uplink, no orders."

"And Lasky? Palmer?"

She shook her head. "No word yet. I was in and out of comms range for a while, taking groups of support staff into the mountains. We were on our way back when we caught your Mayday and started toward your direction. And then this happened. . . ."

Lucas noticed that the two marines who'd been assisting atop the hull were now handing supplies—weapons, ammo, food and water stores—from the lifeboat down to one of the others.

"What about us?" Dimik asked. "What do we do now?"

"We head for better ground, and kill any Banished in our way."

CHAPTER 6

Several days had passed and Spartan Horvath was still trying to wrap his head around what happened.

Two things were certain: the rupture had been unlike anything he'd ever seen or felt before. As far as he knew, the UNSC didn't possess the magnitude of power needed to generate such destructive force. So either the Banished had a new weapon of mass destruction, or it had been Forerunner in nature—and if so, who knew what had triggered *that*. The second undeniable thing: Zeta Halo had inexplicably passed through slipspace during the event, and no amount of astronavigational calculations could tell him or Elfie where exactly in the galaxy they'd ended up.

The days and nights passed quietly, as if the land was in a state of shock. The topography of the Halo ring had been ripped apart, tumbled, and tossed, creating debris piles as high as skyscrapers while large tracts out of the blast and fracture zones remained completely untouched. Dozens of land fragments floated like islands in the break, caught in place by the ring's artificial gravity. And for all he knew, he might be stranded on a similar fragment. His vantage point on what was left of the high-elevation plateau had allowed him to see a good portion of the break in the distance, but the rising topography behind him had created a massive blind spot.

Initially there'd been zero communication, no sightings of another living thing, and nothing crisscrossing the sky. Even the local fauna right down to the insects had gone silent. The effect was disconcerting, and at times he couldn't help but wonder if he was the only one left alive. It was a notion he didn't dwell on, instead putting his focus on linking up with the rest of the UNSC.

He kept moving, stopping only to catch a few winks here and there, then continuing on. He still had a working grappleshot, but had lost his assault rifle during the event and was down to six rounds in his M6's magazine. The damage his GEN3 had sustained earlier remained irreparable and would stay that way until he found a base camp with the requisite technicians and technology.

The day before, he'd finally spotted life about five hundred meters away along the shores of an empty sea—Banished survivors, too slow and weary-looking to be an organized scouting party. He studied the eight Jiralhanae through his display as they fought over who would pilot the three Choppers at their disposal. Taking turns wasn't in the Brutes' vocabulary; only the strongest got the good seats, and they continually challenged each other for the right. The Choppers' giant bladed wheels kicked up a nice trail to follow, day or night, so tracking them at a safe distance was a breeze.

Their pace of travel was slow, dictated by mounds of uprooted earth and debris, deep fractures, and exposed Forerunner substructure, which continued to shift and reposition in a seemingly perpetual process of tectonic repair. By nightfall the

Banished had reached an arid plain, and Horvath was forced to hang back even more. His goal wasn't to confront them, but to follow in hopes they'd lead him to a larger force—a base camp or outpost, anything that might sport a communications array.

And, of course, where there were Banished there might be Spartans.

Eventually the plain dropped into a series of short mesas, canyons, and sinkholes. The conifers that had dotted the landscape all lay broken, blown flat in one direction from the explosion's shockwave. By the time he made it across the plain the Brutes had set up camp at the edge of a shallow box canyon. As he eased up behind a clump of downed trees, the thick evergreen branches and wide trunks giving him plenty of cover, their voices were unusually loud, striking him as odd and unlike their standard cursing and sparring and long stretches of quiet. These voices were excited. Laughter even echoed through the night.

Edging around the debris, he scanned the area around the canyon, switching to thermal imagining. The Brutes instantly lit up on his HUD. A blob of white also lurked at the far end of the canyon. He magnified to get a clearer picture and his heart sank. No wonder they sounded so animated. A herd of small deerlike mammals huddled in one rocky corner, most likely trapped during the upheaval, their way out of the area blocked by debris. Days without food or water—they'd be easy pickings for a hungry pack of Jiralhanae.

Horvath turned and slid to the ground, letting his back rest against one of the large boulders as the Brutes readied themselves for a feast. It'd be the perfect opportunity to strike, instinct was pushing him hard in that direction, but he forced himself to stay put. As much as he wanted a fight, getting back to the main areas of conflict was a higher priority.

The frenzy that ensued made his blood boil.

As soon as he'd been old enough to hit a bull's-eye using both a bow and a rifle, he'd hunted on the plains outside of Kuyik with his father and older brothers. And like the Brutes, if he himself was starving and without his GEN3, he'd be forced to hunt for food. However, unlike them, he had learned to respect the process and be grateful for the gift of food. Disgusted, he muted his audio.

An hour later, he resumed audio to check on the situation. Half the herd was dead and the Brutes were sitting around a fire, bellies full and picking at tendons and bones. He amplified the conversation and was able to listen in as they discussed leaving the rest of the herd alive for later in case they were unable to link up with their clan. Once they decided, the first sleeping shifts began and Horvath himself settled in for a two-hour nap.

Before dawn started to streak the horizon, the Brutes packed out and noisily continued on. Once he verified that the situation was all-clear, Horvath walked through the abandoned camp and then slid down the shallow canyon wall, where the signs of violence pissed him off even more. "Bastards." His curse counter dinged several more times as he picked his way around the carnage.

The remaining herd huddled against the far wall, clearly in shock. He let them be—no need to cause them any more stress—and surveyed the area. There was no way in hell he was going to leave the Banished with a readily available food source to return to, so he began moving aside rocks and downed trees to create an escape route for the herd.

Ninety minutes later the way was clear. The herd was safe to leave, and he was back to tracking the Banished.

And as fate would have it, the next day his efforts to hang back were rewarded.

The small Brute party had rendezvoused with another weary-looking Banished force: a collection of Jiralhanae, Kig-Yar, and Sangheili mercenaries at the edge of a wide chasm where the land had nearly fractured in two. The only thing holding the two pieces of land together was a two-hundred-meter-long land bridge and its underlying support structures.

The two parties began to cross the bridge—a collection of Wraiths, Choppers, and Ghosts churned up dirt as they went, followed by several Banished on foot. Horvath's eye was drawn beyond them to the small trail of smoke in the distance. Full magnification showed the red and gray top of a prefabricated Banished outpost a few kilometers into the hills on the other side of the break—the Banished had been busy, it seemed. And if there was one outpost already dropped from their support ships in the sky, there would most assuredly be others. Carefully he made his way over a mangled section of what appeared to be a Forerunner transport system caught up in downed trees, rock, and large clumps of soil and sod, to follow the edge of the fracture toward the bridge. Once the Banished were across, he'd wait awhile and then continue.

As he neared the land's edge, sharp straight-line winds blew up from the chasm, pushing him back a little as he leaned over to get a better view of the dissected ring. There was at least eight hundred meters of foundation terrain parked on top of a few dozen kilometers' worth of scaffolding, pillars, and support beams that made up the land bridge. Massive conduits and cabling spilled out from either side of the break and dark cavities yawned open, big enough for several *Mulsanne*-class frigates to pass through. But just as astonishing as the scale was the incredible feat of engineering and technology that allowed the ring, even in its broken state, to adjust and maintain its life-support functions, providing gravity and breathable air to the fragmented areas.

He straightened, the wind continuing to buffet him as he gazed out over the break and opened an encrypted transmission. "To any UNSC forces in range. This is Spartan Horvath. Fireteam Intrepid of the UNSC *Infinity*. I've been separated from my team for . . . five days. Working my way around the Banished presence on the ring. If anyone can hear me—"

"*Unknown contacts on approach,*" Elfie cut in.

A dropship stained in red swept in low from the other side of the break, flying over the Banished units crossing the land bridge.

"A Phantom." Horvath took off like a shot, scaling the rubble and climbing over debris as the Phantom slowed to a hover on this side of the break, kicking up dirt and dust as it came to ground at the head of the land bridge.

He stopped near the top of the debris, crouching behind a jumble of broken trees and rocks as the bay door to the Phantom opened and two Brutes jumped out. It was instantly clear that these were no minor foot soldiers, but held a higher position in the Banished hierarchy. One wore about a half-ton of red power armor, a captain, if Horvath had to guess. Big one too. He was without his helmet, which told the Spartan that they hadn't come to this location for a fight, and sported two broken tusks, dark-gray skin, thick gray fur, and a beard striped with white. The other was taller and younger, with jet-black fur. He was nearly three meters tall and clad in the dark-red armor of what might be a Bloodstar. And if so, a significant opponent for sure—the Bloodstars were comprised of highly skilled special ops combatants, and were often Silent Shadow operatives.

What the hell were those two heavy hitters doing here? Horvath edged closer, amplifying the audio range in his helmet.

"Ah. A natural choke point," the captain said, surveying the area. "This is where we build. Order the drop."

"What use is a choke point? The humans are scattered and broken. The battle is already won."

The captain whirled around on the younger Brute. "Do you doubt Escharum's judgment? Keep up that talk and . . ." He paused, his face scrunching up as he sniffed the air, grunting. "We're not alone."

Aw, damn it. "Time to go," Horvath muttered.

Instead of tracking the scent, the Jiralhanae hurried back to the Phantom, likely seeking to scout the area from above. Horvath couldn't face such a vessel head-on, his active camo was offline, and he was currently running thin on weapons and ammo. He couldn't hide either. They'd pick him up on thermal in an instant. Taking quick stock, he could see only one viable option—a little tactical repositioning.

Horvath ran, bringing up a grid of the area on his display. The Phantom rose above the terrain and began circling the area, clearly searching for him. The grid on his HUD showed only one possible vector from his current location, and he instinctively launched toward it.

"Spartan Horvath," Elfie instructed, *"please deviate from your current course immediately."*

"Sorry, Fi, no can do."

He pushed every muscle, his armor, all of it, to the limit, racing to the land's edge.

"You can't mean to—"

Oh, he meant to. And he might be crazy, but—

Without hesitation, he leapt off the edge of the ring and into the open chasm, falling twelve meters and then landing hard on a wide piece of platform sticking out into open space. Metal buckled with the impact and a red shield warning flashed across his HUD.

Surprise stuck in his throat. He hadn't been entirely sure he'd stick the landing.

"Get up. Contact is still on the move."

"Yes, ma'am."

The Phantom approached, gaining speed and overtaking his position as it flew out over the break and executed a 180-degree arc before diving down into the chasm, plasma cannon firing bolts of superheated plasma his way. Horvath pushed to his feet and ran for the interior of the ring.

Banished firepower tore through the scaffolding behind him.

He would've made it too if the idiots hadn't come back around and fired again, hitting the land bridge's support beams in the process. The plasma ate away at the weakened alloy as another bolt hit directly behind him, spraying through additional supports and causing the scaffolding to bend.

The structure began to buckle all around him.

An avalanche of dirt, foundation material, metal, and debris collapsed into the chasm as the land bridge gave way, the weight of it severing its supports completely in two, and completely disconnecting the two ring fragments from each other.

The scaffolding beneath his feet tilted upward as the ring fragment drifted away and began to flip.

"No, no, no." Not good. His boots were losing traction as he struggled to maintain his hold.

A streak of silver caught his eye, flashing through falling debris. *"Unknown contact at eleven o'clock."*

A Forerunner sentinel, aggressive as hell, flew out from somewhere inside the ring and fired a particle beam at the Phantom before slamming into it, gripping hold with its two crablike arms, and using its manipulators to tear into its hull as everything suddenly went vertical. The automated drones were primarily designed to maintain Halo's many support systems but had been known to attack in defense of the ring whenever necessary. This one clearly saw the Phantom as a threat and was responding in form.

As the land fragment continued to flip, the piece of alloy support Horvath held buckled and snapped, and he went weightless. Quickly he fired his grappleshot at the scaffolding still attached to the ring fragment as the entire piece of land went vertical and then belly-up, swinging him into an upward arc and then down at blistering speed along with mounds of loosened debris.

Not again.

He was swallowed up, battered from all sides as his display went black.

He never lost consciousness. He heard and felt it all, rocked back and forth, tossed and tumbled and hit repeatedly by earth and rock and metal. And when the upheaval finally stopped, he lay facedown, held in place by what felt like a mountain of detritus.

His HUD blinked out a few times, lines skating across the display, before finally returning to normal.

"Report," he said with a groan, attempting to push up, but the weight above him didn't budge. "Report."

"Pulling data from sensors . . ."

He waited, staying calm despite the fact that he'd just been buried alive.

What the hell was taking so long?

"Fi! Report!"

"Motion tracker, active camouflage module, and long-range comms remain offline. Propulsion system is damaged and energy shielding is at thirty-two percent. The pressure experienced by your armor in conjunction with estimated average weight of land mass suggests your current position to be nine meters beneath debris."

"Great."

"And you have ninety minutes of breathable air."

Horvath grunted in response, a small note of panic coursing through him. He squashed it immediately, relying on his training instead of giving in to the familiar and unsettling memories of being trapped in his own skin, unable to move, to make anything work. His heavy breaths echoed in the helmet. He hadn't delved too deeply into his past in a long time and absolutely didn't want to start now. That part of his life was over. This time, he wasn't paralyzed; his spine wasn't shattered into a dozen pieces; his body wasn't utterly and completely broken.

No, this time he *could* move. Only a little bit, but it was a start.

His fingers worked back and forth, eventually carving out the tiniest bit of wiggle room, and after a few minutes he was able to move his elbow, some of his arm, and a knee. Elfie displayed a countdown timer on his HUD. Eighty-three minutes.

He removed it with a thought. "Not helping." He was already going as fast as he could. A timer would only get under his skin. "Give me a heads-up at the halfway mark."

"Of course, Spartan Horvath."

It was a painstaking process and took extreme effort to dig and create spaces and pockets to push upward and find a blind path through the debris.

"Halfway mark achieved. You have forty-five minutes before oxygen depletion."

"Plenty of time." He hoped.

Suddenly he hit a small air pocket, giving him more leverage to push aside debris. All around him the land squeezing him in began to relax. His pulse was pounding, his muscles and armor pushed to maximum as he carved a tight path through thousands of pounds of rock and dirt and debris to reach the surface.

Finally his hand broke free, then a forearm followed by an elbow, which he used to leverage himself up. As soon as his helmet was clear, a curtain of dirt slid down his visor, and he was finally out of the dark and into the ambient light of Zeta Halo and the yellow dwarf star nearby. Readouts told him there was gravity and breathable air—thinner than before, but enough to allow him to rip off his helmet and draw large drafts into his lungs.

He stayed there, partly submerged, until he was able to stabilize himself.

"We made it, Fi. We made it." For a while there, he hadn't been so sure. . . .

Horvath pushed the rest of the way out of the ground and finally onto his feet, dust and dirt sliding off his Mjolnir as he straightened. A jumble of downed trees, rocks, and chunks of dirt surrounded his position, preventing him from getting a good look at where he'd landed.

If he could get to higher ground, maybe he could tell where the hell he was and how difficult it'd be to find his way back to that Banished outpost he'd seen. He grabbed his helmet, slipped it back on, and started the climb up the debris. A few creatures scurried in the trees or over the ground, but otherwise it was eerily quiet.

And, of course, once again he was alone.

It took the backside of a half hour to finally reach a cleared high point, and he almost stumbled at the view. "Aw, hell."

He barely heard the curse counter ding this time.

Zeta Halo's ring fragments floated in the break like an island chain in a black ocean of stars. But being flipped upside down as he was, he saw only the fragments' manufactured alloy that made up the ring's outer band. Chunks of mountain, trees, scaffolding, Banished and UNSC vehicles, and base components floated in the spaces between the ring fragments.

In his world, he was considered a big guy even outside of his GEN3, but here? Standing at the edge of space and looking out at the view made him feel infinitesimally small.

Horvath stayed on the rise for a while, staring at the view as reality sank in. He'd have to trek to the opposite side of the fragment to line himself back up to where he had originally wanted to go before the Phantom had showed up and ruined everything.

Weary, he turned and headed back down the rise and toward the interior. "Any power signatures out there?" he asked. Halo installations were littered with energy sources, possessing generators, hubs, and distribution channels throughout the substructure in order to power the colossal ring and maintain all of its functions.

"*Nothing worth noting except a failing environmental containment field,*" she answered.

"How long do we have?"

"*Seven days until complete atmospheric drain.*"

"Plenty of time," he said, letting out a heavy sigh. "Okay, then. Let's see what we have to work with."

CHAPTER 7

Zeta Halo
December 18, 2559
Day 7

TJ Murphy and his lifeboat crew had traveled with Spartan Stone for the last five days through the ring's dramatic landscape, crossing a green river valley webbed with tributaries, before finally making their way up into a damp highland forest. They stuck to higher elevations when possible, hoping to get a glimpse of a UNSC presence. Every once in a while a vantage point opened up, allowing a view back at the destruction.

All those ring fragments suspended between the break, and the ever-present arc of Zeta Halo rising above it, struck Murphy with awe each time he saw it. Having completed several missions on the shield world Requiem during his time aboard *Infinity* and prior, he was well-versed in many things relating to the ancient civilization that had created this ringworld. For instance, he knew Halo installations typically measured over three hundred kilometers across. And from the look of the break, he estimated several hundred thousand acres had fractured, and who knew how many more might lie in front of them. Right now they had no way to know if they were currently working their way through ten hundred or ten thousand acres of floating land fragment or if they were on the edge of the remaining intact ring.

A damp cushion of leaves and pine needles along the narrow game trail made Murphy's combat boots sink deep into the wet soil as he and the rest of the group trekked higher into the foothills. Views of the valley below continually peeked through the spaces between leafy hardwoods and tall conifers, drawing his attention. Three days ago, as they crossed the valley, they'd lost all the marines who had accompanied Spartan Stone during their initial rescue from the lifeboat.

They'd ventured too close to a raiding camp cloaked by a Banished Shroud, a large, beetle-like aerial support vehicle. By the time the Banished revealed themselves and struck, there was no way to outrun the unit of Ghosts led by a Wraith. Murphy and Browning had immediately assisted Ensign Cameron to safety while Dimik provided cover.

It all happened so fast, shoving the injured ensign into a wet, grassy ditch as plasma bolts burned through the air and vaporized the ground a few meters away, sending a shower of superheated soil over the area. Murphy had shoved Browning down too—they had to keep their medic safe at all costs—then raced over the grass with Dimik. But in that short span of time, the single-operator Ghosts had slaughtered all the marines while Stone killed the driver of the Wraith, pulling the Sangheili out of the pilot's seat and then using the vehicle to take out the Ghosts before turning skyward to fire on the Shroud.

After, they'd dragged the bodies into the ditch, not wanting to leave them out in the open. Stone barely spoke. Murphy knew enough about Spartans to know that she blamed herself for their deaths, despite the fact that she'd fought like hell, overcome the equivalent of an armored tank with spikes, and then singlehandedly taken on each Ghost—not an easy feat when they sported twin rapid-firing plasma cannons and were extraordinarily nimble gravity-propulsion vehicles.

Later that day, as they'd started up through the forest, they finally rendezvoused with Spartan Kovan and a small group consisting of two hardened ODSTs, Thompson and Kim; three marines, Mosley, Deleke, and Corporal Foutty, the lone female among them; and two supply staff personnel, Erik Bender and Gavin Jo, who naturally gravitated toward Murphy's crew, integrating with them rather effortlessly.

Days of hiking, hiding, fighting, and surviving by the skin of their teeth.

Rinse. Repeat.

They were busted and bruised and broken. Hungry. Exhausted.

And all he could think about for the last day or so was that he might be getting too damn old for this.

Murphy paused on the trail. The thought had occurred to him plenty of times before. God knew he was feeling all forty years right now—not exactly ready for the veterans' home, but still. Twenty-two years spent in the UNSC. Over half his life. He'd seen countless campaigns, had gotten out of some tight spots and tricky situations, but this? This might be the toughest situation yet.

One of the ODSTs stepped around him on the narrow trail. From the height of him, had to be Thompson; otherwise he and Kim were nearly identical in close-quarters combat gear and cans. Thompson's large pack, loaded with as many weapons and ammo as it could carry, hit Murphy's shoulder, causing him to sidestep too close to the edge of the trail; his boot sank into the mud, collapsing a small section of the trail.

"*Shit.*" He slid down the embankment as the ODST strode on. The weight of his own bulging pack pulled Murphy off-balance and he tipped backward, scrabbling for the nearby evergreen branches to stop his fall.

"Whoa, there . . ." Bender suddenly appeared, snatching a wrist as Browning hurried to grab the other.

Murphy swallowed the lump in his throat. Holy smokes, that had been close. He cast a quick glance over his shoulder. He'd come a long way from the valley below, and tumbling off the steep hillside would've been the end of him.

"Dude, don't even look behind you," Bender said, his helmet falling into his eyes as he and Browning hauled Murphy away from the edge.

"It's not *dude*," Dimik scolded as she came up the trail with her own heavy pack laden with MREs, water, and ammo. "He's a lieutenant. How the hell did you even get on a ship like *Infinity*?"

Back on solid ground, Bender tipped his helmet up with a finger and shrugged. Ever since joining up with Kovan's crew, Murphy had been trying to figure out that one himself; how did a big, strong fella like Bender end up cutting hair on the UNSC's flagship?

"Wasn't my idea, trust me," Bender replied under his breath.

Browning pulled up the shoulder strap of Murphy's pack and settled it back into position. The young medic was staring daggers at the back of the hardened ODST as he disappeared up the trail. "What the hell are those guys thinking?"

Murphy wasn't surprised. "I don't think they *are* thinking . . . about us anyway." The pair that Kovan had picked up along the way to rendezvous with Stone had a one-track-mind mentality right now, and that was to regroup with their squad and wreak havoc along the way. ODSTs didn't play around. The guy seemed oblivious that Murphy had almost bitten the dust, hadn't even looked back.

"You all right, Lieutenant?" Dimik asked, concern clouding her eyes as the last two stragglers, Jo and Cam, came up the trail. Her facial bruises had finally faded to a dull mix of yellow and lavender, and hollows had appeared beneath her cheekbones.

Heat crept into Murphy's face at his rookie mistake. Pausing on the narrow trail had been plain stupid. It was no wonder he'd gotten knocked aside. "I'm good, Dimik." The sooner they all regrouped, the better. He gestured for them to continue. "We're gonna have to hustle to catch up. Let's go."

Dimik, Browning, and Jo took off, followed by Bender. Murphy waited for Cam to pass with his makeshift cane, then fell in behind the wounded ensign, bringing up the rear. Cam's knee injury hadn't quite healed despite several applications of biofoam—and it definitely wouldn't be addressed until they could get him proper treatment. He couldn't carry a rifle at the ready while he walked, but it was still on his back, and Murphy had found him a loaded M6 and holster salvaged off a crashed drop pod.

Dusk was beginning to settle over the area as nighttime marched slowly across the ring, giving the air a slight chill and making the forest scent stronger, the thick decomposing floor layer tangier and the evergreens crisper. It reminded him of autumn weather back home in Lexington when he was a kid. He snorted—how long had it been since he'd thought of his childhood, of life on peaceful ground? Seemed like light-years ago. . . .

The next few hours were filled with the occasional pops of rapid rifle fire, the boom of artillery, and the whir of enemy ships as they streaked across the sky—intermittent reminders that the Banished were never far away.

The spaces between the reminders were occupied by the monotonous drone of footsteps in the woods, the jingle of packs and equipment, and the growing sounds of nocturnal insects as night rolled over this portion of the ring. High above them, daylight moved on a similar ever-constant course, spreading across the Halo installation's inner band. Day chasing night. Night chasing day. Round and round it went. On a clear night like tonight, the daylit arc of the ring hung high in the night sky like a moonlit bridge, providing just enough illumination to manage in the dark if you needed it.

Every once in a while the wind picked up, rustling the leaves and stirring up lovely little whiffs of ripe TJ Murphy, making him long for a shower. Hot. Warm. Cold. Didn't matter.

Bender cast a glance over his shoulder. "What doesn't matter?"

Lost in thought, he hadn't realized he'd spoken the words aloud. Murphy shook his head. "It's nothing."

Eventually they reached a more arid plateau populated by a woodland of ancient evergreens that shot up from a mostly barren forest floor. The trees soared into the dark sky, the trunks so wide it'd take several of the party linking hands to surround just one.

The line stopped and tightened. "We'll rest here," Stone announced after everyone was within earshot. "Fifteen minutes, then we move again."

Thick drooping branches with thin evergreen fronds fanned out from each tree, creating nebulous canopies over the ground. They parked at the bases of a pair of gargantuan trees. Murphy removed his helmet and dropped his heavy supply pack between one trunk's hairy roots as his lifeboat crew, or "boat crew"—as they'd now become, for better or for worse—followed suit. His feet ached, and even though he'd found a seat in the dirt, his muscles still fired pins and needles as though traveling on autopilot.

The nights thus far had been balmy, but this altitude sure made him long for a fire. Not for the light—their helmet and weapon lights along with the glow of the daylight arc above sufficed—but for the warmth and the comfort it provided.

Once he finished a bland energy bar and washed it down with some water, Murphy eased back against his pack, his attention drawn to Spartan Stone standing like some giant guardian on the edge of their camp, always watching, listening, scanning. . . . Her Mjolnir sported a growing collection of deep scratches, burns, and impressive dents, which gave her an even tougher appearance than before, if such a thing was possible.

Somewhere out there in the darkness, Spartan Kovan scouted the way ahead.

"Do they ever sleep?" Bender yawned and removed his boots and socks to inspect the blisters on his feet.

"Spartans can go a long time without needing to sleep, eat, or drink," Murphy said. "It's the armor—the suit and their augmentations. . . . They're designed for situations like this." Sleep wasn't an option for Murphy either. If he tried to get in even a few minutes, it'd only make him feel worse when it was time to move on. Better to stay awake. And staying awake meant some off-the-wall conversations—usually initiated by Bender.

"If only I had an *ounce* of that kind of 'extra,'" Gavin Jo muttered between mouthfuls of an MRE.

Truth if I've ever heard it, Murphy almost said aloud. If anyone needed a bit of extra, it was Jo—someone who absolutely wasn't cut out for this or any other kind of wartime scenario. So far the guy had remained relatively quiet and somewhat shell-shocked, his gaze often far away and pained. He didn't have the strength to carry the heavier packs or engage in any sort of hand-to-hand combat with much success, but he could handle a rifle pretty well and seemed to be a team player, so Murphy had to give him credit. Perhaps the strength and training would come in time.

"They have their weaknesses, though," Browning was saying, watching Stone and lowering his voice. "*Infinity* had an entire team of techs devoted to the Spartans, to monitor their health, their body suits, and their armor. If they sustain enough damage out here, with no techs to back them up . . ." He turned his attention to Murphy. ". . . then they're screwed, right? There's no one to fix them."

Dimik frowned. "How do you know that?"

Lucas wiped a hand across his mouth as he finished up his MRE and shrugged. "Medical departments talk. We *know* things."

"*Ooooh*," Dimik replied mockingly, obviously not impressed.

"We'll find an outpost or set one up ourselves," Murphy said, "move in some salvaged hardware, find an intact ship with a small service bay or two with the right gear . . . God knows, the ring is now littered with them." In the first day of fighting, it seemed like *Infinity*'s entire support fleet had fallen from the sky.

"The techs must be down here too," Jo added. "Somewhere."

"Let's hope so." Because it sure was nice having a couple of Spartans at their backs. Murphy let out a tired exhale, crossed his arms over his chest, and closed his eyes for a second. "Wherever we're headed, here's hoping there's a damn shower."

Dimik sighed wistfully. "And a change of clothes."

"A cold beer or two, or three," Browning said after a moment.

"A double moa burger . . ." Murphy cracked an eye open to see a smile growing across Cam's face. "*With cheese.*"

Oh man, now, that *did* sound good. "You guys are killing me. What about you, Jo?" Murphy asked.

Jo frowned, itching at his growing five o'clock shadow. "A shave would be nice."

It made Murphy want to scratch his own scruff. His gaze traveled over their small group. They were all in desperate need of hygiene. "I suppose Bender can help with that."

"Hey, I don't come cheap." Bender sat up straighter, his expression turning curious as he put his socks back on. "So, Jo . . . mortuary specialist . . . what is it you do exactly? I mean, aside from the obvious."

Jo shrugged. "Honestly, it's mostly the obvious. We provide funeral services and perform the duties of a coroner . . . that sort of thing."

"What about you, Bender," Browning asked, "how'd you end up being a barber?"

As Bender redid the laces to his boots, a smile tugged at his lips. "That's a long-ass story involving a class-three reprimand, a bottle of Tier 7 tequila, a pro wrestler from Actium named Betty Bites the Bullet, and losing one very, *very* important wager." The group began to laugh, keeping the volume low, unsure whether to believe him or not. But that's how it seemed to be with Bender—you never knew whether he was bullshitting you or telling the God's honest truth.

Bender sat back and picked up the much-lauded combat knife Spartan Kovan had given to him, twirling it in his hand for a moment before glancing across to the second tree where the marines and ODSTs rested. "You know, we might not be like those guys over there, but . . . we all have skills."

"What do you mean?" Jo asked.

"Well, take Dimik for example. She knows everything about

preventing fire, explosives, plasma burns . . . which means she knows how to start them too."

Dimik thought about it and shrugged. "True."

"Browning here can stitch us all back together. I'm handy with this beautiful thing. And you, Jo, I'm guessing you know a thousand ways a person can die . . . in my book that makes you pretty lethal if you need to be."

"Also true," Jo responded, "though my expertise doesn't translate to alien species."

"Semantics. They have similar bodily functions—they eat, they breathe, they breed . . . they bleed, their organs are—"

"Ugh," Dimik said. "Let's not go there. What about you, Cam? You're a pro at comms."

Cam put his hands behind his head. "Which doesn't help at all since we're radio silent. But I was all-star track back home and won the annual Bow to Stern relay on *Infinity* twice." He stared up at the pine branches, thinking. "I guess you could say I'd be damn good at running away, if not for this major setback." He gestured to his knee. "Just call me the weak link."

The whole team made noises of denial.

"Nah, it'll heal," Browning said. "It's only been five days, and when we find better salvage, better med-tech, it'll be good as new."

Murphy didn't miss the tick in Cam's jaw and the pain that hid beneath his sarcasm. It was well-known in certain circles that Isaiah Cameron's father, grandfather, great-grandfather, two uncles, and four cousins had served or were still serving the UNSC with distinction—nothing like having an admiral, two five-star generals, and a couple captains in the family tree to make you feel the pressure—and to make matters worse, Cam had been demoted from junior lieutenant to ensign about a year prior. Murphy still wasn't clear on the details, but he felt for the kid nevertheless. "If you're good at running," he said, "then you're perfect for sabotage. If we need anyone to plant one of Dimik's explosives or cut a brake line or lift a nice munitions launcher from a Banished supply camp, we know who to turn to."

"I said I'm good at running, not crazy."

Silence descended on the group until Bender piped up with a wide smile he could barely suppress. "We have five minutes left. Let's talk about Kovan."

A mix of groans and muffled laughter followed. It was a favorite subject of Bender's during the long stretches of travel.

"She gave you a knife, Bender, not her heart," Dimik said bluntly.

"It's just the first step, though. First a knife . . . then a Sidekick . . . then who knows where it might lead?"

Murphy shook his head, grinning. Honestly, he couldn't tell if the guy wanted to bring levity to the group or if he truly had a crush on the Spartan.

"Besides, I'm a sucker for a good accent and aloof women."

Dimik burst out laughing, eyes crinkling as she covered her mouth to stay quiet, and shared a look with the others. "Who the hell says *aloof*?"

Bender grunted back, trying not to laugh through his response. "I couldn't think of a cooler word."

"Here's one for ya," she replied. "It's called 'not interested.'"

The rest of the group chuckled.

"That's two words. And say what you want, but Kov—"

A loud *whoosh* cut through the makeshift camp.

Murphy sat up as the rest of the team turned toward the noise. It seemed to happen in slow motion, the battle axe coming out of the darkness, going end over end, its embedded red light creating an arc of color as it went straight through camp and lodged into Mosley, pinning the marine to the tree where he sat.

As soon as it hit, the sound reverberated through Murphy's body like a bolt. He was on his feet, rifle in hand as Spartan Stone turned and charged through the center of camp at a dead run, coming up hard against a Brute as he stormed toward them. They hit each other with enough force that Murphy felt it in his chest.

He tossed Cam his rifle as the others scrambled, snatching up their weapons and helmets. Another massive Jiralhanae emerged out of the darkness in armor splashed with the red markings of the Banished. Flanking him were eight avian predators—Kig-Yar, better known on the battlefield as Jackals. Immediately, dread slid into Murphy's gut. He'd seen his share of aliens, and plenty of Kig-Yar, but these . . . they didn't look right. They were thin and haggard, but it was their eyes that worried him. They were intense and bright, almost too bright, too . . . hungry.

Shit.

Rounds spat off in quick succession, the marines firing at the second Brute, though it did nothing to stop his approach. The Jackals fanned out and eased back into the forest, returning fire, the pink glow of their needlers giving away their positions. "Murphy, deal with the Jackals! We've got the Brute!" the marine corporal shouted.

"You heard her! Let's move. Stay together!"

They used the gigantic trees for cover and tried to keep close, but the Jackals actively maneuvered to separate them like a pack of hyenas culling the weak from the herd. Out of the corner of his eye, Murphy saw a body fly through the air, flung by the Brute under siege. When it landed on the ground, a Jackal appeared out of the blackness and savagely tore into him.

There was no time to be afraid or shocked. "Stay together!" he yelled again. His team moved to join up as the bark of a nearby tree exploded. The beams of the tactical lights on their standard-issue helmets only went so far, but the lamp on Murphy's rifle scope hit upon a pair of glowing eyes and he instinctively fired. "Their eyes—they're reflecting light in my scope! Aim for the eyes!"

The branches rustled above them and two Jackals dropped onto Bender and Jo, jaws snapping wildly. Before he could fire, sharp claws dug deeply into his neck and yanked him backward so forcefully that he dropped his rifle. The warmth of his own blood spilled over his skin as claws like daggers pushed deep into muscle and dragged him farther into the darkness.

As he struggled, he caught sight of Dimik and Cam backed against a tree, trapped by a line of four Jackals, and out of ammo while Browning was nearby unloading.

"Browning, your gun!"

Browning swung his head around and found Murphy in the darkness, tossing the rifle.

He caught it, flipped the barrel, and fired a round past his shoulder. While his combat helmet mitigated some of the concussive force, his eardrum reverberated painfully as the round struck the avian predator in the face, spraying Murphy with alien blood and brains, and bits of skin and beak.

The claws released. Murphy dropped to his knees, gasping, stomach turning as he flipped the gun back to rights and fired several rounds into the Jackal over Bender, killing it and scattering the others in front of Dimik and Cam.

His headlamp lit on another Jackal as it pulled Jo into the darkness by the back of his combat vest. Jo flailed wildly, struggling to find purchase on the ground and instead finding

Bender's combat knife. As soon as it was in his hand, he stabbed at the Jackal's forearm, causing it to stumble and fall flat on its face. Using the arm as leverage, Jo crawled onto the Jackal's body and plunged the knife into its side, chest, and finally neck with rapid, panicked strokes until it ceased struggling.

Murphy pushed to his feet and tried like hell to ignore the overwhelming ringing in his left ear as he looked back at camp, where Stone exchanged punches with the Brute while his partner terrorized the marines with its bare hands, ripping apart one and slamming another against the tree trunk. Kovan suddenly entered the fray, the long barrel of her sniper rifle up and aimed as she fired into the Brute's face, the 114 mm round exploding flesh and bone, the report cracking through the forest. He backpedaled, falling nearly headless as she spent her ammo, but she was far too late to save any of the marines.

Stone meanwhile ran to the bloody axe that still pinned the first fallen marine to the tree. She leapt over the victim, grabbing the axe handle and wrenching it free as her momentum carried her up the tree trunk, where she springboarded off, sailing over the pursuing Brute's head and bringing the bladed weapon down into his neck.

With a roar stuck in his throat, the Brute dropped dead next to his brother.

The ensuing quiet settled like a pall over the forest.

Fuzz edged Murphy's vision and his balance wavered. He slumped against one of the trees. "Sound off!" He closed his eyes and held his breath, praying every single one answered back.

"Lieutenant, are you hurt?" It was Browning, but the voice sounded as if it were coming from underwater.

Murphy waved him off. "I'm fine." He gripped his rifle tighter and tried to straighten, knowing he had to stay alert. They had no idea how many Banished were out there, waiting, hidden in the ring's shadows or with the aid of alien cloaking technology. "We need to get back"—he wasn't sure if anyone heard him, but that might have been Dimik's voice responding. . . .

A hand came out of the darkness and gripped his elbow. "Here, let me help you." It was Cam. "Everyone is accounted for."

Adrenaline continued to flow through Murphy's veins as he led them back to camp, and he said a prayer of thanks that there was still some left in the tank; it was the only thing keeping him upright and alert, though it faded once he saw the two Spartans.

Stone and Kovan knelt in the dirt, heads bowed, amid the bloody remains of the marines and ODSTs. The crew stopped with him and stood there silently, breathing heavily, covered in blood both human and Jackal, trying, like him, to make sense of the scene.

The image burned into Murphy's brain.

"This is bullshit," Bender cursed softly, breaking the spell as he moved away to sit down and put his head in his hands. Cam went behind a tree and proceeded to vomit. Dimik wiped tears from her eyes, her lips drawn into an angry quivering line as she joined Bender. Browning's hands were shaking, but he grabbed one of the med kits they'd salvaged and headed over to the carnage, despite the obvious—there were no survivors to help.

Only Jo remained at Murphy's side, the guy standing there in shock, covered in purple blood, shaking like a leaf, eyes wide and helmet askew. His hand gripped Spartan Kovan's knife so tightly that it too trembled.

Murphy moved in front of him and slowly took the wet blade away, then put his hand on Jo's shoulder. He tried to find words of comfort, but what the hell could possibly be said after this butchery? So he just stood there until Jo focused on him.

Jo's eyes blinked rapidly, his pupils dilated. "I'm not a killer. I'm not a killer." A sharp, anguished laugh bubbled from his lips. "I'm not a killer, I'm not . . ."

Murphy understood all too well. It wasn't hard to pull a trigger and shoot from a distance, but it was a whole lot different in close quarters, body to body, fighting to the death.

Spartans Kovan and Stone rose in unison. Stone's head turned Murphy's way, and for a moment he could see his small reflection in the sheen of her visor. She jerked her helmet, motioning him for a word while Kovan and Browning tended to the dead. Jo wiped his face, lifted his chin, and slowly walked over to offer his help.

At the edge of camp Murphy joined Stone as she stared off into the night. "Kovan picked up a transmission on the ridgeline." Ah. That would explain her delay in returning to camp. "Looks like Makovich found us our rendezvous point. The *Mortal Reverie*."

"She's intact?" he said in surprise.

"About a day's journey, depending on terrain. In pretty decent condition from what we hear. We'll get you guys there in one piece." Her voice was brittle and edged with guilt.

"Your armor is taking a beating, Spartan. How you holding up?"

"Don't worry about me."

"Your motion tracker is offline, isn't it? And probably your targeting sensors too." Otherwise, she damn well would have seen the enemy coming.

"I know what you're getting at, Murphy. Don't make excuses for me."

"Why not? They're legit. You and Kovan . . . you're running on borrowed time just like the rest of us, and working with gear that's taking some intense damage and no goddamn way to repair it. We're all doing the best we can, including you."

"Yeah, well, my best sure as hell isn't losing people to the Banished." With that, she marched away.

Sighing, Murphy watched her go. Spartans held themselves to impossibly high standards. They took the slightest perceived failure personally and they always made amends. Hyper-responsibility was a mountain all Spartans carried . . . but then, he supposed they were designed to carry mountains.

CHAPTER 8

The first glimpse of the *Mortal Reverie* struck Lucas with awe. He paused along the mountainous ridgeline with the rest of the team. He was no expert, but it seemed like a good location, dominating the end of a pass littered with a few sparse grass patches and thin alpine trees clinging to loose soil, rocky outcroppings, and strange hexagonal stacks of Forerunner alloy that rose from the ground in groups and seemed to slowly shift and adjust. They were still several klicks away, according to Murphy, but from their higher position on the ridge, their view was unobstructed.

The frigate lay at the edge of an unnatural cliff where a fracture had split part of the mountainous area in two, her bow hanging over the open chasm. Her center was buckled and part of her belly had lodged deep into the landscape, as though she'd hit the ground hard and fast, plowing her way through to the very precipice.

The overwhelming relief at seeing her weakened his legs and actually hurt his chest; after what had happened in the woods,

Lucas was surprised he could feel anything at all. Despite his cuts and bruises and exhaustion, the entire journey he'd been feeling numb and dumbfounded that their small crew had actually made it out alive while others more trained and able had not.

Survivor's guilt settled firmly into place as he remembered each loss from the moment *Infinity* had been attacked.

Spartan Horvath followed on the heels of those memories, and Lucas wondered if the lifeboat's would-be rescuer had survived the ring's destruction, if he continued to search for them, if he'd found the empty shuttle, or had met a terrible fate at the hands of Banished patrols and scavengers.

Jo stopped next to him, interrupting the direction of his maudlin thoughts. The petty officer was extremely pale and gaunt. Everything about him shouted that he was done, mentally and physically. Some of the intense shock of the brutal forest attack had worn off, and they'd washed away as much Jackal blood as they could without wasting too much water, but traces of purple still clung dark and crusty in the crevices of Jo's skin and stayed dried on his clothes. His dark eyes were lost, dazed, consistently red-rimmed.

"Surprised we made it," he remarked in a flat tone.

Lucas plastered a hopeful expression on his face even though he too wasn't feeling especially bright. "It's going to be good," he said as they continued walking, Bender and Dimik ahead of them, Murphy and Cam behind. Spartan Stone was keeping pace at the head of the pack and Spartan Kovan was more visible this time, following Murphy but keeping to the higher rocks. "We'll regroup, you know? Clean up, shave, finally sleep without looking over our shoulders all the time, eat warm food . . . things will turn around."

Jo snorted. "It'll be a miracle if we survive. We're scattered and outnumbered . . . and we don't even know when or if help is coming."

Lucas didn't know how to respond to that, mostly because deep down, he couldn't argue with Jo's logic.

They went a few more steps before Jo said, "I'm sorry. I'm just being realistic—to a fault, I know. And trust me, I've heard it my entire life. No one likes to hear the truth or look at the world through unfiltered lenses. I don't like it either," he said hoarsely, "I hate it—I hate . . . *this*. But—"

"It's not in your nature to sugarcoat things. That's why you're good at what you do. Just the facts, right?"

Jo glanced over and Lucas was surprised to see that his eyes had grown glassy and his mouth was spread into a thin, grief-stricken line. He dipped his head, grateful to be understood. "Right." An errant tear slipped down his cheek, carving a clean trail through days of dirt, smoke, sweat, and blood. "So, what's left to hold on to for a person like me?" He laughed and wiped it away. "I hate this goddamn place."

The true weight of what Jo was going through hit Lucas hard. Jo didn't want to feel the way he did—who would? But if you lived in the land of raw facts and unbiased odds—if that was just part of your DNA—then it sure was going to be a struggle to find hope amid the chaos and grief and the constant stresses of war.

Lucas's training had included PTSD, of course. But seeing it firsthand over the past few days had made him realize how unprepared he was to be the effective medical figure everyone needed him to be. At twenty-five, he was the youngest one on the crew and at times felt like he had no business helping anyone at all.

He hadn't realized he'd stopped walking again while Jo continued without him.

A tight sensation squeezed Lucas's chest. He was familiar with this feeling—the anxiety that came from questioning his worth, whether he was good enough to make a difference, to survive. Imposter syndrome, they called it. All he'd ever wanted to do was save people, and right now he certainly didn't think he had what it took.

And also right now, just like Jo, he wasn't sure if that was even possible in the end.

The air was thinner up here and cooler, grayer. Lucas drew it deeply into his lungs and released it slowly, attempting to push out the doubts. No matter the outcome, he'd do what he could, ease pain and suffering, offer a shoulder to cry on. A little attention and comfort could go a long way—he'd seen it up close, knew it to be true after growing up in a house full of nurses and caregivers. He'd focus on those things and take it one step at a time. And leave the big-picture worries for the ones in charge.

"You all right?" Murphy asked, catching up to him. "You've stopped twice."

Murphy was just as dirty and beaten and exhausted as the rest of them, yet through the busted lip and scruff, the nasty bruise under his left eye, the deep claw marks on the side of his neck that continued to ooze blood, and the weight of the pack he carried, he still managed to project an aura of ease. And always that slight quirk to his mouth or humorous glint in his eyes.

It struck Lucas how much the lieutenant reminded him of his father—probably the worst realization to have when he was already swimming in emotions. He swallowed that line of thought down real quick. "Nothing's wrong. Just . . . I don't know, thinking, I guess."

Murphy eyed him for a long second. "Take my advice and save the thinking for later after you've had some time to rest, okay?" He clapped him on the shoulder and gave a small squeeze.

Lucas responded with a nod of appreciation, then turned his attention to Cam as he approached. "How's the knee today?"

"It's looking forward to getting into *Reverie*'s med bay." Cam actually cracked a smile and continued walking, more positive than he'd been in days.

"Come on, Doc," Murphy said. "Chin up. The *Reverie* is waiting."

The *Reverie* is waiting.

And that was the best damn thing he'd heard in a very long time.

CHAPTER 9

UNSC *Mortal Reverie*
Zeta Halo
December 19, 2559
Day 8

As they made their way off the ridge and into the pass leading toward the downed ship, the team and their two Spartan escorts tightened into a group, and Murphy got his first sight of an active UNSC presence. Goddamn, it was good to see.

The mood of the entire team automatically brightened.

Once they passed through the first armed barricade of interlocked titanium sheets, the sheer size of the *Mortal Reverie* began to reveal itself, perched in the rocks and looming above them. The broken behemoth filled Murphy with relief and happiness. All things considered, she wasn't in bad shape, and that meant supplies, provisions, tech, medical, armory . . . it was all there. She was so damned beautiful that he choked up a bit.

A burly warrant officer with his arm in a sling greeted Spartans Stone and Kovan. "Sure good to see more Spartans joining the fold. Commander Hensler and Spartan Griffin are in the command center, waiting for your report." The two super-soldiers proceeded without a backward glance.

Murphy saluted the wounded WO. "First Lieutenant TJ Murphy," he introduced himself before turning to the team. "I've got Mortuary Specialist Third-Class Gavin Jo; Retail Services Specialist Erik Bender; Safety Specialist Robin Dimik; Comms Specialist Ensign Isaiah Cameron; and Marine Combat Medic Lucas Browning."

The officer recorded their names and ID numbers into his datapad. "Thank you, Lieutenant. Staff Sergeant Park will assign clean uniforms and gear, sleeping quarters, and shower passes. Once you've all cleaned up and eaten, she'll assign you to a task group. All bags, weapons, and ammo can be dropped with her as well and contents parsed out to the appropriate supply departments." He glanced up, acknowledging each one of them. "Glad you made it—welcome to *Mortal Reverie*."

Murphy turned to the group, his chest swelling. These guys had been through the worst kind of hell, and he was damned proud they'd come this far. He gave them an encouraging smile. There were a few pairs of watery eyes, and thanks passed along to the warrant officer, before they continued through the barricade.

Once they were clear and had gone several paces, the team stopped and regarded each other for a long, solemn moment; then Dimik let loose with a wide, dimple-filled grin, and it was like the sun had come out. The dawning realization that they'd actually made it to a safe place was now palpable and even Jo cracked a disbelieving smile.

"We made it, you bastards," Bender said, and hooted, and smiles turned to laughter.

Dimik reached over and pinched him. "You know you can go to the brig for calling the lieutenant a bastard, right?"

Murphy laughed. "I think he gets a lifetime pass. You all do. Come on, let's get settled in."

As they approached the staff sergeant's post, another small group was just leaving the area and entering the ship. The sergeant was surrounded by duffel bags and crewmen loading those bags and other salvage into bins for sorting. When she finished on her datapad, she glanced up, meeting his gaze and saluting. "Lieutenant Murphy."

He returned the honor. "Sergeant Park."

"I've got all the info from the warrant officer, so go ahead and leave your things—you can keep anything personal if you have it." She reached into a bin and began handing out fresh uniforms. "If you have any tags from the field, they go in that bin."

The team exchanged glances. The bin in question was near her feet, and filled deep with dog tags. Murphy's heart gave a painful lurch, and he understood immediately that all the groups arriving had done the same thing—collected the tags from those they'd either lost or come across, keeping them safe until they found a home base.

"Jesus," Bender whispered, and for a moment it felt like time had paused as they stared at the impossibly large collection of tags. There were so many.

Murphy dropped his bag and withdrew the tags they'd been keeping safe and carefully placed them in the bin with the others.

"To conserve resources, we have a lock on water usage. I've entered your names and ID numbers into the database and you're now in today's rotation. We have two locker room facilities for your use that require ID for entry. All other sites have been closed, including personal bathrooms and sinks in quarters, so don't try to use one—if you do, you're on bathroom duty, and trust me, you won't like it. Got it?"

"Yes, ma'am," everyone replied in unison.

She gave them a quick smile, attempting to show some friendliness, but Murphy could see she was dog-tired and must've been at it a while. "On behalf of Commander Hensler and the *Mortal Reverie*'s crew, welcome aboard. Your quarters will be Deck Three aft, Section H-5, and the mess is main deck central. Stay out of damaged areas unless expressly permitted, and Decks One and Two are completely off-limits. The group before you will be heading to the showers, so eat first and then get cleaned up. Ensign Cameron, we expect you in the med bay for treatment after you eat. Browning, make sure he gets there."

"Yes, ma'am."

"Anyone else with injuries, join them." She threw a glance at Murphy's deep claw wounds. "That includes you, Lieutenant. Take advantage of the care before it runs out. You'll get the night to rest, then come see me at zero six hundred for assignments. At that time, please make sure to relay any skills or hobbies you possess outside of your current occupation—mechanics, game hunting, cooking, et cetera."

They waited for more, but she jerked her head to the ship. "That's it. Enjoy the meal."

After salutes were exchanged, they headed inside, and made a beeline for the mess.

The order in and around the *Reverie* gave Murphy a sense of comfort and stability and belonging. The military had been his life for so long that being aboard the ship was as close to a homecoming as he could get. Not since the Covenant War had the feelings hit him so strongly. Out there, in combat, in chaos, in the utter shitshow of the last few days . . . he had no idea how he'd held it together, but now that he was here, safe for the moment, the true gravity and emotion and grief swelled over him all at once.

As the others filed into the mess hall, he paused at the entrance and reached for the bulkhead for support. His limbs felt unsteady and his heart raced. His throat closed up and his eyes began to sting. He squeezed them closed and pinched the bridge of his nose, measuring his breathing, trying like hell to keep the horrific images and losses from flashing one after the other through his tired mind.

Suddenly hands were on him, one on his shoulder, another gently pulling his hand off the bulkhead and supporting his elbow. He opened his eyes, expecting that Browning or Cam, mostly likely, had come back—but it wasn't just one; the whole crew had gathered around him. No words were needed; they'd all been there, all understood. And they would never forget.

"I'm okay," he assured them, knowing without question he'd lay down his life for any one of them. "I'm okay."

"Yeah. We know," Browning said.

"I think you're the most *okay* guy I've ever known," Bender added.

"None of us would've have made it here without you, Murphy," Cam said, Jo nodding in agreement next to him.

Dimik met his gaze, her eyes turning soft and gentle. "Come on, let's go in and stuff our faces."

Murphy stood straighter and drew in a rallying breath. "Never been more ready . . . after you."

The mess proper contained three groups of survivors, all in working coveralls. They glanced up at the new arrivals, and Murphy found himself searching for familiar faces, noting that the other groups were doing the same. They were busted up and bruised, but nonetheless clean and with full bellies from the looks of their empty trays. Seeing them made him silently ponder the fate of his comrades—the Pelican unit had been a tight-knit community, and part of his family for well over a decade.

But now he saw no one he knew among them as he followed the others to the counter, grabbing a tray for himself and one for Cameron, sliding it on the rail in front of him. Like water, food would be strictly regulated. They'd get whatever was served, and at this point, who cared what it was.

Murphy almost wept right there on the line when one of the counter servers slipped two slices of plain cheese pizza onto his tray. Two beautiful, perfect cheesy triangles. He blinked as the sting of tears once again hit the backs of his eyes. He must be losing it to get so emotional over some damn pizza. He glanced to his right. Dimik was staring down at her own slices with the same look, and he realized it was more than just food—it was a symbol of home, utterly comfortable and completely human.

Moving along, he received a spoonful of fruit—a mix of blue grapes, Sedran red fruit, and a selection of citrus. A soy-based protein square rounded out the meal, along with a bottle of Rejuvenole-10, a high-vitamin and -mineral boost.

The next fifteen minutes passed in a daze. Grunts and groans issued around him, but nothing mattered except crust, red sauce, and cheese. It went by way too fast, of course. He could eat another ten slices easily, but had to satisfy himself with the fruit and the protein square, which in the end was extremely filling.

The name *Lasky* suddenly reached his ears. Murphy perked up, trying to overhear the conversation from the nearby table, but couldn't discern anything.

"You heard that too? Lasky?" said Bender.

"I guess they're wondering the same things we are. What happened to the captain, to *Infinity* . . . is help coming?"

Murphy knew several people who might know the answers. And they were currently gathered in the command center. "You three head for the showers," he told Dimik, Bender, and Jo before addressing Browning and Cam. "You two go on to the med bay."

"What about you?" Browning gestured to his Jackal wounds. "Those need to get taken care of."

"I will. But first I need to figure out what's going on." And he'd provided enough support to the Spartans over the years that getting some answers from them now shouldn't be a problem.

"Let us know when you do," Dimik said. "There's nothing worse than being in the dark."

"Will do. And until then, get comfortable. This is going to be home for the foreseeable future."

And as far as temporary homes went, they'd hit the jackpot.

CHAPTER 10

Horvath had spent the last couple days scouring the small island fragment. He'd been able to make it from one end to the other in less than half a day, and had crossed several times, creating a grid and using the highest vantage points to build a lidar of the topography, which was mostly edged with debris and forested in the interior, with a wetland basin in the center that was slowly draining water out into space. So far he'd found nothing that would help him get across open space and back to the larger ring fragment where he'd seen the Banished outpost.

Once he finished exploring the basin, he planned to scale down the outer edge of the island and head inside the fragment's substructure.

"Picking up a life sign twenty-six meters from your location," Elfie stated. A small dot appeared on his HUD deep in the basin. *"It's too far and intermittent to determine species."*

It was the most promising thing he'd heard in days.

Energized, he made tracks to the location, heading through the higher-altitude forest, down a steep ravine, and into the lower hills.

The hills gave way to the basin area and wetland habitat where fat green vines weaved their smooth limbs through tall shaggy-barked trees, making the passage dark and difficult to navigate.

As Horvath pushed through the tangle, he carefully monitored his display to stay on solid ground versus veering off into camouflaged sections of deep sludge. Things slithered and rustled through the habitat and his every move was watched from above by large brown birds with talons that enabled them to grip tightly to the trees, and long legs, beaks, and feathers that perfectly mimicked the bark and twigs and leaves around them.

As he closed in on the signal, a picture began to build. "You've got to be kidding."

A Phantom came into view in a burned-out circle of vegetation and broken trees, pointed ass-down and listing portside. The stern, portside, and most of its central body were crushed into the ground. Horvath paused, cocking his head and giving a grunt of satisfaction. So he hadn't been the only one caught up when the land mass flipped.

He continued his approach, examining the image building on his display. The engine was pulverized and buried in muck, but there might be some salvageable parts he could use to get him back where he needed to be.

And then he saw the sentinel trapped beneath the starboard hull aft. Seventy percent submerged. One of its crablike, alloyed appendages and just the top of its rounded central head stuck out of the mud. "Now, *this* might be useful," he said, picking up the pace. Forerunner drive systems, like the ones used by sentinels, were remarkably versatile and could often be adapted to provide lift and propulsion—that is, *if* it was still functional and Elfie could access its power and control systems.

Once he reached the site, he went immediately to the sentinel, squatting down to scan the Forerunner security drone. No power sigs, but there had to be a gravity unit and an impulse drive buried beneath the mud and the Phantom, which was just the kind of thing he'd been looking for.

"Life sign reads trapped Jiralhanae."

His lips spread into a smile. "Did . . . you just make a joke, Fi?"

"Just being thorough in my report," she answered, but there was definitely a trace of humor in her tone, which was nice to hear. She was programmed for it, but hardly made use of it.

As for the Brute inside the Phantom—the enemy could rot for all he cared. He had better things to do.

Unfortunately, much later, Horvath realized he might have to care a little bit.

Almost an hour had passed in his attempt to free the sentinel. He was strong, but not even an augmented Spartan-IV in GEN3 Mjolnir power armor could lift and hold a Phantom out of the mud while retrieving a sentinel stuck in the same muck. He'd managed to rock the Phantom ever so slightly, but the mud kept sucking it back down. He needed a second pair of hands, or to face the fact that he might never get off this island.

Annoyed and tired, his stomach actually growling for the first time in ages, he marched away from the wreckage. He was wasting his time here. There had to be some kind of Forerunner tech in the substructure that was a better option than this.

There wasn't jack in the substructure—at least, nothing that he'd been able to find in the last few days. Anything not nailed down, along with a good portion of substructure, was currently floating peacefully in space just below the island fragment. It would take weeks to work his way through the rest of the twisted underbelly.

"Three days before atmospheric depletion," Elfie reminded him as he returned to the edge of the basin.

"Yeah, I'm well aware." He stared at the wetland jungle with reluctance. Time was running out.

What other choice was there? He'd have to rescue the damn Brute.

As stubborn as Horvath was, he didn't plan on losing his life over pride and hatred for the enemy.

With a very reluctant sigh, he made his way back to the downed Phantom.

With a simple jump, he grabbed the edge of the open starboard bay floor, boosting himself to his feet and then angling down the steep slope into the Phantom's cargo hold, the stench hitting him immediately. "Increase filter," he said, grateful for his helmet's ability to deal with air, toxins, and smells.

His headlamp lit the black space, revealing the crushed portside interior and the captain he'd seen days ago dead and covered in flying insects, lying amid a pile of damaged supply crates and grav carts. Anything loose had been thrown violently to that side. The life signal on Horvath's HUD pointed to a spot through the gangway and just behind the cockpit, where a form was trapped between the buckled aisle and a jump seat, but he ignored it for the moment and instead rooted through the interior, picking up a decent collection of weapons—a couple needlers, a ravager, a skewer, and a few plasma rifles and carbines. From the captain, he lifted an explosives launcher called a brute shot. After gathering the weapons, he started in on the supply crates, surprised to find them full of excavation tools, everything from plasma cutters to gravity plates.

Two of the crates held a selection of stone reliefs.

Curious at the unexpected find, he removed each artifact and laid it on the bay floor to get a better look. The stones appeared crudely excavated, as though laser-cut out of a larger slab or directly from a natural stone wall. Each contained a collection of symbols etched onto the surface. Some of the pieces were curved at one end, and when placed together formed a half circle.

There was no apparent technological value to what the Jiralhanae had excavated. The value had to lie in the material itself or in the symbols carved onto the surface. "Fi, run the symbols through the database and ID the stone."

"The material is a granite composite—quartz, plagioclase, feldspar, and biotite," she reported. *"There appears to be no match presently on record for the symbols. Origin unknown."*

He squatted and ran a hand over the symbols. They appeared incredibly old and prehistoric in composition. "Nothing in the Forerunner database?"

"No."

Over a thousand centuries ago, a network of Halo weapons had been designed to cleanse the galaxy of all sentient life in an effort to defeat the Flood parasite. But they'd also served another purpose: as repositories housing collections of species from across the galaxy, preserving life in order to reseed the galaxy once the threat of the Flood was gone. Whatever language was etched into the stone fragments might be an early form of Forerunner language or from one of the species the Forerunners had collected and housed on the ring.

Horvath stared at the dead Brute for a long moment before

getting up and inspecting the body, shooing the small black insects away. On the Brute's left-arm gauntlet, a crushed datapad yielded a destroyed data chip. He tossed it and turned the heavy corpse over, only to be let down again. Was it too much to ask for a jump pack? With a disappointed sigh, he grabbed the Brute by both wrists, pulled him up to the cargo hold's edge, and then shoved him off before leaping down and dragging the body far out into the basin.

Once that was done, he returned and gathered all the handheld weapons he'd collected, tossing them into a crate and carrying them off the vessel and high up in the ravine for safekeeping before returning to the Phantom for the survivor.

The massive black-haired Jiralhanae he'd seen with the captain near the land bridge was indeed trapped on the floor between the crushed hull and a damaged jump seat. A section of floor had been forced up in the aisle, creating a wedge against the jump seat, effectively pinning the Brute's large body with his arms trapped at his sides.

While Horvath had been stomping around the Phantom, the Brute had remained silent, but it wouldn't be long before things got a little louder. As he ducked beneath a section of loose hull, his headlamp illuminated more of the enormous beast, lighting on shiny black eyes that quietly glared daggers in his direction. Its chest rose and fell with powerful, audible breaths.

Elfie projected a deep bio scan of the Jiralhanae behemoth on Horvath's display, revealing a dislocated shoulder and three cracked ribs from the impact.

Beyond him in the cockpit, a Brute copilot had been smashed between the hull and console while the Jackal pilot lay draped over the arm of its own seat. Horvath moved into the cockpit and shoved the pilot to the side to give enough room to lie on his back and pull off the panel beneath the console. "Okay, let's see what we've got."

On his display, Elfie automatically constructed a blueprint to give him a clearer picture of what he was viewing. *"What are we looking for, Spartan?"*

"Anything that might tell us what the Banished have been up to. Ah. There it is." He reached through cables to the circuit containing the Phantom's flight recorder, and retrieved the intact data chip inside. "Analyze all flight paths over Zeta Halo," he said, slipping the chip into his helmet's data port. "And let's recover the nav logs while we're at it."

"That will be impossible, Spartan Horvath. The navigational log is severely damaged . . . however . . . I am able to retrieve the last forty-eight hours of flight path."

"What about comms logs?"

"Unsalvageable."

"All right. Weed through whatever you can."

He pushed out from under the console and returned to the lone survivor, kneeling and picking the Jiralhanae's helmet off the floor. He rolled the heavy piece of armor around in his hands. After a moment, he cocked his head, regarding the Jiralhanae thoughtfully. With that fancy Bloodstar armor, there might be a propulsion pack hiding at the Brute's back that he hadn't noticed before, and if that was the case, then he could ditch recovering the sentinel, and just kill the Brute and—

Damn it. No jump pack.

Horvath dropped the helmet and draped an arm over his knee, huffing. "I really hate to do this," he said, shaking his head. The Jiralhanae's giant body went still, indicating that his translation software was working just fine at least. "But"—the words were like glass in his throat—"I'm going to have to let you live."

The Brute's eyes widened, but it was only a brief moment before indignation and fury shone hot in his gaze. Horvath grinned. How it must burn the Jiralhanae from the inside out—that a Spartan was showing him mercy.

"I've been all over and inside this chunk of the ring," he said slowly. "You and me—we're the only ones here, and in three days, gravity and atmosphere will cease to exist. So here's how this is going to work: we're going to free the sentinel that this piece of junk is currently sitting on and use its impulse drive to get us out of here."

He let the words hang in the air, feeling unclean and itchy for having made such a suggestion to the enemy, one who would rend him limb from limb given the slightest opportunity.

A slow and impossibly deep chuckle built in the Jiralhanae's chest, filling the space.

Horvath straightened. He already knew how this was going to play out and would have to go through the motions to get what he wanted. He turned his back and walked away, ducking under the broken hull as the Brute finally spoke.

"A truce, then, human."

The obvious lie made Horvath roll his eyes. But he returned to the Brute, dipping his head and choking down his reply. "Yeah. Until we make it back."

A vicious smile emerged, revealing a nasty set of fangs. "And then I kill you."

Funny. That's exactly what Horvath was thinking.

The Jiralhanae, however, wasn't going to wait until after they made it back. Horvath drew the cool, filtered air into his lungs and released it. Shit was about to get messy, which was fine by him.

He'd been exasperated for days anyway and could use a good fight.

With renewed energy, he kicked the wedge in the floor until it broke and flew into the cockpit. As soon as it was gone, the Brute started pushing at the jump seat with his elbow. The metal groaned. Horvath grabbed its frame and pulled until the bolts popped out one by one and the seat moved just enough for the Jiralhanae to free his shoulders, then his arms.

Horvath moved back, energy flowing and ready as the Brute got his feet under him, and straightened to his full height. And despite the dislocated shoulder and cracked ribs, he charged.

Giant arms wrapped around Horvath's waist, lifting him up and then slamming him against the piece of hull that hung into the aisle. He heard the telltale *snap* indicating that the force had slammed the Jiralhanae's shoulder back into place. They crashed through and rolled into the bay. He gripped the side of the Brute's damaged chest armor, ripping a section free before landing a hard blow to his injured ribs and feeling a small, satisfying crunch.

The Brute rallied by seizing his shoulders and slinging him across the bay; the pummeling went on for several minutes until Horvath's lungs burned and armor integrity warnings skipped across his display. Neither he nor the Jiralhanae was able to stay steady on his feet, but Horvath was in much better shape overall. Every blow he landed was aimed at his enemy's ribcage. Finally the Brute held up a wavering hand, and slurred, "A truce, demon."

If he'd had the breath to laugh, he would have. But all he could manage was "That's what you said earlier, and look where it got us."

"On . . . my honor, human. A truce."

Horvath hesitated, and said before slumping against the bulkhead, "Knew you'd see things my way."

CHAPTER 11

Zeta Halo
December 24, 2559
Day 13

Spartan Horvath sat on the hillside, staring at the smoke curling up from the basin, his helmet resting in the grass beside him. Gorian, as he'd come to know the Brute's name, must have caught a couple of snakes or birds to tide him over, and started up a campfire.

It had taken two days, but together they'd finally succeeded in leveraging the starboard side of the Phantom about twelve centimeters out of the mud with a couple substructure beams gathered from the edge of the island. It was enough to start digging around the sentinel. Dead tired and needing a break from the constant vigil of watching his back, Horvath had hiked out of the wetlands and high into the hills.

From this vantage point, the view stretched clear to the edge of the island and out into space, where only a few pinpricks of starlight flickered in the blackness. There wasn't much out there— which worried him more than he'd care to admit. He'd made this hike a few times now, sitting on the hill and wondering just how isolated they were in the galaxy.

As far as Christmas Eves went, this wasn't the worst one he'd spent, though it might just be the loneliest. Plus, he was pretty sure Gorian hadn't even gotten him a gift.

Horvath scratched his growing beard as memories of Fireteam Intrepid filled his mind, sitting in the lounge on S-Deck with the team, toasting the holiday, talking shit, making stupid bets, planning their next prank. They were chaos-makers on and off the job, and he'd loved every minute of it.

Unsettled, he donned his helmet and headed down the hillside. Might as well see how much he could poke the Brute and liven up the holiday.

Gorian sat on an empty supply crate in front of the fire, his massive black shoulders slumped forward. A large plucked bird hung over the flames, suspended from a limb balanced on two tripods, while a couple thorned snake heads and skins lay at the edge of camp. Horvath kicked one aside as he entered the area, and sat across the fire. The Brute picked a snake bone from his dirty mouth, tossed it over his shoulder, and then pulled the bird from its pole to sink his fangs into one of the wings, the crunch of bone and meat drifting across camp.

"As soon as we're off this fragment," he grumbled between chews, "I will enjoy killing you." A line Gorian repeated frequently.

"Keep talking like that and I might start thinking you like me."

"Why don't you take that helmet off or eat anything?"

"Who says I don't?"

The Jiralhanae grunted, eyes narrowing as he paused in his feast to hold a hand out, palm up. The leathery expanse flexed, the fingers curling into a tight fist as he intoned: "Atriox once crushed a Spartan helmet with his bare hand."

"Well, Atriox isn't here. . . ." Horvath paused thoughtfully. "In fact, I'm betting he's probably good and dead by now."

Gorian went still, then pointed the mauled crane wing at him. "Careful with your words, demon."

Ah. He'd hit a nerve. Naturally, he had to do it again. "The Banished will never take the ring."

An amused grunt issued from deep within Gorian's throat. He polished off the wing, juice and fat sticking to the fur on his chin, and then wrenched open the bird's chest, biting into one side. "There are more of us here than there are of you. More weapons. More ships. And soon we will control not only the ring, but the—"

Now, that caught his attention. What else was there? What were the Banished up to?

Gorian laughed slowly. "You humans have been here for years, studying with your feeble minds, and yet you know nothing about what this ring is capable of or what it holds."

"And you do?"

"Why else would we be here?"

Not exactly a giant revelation, but Horvath was starting to think it might have something to do with the artifacts the Banished were so interested in. "So what's the endgame, then? You take control of the ring and whatever else is here . . . and then what? Do you even know why you're fighting?"

"War." He ripped off a giant chunk of meat. "It is the lifeblood that feeds the Jiralhanae soul. There need be no other reason than that." He took a moment to study his opponent. "You think you are different? Is it not *your* lifeblood as well? What would you do without war, Spartan? Who would you be?" He grunted and went back to eating. "Nothing. Nothing at all."

The fire spat sparks into the sky. Horvath watched them rise, mulling over Gorian's words, when a chunk of bird meat hit his Mjolnir armor with a splat and slid down to his lap. "*What the hell?*" His curse counter dinged as he picked the meat up between two fingers.

Gorian's smug laugh was low and deep. "We still have a truce, Spartan. All warriors must eat. When I do kill you, it will be a fair fight. It won't be because you are weakened by hunger."

The bird was rare in the middle and turned his stomach. Immediately he flung it back at the Brute, smacking him square in the mouth. A wide grin split Horvath's face and laughter bubbled from his own throat, loud and clear via his helmet speaker. *Go chew on that, asshole.*

Gorian flung it to the ground and leapt to his feet.

Horvath responded with a very satisfied and lengthy sigh. "Merry Christmas."

"I know not what you speak of, this merriment."

"You wouldn't," Horvath muttered.

Gorian returned to his seat and regarded the Spartan quietly before saying: "Long before the Great Immolation, in Jiralhanae prehistory, females were tasked with raising and training the fearsome *kateukal* warbeasts, with killing the mother and raising the pups, allowing them to sleep in their beds, nurse at their breasts, to bite and nip at their heels, and fight with their own offspring. They yapped and yapped, fierce, but small and stupid for many, many years, so that no male Jiralhanae could bear to dwell in the settlements while the pups were there. . . ." Gorian chuckled softly, then leveled a dark stare across the gloomy campsite. "*You* are such a pup."

Horvath snorted. "And here I thought Brutes didn't have a sense of humor."

Gorian continued his meal, evidently too hungry to be bothered by the Spartan's response. Horvath let the silence sit for a moment as the restless feeling from earlier suddenly reemerged. Gazing at the night sky, he wondered what his team might be doing at that very moment. . . . "So what happened to the pups after those many, many years?"

"They grew to maturity and became legend."

"That's what I thought." He pushed to his feet, surprised to feel his muscles aching. The sooner he got off this island and back to a UNSC presence, the better. Everything from his Mjolnir to his operating suite needed repair.

"Where are you going, Spartan?" Gorian demanded.

Horvath ignored him and headed for the ruined Phantom. The supports they'd recovered were now sunk deep into the mud and leveraged beneath the hull. He bypassed them and climbed into the vessel. Within the bay area, he found a few pieces of bulkhead plating that hung from the ceiling. After ripping one out, he tossed it out the bay door, then went back to retrieve another before returning to camp with the pieces.

With his helmet's headlamp beam shining on Gorian's face, he threw a piece of the Phantom's plating at the Brute. It stuck in the soft ground a hair's breadth from his leg. "Here—if you're done stuffing your face, you can help dig."

Gorian didn't move as Horvath turned and made his way back to the Phantom. The Jiralhanae's pride wouldn't let a Spartan dictate when he rose or rested, so the bastard waited a good twenty minutes before he finally decided to join in on the task at hand.

They dug in front of the sentinel, making a channel to pull it laterally from the mud.

"Don't jab the plating in too far when you dig," Horvath grumbled. "If you hit the impulse drive, this'll all be for nothing." It was the same reason why he hadn't used the recovered plasma cutters.

"I'm not going to damage the drive. You think I'm stupid, Spartan?"

"Uh. Yeah." He tossed a plate full of mud over his shoulder with way more force than necessary. "I mean, you stepped right into that one, so . . ."

Gorian glanced down at his feet and snorted. "As usual, your words lack sense. Keep digging and be quiet, little pup."

He glared at the Jiralhanae, wishing Gorian could see just how much hatred was being sent his way. "You're going to miss me when this is all over, admit it," he said, gritting his teeth and refusing to be baited.

"Like a plasma mortar to the gut."

The laugh was out before Horvath could help it. Gorian chuckled and kept digging, no doubt amusing himself with when and how he'd finally make his move. Horvath had wisely been doing the same thing.

Once the sentinel was free and working, who would be the first to strike?

For now, they were both playing it safe. No reason to do the work of two. As hard as it was, waiting until it was absolutely clear that he had a working, viable way off the fragment was the best bet. And Gorian, with his broken ribs, would play a waiting game too, if he was smart.

A clump of mud where he'd been digging suddenly dropped away, revealing the metallic gray body of the sentinel. "Hold up," he said. "I think we can start pulling now."

They gripped the alloy arm and carefully extricated the two-meter-tall drone from the stubborn muck, then tugged it easily up onto higher ground.

In every Spartan armor's operating system was a memory core with schematics of nearly all known alien technology. Horvath now made use of it, keeping Gorian in his sights as he squatted and scanned the drone. It didn't seem to be damaged, but was simply offline. He sat back on his haunches, turning off his exterior audio.

"What are we looking at, Fi?"

"Aggressor sentinel. Intact. Currently in survival protocol shutdown. Once rebooted, it should come back online. Unfortunately, when that happens, it will automatically reconnect to the installation's directive system and will likely consider you and the Jiralhanae a threat. And then it will attack."

"Great," Horvath said, gritting his teeth. "This'll require some surgery, then."

"Well?" Gorian said impatiently.

"Well, the good news is it's undamaged . . ."

"Go on . . ."

"But we can't reactivate it until we sever its connection with the ring and change its core directive. Otherwise, if it communicates with the monitor's network defenses, we'll be in a world of hurt." And never get off the island.

"It won't communicate with the monitor."

"How do you know that?"

"Look around you, Spartan. The ring is broken, fragmented. The monitor shows no resistance to our presence or yours. It offers no defense."

"Then how do you explain this guy?" But Horvath realized

the answer before he finished the question. Survival protocol. The land bridge collapse must have triggered the sentinel to attack. It didn't mean that Zeta Halo's monitor wasn't aware of what was happening or that it was no longer in contact with its defense network. It just meant that, for whatever strange reason, it was not involving itself in the ring's affairs—at least, not that he'd seen so far.

"There is no monitor here to interfere," Gorian said. "We need only to activate the machine."

Horvath rolled his eyes. "I'm not about to take that risk after all we went through to retrieve the damn thing. It'll only take a few minutes." Annoyed, he switched back to Elfie, ignoring yet another ding. "Can you get in and assume control?"

"Yes. But assuming complete control is unlikely. Without authentication, there are limitations. However, I may be able to momentarily suspend its operating directive through the reboot stream."

"For how long?"

"Ten to fifteen minutes, perhaps."

"And the network?"

"You must manually disconnect the quantum processor from its hard-light optics filament. This will sever the network link. You'll also need to destroy the hard-light generator, or it will seek to repair itself."

As she spoke, Horvath continued scanning the sentinel's schematics. The situation was getting far more complicated than he'd like. It looked like timing would be the key.

"Once we're at the edge of the ring fragment, I will adjust telemetry from that location and put the sentinel on a direct path across space to the desired ring fragment."

"What does the little voice in your head tell you, Spartan?"

Horvath turned his visor toward the Jiralhanae. It told him that they had to drag a Forerunner sentinel across kilometers of landscape without trying to kill each other and then make a Hail Mary leap into open space. "It says grab an arm. We have work to do."

CHAPTER 12

If anyone had told him he'd be standing on the edge of a broken Halo ring with a sentinel and a Jiralhanae Bloodstar by his side, Tomas Horvath would've clapped that person on the back, bought him a round, and had a good laugh.

Nothing should surprise him anymore.

And yet the view into open space stole his weary breath. The dark-gray outer rim of each Halo fragment hovered in a break the size of a large continent, all trapped in the ring's artificial gravity along with millions of tons of debris. Below his feet, kilometers of jagged metal extended from the broken substructure; beyond that, the distant curve of the ring revealed a glimpse of its signature earthy hues.

Gorian stood still and quiet, chin up, his massive helmet tucked under his arm and his eyes cast over the scene like some armored beast king surveying his kingdom. The Jiralhanae warrior had promised to kill him countless times—was probably thinking about it even now—but Horvath had to believe that the Brute wanted to get back to his own situation as much as he did. Any attempt on his life wouldn't happen here. But as soon as they made it back to that dark fragment in the distance, all bets were off.

His gaze settled on the largest fragment. Seeing it out there floating in the vast debris field made a deep longing well in his chest. The punch of emotion came as a surprise, the intensity of it, the driving need to reunite with his team, with his fellow Spartans, with the crew of *Infinity*, with any human being.

"You ready?" he asked Elfie.

"Ready when you are."

Using the work-through on his heads-up display, he knelt next to the sentinel to trigger the access panel, his touch activating the alloy and causing embedded machine cells to shift the alloy from metal to hard light, which then dissolved into nothing at all. Horvath carefully worked his way into the drone's guts, severing the superfine fiber optic from the quantum processor, and frying the hard-light generator in the process. Simple process if you had the schematics and a state-of-the-art artificial intelligence guiding your hand.

"Okay, that should do it." With the connection severed, it was time to start the reboot. "You're up, Fi."

"I'm in," Elfie announced a second later. *"Operating directive is momentarily disabled. It will correct itself in approximately eleven minutes. Telemetry is set."*

They had eleven minutes to get across open space, avoiding debris along the way, and land on the inner side of the fragment. There was no room for error. Horvath straightened and stepped back. "Don't mess this up," he warned the Brute.

"Concentrate on your own task, pup. You'll be meeting your gods soon enough." He snarled. "Be ready."

"Count on it."

Slowly the sentinel came to life, hard light spilling blue from its core as its impulse engines lit and antigravity lifted it effortlessly off the ground. No turning back now. He grabbed one of its arms with both hands. "Telemetry is set," he told the Brute. "We have a clear path through the debris. On the count of three."

Without a word, Gorian pulled his helmet over his head and took hold of the sentinel's other arm.

"One . . . two . . . *three!*"

As one, they executed three running steps and leapt off the edge of the ring fragment, free-falling into space, soaring down past kilometers of protruding lattice and substructure before the impulse drives kicked in, sweeping them out of the fragment's artificial gravity and into an arc that aligned with the inside curve of the Halo ring.

Felt good to be right side up again.

Horvath's heart raced and adrenaline surged through his system as the sentinel made a blistering trail through the debris field. He'd done some crazy things in his time, but this was in another league altogether. His HUD fed constant updates, providing a moving grid of wreckage along their flight path.

Over halfway there now, he could already see their path through to the main fragment.

Gorian no doubt could as well.

Horvath glanced across the sentinel's exterior to see the Brute's head turned in his direction.

Not good.

Before he had time to react, Gorian struck with a large armored fist. Horvath blocked the blow with his forearm, but their movements caused the drone to spin and the force flung him off into open space—

"WATCH OUT!"

Immediately Horvath rolled, barely missing a blur of gray metal as it streaked by. Determined, he calmed himself and focused, straightening his body as he dove for the fuselage of a burned-out Seraph, using it to springboard with all his might forward to link back up with the sentinel. He missed, but managed to snag the heel of Gorian's right boot.

Got you.

And damned if he'd let go.

The muscles in his hand and forearm tightened until they burned, but he held on, using all his strength to maintain his grip as the Jiralhanae tried to shake him off. With extreme effort, he managed to throw his other arm up and snagged the knee joint in Gorian's armor. With a loud grunt, he pulled up, finally able to latch a hand on the sentinel, then used the other to pound at the Brute's injured side.

Gorian lost his hold and rapidly tumbled out of Horvath's immediate line of sight.

"Eight o'clock," Elfie said quickly.

Gorian leapfrogged across the barrel of a shorn-off artillery cannon and reconnected, grabbing the sentinel by the arm once more. Horvath braced for the collision, doing everything in his power to maintain his hold while defending against the warrior's ensuing blows, and landing some of his own, as the drone flew them directly into the pitch-black maw of a skyscraper-size chunk of floating substructure. They emerged on the other side, the main ring fragment's exposed layer of soil, solid rock, and lattice foundation looming directly in front of them. Damn it, they were coming in too low.

"Telemetry is off!"

"*I am aware.*"

With meters to spare, Elfie executed a hard correction upward, the sentinel clipping the edge of the main fragment and sending them into a dizzying spin. Horvath hugged the drone's arm to his chest as they crashed through the ruins of a Forerunner tower, then brushed the tops of several trees as they dropped lower over an area dotted by tall sandstone pillars, hitting several and driving through meters of the soft rock, and then shooting out over a couple kilometers of mud flats before slamming deep into the embankment of a dry creek bed.

As protective as his Mjolnir armor and ballistic gel tech suit were, the impact reverberated straight through Horvath's body, ringing muscle, tissue, and bone like a bell. He couldn't catch his breath. Equilibrium was way off, and his left side was screaming. Elfie's voice echoed with reports, but he couldn't process what she was saying.

His chest rose and fell rapidly and his lungs strained for oxygen. His limbs felt like lead—his mind urging him to move, but he simply couldn't make the action occur.

"*. . . and there are multiple contacts on approach. Your wounds are severe. Spartan Horvath, can you hear me? Please respond.*"

As bad as it all sounded, at least her words were starting to come through crystal clear.

"How bad is it, Fi?"

"*An alloy shard thirty-five millimeters in diameter is currently sitting between your upper intestine and spleen. Both artificial organs are damaged and you need immediate medical assistance.*"

He let his head turn to the side and was greeted with the sight of Gorian, a few meters away, slowly pushing to his feet and ripping off his helmet. The Jiralhanae's giant shoulders heaved as he pounded his chest twice and stared up at the sky, giving a great roar that ebbed into laughter.

"*Spartan Horvath, incoming contacts. . . .*"

"Yeah, I hear you." If he could just roll to the side and sit up—

Gorian strode over, casting a massive shadow across Horvath's display. All he could do was watch as the dark Jiralhanae face bent down and peered into his visor. The Brute's thick leathery brow furrowed as he assessed the situation. A sneer pulled his lips back from sharp teeth and a smug glint lit his eyes. And then Horvath felt the Brute grab the metal shaft protruding from his side.

"AH! GODDAMN IT—"

Sharp spasms of pain radiated from the wound, stealing his breath and stiffening his body. Tissue tore anew as the bastard ripped the metal out and flung it to the ground with a grunt. Bile rose to his throat, stuck there with a rush of curses as the Jiralhanae bent down and gripped Horvath's helmet, drawing him forward into a sitting position.

"How disappointing. . . ." he snarled, showing his fangs and pausing a long moment before saying, "Next time then, stupid little pup. Next time, perhaps it will be a fair fight."

Gorian shoved him back to the ground and, without another word or threat, retrieved his helmet, stepped over Horvath's head, and disappeared up the embankment.

"*Biofoam and medical gel have been injected into the wound. The tear in the tech suit has been localized and nano-repair procedure begun. Once the patch is applied, you'll have—*"

"I know," he murmured weakly as sweat beaded on his brow. The nano patch was only a temporary fix.

The clouds above him went fuzzy at the edges before sharpening into focus.

With a shaky hand, he removed his helmet and took in the fresh air with loud, audible gulps, stunned by the pain and the fact that he was still alive, had made it back on the slimmest of chances, and Gorian hadn't taken the opportunity to kill him outright.

He was a sitting duck out here in the open, though. Horvath gritted his teeth and forced his body to roll to his uninjured right side. Then he tucked his legs under him, brought his elbow to his chest, and used it to push himself over into a crawling position. "Hang in there," he muttered to himself, swaying and cursing as his gut twisted into a tight, sour ball. "Don't be sick. Don't you dare. . . ."

He snagged his helmet and began inching with it up the embankment. It wasn't even steep, but by the time his shoulders breached the top, he was trembling and cold and couldn't continue. The view before him stretched out like a mirage; in the center was the hazy black-and-red figure of Gorian growing smaller and smaller as the Jiralhanae crossed an expansive mud flat.

He blinked a few times more, but his vision wasn't cooperating, so he donned his helmet and magnified the scene through his HUD.

Beyond Gorian a large group of Banished Choppers, Skitterers, and Wraiths was rolling across the area kicking up a significant dust cloud. Escorting them from above was a unit of Banshees, a Blisterback, and a Phantom; the latter peeled away from the group to approach Gorian's retreating form.

As the Phantom executed a turn and began to set down, a tall Sangheili appeared at the edge of the side bay door. Decked in a sleek black combat harness with red accents, the warrior gave off a sinister vibe and certainly got Horvath's attention.

Gorian leapt onto the descending ramp, then paused, turning his hulking body slightly to look back in the direction he'd come.

It felt like the Brute was staring him directly in the eye.

Horvath held his breath. All Gorian had to do was give the word and it would all be over. But surprisingly, the Bloodstar continued up the ramp. The bay doors closed, and the Phantom rose into the air, returning to the group.

Horvath slumped to the ground, unable to hold himself up anymore, his head heavy and his body growing colder. Fi's voice echoed in his ear but the sound never quite translated into words. Exhaustion slid over him like a two-ton blanket, drawing his consciousness down into oblivion.

CHAPTER 13

TJ Murphy caught the towel and held it to his bloody nose. The stars dancing in his field of vision slowly faded, replaced by Dimik's form, hands on hips, breathing heavy, sweat covering her face and dampening her tank top.

At least he'd made her work hard for the elbow to the face.

The rest of the boat crew was in similar shape but had taken seats on a couple cargo crates to watch the latest sparring session. In the last month or so, they'd settled into a regimented life, and were slowly being transformed into the kind of soldiers necessary for the environment—a fight-dirty, use-anything-at-your-disposal, guerrilla-warfare kind of force; knowing how to survive out there in the wild while constantly badgering the enemy.

"Sorry about that." Dimik wiped her face and took a long swig of water.

She didn't look that sorry.

"It was a good move. Your instincts are spot-on." In fact, she could go another two rounds from the looks of her. Murphy retreated to his side of the makeshift training ring—an area outside the *Mortal Reverie* sectioned off by a random collection of supply crates, cargo bins, and salvaged parts—and tugged his standard-issue UNSC T-shirt over his head. Had he not pulled away sooner, his nose would be bleeding profusely. His reflexes were getting slower, it seemed. He leaned against a crate and chugged water before wiping his forearm across his mouth.

It had been a long training session. Spartan Kovan had stopped by at his insistence to give them some pointers, and then Murphy had taken over after it became abundantly clear that teaching would *never* be in Kovan's wheelhouse.

But apparently teaching was in his, or so he was told.

Since *Reverie*'s aerial support vehicles had been deployed from the ship during the initial Banished ambush, there was essentially nothing for him to fly. And even if he had something, it would not have been wise to take it out for a spin. For reasons Murphy didn't understand, the Banished had been preoccupied with another part of the ring and the UNSC personnel who'd taken shelter in *Reverie* were not eager to jeopardize that fact. So he'd been tapped to provide military training to all supply staff and nonmilitary personnel.

Bender worked as a barber and mechanic, servicing the small number of Warthogs, Mongooses, and battle tanks that had survived the crash. Dimik had become part of the group assigned to weapons and ordnance stockpiles, and Browning and Jo helped out in the med bay and wherever else they were needed while Cam worked on the bridge as a comms specialist.

"So what's the latest with comms?" he asked Cam.

As far as they could tell, the Banished had destroyed most of the sophisticated array of battlenet commsats that *Infinity* had quickly launched upon ambush. Without those, there was no overwatch and no way to achieve a complete coordination of movements and engagements from a central command standpoint.

Their goal these days was to restore the local link between the small number of FOBs, or forward operating bases, that were spread thin across this massive sector of the ring fragment. The bases had been hastily deployed to monitor Banished activities and launch incursions against raiding parties, supply depots, and other manageable targets, but now only a handful remained within UNSC control. The Banished were utilizing a number of signal disruptors and broadcast towers that continually interfered with their short-range comms and made long-range communications nearly impossible. And when they could broadcast, they risked revealing their locations and bringing the Banished might down upon them. It was a constant game of cat and mouse, of cycling through time and signals to avoid detection and achieve sporadic radio contact.

"Not much has been going on," Cam answered, absently rubbing his repaired knee. "*Reverie*'s local reception hasn't been holding steady into the Red Zone. We've got one tech trying to rebuild a sensor completely from scratch, and only one working quantum printer for the whole ship."

As far as they knew, the *Mortal Reverie* was the most intact ship in the area. And while her slipspace engine was shot and large portions of her were damaged, she was a good resource, full of supplies, rations, power, fuel, weapons, ammo, and enough hardware to repair most anything.

"Any word on the captain?" Bender asked.

A daily question that occurred all over the ship without fail. Captain Thomas Lasky had all but vanished. Last reports had Fireteam Taurus escorting him into a dropship aboard the flagship. Spartan Hudson Griffin, who led Taurus and had taken on an operational leadership role among the UNSC survivors, confirmed that much to be true. After that, however, no one knew. But if the captain was found, it would certainly be a massive morale boost for survivors all across the ring.

A few days after their small band had arrived, they'd learned through stories shared in the mess hall that while they'd been trapped inside the lifeboat, the ring had made a slipspace jump as it fractured. Murphy clearly remembered the distinct tang in the back of his throat, the electric static on his skin. But more than just the jump, it meant that any Mayday the UNSC *Infinity* might have sent out before she was destroyed would be useless. Zeta Halo had left its location and could be clear across the galaxy, or even outside of it, for all they knew.

It could very well be that no one back home in UNSC territory had any idea what had happened to them. And if that was the case, then no help was ever going to come. The only way out of this was to help themselves.

It was a topic discussed often by those in command of *Reverie*'s forces—whether they could salvage and restore a commsat, send a wavespace Mayday, or recover a ship with the proper technology, any way to let humanity know what had happened, that the Banished were a bigger threat than anyone had realized. That they'd found their way to Zeta Halo and were fighting to take control of the ring.

A collection of heavy footsteps echoed from within the *Reverie*. The team climbed onto the crates to get a decent view as several Spartans along with Commander Etana Hensler and her aides exited the ship.

Over the last few days, the Spartans had been coming and going with more frequency. Yesterday they'd gathered in the command center for quite a while, and today they'd done the same.

Murphy couldn't shake the feeling that something big was about to go down.

The Spartan group stopped and conversed with Commander Hensler. Then four heavily armed super-soldiers separated from the rest and headed down the pass toward the barricades. The mood went somber. Everyone working paused as though sensing the same thing. When they started saluting, Murphy knew in his bones the situation wasn't good. He and his own team straightened and saluted, holding the position until the Spartans were out of sight.

"What the hell is happening?" Jo asked.

"I don't know." But he sure was going to find out. "That's it for today. Get some chow and then get back to work." He hopped off the crate. "And let me know if you hear anything in the mess."

CHAPTER 14

Spartan Stone sat on the highest rock overlooking the only pass that led to and from the *Mortal Reverie*. Fellow Spartans Griffin, Malik, Panago, and Sarkar were heading out. She'd already said her farewells, sent them off with a bit of luck, and now she perched on the rocks high above, trying like hell to ignore the sinking feeling in her gut.

While on recon with Kovan in the Red Zone a few days ago, she'd known without a doubt that their intel would be the catalyst for what came next, and as soon as Kovan made the report and gave her assessment, the die was cast. Every Spartan listening in at *Reverie*'s command center knew what Spartan Griffin would say in response whether they agreed with it or not.

There was no denying the facts. The Banished were continually in competition, clans infighting and angling to elevate new leaders. The only thing keeping them in check was the grizzled Jiralhanae war chief known as Escharum. Without the unity their seasoned leader provided, they'd lack the necessary cohesion and strategic capabilities to defeat the UNSC's quickly massing forces. And if all-out war eventually broke, such disunity meant that the Banished would be vulnerable.

So, Escharum had to be eliminated.

It was the only way to break the Banished into manageable pieces and make sure they didn't gain control of the ring.

Breaching the warlord's newly erected stronghold and fighting through his guards might be a near-impossible mission, but if just one of the Spartans could slip in far enough, get a shot off—the right one at the right moment—then the rest of the UNSC trapped here on the ring would have a fighting chance.

And that was enough. That one chance made the risk worthwhile.

Spartans were explicitly made to take these kinds of risks: last-ditch operations that held the fates of so many others. They'd brought down countless Covenant factions, succeeded in one black-ops mission after another relying on nothing more than their skill, their armor, and their teammates. Yet despite that track record, Stone felt uneasy watching them go.

She wished she'd drawn one of the short straws. And she wasn't alone in that desire. Spartans were a family; they looked out for each other, died for each other, and never, ever shied away from the impossible—rather, they grabbed on to it wholeheartedly. Thus, staying behind was a special kind of torture.

She heard Kovan long before her teammate appeared on the ridge. But that was only because Kovan hadn't bothered hiding her approach—if she had, Stone never would have seen or heard her coming until the very last second.

The sniper specialist leaned against one of the rocks, removed her helmet, tucked it under her arm, and watched the other

Spartans move down the pass. Her expression was blank, her profile set in a stern line—nothing new. They'd been together since Fireteam Shadow's inception, long enough that, despite the blank expression, Stone could read Nina Kovan, aka the Stoic, like a book.

During their time marooned on Zeta Halo, Kovan's short blond hair had grown some, leaving it a little wavy, and the chilly air caused the pink to come easily to her pale cheeks. Nina Kovan was as tough as nails, though. No one gave her a hard time. She never messed up, never missed, and never responded to sarcasm. It drove the other teams crazy—she was a nut they could never crack.

And everyone admired her for it.

"Stop staring," she said gruffly without looking at Stone.

Stone removed her own helmet and set it down beside her. "Your intel was good. The suggestion to go after Escharum was key. You know it. I know it. They know it." Something had to give.

But if something went wrong, Kovan would take it the hardest. She'd never let it show, of course, or let it affect her work in the slightest; nevertheless, a heart did exist within that hard exterior, and no amount of gene therapy, augmentations, and cybernetic implantations could ever change that. They might be Spartans, trained to be the most elite frontline combat force ever created, but they were still human.

"You get that bad shield sensor repaired yet?" Stone asked. While the *Reverie* was equipped with a small Spartan bay, it was currently without a qualified Class-61 technician, so they had to make do with an engineering scientist among the survivors to assist in repairs for their GEN3 Mjolnir armor and operating systems.

Kovan shook her head and finally glanced over. "Your motion sensor?"

"Nah, it's too fried, and Makovich got the last one in storage. One of the engineers is attempting to make another. Just takes time. Could use a fix on this dent, though. . . ." Stone worked her shoulder. Ever since the nighttime fight with the Jiralhanae in the forest, it had given her trouble. One of his blows had created a dent in the titanium composite plating over her right shoulder blade, which now caused it to press against her bodysuit—not enough to pierce it or prevent movement, just enough to make it really annoying at times. She was sure the Brute must've employed some kind of a power-assist gauntlet when he'd struck her.

Griffin's team had now disappeared down the pass, but she kept her eyes trained on their last location. There were other Spartans out there, patrols tracking the group, providing overwatch, but eventually the strike team would be on their own.

If they had any chance at all, they had to approach their mission with the utmost discretion.

As Stone hopped up and grabbed her helmet, she saw Kovan make a face. "What?"

The Stoic eyed her for a second. "Why is it you can sit still for hours during recon, and yet—"

"Recon *is* doing something." Sitting on the rock and losing herself in what-ifs was not.

"You once sat for six days in the same position monitoring that Sangheili zealot on Talitsa."

"Yeah, and still never came close to Shadow One's record."

"We can't all be champions," Kovan replied with a smirk.

No one had seen the other two members of their fireteam or heard anything on any channel. Every survivor who arrived at *Mortal Reverie* made a report, and within those there were no mentions of any Spartans matching Shadow One's or Two's description.

"They made it off the ship," Kovan reminded her, "made it to the surface."

"Probably trapped on one of the ring fragments," Stone said. "Otherwise they'd be here already."

"If they are trapped, you can bet wherever they are, they've already finished clearing out the Banished."

Stone smiled. "No doubt."

To say Fireteam Shadow was tight-knit was an understatement. They'd gotten together just after the final year of the SPARTAN-IV program's experimental phase. Nearly ten years working in the shadows as a unit had made them extremely close. They did the work that allowed other teams to deploy in the right locations, with the right gear and the right intel and targets. Shadow was a specialized unit unto itself, and now, like the ring, it was fractured.

"Once Escharum's out of the picture and the Banished are on the run, we'll search," Kovan said. "We'll find them."

And they'd never *not* found a target once the hunt began.

With the Banished in disarray, patrols of the Red Zone would weaken, choke points would be abandoned, and more of Zeta Halo would open up to what remained of UNSC forces.

One step at a time.

Stone slipped on her helmet. "How'd your training session with Murphy's team go?"

"Murphy's got a knack for teaching. They're coming along."

"That wasn't what I asked."

Kovan sighed. "Let's just say they don't appreciate my bluntness . . . except that odd one . . . Bender, doesn't seem to mind."

"Never should have given him your knife."

"Mmm. That's what Murphy says."

Stone grinned widely behind the safety of her helmet as Kovan donned her own. She could just imagine the Stoic trying to teach a group of retail services and supply department personnel how to be lethal killers. "Let me guess—your lesson went something like: *Point. Shoot. There. Done?*"

Kovan shrugged. "What else is there to know?"

Come to think of it, she had a point.

CHAPTER 15

UNSC *Mortal Reverie*
Zeta Halo
January 31, 2560
Day 51

Word had spread throughout the *Mortal Reverie* that an assassination attempt on the Banished leader, Escharum, was under way. A week had gone by since the Spartan team, led by Hudson Griffin, had departed, and the mood around camp was somber, everyone on edge, hoping for success and praying this would be the end of the stranglehold the Banished were establishing across the ring. Since then, Berthold Vettel, another Spartan from Fireteam Taurus, had joined Commander Hensler in Griffin's stead, helping provide leadership over *Reverie*'s forces.

While Murphy hadn't gotten direct access to the command center, Spartans Kovan and Stone did their best to keep him up-to-date, and finally today, as Kovan passed the training area on her way into the ship's midsection bay, she'd given him the heads-up. A transmission from Griffin had been received. Of course, that made concentrating on anything else impossible, so when Dimik arrived with a stockpile of munitions for today's training, he tasked her to lead the group of recently arrived survivors in weapons drills. "I'll fill you in later" was all he said in response to her questioning look.

Murphy poured a splash of his drinking water into the palm of his hand, rubbed it onto his sweaty face, and quickly dried off before heading into the bay, up the lift three levels and then out into the corridor leading to the command center inside *Reverie*'s bridge.

The minutes crept by as he paced the corridor and then leaned his back against the bulkhead. Occasionally, loud voices echoed from inside the bridge, but nothing he could translate into intelligible words. Pace, rest. Pace, rest. At least an hour went by, and the ominous feeling he'd had ever since the assassination team left grew by leaps and bounds.

He'd always been that way—his instincts and intuition, even as a child, hardly ever leading him astray. And as much as he wanted to deny what he was feeling, he knew better. Pacing again, Murphy bit his bottom lip, hoping he was wrong for once. If Escharum was killed, if the UNSC could gain control of this ring, they could find a way back to civilization, reunite with home base, regroup, and heal from their devastating losses.

Finally the door slid open and a couple dozen Spartans began filing out of the bridge. With grim faces, they marched past him, the sound of their armored footsteps on titanium flooring echoing like drumbeats throughout the corridor.

Trying to find Kovan in a sea of Mjolnir-clad giants wasn't easy, but he finally got a glimpse of faded jungle camo and pale hair. "Kovan!" Her head turned slightly in his direction, but only for a brief moment.

He waited until the last Spartan left the command center, then fell in step behind the group, following until they dispersed in the midsection cargo bay, some moving deeper within the ship while others headed outside, but the mood was definitely one of purpose and resolve.

Just outside of the bay, Kovan separated herself from a pair of familiar Spartans: Vettel of Fireteam Taurus, unmistakable in his red Mjolnir, and Makovich, whom Murphy knew well—the Fireteam Windfall leader was hands-down the best pilot he'd ever seen and was something of a hero to the flight squadrons on *Infinity*.

Murphy hurried to catch up to Kovan outside as all around him orders spread and crews were put into action. "What are we preparing for?" he asked.

Normally, reading Kovan's expressions was an exercise in futility—she had an excellent poker face—but not today. Her mouth was grim and concern clouded her eyes. "The mission failed." She slowed her walk so Murphy could keep pace. "And we just got word from Stone out in the field. Escharum is going to hit back, and hit back hard. He has our location, and he's massing an army of Banished. They'll be here by nightfall."

Stunned, Murphy went full-stop. All he could do was blink as her words coiled in the pit of his stomach. He glanced around the camp. A couple hundred hodgepodge personnel against an army?

Kovan paused, helmet tucked under her left arm, and stared down at him for a hard second. "Don't focus on the odds. We all know they stink. Just focus on what we have to do now. We hold the ship. *Reverie* is ours, and we sure as hell can't lose it and its resources."

That was all good and everything, but . . .

He moved closer, lowering his voice. "How the hell can we hold the ship with—?"

"We have our orders."

It was all happening way too quickly to process. He was still trying to get a mental handle on the news, and her apparent lack of empathy only flustered him more. Murphy stepped back, shaking his head in denial. "No. No, what we *have* is a goddamn nightmare."

Mortal Reverie had a good group of soldiers, made up of navy, army, marines, ODSTs, and Spartans. They had seen countless engagements and gotten out of impossible situations, but the rest of them? The UEG personnel, the scientists, the retail specialists, the support staff—people who had no experience going head-to-head with a Grunt or a Jackal, much less a relentless Elite or vicious Brute—were supposed to handle an all-out brawl with a massive Banished force?

"Kovan. Half the people here have never even seen a real battle," he said tightly.

She held his gaze for a long second. "Then let's hope you've trained them well."

A sharp, disbelieving laugh shot from his mouth. Kovan was blunt, but right now she was sounding pretty damn callous. "You *know* I've been training them well, but it doesn't mean they're ready for this." He'd been doing the best he could, but some of the newer arrivals were still too wet behind the ears or traumatized by what they'd experienced out on the ring, and the others—those who had been with him for a while, even his ragtag boat crew—wouldn't be prepared for something like this.

Her expression softened somewhat. "Look . . . I know this isn't what anyone wants to hear. But we can't change what's already happened and running away from *Reverie* isn't viable—we both know that. If they can't dig in and fight here, there's no way they'd survive out there. We face the enemy's attack head-on and we do it from *Reverie*. There's no other option. I'll try to keep an eye on your crew. Just make sure they're as ready as they can be, okay?" She slipped her STORMFALL helmet over her head and moved on.

Murphy dragged a hand through his hair and let out a shaky breath as the weight of what was coming bore down on him. Nightfall would be here before they knew it. They didn't have much time. With a muffled curse, he turned and made his way back inside the *Reverie*, heading for Deck Three and rubbing his chest to try to alleviate the sudden burning sensation. He'd never felt worry like this for a team before—never needed to—as he'd always had the full weight of the UNSC behind him.

"Get it together," he muttered to himself, clearing S-Deck and then heading down the corridor to Section H. Kovan was right. Orders were orders, and losing a resource like *Reverie* would be devastating to their efforts. They'd be scattered again and might never regain a foothold like the one they had now. Ready or not, they had to hold her.

Word, it seemed, had already traveled. In the lounge area and the passageway leading into the sleeping quarters, teams were busy prepping, shoving personal effects away and pulling standard combat gear over their coveralls. He caught sight of Browning and Jo exiting their shared quarters, Browning already in full combat gear and Jo just slipping an arm into army-issued chest armor while he'd already donned standard VZG7 armored boots and leg protection.

"Is it true, then?" Jo asked, catching Murphy's eye as he adjusted the side straps to his chest armor.

Murphy flattened himself against the wall as a group hurried down the passageway and headed out of the lounge. "Yeah. Yeah, it's true. We have about six hours," he said, falling in step behind Jo and Browning as they left. "Time to get your game faces on."

Because by nightfall, hell would rain down on all of them.

CHAPTER 16

UNSC *Mortal Reverie*
Zeta Halo
January 31, 2560
Day 51

Night arrived on the heels of thin gray clouds that settled into the ravines and hovered around the cliff tops. The air became still and cold and quiet, every bump or knock echoing in the poised atmosphere. All personnel were armed and in key positions around the exterior of the ship. Barricades had been fortified and ammo and resupply stood with runners at the ready. Inside the ship, gunners manned what remained of *Reverie*'s Rampart point-defense guns while Commander Hensler and Spartan Vettel were prepped to coordinate movements of personnel and Spartans.

Murphy stood in the armory. It'd been a long while since he'd geared up in infantry body armor. He grabbed a standard CH252 helmet complete with its own heads-up display and comms system. What he wouldn't give to be behind the controls of a Pelican right about now. The idea of close-quarters killing made his heart pound a little harder in his chest. The idea of being outnumbered a hundred to one made it worse. It came down to this—making their stand, knowing their chances.

Which weren't exactly good.

There wasn't time to relocate safely. If they ran now, they'd be easy pickings with little ability to organize any resistance. So they'd stay and fight, and hopefully put a dent in the Banished forces. It was something at least. And maybe someday they'd be remembered for staring hell in the face and standing their ground anyway.

He picked up an MA5D assault rifle and as much ammo as he could carry, then left the armory trying like hell to *not* think about his life up until now, all his achievements and blessings, his failures and regrets.

An eerie quiet lay over *Reverie*'s central corridor. Murphy's footsteps echoed loudly and ominously, making his skin prick with goose bumps. Disturbing the silence reminded him of all those times arriving late to church as a child when the service had already started. When he neared the bay and heard the familiar sounds of activity, it drew him like a warm fire.

On the ground outside the bay, a domed medical tent had been erected and the engineering scientist who'd been acting as the Spartans' technician directed the setup of a temporary repair station, while Jo and Browning made a staging area for quick triage. Murphy joined them. "All set?" he asked. "You have enough ammo and secondary weapons?"

"Yep, it's all taken care of," Browning answered, busy opening a crate of emergency medical packets for soldiers to take into the field while Jo maneuvered a crate of biofoam canisters into the tent. "The others are already at post." The doc handed out EMPs to a squad as it passed by.

Murphy couldn't help but notice the doc's shaky hands and how his offered smile to each soldier trembled slightly. He seemed far too young and innocent to be part of this picture, even though Murphy himself had only been eighteen when he joined the UNSC and twenty when he saw his first engagement, several years younger than Browning in fact. Yet somehow, despite the past, the current picture seemed wrong. Once all twelve members of the squad had received their packets, Browning drew in an audible breath. The kid was about to have his hands full, and Murphy had done all he could in the time he had to prepare him. Still, he couldn't help but say, "If Commander Hensler or Spartan Vettel call for retreat—"

"We head up the ridge like we talked about," Browning replied, nervous energy pouring off him even though he was trying hard to hide it.

"Right." Murphy squeezed his shoulder.

"How the hell do you guys do this?"

Murphy glanced around the well-lit area. "Wish I knew. Been around awhile, I guess—seen and done some crazy things."

"Aren't you scared?"

"Of course I am. Trust me, the fear is there, but you just learn to ignore it, manipulate it, lie about it, use it, whatever you need to do in order to get you through. . . . Isn't that right, Kovan?"

"Spartans fear nothing," she replied matter-of-factly as she exited the ship nearby, carrying an MA5D rifle in one hand, an M41 SPNKR rocket launcher in the other, two M6 Magnums on her hips, an S7 sniper rifle on her back, and a boatload of extra ammo and grenades. She paused, towering over them, illuminated by *Reverie*'s auxiliary lights. "Remember what I taught you?" she asked with a note of humor in her tone.

Browning let out a soft laugh. "Point and shoot?"

"You got it."

Murphy shook his head as Jo finished his task, joining them as Kovan gave a curt nod and headed up the steep side of the pass and over, disappearing into the darkness.

"Hey, Doc! I need you for a second!" Sergeant Park called from the bay.

Browning hesitated, wanting to say more, but Murphy gestured toward the sergeant. "Go on, get out of here."

Watching Browning jog away, weighed down in his body armor and gear, reminded Murphy too much of the height of the Covenant War, never knowing from one battle to the next who would live or die, whether to say good-bye or see you later or to not say anything at all and then wish you had.

Reverie's external lighting went dark and the PA system whined through the exterior speakers with Commander Hensler's strong voice. *"All crews, battle stations."*

The Banished frontline force must have been spotted. There was little time left now.

"So that's it," Jo said, attempting to latch the chin strap to his helmet, but his fingers were trembling too badly.

Murphy brushed his hands aside and latched the strap, then quickly checked over Jo's gear to make sure all was in order before giving him a good slap on the helmet. "All set."

Jo's Adam's apple slid up and down with a hard swallow. "I'm not set, though. . . . I don't know if I can—"

"Hey." Murphy grabbed Jo's shoulders, but then found himself at a loss for words. He wanted to reassure him, to tell him everything was going to be okay, but they both knew the reality was pretty grim.

Jo drew in a steadying breath, lifting his chin a little higher. "Thanks, Murphy, for everything. . . ."

It was the kind of acknowledgment that held more than just the here and now; it extended over the course of their time on this accursed ring. "Thank me later." And with that, he gave Jo one last pat on the helmet and headed down the pass to the second barricade.

Grim outcome or not, screw the Banished. If he could send even a handful of them back to hell, then he'd go out with a smile.

And, hey, at least he'd gotten to enjoy pizza one last time before cashing in.

All support staff teams were stationed with an experienced squad. Murphy and his crew had been assigned to one of two barricades erected in the pass. They'd make their stand at the secondary barricade with two mixed units consisting of marines, army, ODSTs, and six Spartans—two of whom, Makovich and Sorel, he recognized from their armor. A couple of Wolverine anti-aircraft tanks were stationed in front of the barricade. The primary barricade was similarly erected, but maintained a larger force of three Spartan teams of four, along with additional equipment. Beyond the primary barricade lay a minefield, and additional units, Spartans, and a handful of Warthogs and Scorpion battle tanks lined the ridges along the pass. And while that would help ground forces, it would do little for air support. That's what *Reverie*'s guns were for.

By the time he made it to the barricade, Murphy was out of sorts and agitated. He took his place on the barricade next to Bender, slipped his helmet on, and drew the cold air deeply into his lungs, before tipping his head sideways and knocking Bender's helmet with his own—a simple sign of camaraderie. It was game time. Bender glanced over and grinned, then passed the gesture on, and it went from him to Dimik to Cam and on down the line, the knocking echoing out into the still night.

Seven minutes later, the Banished arrived.

Their vast ground forces, directed by a heavily armored Jiralhanae at the rear, swept up the pass with a hard-driving fury, the fog alight with a red glow of overclocked Banished vehicles and weapons. Suddenly *Reverie*'s point-defense guns engaged in a series of earsplitting blasts as enemy air forces appeared in range, the sound striking thunder in Murphy's heart and signaling the beginning of chaos.

The primary barricade began letting loose. Heavy fire streamed from vehicles and weapons as the minefield lit up the Banished front line.

"*Hold steady!*" Murphy called, keeping a steely eye on the edges of the primary barricade and the ridgeline above the pass. His finger tapped anxiously against the side of the rifle's trigger. . . . *There.* A swarm of Choppers had breached one side of the barricade while a unit of Grunts and Jackals was leading a charge down the ridgeline. "*Fire!*"

All thought and emotion gave way to a highly condensed tunnel vision of focus.

Point and shoot.

CHAPTER 17

UNSC *Mortal Reverie*
Zeta Halo
February 2, 2560
Day 53

"*Pull! Pull, goddamn it!*" Lucas's voice broke, hoarse from a day and a half of relentless fighting. Exhaustion permeated his mind and body, but he forced the words out the same way he compelled his body to keep on going. Artillery echoed overhead, the ground shaking violently as plasma mortars slammed into the edge of the pass nearby. Rocks and soil rained down, pelting his helmet and bouncing off the wounded Spartan lying at his feet.

The medical-grade gravity plate he'd stuck to the warrior's faded black chest plate was too damaged to lift the Spartan completely, only making the unconscious patient light enough to drag over the dirt, and still Lucas couldn't accomplish the task himself. If he could just deliver the Spartan to the med tent or at the very least get him or her out of harm's way—

"He's too heavy!" Jo shouted across the body, dropping the Spartan's arm and looking desperately around the battlefield for another option as plasma bolts peppered the ground only meters from their feet. Determined, Jo pulled his rifle around to the front of his body and ran toward an abandoned Warthog. Lucas realized immediately what the PO intended. If they could hook the Spartan to the Warthog, they could drag him to the med tent.

But before Jo reached the vehicle, it was hit by a plasma mortar, sending it tumbling into the side of the pass as a toxic red residue ate away at the damaged Warthog. Immediately Jo slid to a stop and covered his face, scrambling back the way he'd come.

Lucas tugged on the Spartan again as the futility of his efforts cracked through the shell he'd built around himself. The shell allowed him to compartmentalize and focus on the wounded, on retrieving and treating soldiers, instead of on the battle being waged around him. But now the two were melding. The dead and the dying were too many, explosions and screaming and endless combat all closing in on him and making it hard to think.

A Sangheili hit the ground a few meters in front of him, snapping Lucas out of the battle haze. Immediately a Spartan dropped onto the alien warrior and stabbed a ravager bayonet deep into its gut, twisting and then ripping it free and sending a spray of purple blood arcing through the air. Without missing a beat, the Spartan fired the ravager's incendiary bolts into the bladed wheel of an oncoming Chopper. It instantly veered off course and crashed into the burning Warthog.

The bright explosion put the super-soldier in the spotlight, and Lucas realized it was Spartan Stone. Jo hurried around the dead Sangheili and slid to his knees on the other side of the unconscious Spartan.

Stone reached down and grabbed the wounded Spartan's shoulder armor, yanking with one hand while firing her rifle with the other as she pulled the patient toward the medical tent. Lucas pushed to his feet and jogged to keep up, trying to stay focused, to lay down cover as they made their way closer to the *Mortal Reverie*.

The ship was lit up by her artillery guns and the barrage of fire from the Banished air support that just never stopped. The guys relentlessly firing those UNSC guns were insane. Heroes. Without them, no one here would've lasted beyond a day.

Almost there.

The smoky air in front of them warbled for a second with the now-familiar signature of a personal cloaking device. Stone dropped her hold on the unconscious Spartan and threw up a defensive arm as a Sangheili warrior solidified and slammed into her. She went down on one knee. Lucas stumbled forward at the sudden stop as an earsplitting *boom* resounded from a nearby mortar hit. Jo had fallen onto his rear and was attempting to right himself and aim his battle rifle at the Sangheili as it raised its now-activated energy sword over Stone.

Heart in his throat, Lucas reached for the knife at his belt and surged forward, shoving it as hard as he could into the break of the Sangheili's leg armor.

The alien roared, backhanding him across the dirt, but it was all Stone needed to land an uppercut to the Sangheili's jaw and then an M6 in the face until he fell dead.

Stars danced in Lucas's vision. Agony pulsed across his face, and blood and grit pooled in his mouth. He tried to lift his head but couldn't seem to move.

"Doc!" Stone yelled. "Snap out of it! *Browning!*"

Snap out of it. Snap out of it.

His vision slowly righted, revealing a marine lying a few meters away in the dirt, arm below the elbow crushed, chest heaving, and blood spurting from his mouth. *Need to get him a tourniquet. Stop the bleeding. Internal injuries—* The marine suddenly went still and stiff, and then his entire body relaxed.

"Lucas!" Jo called over the din.

Lucas shook the fog from his brain and began crawling back to Stone and Jo, keeping his eyes on the Spartan like a lifeline as two red bolts of superheated plasma soared over his head and hit Stone dead-on. Her Mjolnir armor shimmered, mitigating the blasts, but the impact sent her stumbling as a heavy boot slammed into his side, knocking him back. For a second he couldn't breathe and thought for sure his ribs were about to crack, but the body armor held as a Brute stepped around him and kept on walking toward Stone, firing repeatedly as she dodged for cover.

Over the body of the fallen Spartan, Jo was now on his feet, struggling to reload his rifle.

Somewhere through the chaos he heard Murphy yelling and turned to see two UNSC marines running toward them, covered in grime and blood, the whites of their eyes flashing as they aimed their rifles at Jo.

No, not at Jo, but behind him in a cloud of smoke.

Jo lifted his head, hearing the shouts.

Lucas's jaw dropped open in horror.

No, no, no—

Time seemed to stop as the tip of a blue energy sword appeared through the lower right portion of Jo's chest plate. His eyes bulged in shock, his mouth opening, but nothing came out. Behind him, a Sangheili in crimson armor emerged. A split second later, a shadow fell over the alien warrior and a Spartan in camouflage armor landed on its back.

Kovan.

She came down on his shoulders from the ridge above, wrapping her alloyed legs around his neck, grabbing his helmet and twisting with all her might. The Sangheili ripped the weapon out of Jo and the man collapsed to his knees next to the fallen Spartan as Kovan twisted and twisted until the alien's neck snapped.

Hot tears rose to Lucas's eyes as he crawled over the prone Spartan to reach Jo.

Blood was already flowing from Jo's mouth and nose as he slumped to a sitting position. "Come on, Gavin . . . hang in there, okay?" Lucas said, voice shaking, a million things running through his mind, how to address the wound, the best treatment . . . If he could just get Jo inside the *Reverie*, there might be a chance despite the tiny voice in the back of his head that told him otherwise. Refusing to give up or listen to that voice, Lucas hurried around Jo's shoulder and grabbed his collar to start dragging him toward the ship, but just as he did, a large swath of the starboard side of *Reverie*'s hull exploded in a shower of plasma and melting titanium.

Superheated bits of burning detritus filled the dark sky and collided indiscriminately with enemy and friendly forces alike, covering the battlefield in an ashen gloom that obscured nearly everything. *Reverie* had been compromised.

At that moment, he knew it was over.

It was all over.

"Get up!" Kovan shouted. "We need to move!"

Murphy and Bender slid down next to them, their faces covered in soot and blood.

"Bender, put pressure on the wound!" Lucas ordered. "Murphy, help me lift him!"

Murphy took one side and Lucas the other.

Jo kept slapping them away. "Stop," he managed through gurgling. ". . . stop. I'm done. You have to go. Just leave me. Go."

"Screw that, no way," Bender said. Behind them, a pack of Jackals eased closer and began to fire on their position, but were struck down by Cam and Dimik as they raced across the open pass.

"Help me get him—" Lucas tried to tell them, but Jo squeezed his hand.

"Go," he gasped. "Please. I'm done. I'm done. . . ." He coughed up more blood and his face went white. His pupils were dilated. His breathing came in faint, slow whistles. The energy sword had cauterized the initial wound, but it had also created a domino effect inside his body as his organs and tissue suffered residual heat damage and vessels and arteries were effectively blocked. "Go, so I know . . ."

So I know you made it. He didn't need to say it aloud for Lucas to understand. Gavin wanted them to survive, to know before he died that they had a chance, at least. He didn't want them to lose their window to retreat into the hills.

But how did one leave a dying soldier, a friend, on the battlefield?

Lucas couldn't move. No one could. It went against everything they stood for.

Kovan made the decision for them, grabbing Lucas by the shoulder harness and yanking him up. "I said, *let's go.*" She turned sharply toward Jo and he tried to dip his head, to tell her that yes, this was the right thing to do, before his gaze went blank and his head fell to the side.

She pulled Lucas away. "Murphy!" she yelled harshly.

And then they left.

They just left Jo lying there.

There was no safe place to fall back to. With *Reverie* burning, Banished aircraft now flowed overhead en masse. Chaos closed in from all sides, fire, explosions, the smell of fuel and mortar and dirt . . . the screams and shouts, the alien roars and chatter and even laughter as survivors were brutally cut down, or run over by Choppers and Wraiths, or herded off the edge of the cliff by force—some leaping by choice.

It was a massacre.

The survivors were gathering as much hardware as they could carry—from the ground, from the dead—and still the Banished didn't stop, ferociously pursuing them through the dark.

Lucas no longer looked back—he just ran.

Ran with everything he had, until his body was screaming, and his lungs and muscles were on fire.

CHAPTER 18

They ran for what seemed like hours, using the darkness and the landscape's natural cover to their advantage, but they were never far from the threat of Banished scouts and trackers. Many times Spartans Kovan and Stone split from the group to engage the small pursuit parties, to save as many personnel as they could, to give them time to hide or flee farther into the mountains.

Stone had disappeared a short time ago after hearing shots nearby, leaving Kovan to lead them at a blistering pace through a maze of alpine trees and rocks tucked among the enigmatic hexagonal stacks of Forerunner alloy that punctuated the area.

And while he was no Class-61 technician—not even close— it was clear to Lucas that Kovan's energy shielding was nearly toast. The plates on her Mjolnir armor were blackened and damaged in places, the left side of her helmet was dented in, and she'd taken a direct hit in the back from a mangler. Even a Spartan had limits, and Lucas couldn't help but wonder if she was nearing hers. Though she certainly wasn't struggling in the endurance department.

Unlike the rest of them.

He stumbled over loose rock and went down on one knee. Bender grabbed his elbow from behind. "Come on, Doc, keep moving," he said quietly.

It was too much effort to reply. He could barely breathe as it was, his heart galloping wildly in his chest and his lungs strained. Bender urged him forward, and Lucas put one foot in front of the other. *Keep moving. Keep surviving.* That was all he could do now. That was all any of them could do.

After edging along a series of sheer rock walls and stacks, the line slowed. Lucas closed the gap between him and Cam. Ahead, between an alloy stack and a rock face, Kovan had found a gap. She ushered them into the narrow passageway.

The interior air was cold and damp and earthy. He stumbled again, but this time caught himself on the wall and used it as a guide as the group moved farther into the crevice.

They gathered in the back of the gap, the area no bigger than the lifeboat that had taken him from *Infinity* down to Zeta Halo's surface. Lucas sat on the hard ground, shaking so badly his teeth rattled. Pins and needles fired through his fatigued muscles and every breath pained his lungs. He could feel the others around him and hear the heightened sounds of their breathing, and the shuffle and clink of bodies and gear. All this time, he'd assumed they'd stayed together during their escape and flight into the mountains, but now he wasn't so sure. "Is everyone okay?" he whispered, removing his helmet.

A few grunts and affirmatives echoed.

"Sound off," Murphy said.

Bender, Cam, and Dimik answered back. "Browning here," Lucas said. Jo should be the next one answering, and yet . . .

Silence fell on the group and Lucas knew he wasn't the only one thinking of their fallen comrade.

"Stay here until I come back," Kovan said, moving toward the exit. She took two steps—and then her shadowed form suddenly froze. Lucas straightened in alarm, afraid the Banished had found them, but to his shock, Kovan fell flat on her face.

Lucas pushed to his feet and stumbled over the others to reach her side. He grabbed a low-spectrum light strip from his harness and snapped it. She was down, all right, and attempting to use her right arm to push up, but then cursed and fell back to the ground. "Kovan," he whispered, stepping close and kneeling by her torso as Murphy joined them. "How can I help?"

"You can't." Her voice was strained and utterly pissed as she punched the ground with her fist. "There's a . . . ballistic gel layer in my tech suit. It adjusts to pressure and impacts, but it's gone rigid on the left side. The density regulator is malfunctioning. Took a hit to the core mechanism back at the *Reverie*."

The mangler shot, Lucas guessed.

"Shit," Murphy whispered.

"The Banished are using some kind of signal jammer . . . I can't reach Stone," she said.

"What's wrong, what's happening?" Dimik asked.

"Shhh!" Bender whispered.

The Banished were so damn close. Deep Brute voices, Grunt chatter, and the harsh avian caw and squawk from Jackals carried easily through the chilly air.

"Search everywhere!" Angry-sounding Jiralhanae orders echoed through the translation software in Lucas's earpiece. Having originated from the Covenant, the Banished's primary language was native Sangheili, though it bore a heavy Jiralhanae

dialect—Lucas's earpiece picked up the sound and translated it all almost instantaneously. *"Leave no stone unturned! They are here somewhere!"*

It was tight in the small cave. They'd be found soon and that would be the endgame; there was no way the Banished would miss it once they moved in closer. Lucas shifted his gaze to the entrance. If they were discovered, there'd be nowhere to run; it would be a slaughter, and they sure as hell hadn't come this far for it to end like this. Not if he could help it. Lucas lifted his head and met Murphy's gaze across Spartan Kovan's prone form. Nervous energy began seeping into his bloodstream. He bit his lip as his thoughts let loose, and once they did, there was no reining them in. He shoved the light strip into his pocket, and before Murphy could open his mouth or reach over Kovan to grab his arm, he was up and running.

No thought to it. He just ran.

He might not be able to save them all through medicine, but he could in this way. And wasn't that the whole point of why he'd joined the Corps anyway?

He heard them hissing his name, calling him back, but Lucas was closest to the gap; it had to be him.

He emerged from the cave and then stuck to the ledge, following it a safe distance away before darting down through the trees and out into a grassy clearing. His heart pounded so hard he was pretty sure it would seize up just like Kovan's suit. Adrenaline took over; he was shocked he still had some left. He knew he was running but couldn't feel anything, almost as if his feet were barely touching the ground.

The Banished search party was across the clearing, searching in the trees, so he made a beeline for one of their Ghosts parked near a rocky outcropping. It was just sitting there. Alone. He might've laughed at the absurdity of it, but was pumping too much air in and out of his lungs for anything else to come out.

Light-headed, he leapt into the operator's seat of a vehicle he'd seen many times before, but had no idea how it worked. His hands began to shake as he fumbled for the controls. His head went light, his vision temporarily blurring.

Come on, come on!

He grabbed what looked like a throttle and squeezed. Nothing happened. Then he pushed it, and the vehicle launched forward with a deep humming noise.

As one, the small party turned toward the sound, giving Lucas their full and undivided attention. Panicked, he shoved the throttle all the way forward—a big mistake, as the vehicle went tearing across the clearing and slammed into an embankment, but he was clutching the throttle so tightly that he never actually let go, so it climbed up the embankment and shot out over the grass, eventually crashing into the trees beyond. Smoke and sparks sputtered from the engine.

Lucas shook off the fog, releasing his death grip, and jumped off, darting into the trees, the entire scouting party now after him instead of heading in the direction of the others.

He'd done it. He'd actually done it.

And then pinkish crystal needles staked the ground beside him, making him veer off in shock and straight into a solid wall. He bounced back and hit the ground as the wall—no, a Brute— leaned forward with a sneer and plucked him high off the ground by the scruff of his neck.

Oh God.

Its massive and terrifying face drew closer, lips curling into a vicious smile, revealing two perfect fangs and two perfect tusks. "What have we here?" It chuckled, the sound so deep that Lucas felt the vibration of it ring through his chest.

"Save that one," one of the other Brutes said, approaching. "Escharum needs a few humans alive. Do not forget our orders."

"Surely he can miss a puny one such as this."

"Which is what you said about the last dozen. They are *all* puny, all worthy of death, but think before incurring his wrath. Our clan has been warned already."

"Fine—toss him in the war-skiff."

Lucas didn't think they'd literally toss him, but that's exactly what they did—dragged him back across the clearing and threw him through the air like a bag of supplies into the back of an open transport vehicle, a large Banished skiff designed for hauling. A sharp stab of pain shot through his shoulder, but he scrambled up and tucked himself in the very back corner.

No matter how scared he was or how badly his body was breaking down, when he realized the search party was indeed moving away from the boat crew's location, Lucas wanted to shout for joy.

At least he could say he'd done one brave thing before he died.

Kovan growled inside of her helmet and beat the ground with her good fist. *"Hurry up!"*

"The damage to the density regulator is due to a short in the core mechanism," Mouse said, her soft tone steady and unhurried. *"A reboot might reset core functionality, but it will not repair the regulator completely."*

The sound of the Banished giving chase echoed in Kovan's head and fueled her anger. The doc was out there, running for his life, that idiot. How could he have done something so stupid?

"Fine. Whatever. Just do it!"

Almost immediately, her HUD display went dark as her GEN3 operating system powered down.

In the absolute quiet, the stark possibility that Browning was already dead swirled around in her mind and sat heavy on her chest. *She* was the one who was supposed to fight for them, protect them, and keep them going until help arrived. Instead, a twenty-five-year-old rookie medic had schooled everyone on what courage really was.

What an utter shitshow. From the moment *Infinity* dropped out of slipspace, things had gone sideways. For a brief time she'd thought the *Mortal Reverie* would be their saving grace, their turning point. Memories of the fight populated in the dark like holo-images, one after another, each one desperate and horrific. Far too many friends lay dead on the battlefield, the ground littered with Mjolnir, with the strongest, most formidable fighters humanity had to offer. . . .

Her display finally lit up as Mouse said, *"Reboot complete. Gel viscosity returning to baseline. Density regulator currently showing a forty-four percent drop in functionality."*

Which meant from here on out, she'd be skating on thin ice. The next time her bodysuit reacted to extreme pressure or impact, there was a good chance it'd seize up again. And to make things even dicier, the suit might also react randomly, as it had this time. How was that for living on the edge?

The hydrostatic gel layer relaxed from its rigid state, releasing her left side from its protective grip.

About goddamn time.

Immediately Kovan was on her feet, cold determination filling her with resolve. The doc had a ten-minute start on her. She strode to the cave exit and paused to glance over her shoulder.

"Stay here until I come back to get you, understood?"

She slipped out of the gap before they had a chance to answer. Her customized STORMFALL armor provided a nice bit of camouflage cover as she crept along the rocks and made for the woods, blending in perfectly with the tree line. Small skirmishes across several square kilometers echoed sporadically through the predawn—ground vehicles, gunfire, mortar blasts, aerial assaults, and screams. Plenty of those to go around.

Kovan put herself in Browning's shoes and made for the easiest and fastest direction he might have taken to lure the Banished away from the cave. She found several sets of Chopper tracks that had dug deep furrows in the ground and a crashed Ghost, but no sign of the doc and no Banished mercenaries either.

Her search of the immediate vicinity proved fruitless and her short-range comms were still hindered by disruptors. Stone was out there somewhere, and Kovan could only hope they reconnected soon.

Farther afield, she came upon a small group of Jackals flushing a handful of marines out into a large field. Her concerns faded into the background, replaced by training and muscle memory. Quickly she scanned the landscape, eyeing a tall outcropping perfect for her purpose. Moving stealthily through the trees and up the rocks took only moments. Once she reached a decent ledge, Kovan unshouldered her sniper rifle, crouched, and sighted, timing her rounds with the sounds of vehicles and gunfire, giving her more kill opportunities before being herself discovered.

She picked off each Jackal with rapid precision, her rounds cracking through the air like lightning until she ran out of ammo and the field was painted with alien blood and the marines had fled into the darkness. Then she hustled down, eased her way to the next location, scavenged ammo, and started all over again.

Unfortunately, she never found Browning or Stone.

As dawn shifted to day, Kovan cleared another copse of trees, the landscape giving way to a grassy slope connecting with the pass that led down to the valley in one direction and up to *Reverie*'s location in the other. While she couldn't see whatever remained of the ship from this lower elevation, a hazy glow hovered above its location.

Much as she hated the idea of using another Spartan's gear to repair her own, it was standard protocol in wartime scenarios. If she wanted to stay in the game and be effective, she'd have to go back. If one fallen soldier's gear could save another, it had to be utilized. If she had been KIA, she damn sure would want any of her Spartan brothers or sisters to take what they needed in order to continue the fight.

An hour later she paused on a rise overlooking the *Mortal Reverie*. The sun peeked over the snowcapped mountains and spilled down into the ravines and fractured chasms, glinting off exposed Forerunner alloy and the heavy dew that lay on the ground.

A nightmarish scene bathed in the fresh light of day.

But Kovan didn't shy away from it; rather she magnified her HUD, ignoring the Banished force that lingered around the ship and inside the bay as they picked through *Reverie*'s supplies. Her focus was on searching for survivors, for friends and fellow Spartans, but she didn't find a single Spartan, alive or KIA, even though she'd seen many of them fall.

Which meant the Banished had taken them from the scene, making any potential gear collection impossible.

Escharum was turning out to be an extremely cunning adversary.

CHAPTER 19

An entire day had passed in the cave and night had settled in again. It had grown quiet outside, but Murphy knew the area wasn't completely clear yet. There'd still be a few Banished packs out there, lingering, waiting for any survivors to show themselves. His gut wrung itself like a wet towel, his hunger severe. Exhaustion had him fading in and out of sleep, and cold had seeped into his bones.

No one had spoken much since Kovan left. They were too tired, too traumatized and broken, lost in their own thoughts and memories of the *Reverie*.

Dimik had snapped one light strip, barely enough to illuminate the gap, but enough to make out faces in the dark. Murphy tried not to look too hard. The bleakness and shock and grief carved into their features stirred something desolate inside of him, like staring at his own reflection. Right now he couldn't acknowledge his similar feelings, couldn't delve too deep. He had to stay strong, had to lead, and wouldn't let them see that inside he was just as broken as they were.

"How long are we going to wait?" Bender whispered. "I'm losing my damn mind here."

Murphy would be lying if he said he hadn't been thinking the same thing. How long would they—*could* they—wait? The way things were going out there, Spartan Kovan might never come back.

Cam and Dimik sat shoulder to shoulder against the wall, still swallowed in combat gear, their helmets on the ground beside them. Bender had gotten up to stretch his legs despite the cramped space.

Weary tears pooled in Dimik's eyes as she rubbed them hard, streaking smoke and dirt across her face. "Goddamn it," she cursed softly, her head falling back against the cave wall. Her throat worked as she struggled to swallow her emotions. "It's like a nightmare we can't get out of."

Cam bumped her with his shoulder, offering a tiny bit of comfort. "Hey, we made it this far."

She sniffed. "No. You're right. We made it this far. . . ."

Murphy picked dried blood out of his ear as Bender moved toward the exit, peering out. "If she doesn't come back . . . we'll let things settle a little longer and then make way."

And then they'd need to start thinking about surviving out there in the wild long-term. Zeta Halo was filled with resources. They might not be used to living off the land and scavenging for supplies and weapons, but they'd have to change their mindsets. Help was a long way off, if it ever came at all.

"Should be some rations in the wreckages nearby. And if not that, some game or plants or something out there we can eat," Bender continued. "There's also the *Reverie*—that might still be intact."

"And crawling with Banished. My guess is they'll set up there long-term just like we did. It's a good location and she's still full of salvage, tech, and supplies," Murphy pointed out.

"Wherever we go, we need to find food. At this rate if we need to run again, we'll be too weak to go half a kilometer before collapsing," Bender replied.

"He's right," Cam piped up. "We need to eat. And more immediately, we need to drink."

Dimik caught Murphy's eye and shrugged. "They're not wrong."

While he agreed with them, he wanted to give Kovan a little more time. Going out there without her was a risk he wasn't keen on taking, not unless they absolutely had to. "Look, Kovan said—"

"We know what she said," Bender interrupted, "and she could be dead for all we know."

Just then a tall shadow fell over the cave's entrance. *Shit.* Murphy reached for his rifle as Bender had his M6 in hand and aimed. Spartan Kovan ducked inside, carrying two bloodstained rucksacks. "You were saying?"

She dropped the bags at Bender's feet.

Murphy leaned forward and tugged at the opening to one of the rucksacks. Energy bars, MREs, water rations, and medical supplies. Magazines and weapons filled the other. His first inclination was to ask where she'd gotten such riches, but his time on the ring had taught him that the answer was often hard to hear—and in this case, the still-wet blood on the bags told the tale. Too many times in the past they'd pulled items like these off the dead, and the task never got easier. "Good work, Kovan."

"Hardly," she said.

"Remind me never to underestimate you again," Bender muttered, dropping to his knees as the others gathered around the bags, immediately tearing into the bars and gulping mouthfuls of water.

They were going to make it another day.

"Area is starting to cool down," Kovan told them. "We'll lie low here until morning, and then we move."

Murphy tore into a chunk of energy bar. "To where? Is there a rally point?"

"No."

When it was clear she wasn't elaborating, he pushed. "Kovan . . . ?"

"There is no rally point, Lieutenant. There's no one to rally *with*. We're completely on our own now."

CHAPTER 20

Lucas Browning had been in the holding cell for six days now as it filled up with prisoners, some of whom he recognized from the *Mortal Reverie*. They were in all states—from the severely wounded and critically injured to those who'd escaped harm and were simply weak and starving. No one was afforded medical treatment and it was impossible to administer care from within the cell—all he could do was offer a bit of comfort when the guards weren't looking. He'd learned early on to stay quiet and stop asking each new prisoner who had lived and who had died on the battlefield. Talking meant garnering the attention of the Brutes, garnering attention meant beatings, and no one came back from a beating.

He spent most of his time in the corner, head down, trying to stay warm and ignoring the gnawing in his stomach. Day after day, not much changed, so he was stunned when the Brute in charge of his block appeared and deactivated the translucent red energy barrier.

Their jailer sneered, revealing stained fangs framed by even dirtier upper and lower tusks. He was short for a Jiralhanae, but wider than most, with meager armor and dark-gray skin. He was lazy too, spending most of his time outside the cell, leaning against supply crates napping, stuffing his face, or getting in shoving matches with the Jackals that came and went.

"On your feet, vermin," he said in basic English.

About twenty of them rose and began filing out of the cell. Those who couldn't stand were dragged out by the jailer's Kig-Yar underlings.

Hunger made dizziness cloud his vision and weakness threatened his balance. Once a day, Lucas had been fed a random meal of unidentifiable slop, or salvaged energy bars, or sometimes nothing at all if there wasn't enough to go around, along with a canister of water, and he was feeling the effects now as he and the other prisoners were led from the prefabricated base structure that housed the cell. The entire area was walled off by tall alloy barricades, and more structures dotted the uneven ground, serving many purposes—barracks, munitions depots, cells. . . .

In an open area, they were stopped. A cool breeze blew through the outpost, making Lucas close his eyes and appreciate the sensation on his skin and the freshness in his nostrils. After six days in the rank stale air of his cell, it was a welcome change. Though he couldn't see what was happening at the front of the line, he figured it must be some kind of inspection or interrogation. Every time the line moved, he'd see a Brute drag a prisoner to the right and toss them into another holding cell.

By the time Lucas made it to the front of the line, he was numb. Anticipation and fear should've had a tight grip on him, but after everything he'd been through, all he could muster was vague curiosity. He knew he should be scared, but there was only so much a body and mind could take.

At least, that's what he thought as he stepped forward and lifted his gaze. His mouth went slack, those dull emotions he'd been feeling flaring bright as his heart broke into a million pieces. His mind stumbled over the sight, unable to process what he was seeing, unable to reconcile the immense betrayal.

The one inspecting the prisoners was human.

"Strip," the inspector said in a bored tone, barely glancing at Lucas.

The man was in his mid-thirties, tall, wearing a soiled white lab coat. His hair was long and straight, pulled back into a tail. His face was hard-angled, eyes cold and indifferent as they swept over Lucas. He gestured to one of the Jackals flanking him. It stepped forward. Memories of vicious snapping jaws and hungry eyes flashed across his field of vision, making him recoil. But the Jackal simply latched a claw onto his arm, digging in painfully, and using his other hand to cut Lucas's clothes with a blood-soaked knife.

Horrified, Lucas snapped to and began struggling.

"You can do it yourself, or they can do it for you," the inspector said, leaning casually against a stack of munitions crates at his back.

How could he be so indifferent? Lucas expected this kind of detached coldness from the Brutes and Elites, the Jackals and Grunts . . . but a human? In his time spent at *Mortal Reverie* he'd heard talk that, while the Banished had once welcomed humans into their ranks, there was growing discontent ever since the Jiralhanae homeworld and its two populated moons had been completely obliterated by the rogue human AI Cortana. There'd been reports that there was ongoing and sometimes lethal contention between many Brute clans and the small number of humans within the Banished.

That this one was here and working alongside the Jiralhanae told Lucas that he must have earned enough respect within the Banished hierarchy to avoid Brute vengeance.

The Jackal approached him again with the knife, but Lucas shrugged him off as the sting of tears rose through his nasal passages and hit the back of his eyes. "I'll do it myself." There was something even more demoralizing than being cruelly disrobed by the Banished; it was being stripped of his dignity in front of his own goddamn kind. But he did it anyway. Shaking all over, he pulled his shirt off and stepped out of his pants. He was checked for injuries, then told to re-dress, his shirt now torn but at least his pants were in decent shape. His shoes, however, were taken.

"Occupation?" the inspector asked.

"Screw you." Hot tears slid down his face.

"He doesn't have the physique of a soldier," the inspector noted to the Jackals in Sangheili, ignoring the insult. Presumably it hadn't been the first. "Keep him; he's probably a scientist or a doctor." The traitor stared at Lucas and smirked. "It's your lucky day."

Even though it went against his oath to do no harm, Lucas had never wanted to kill anyone in cold blood more than this man right now. He could only hope he'd get his chance at some point.

One of the Jackals cackled in response to the inspector's remark. Lucas was taken to the left and up an embankment to another prefabricated holding cell overlooking the area. Dazed, he shuffled inside the empty cell and then turned around. There were eight others left in line, and he watched with grief as they reacted to the inspector with the same emotions—some enraged, screaming, lunging for him and being beaten for their efforts, while others broke down, completely demoralized.

Early on he'd heard the Brutes call this place the Redoubt of Sundering, a "processing place" for prisoners. Its definition might've sounded managerial in nature, but that didn't even come close to the truth. As the day wore on, Lucas witnessed exactly what processing meant. The Redoubt was a place of culling, separating the soldiers and injured from the uninjured, eliminating the weak and the dying from the herd before the rest were sent nearby, to a place called the Tower.

No one but Lucas passed that day. From his vantage on the embankment, he had a decent view of the outpost and of the other prisoners now gathered in the cell across the open area. Maybe somewhere in the back of his exhausted mind he already knew what their fate would be; he just wasn't prepared for the sight of their mass execution.

The inspector and his companions left the area as a Grunt wobbled into view, talking to itself as it passed the occupied cells that Lucas could see and casually tossed in a methane canister. The creature never stopped walking or talking, just threw it in and carried on, leaving a noxious blue/green cloud to fill the cells, obscuring the prisoners. Lucas heard a few desperate screams, but they were cut short, replaced by the sound of choking and coughing. But it was the red energy barrier that suddenly lit up with the outline of bodies as some tried desperately to push through that sent him to his knees.

It was over in seconds.

Nothing left but silence, stillness, and the wafting stench of methane.

That could just as easily have been him in there. And yet, despite what the inspector had noted, he really didn't feel so lucky.

Every week or so now, countless more prisoners went through the line to be inspected and culled while Lucas remained in his lofty cell overlooking the horrific spectacle. Hate and hopelessness festered inside of him, and he burned with rage. He saved lives, it was who he was—but he swore if he ever got out, ever had the opportunity, he'd kill the inspector first and foremost. And he'd enjoy it. Oh, would he freaking enjoy it.

There were days when he wanted to scream, but never did, and holding it in was just another kind of burn. At night, the burn gave way to the hellish replay of the *Mortal Reverie*'s last stand, Gavin Jo's death, and Lucas's inability to save him then or in the many opportunities presented in his dream state. He withdrew more and more into himself, so much so that he found it difficult to look at or speak to the handful of other prisoners who had also made it into his cell.

It was in the third or fourth week, he wasn't quite sure anymore, that the Brutes brought out the Spartans. Five of them dragged limp into the open area, either severely injured or dead already—it was impossible to tell, as they were certainly unable to fight back—but Lucas prayed for their quick and merciful demise as the Brutes, Jackals, and Grunts set about dismantling the precious Mjolnir armor, ripping it off in the crudest, most damaging ways possible—manglers, plasma cutters, brute force.

And if the Spartans hadn't already been dead, then it happened sometime during the dismantling. Afterward, their bodies were pummeled, used as target practice, disgraced, defiled . . . treated like trash.

He'd thought he'd seen the worst of the Banished during the battle of the *Mortal Reverie*. Instead, that was just a primer to the depths of their cruelty.

He was quite certain now that the Banished had specifically chosen a human to process the prisoners. Being betrayed by one of your own kind was far more destructive to the psyche. It was psychological warfare at its finest. It probably wasn't even random that Lucas's holding cell overlooked the execution area.

They were being demoralized to the point of compliance. And that was the entire point. The Banished weren't simply defeating their enemies in battle; under Escharum's leadership, sophisticated tactics were employed to crush them mentally as well. Total domination.

And it worked—by the time Lucas and the others were being loaded onto a transport to the Banished's long-term prison, the Tower, emptiness filled the spaces where hope and promise used to dwell. It was so complete that he no longer had the waking, terrible flashbacks of the *Reverie* massacre and Gavin's death. Everything was muted, grayed out, and distant. He barely noticed the environment, more focused on watching his dirty bare feet move one in front of the other as he was shuffled along outside and across the outpost to the waiting transport.

Two low-ranking Brutes, by the looks of their armor, accompanied them. "Such work," one of them grumbled, shoving Lucas forward and onto a transport vessel with open sides. "And for what purpose?"

"It is beneath us," the other agreed. "Punishment to be their caretakers when we have done nothing to deserve it. Kill them all, I say."

His partner glanced menacingly over his shoulder, and Lucas quickly cast his eyes downward and scrambled to sit in the center of the vessel with the others. Meeting a Brute's gaze, he'd learned, was a challenge met with instant death. "They die with barely a touch," the first Jiralhanae said with disgust. "We can hardly be expected to keep them alive long enough to make it to the Tower."

"Fragile, are they not? Squeeze them too hard, step on them, hit them, and all they do is die. They are as useless as fur lice."

A Sangheili pilot began start-up procedures, and in short order the transport lifted off. They hadn't even bothered putting restraints on the prisoners, so sure they were that if anyone attempted to escape, they wouldn't get far. It almost felt like a dare, just another excuse to kill them if they made a break for it.

Lucas tried not to think about what life would be like at the Tower; he kept his head down and let his weary mind rest until the transport eventually landed. The prisoners were ushered off the vessel and beneath the massive legs of the Tower's support beams. His instinct was to look around, but really what was the point?

One of the Jiralhanae shoved him from behind and he went sprawling, landing on his knees and elbows. He was so tired of being pushed and shoved and handled that it brought tears to his eyes.

"Get up!"

A massive hand curled around the top of his head tightly and plucked him off his feet. His neck muscles stretched and something popped in his spine.

"Itacus!" a booming voice with an air of authority called from the open ground floor of the Tower. The Brute turned but didn't release him.

"Alive, remember."

The Brute cursed, holding Lucas directly in front of his face. The beast's breath was atrocious and made his stomach curl. He grinned and then opened his hand wide, dropping Lucas like a stone. "Welcome to the Tower, maggot."

The Tower was a menacingly large square keep held off the ground by massive landing supports. Like most of the other Banished structures Lucas had seen, this must have been dropped into place by one of the Banished's capital ships, allowing them to assemble and fortify it quickly. It had a central gravity lift and ramps around the inside perimeter leading to each level. The top level, he soon learned, was the domain of Chak 'Lok, warden of the Tower.

While Lucas was a low-level prisoner, the day he arrived he'd been taken to the top, shoved into a dirty, bloodstained chair in the middle of a room bathed in red light, and questioned by the warden. The room had turned his stomach, the stench of blood and rot and excrement overwhelming and instilling an immediate panic.

He'd expected to meet a vicious-looking Jiralhanae, not a tall Sangheili in gleaming gold armor, but Chak 'Lok was no less intimidating. The Warden considered torture to be an art form, and as soon as he'd brought out the plasma cutters, Lucas fainted. The next thing he knew, he woke alone in an enclosed cell, still in one piece. Maybe passing out had been his saving grace, but it wouldn't help him the next time.

Hunger pains gripped his insides. Every couple of days, someone would come and toss in scraps and bones of some animal, none of it ever properly cooked. Occasionally he got some kind of slop. It smelled horrible, making him curse with disgust, but the guy in the next cell heard and tapped on the wall. Lucas had moved over and let his head fall against their shared wall.

"Just eat it." His neighbor was male with a deep voice and a kind tone. "It won't kill you."

Lucas had scoffed at that. "Too bad."

His neighbor responded with a scratchy laugh, obviously relating to the sentiment. "Keep fighting, soldier. You never know when help will come."

Tears had sprung to Lucas's eyes. "Help isn't coming. There's nothing left. We're all scattered and outnumbered."

"What do you mean?"

"After the battle at *Mortal Reverie*—"

"You were there?" the stranger asked intently.

"Mmm. Was a bloodbath. The Banished, they outnumbered us a hundred to one. We didn't stand a chance. We never did."

"And the Spartans?"

"Fought like hell. Never seen anything like it. I don't know. . . . Saw a lot of them die. Have no idea how many. Me and my friends, we escaped with two of them."

"Which two?"

"Stone and Kovan."

"Ah," the man remarked, then said on a heavy sigh, "The *Reverie* is lost to us, then."

"She's been lost over a month now. . . ." If the guy didn't know about *Reverie*, he must've been captured early on or picked up in another sector. Lucas's curiosity stirred. "Who are you?"

So much time had passed that Lucas wasn't sure if he'd get an answer at all, but finally his neighbor replied, "It's better if you don't know."

Lucas slumped against the wall and pulled his knees to his chest, fairly certain that whoever was next to him had to be of significant rank for him to say such a thing. He let the answer lie, appreciating the protection his neighbor was trying to afford him. It made him think of the boat crew—of Murphy, Dimik, Cam, and Bender—and how they'd all looked out for each other from the moment they'd met. He missed them. He didn't want to—hell, he didn't even want to remember them because it all hurt too much. Yet he couldn't seem to help himself, and for once he let his guard down and let the memories free.

Where were they now? Dead? Alive? Imprisoned somewhere like him?

No, they'd made it. They were out there right now, giving the Banished hell. He had to believe it, needed something to hold on to, so he held on to that. It might be the only thing that kept him going.

CHAPTER 21

Zeta Halo
March 3, 2560
Day 82

They came upon the abandoned forward operating base at dusk.

The FOB had been dropped in a good spot, tucked in a grove of pines with a rocky point at its back. The boat crew didn't talk much; after a month of surviving on their own, they knew the drill, making a sweep of the area, searching the prefabricated platform for supplies . . . They'd found a few of these hastily established bases in the time since the aftermath of the *Reverie*. Some were even occupied by small squads like theirs, but reunions were brief—a day or night at the most, sharing news and information and supplies, but always they moved on. They'd learned, as many others had, that smaller groups survived better and could evade more easily, hide quicker, and achieve peak results.

An ongoing leaderboard had been circulating by word of mouth. Unofficial squads kept track of kills and the chaos they engineered. Gravediggers, a ragtag unit of super-hardened ODSTs, had been extremely effective at taking out Banished supply runners and raiding parties, while a group that called itself

Hatetriox successfully destroyed towers and bridges and other Banished structures.

Spartan Kovan was off scouting the area while Murphy took point like always—they'd developed a tidy sequence to their wanderings. "Looks like the console is useless," he said, noticing the lump of melted alloy and circuitry. "Cam, see if you can get anything from the comms unit. Dimik, Bender, give me a hand with the fallen."

Murphy felt like he was always on autopilot these days, and this scenario was no different. Gathering the dead, taking their tags, setting up camp, salvaging for supplies, remaining on high alert. Rinse. Repeat.

And he often wondered how long they could keep it up.

According to the military calendar, today was the anniversary of the end of Covenant War. On March 3, 2553, humanity had gathered at the final battle site on Earth to memorialize three decades of fighting, often with their backs to the wall against a far superior enemy. And now, here they were, seven years later, still fighting and still with their backs to the wall. For most of Murphy's life humanity had been struggling against some kind of existential threat or another. Some things apparently never changed.

Bender pulled his scarf over his nose, coughing and letting out a small gag. "Looks like these guys have been like this for a while."

"Yeah, so let's stop talking and get this done quick," Dimik said.

They collected tags and then grabbed wrists, dragging each corpse across the hard ground to a place behind some rocks. It would have to do.

Cam was rooting through burned supply crates when they returned, but Murphy would be surprised if the ensign found anything useful—the place had seen some heavy combat, too damaged even for the Banished to set up shop. "This is a bust," Cam muttered disappointedly. "No ammo, munitions, rations . . . nothing."

Murphy jumped onto the platform and took a seat near the crates, unwinding his scarf and giving his beard a good scratch before bending over to untie the laces to his boots. The soles had begun to separate and the combination of wet, dry conditions as they stayed on the move constantly kept his feet damp and blistered. As he started to peel the socks off his feet, a couple of loud *thuds* hit the platform.

A pair of combat boots lay on the surface, Dimik standing on the other side with a lift to her brow that said: *Don't even.* She tossed a pair of socks on top. She'd been tough before, but had grown even more hardened and adept over the past few weeks on the run. Murphy often thought she'd make a damn fine Spartan recruit. Bender too.

She made a *gimme* motion with her outstretched hand. "Come on. Hand them over."

A deep sigh escaped him. The idea of wearing a dead soldier's boots had prevented him from scavenging new ones until now. But he knew it was time. He picked up the old footwear and slung them across the platform.

"Thank you. About damn time." She grabbed the offending boots, walked to the edge of camp, and flung them as far as she could.

Cam had moved on to the FOB's standard comms antenna, on his knees to better reach the access panel. Eventually the familiar sound of static filled the air and the others gathered around the platform as the ensign tried to tune in. Short-range communications were all they were able to utilize, and those had to be used sparingly on the occasions they broke through the Banished disruptors. Unfortunately what came through as Cam searched frequencies was far from useful. As soon as the familiar voice whined through the speakers, they collectively rolled their eyes.

"Not this asshole again," Bender said.

The Grunt calling himself Glibnub broadcast daily from comm towers all over Zeta Halo, selling Banished propaganda designed to demoralize any human survivors who might be listening. And he enjoyed his job tremendously. Even the Banished were paying attention—relishing the broadcast as though it were an old-time favorite.

"Do you ever wake up in the morning and think today is going to be a better day?" The Unggoy's nasally voice went dead silent for several seconds before bursting out in a long, annoying laugh that went on and on until he was out of breath. *"Yeah, didn't think so!"*

"Can't believe no one's put a bullet in his head yet," Dimik said, shaking her head.

Whoever did would immediately get to the top of the leaderboard as well as holding bragging rights forever. It was something they all talked about when meeting other groups and sharing intel. One of their Most Wanted was the irritating Glibnub, holed up somewhere deep in Banished territory.

"Now, this one's for all you lovers out there," the Grunt said, taking on the affectation of a late-night Waypoint host. *"Private First Class Owens, a certain gunnery sergeant, didn't finish filling out his UNSC Personal Relationship Request. . . . Apparently, humans need permission to mate. Who knew! AHAHAHAHA! I have news for you, pal—request denied! Can't mate when you're dead!"*

"Turn it off," Murphy said, MRE in hand.

As the group ate, Cam continued to cycle through channels. After a while, he caught on a few spotty words. He leaned closer, frowning, listening.

"What is it?" Kovan asked, returning to camp.

"Broad-channel message, on repeat and pretty spotty. Let me see if I can clear it up a bit . . . okay, this is as good as it's gonna get."

As Murphy continued eating, the message played and he sat up straighter. He knew that confident voice. Sounded a hell of a lot like Spartan Sorel. ". . . *all UNSC forces per . . . Rubicon Protocol has been initiated . . . must do whatever is necessary . . . out of Banished hands . . .*"

"Rubicon Protocol?" Dimik asked. "What's that?"

"Asset denial. It means we do whatever is necessary to keep control of Zeta Halo out of Escharum's hands." Kovan removed her helmet and set it on an empty supply crate. "The Rubicon Protocol means we don't need permission, don't have to wait around for orders. We've been given free rein, permission to act, to do what's needed, wherever and whenever we can."

Murphy nodded. "So we don't just survive—we make life a living hell for the Banished. If that means armed conflict, or poisoning their water supply, or blowing a munitions site . . . we do it, every and any chance we get."

"Guerrilla warfare," Bender said.

"So basically what we and a bunch of us have already been doing for the last month," Cam said, unimpressed.

Murphy gave a soft laugh at that—they'd certainly been a thorn in the Banished side, however small. "We're the last line of defense. The ring is repairing itself—we know that, we've seen it—and once it's operational again, there's no way in hell we can let the Banished control a weapon like this."

"Just what kind of weapon are we talking about, exactly?" Dimik asked.

Kovan glanced around the group. "If the Halo ring fires, it wipes out all sentient life within a twenty-five-thousand-light-year radius. And when its pulse reaches the other rings, it could erase all thinking life from the galaxy."

Dimik's eyes went wide. "Come again?"

Bender leaned forward, looking just as shocked. "Jesus. No wonder they're after it."

"I think it's more than that, though," Kovan said thoughtfully. "The ring isn't just a weapon—it's a habitat, and not a bad one, at that. Because of Cortana, the Jiralhanae lost their homeworld and both of their moon colonies . . ."

"They're looking to make this their home, you think?" Dimik asked.

Kovan shrugged. "It's what I would do. Whether they came here for that reason or they were after Cortana for payback, making Zeta a highly defensible outpost and getting their revenge all in one go . . . How can they resist?"

"If that's true, then it makes our job even harder," Murphy said. "They'll dig in and fight at all costs to keep the ring."

"You guys realize, with this Rubicon Protocol in effect, it means we're on our own," Cam said. "It means help isn't coming. We *are* the help."

Murphy had silently hoped differently, of course. If they could gain a foothold, find a little luck, then maybe, just maybe fortune would smile on humanity's side and help would indeed come. They just had to hold out. . . .

"However you look at it, we can either give up or we can go all-in and give the Banished hell," Kovan said. "And I know damn well which one I'm choosing."

"Me too," Dimik replied. "All-in."

Murphy watched each of them answer in kind, no question, no hesitation, until they were staring at him, waiting. All-in didn't just mean they'd give it their best shot—that was a given—it meant they understood how enormous the stakes were and were still willing to give everything, including their lives. It didn't get any more humbling than that.

They were crazy in the best possible way, and he most definitely could relate. After a deep exhale, he gave a nonchalant shrug and a lopsided grin. "All-in."

CHAPTER 22

Spartan Tomas Horvath had lain unconscious for several days on the edge of the mud flats after Gorian ripped the near-fatal metal shard from his side. After he woke, he stayed another week or so, his biomonitors inducing a semicomatose state, slowing down his brain function, metabolism, core temperature, and circulatory system while the medical systems within his armor engaged in the regeneration of his torn insides.

Once he was able to stand, he'd been on the move—albeit slowly at first—sticking to the shadows and feeling real hunger for the first time in a long while, and surly because of it. Those emergency high-caloric nutrient supplements fed directly into his system during his healing process had been the barest minimum to keep him alive. It was enough to get him across the kilometers of mud flats and to a more familiar landscape, but it sure as hell wasn't filling.

In the weeks that followed, his strength returned and he became adept at hunting the area's population of striped gophers and land birds for food, and finding abundant water sources in the lowlands. Thanks to the Banished, no doubt, some of the larger fauna on Zeta Halo had been eradicated from this part of the ring, effectively hunted to the point of extinction. This was the Banished's *modus operandi*: indiscriminately ravage a location's resources until it was bare and then move on. For the time being, he'd have to make do with smaller game.

He'd definitely landed off-target of where he had originally intended, but he still counted it as a success—that he'd made it across open space at all was a miracle. Now the challenge, once again, was finding his way back to a UNSC presence.

And at every opportunity, he took out the Banished, becoming somewhat detached after a while, a lone wolf hunting the enemy, picking his targets, stalking them, taking them down one by one and then disappearing. He was smoke and shadow; they never saw him coming and he never left anyone alive to see him leaving.

All the while he stayed on the move and, with Fi's help, sought the location he'd discovered in the Phantom's flight recorder. He often referred to the data he'd stolen from the crashed vessel, trying to get a lock on position, using the landscape, building his own map, looking for the ruins from which the Banished had extracted the stone artifacts.

It was the only known location he had to go on, and he was certain it'd bring him back into the Banished's—and, he hoped, the UNSC's—main playing field.

After so much time searching, he'd finally found it on the edge of a flooded plain populated with a series of tall, connected mesas. It was a site of intense destruction, the once dry plain evidently having been splintered by the initial ring fracture, causing the ground to drop dramatically in places, leaving the mesas behind and allowing water from a higher-elevation lake to drain into the depressions.

The weather over the plain was tumultuous. Storm clouds appeared to be stuck in a perpetual pattern of rotation, producing harsh winds and churning the water below. Horvath bent his head against the wind and made his way across a narrow strip of land connected to the first mesa, where the vegetation and sparse trees eventually gave way to stone and mud-brick foundations and the ruins of several large stone rings partially buried in the ground. Sure as hell similar to the artifacts he'd found in the Phantom.

"Let me guess, nothing in the database?"

"That is correct," Elfie answered.

And no sign of the Banished. The area had been harshly excavated, pits of turned earth and stone, evidence of their occupation lying discarded among the ruins—empty crates, spent shells, campsites, trash, and even abandoned excavation tools.

Horvath had no idea what he was looking for, so he walked the large site in a grid pattern, fighting the wind and the small sporadic dust funnels that formed and withered, until he found a deep pit where one steep side revealed the unearthed walls of an ancient building. Following a sloping section down into the pit, he noticed depressions in the path. Definitely made by an excavator.

From the bottom of the pit, the façade of the ancient building rose three levels, its peak well over ten meters above him. He regarded it for a long moment: the precisely stacked stone blocks, the window openings and ornate archways over each one, and the crudely smashed opening in the center of the façade. The Banished obviously weren't interested in preserving the site. "Well, let's see if we can figure out what they were after."

Horvath stepped over the rubble and into a dark, cavernous space. His light activated, illuminating a stone floor with a few remaining pieces of floral mosaics decorating the edges. The wind from outside echoed in the space, creating a hollow and mournful sound. At the far end of the chamber was another crude hole, a shaft large enough for a Jiralhanae, extending downward. Horvath ducked inside, moving into the bedrock, finally emerging a level below into a series of rock-cut chambers, littered with excavation debris.

"*I'm detecting a faint life signature,*" Elfie said. "*It is human.*"

Horvath paused in midstep, a stunned breath caught in his throat. He hadn't seen another human being since Zeta Halo had fractured. "Are you sure?"

"*Positive.*"

His display lit with a grid of the chambers, and a green dot marked the spot. Each step sounded loud in the cavernous space, and his helmet lamp illuminated only a small portion of the area as hope carried him closer to the dot. He cleared the grid from his display as an unrecognizable heap tucked against the wall came into view.

It was either another sensor going to hell or it really was a human, and a living one at that. His hope faded as he approached and knelt, removing his helmet and immediately regretting it. The horrific smell of human rot stung the back of his nose and stuck in his throat.

His helmet light stayed on, proving a means to inspect the mass of matted hair, and what looked like a bony shoulder. He reached out, gently pulling the figure over. His heart gave a painful bang. It was a woman, her skin sunken, papery-thin, and bruised; in some places old, open wounds festered. She wore a nondescript black operative suit stiff with dried blood. Both legs had been broken and set at odd angles, and three fingers on her left hand were missing.

Her wounds were in such varying stages that it was clear she'd been tortured over a long period of time. And then the Banished had left her here at some point to die.

He ran a hand down his beard, letting out a heavy sigh. That someone had endured this, and still lived . . . his scanners weren't necessary to tell him that she was at death's door and there was no coming back from it.

Her eyes moved beneath the lids as a faint moan lodged in her throat.

"I'm not going to hurt you. I'm Spartan Tomas Horvath of UNSC *Infinity*. You're safe. You're safe now."

Her right arm lifted. Horvath reached out and grabbed her flailing hand, surprised by her grip. He could sense her desire to communicate and moved her as gently as he could so that she was propped up somewhat.

Her breathing was labored as she sought enough strength to talk. "I'm . . . ONI . . . asset recovery . . . came here on the second exploratory expedition two years ago." So she'd been here long before the Banished came. Since the first expedition, in 2555, Zeta Halo had been home to a few thousand military and science personnel. And surely others were still here, hiding, surviving, fighting. . . .

ONI asset recovery teams were highly skilled combat specialists, trained to navigate and survive in any number of hostile territories and environments while hunting the highest value assets— a quarry that often included ancient Forerunner relics. They were badasses through and through, and seeing one brought so low filled him with anger.

"The Banished . . . the ones called . . . Jega . . . Gorian . . . they—"

At the mention of a name he knew well, Horvath clenched

his teeth and had to keep from tightening his hold on the agent's hand. It didn't surprise him, though, as it was Gorian's intel and his Phantom full of artifacts that had led him here. "Captured me months ago. . . . Stole my research—"

He should have killed the bastard the moment the sentinel regained power.

"—been to one site after another and back again. Finally dumped me here . . . but I know where he's going next." She released Horvath's hand and pointed to the cave wall beside her where she'd been curled up. "It's there . . . the way to one of the Conspectus network hubs. They'll go there next for answers."

"Why there? Answers to what?"

"It's a data storehouse. It contains system protocols and records of all the activity on Zeta Halo—status reports, event logs, maintenance, communications. . . ." She paused to catch her breath. "Even access to its defensive system. It's all stored in local information hubs throughout the ring. There's so much more to this Halo . . . so much we still don't understand." Her eyes rolled back into her head.

"Hang in there," he said softly, hoping she could hear him.

He sat with her for a long time, until finally she gathered enough strength to speak once more. "Do whatever it takes . . . don't let the Banished find the data . . ."

She was fading again, but managed to lift her right hand and slap it against the cave wall as though that explained everything. A tear slipped from her swollen eye.

She'd been sent by the Office of Naval Intelligence to Zeta Halo in order to retrieve Forerunner artifacts of critical importance, and she'd found something else—something the Banished were now after too.

"Horvath?" Her throat worked and another tear slipped out. "I'm sorry to ask. . . ." Her head tipped to the side so she could see him more clearly.

Perhaps some small part of him knew she'd ask even before she said it. He would do the same if roles were reversed—yet when it came down to it, he wasn't so sure he could grant her request. He shook his head, unable to form an adequate reply, but she kept looking at him, pleading without words, letting her hope sink into him and through all of his doubts and denials.

"They've already killed me," she said, reading his thoughts.

His head hung. "No, I—"

"Give me your weapon, then."

Goddamn it.

Horvath hesitated, gritting his teeth in denial. He was supposed to save people, not provide them with a way out. Yet how could he just walk away and allow her agony and suffering to continue? How could he not grant her this mercy?

Being an ONI operative, she wore no name tag on her clothes or gear, no dog tag to identify her; in any other instance if he asked an operative in the field for a name, the agent would laugh in his face and ask him if he'd failed basic training. But this circumstance was quite different, and if he was going to help her, then he damn well wanted to know who she was. "You got a name?" he asked gruffly, withdrawing one of the M6s from a mag-clamp on his side, checking the magazine and chamber. Then, cradling her right hand, he placed the gun in it and guided her fingers around the grip.

"JAEGER," she strained.

"How about a real one?" Horvath knew an ONI codename when he heard one and he refused to let it be her lasting identity.

A small smile pulled one corner of her wounded mouth. "Stalling. Kate Stalling." She tried to lift her arm, but the gun was too heavy to manage, so he helped her until her arm rested on her chest, the barrel pointing toward her chin. "Thank you," she whispered in relief. "Leave it with me. I'll wait until you're gone."

Horvath met Stalling's glassy eyes and gave her a deep nod, marveling at her strength and fortitude, then grabbed his helmet and left the chamber. He climbed out the way he'd come in, hearing the howl of the wind before he saw daylight spilling down the shaft. The sound pricked the hairs on the back of his neck as he cleared the main chamber and stepped out into the pit.

Every second that passed, every step he made or breath he took, might be punctuated by the crack of the M6. He tried not to think about it, or wait for it, and instead walked up the slope and headed through the strange stone rings and ruins to the edge of the mesa. The wind whipped at his hair and left a cold sting on his face. Thunder echoed from the dark storm cloud above, and the waves below crashed against the mesa walls.

He stared at the tumultuous view for such a long time that when the gunshot finally rang out, it startled him enough to make him flinch. The birds in the nearby trees took flight, soaring to safer foliage as the finality of that violent noise rang in his head.

Horvath sat, letting his legs dangle over the edge and his posture relax. That final, awful sound—one he'd heard so many times in his life—tried to bore its way inside him, to make him think not just of Kate Stalling but of all those he'd lost along the way, those more recently on *Infinity*, and those he could no longer reach—his team, his fellow Spartans, even his heroes like the Master Chief. . . .

Blue Team had been on *Infinity*. Were they still up there? Or had they found themselves in the thick of things down here on the ring? Was the Master Chief even now fighting his way through Banished ranks and laying the groundwork for victory? Or had he met a far worse fate?

Horvath gazed out over the water and beyond the spinning supercell cloud that hovered over the mesa, to the clear horizon and the faint glimpse of the ring curving upward. The area was so vast, thousands and thousands of acres broken into pieces, everyone impossibly scattered. . . .

Some days it felt like he was taking two steps forward and one step back, but now Stalling had given him hope. If there was an information hub with every event recorded, every status logged, then that meant the slipspace event would have been logged as well. Where they'd ended up in the galaxy would be noted. And if he could find coordinates and get a message out, to let the UNSC know what had happened to *Infinity* and what was happening here on the ring, then reinforcements would be inbound and the Banished would finally experience the full retribution they deserved.

Sounded great in theory, but the Banished had a huge head start and aerial vehicles at their disposal—they might already have the critical information they sought.

Not one to dwell on the obstacles for too long, Horvath rose and made his way back down to the chamber, where he carefully moved Stalling's broken body to inspect the crudely scratched symbols and the map she'd made on the wall. He recorded the image—"See what you can make of the map," he told Fi—and then used a nearby rock to scratch out its existence.

That done, he gathered the ONI agent in his arms and easily carried her back to the surface, where he buried her in a spot overlooking the water. He'd find the Conspectus hub Stalling mentioned and make sure her sacrifice would not be in vain.

The map would keep him on the trail of Gorian, and more than anything, Horvath wanted the Brute's blood on his hands.

CHAPTER 23

"*Bender, you got eyes on them?*" Murphy's low voice buzzed through the team's salvaged comms.

Spartan Kovan magnified by five, meticulously scanning the target area from eighteen meters above the ground in an ancient evergreen. As she unslung the SRS99-S5 sniper rifle, she left one leg hanging over the thick tree limb, drew the other up, and then rested her rifle-bearing forearm on her knee for added stability. She cocked her head in a stance that was as natural as breathing and sighted through the S5's standard scope, once again wishing she hadn't had to ditch her custom sniper rig, Abbey Lime, during the attack on the *Mortal Reverie*.

This weapon she'd picked up a few weeks ago from the edge of a blackened-out missile crater—a lucky find, but it didn't compare.

"*I got nothing,*" Bender replied.

"*Kovan?*" Murphy asked. "*You see them yet?*"

Cam and Dimik hadn't reappeared from setting the salvaged C10 charges along the perimeter of the biggest Unggoy camp they'd come across to date. The area had two portable atmosphere pits the size of heavy Scarabs. Dug into the ground and fed by cylindrical methane tanks, the pits were covered by white reinforced tents and airlocked to prevent leakage and provide access in and out of the enclosures. They were designed to mimic the Unggoys natural atmosphere, a place where they could ditch their portable methane tanks and move freely without asphyxiating in Zeta's oxygen-rich environment.

All that methane just waiting to blow sky-high . . . Naturally, it made the perfect target.

Movement near the trees caught her eye. *"They're coming, southeast tree line."* Cam and Dimik were hauling ass back to the cover of the rocks. *"Should be in range in five seconds."*

As soon as they hit comms range, Murphy made contact. *"Hurry it up, you two. We're running out of time."*

Soon the large detachment of Grunts relaxing in the pits would be replaced by another incoming unit. For three days they'd watched the routine, and now it was just a matter of timing.

Two birds. One stone.

Multitasking was something she and Murphy had in common, and it made them a pretty effective team. Though, to be fair, there was no one more skilled at it than Bonita Stone. Kovan shoved the thought of her missing teammate away; they'd been good at so many things, yet reuniting didn't seem to be one of them. She hadn't seen or heard from Stone since fleeing the *Mortal Reverie*.

"In position," Cam said between breaths.

"Once this thing blows, remember the plan," Murphy said.

Blowing stuff up wasn't the part that worried her; it was what came after.

When she and Murphy had devised their latest raid, making the decision to hunker in place—instead of running like the

Banished would expect them to—had been the smartest tack to take. It still was. But it was also risky. With the Grunts' playground only a klick away from a heavily guarded Banished armory, they'd had little choice. Blowing the camp and then running, scattering, and potentially being chased down by highly armed enemy guards was tantamount to suicide.

So the decision had been made to not give the Banished a target at all.

They'd strike, then conceal themselves close to the site in the foxholes they'd been digging beneath the rocks over the last three days, and wait until the dust settled.

After that, they'd hike out and head northwest.

Kovan spied the exchange unit waddling through the pass in a cloud of methane. *"Look sharp. They're here."*

Thirty Grunts passed through the heavily guarded barricade and approached the pits. Just a few more meters to go . . . Kovan settled her thoughts and relaxed her body.

The detachment separated into two groups and came to a halt at the pits' airlocks.

There was a good chance Kovan's round would ignite the methane by hitting something metal inside and creating the spark needed, but no point in taking chances. If they were going to risk their lives, they'd make damn sure the campsite lit up the sky. If the last couple months had taught them anything, it was to make the most of every opportunity, and wreak as much havoc as possible. Maximum damage, all the time.

"Taking the shot in three." Slow exhale out and . . .

"Now," Murphy whispered into comms.

Kovan's high-velocity armor-piercing round cracked through the air and pierced one incoming Grunt's methane tank just as he was about to enter the tent. The HVAP round continued straight through the tank and sliced into the first tent as the C10 explosive charges blew the second tent. The whole damn campsite went up with an earsplitting *whoosh*. The ground shook and the trees rattled, sending birds scattering from their branches. The sky turned dark as a fiery plume of methane mushroomed into the air.

"Kovan, get the hell out of there," Murphy said. *"See the rest of you this time tomorrow."*

Kovan waited until the team signed off; then she climbed down the tree, her right leg feeling a little stiff again, jumping the last seven meters and then taking off at a dead run toward the Banished armory. Keeping an eye on their movements was critical. Bits and pieces of the Unggoy camp rained down through the trees, steaming methane clumps splattering onto the forest floor.

The forests had become her cover of choice—ancient, thick evergreens, some as tall as ten stories, provided excellent cover and vantage points, and they populated this part of the ring in large tracts interspersed with arid, mountainous terrain.

Kovan reached her second bird's-eye location and climbed to a limb twenty meters above the armory where she had a clear view of its high, well-protected fabricated walls, patrolled by Brutes along with a small group of Elite mercenaries. There was just enough time to get settled before the Banished guards at the armory mobilized and exited the barricades, piloting a couple of Choppers and seven Ghosts by her count. From her position, they looked like red insects spilling through the woods.

She kept her eyes on their passage as they made it to the Unggoy pit. After realizing there was nothing left of the Grunt campsite, they split into four groups to search in an outward sector pattern.

The boat crew would already have retreated into their dugouts beneath the large boulders surrounding the Grunts' campsite. No comms, no signals of any kind to give them away. They'd lie low for twenty-four hours; then, if all was well, Kovan would make contact. If it was safe to travel, they'd meet up and head out. If not, they'd wait another twenty-four hours and try again. There was enough food and water for each of them to last a few days, and they'd definitely learned how to make it stretch, all knowing intimately what it was like to go hungry—their bodies these last few months becoming lithe and strong and capable of existing on less as a result.

Being a Spartan for nearly a decade, Kovan had forgotten what it was like to be vulnerable, to be without the resources of the military at comms' call, without augmentations and billions of credits in hardware at one's disposal. Seeing her companions persevere was nothing short of heroic and inspiring. On days when her bodysuit's density regulator went on the fritz and the suit tightened painfully around her leg and arm, it kept her going. *They* kept her going.

But she knew she was on borrowed time. The next time the suit froze up, it might be her last. Stuck in the GEN3, unable to get out, wasn't something she wanted to think too much about. All she needed was a replacement chip to the core mechanism that controlled the regulator and someone to help her install it, but so far finding a replacement hadn't been in the cards.

It was wait or else ditch the armor altogether, and she wasn't quite ready to give up her Mjolnir just yet.

Ammo was running low too. Once they started north, they'd have to make a few salvage runs and see what was out there.

The guards continued moving away from the campsite, and she suspected it wouldn't be long before they gave up the search entirely. So far the plan was working beautifully. Her gaze continued over the landscape, beyond the dispersing smoke cloud, and over the foothills, the fractured cliffs and mountains, and the empty sea, to the ever-curving shape of the Halo ring with its hues resembling the surface of thriving blue-green worlds.

It made her wonder if, somewhere else on the ring, her team was seeing a similar view. Stone was somewhere in this sector—had to be—and the others were together, she hoped, surviving, doing their best like everyone else. At every FOB they'd stumbled upon, Kovan had left a report of their actions, anticipating the same or maybe a message.

Just once . . . to hear their names in a report or a fractured transmission.

But she never did.

With a tired sigh, she leaned against the tree trunk to settle in for the long wait.

Daylight was beginning to fade. Night would fall soon. And she'd still be here. Waiting. Watching. Always watching.

Throughout the night, the Banished guards made several forays through the area before finally giving up and returning to the armory. They never bothered searching on the doorstep of the explosion site.

Twenty-four hours later, she made contact with Murphy, and they moved on.

CHAPTER 24

Since fleeing the site of *Mortal Reverie*, Spartan Kovan and the boat crew had gone southwest, then east across the ring fragment, using the ship as their north star to orient their direction of travel. At first the track they'd taken had been a means of survival; once the Rubicon Protocol had been enacted, it had been determined by whatever Banished locations or groups they'd come across.

They'd seen several Banished aerial transports heading in a northerly direction in recent weeks, so that became the new direction of choice.

Kovan stayed twenty meters above the crew on the rocky slope, tracking parallel and gaining the better vantage while the others took the easier path up into the mountains. Sometimes their laughter would carry with the wind, and for an odd moment or two she longed to be part of their banter. It made her miss the companionship she'd had on *Infinity*—the Spartan deck was always a lively place. The fact that it might not exist anymore . . .

Even now, after all this time—it felt unreal.

Along with the Spartan losses, the loss of Gavin Jo and Lucas Browning continued to weigh heavy on her shoulders, and despite going over their deaths in her head a thousand times, she'd come to the conclusion that she'd failed them. More often than not, it was because of them that she maintained her distance from the group, knowing another loss would hit her too hard.

Kovan heard the Banshees three klicks off.

And they were coming in fast.

"Take cover," Kovan told the team over the standard-issue infantry squad comms Cam had salvaged weeks earlier. Rudimentary compared to the GEN3 communications suite she'd once been able to utilize. Instantly, Murphy, Bender, Cam, and Dimik scattered and hid as a unit of the Banished aircraft soared over the mountains.

When they were gone, Kovan gave the all-clear.

"That's the fourth flight today," Murphy said.

"All heading in the same direction."

The team picked up their pace and, after a few hours of hard hiking, they made it to a higher elevation where the air was cooler and the trees thinned out. The terrain became flatter too as they trekked across a plateau pocked with small canyons and valleys and a few thin ring fractures that left deep chasms and exposed Forerunner substructure. As dusk gave way to night, they stopped to make camp in a protected canyon and Kovan hiked down to rejoin the group.

They were sitting down eating when she arrived, giving her a few glances and nods of greeting, but more interested in the food. She couldn't blame them. Her stomach growled as she took a seat on one of the rocks. "What's the ration status?" she asked Murphy as he picked through his rucksack and tossed her an MRE.

"We'll run out in two or three days."

"I saw a few deer in the woods below us," Bender said, stuffing his mouth with a nondescript, rather pathetic-looking sandwich. When no one replied, he said, "We're going to have to use fire sooner or later."

True, but no one wanted to debate it yet again.

And no one wanted to bring the Banished down on their heads with a campfire either. Feeding themselves would eventually mean putting themselves in danger. And one imperative would win out over the other.

Cam's head lifted. "Shit. Is that another transport?"

"Scatter," Kovan said, jumping up.

This time it wasn't just a small unit or a couple of light vessels, but an entire force: several Banshees, Spirits, and a couple of heavily armed Phantoms crossed the darkening sky and trembled the loose stones at their feet.

After they passed, Dimik got up and walked to the edge of camp. "There's more down in the valley." In the pass below, ground vehicles followed a similar direction as the aerial vehicles, kicking up dust as they went.

Bender joined her to watch the procession. "What the hell? We haven't seen movement like this since *Reverie*."

"Only thing north that we know of *is* the *Reverie*," Cam said quietly.

And they hadn't been back to that area since the initial attack.

"Hold that thought." Kovan snagged her helmet and then made tracks across the plateau and up the rugged mountain slope so she could get a look out over the landscape.

By the time she reached a high set of boulders and climbed to the top, her breathing was labored. She walked out onto a large rocky promontory and magnified her visor on the tail end of the aerial group. Cam was right—the Banished continued due north and seemed to be headed back to the *Mortal Reverie*'s location, or at least somewhere close to it.

When she returned to camp, the others were already packed up and waiting, game faces on.

"We'll stick to higher ground for the time being," she said. "Let's go."

Another couple days of travel, and Kovan found a nice spot to recon the surrounding mountains while the others were making camp. This time she was hunkered in between two boulders, using the scope on her S5 to survey the area. While she'd never been in this location before, the terrain was starting to become more familiar, more woodsy and green. Occasionally she came across burned-out Banished vehicles and evidence of older ground fighting.

And then she hit on a smudge in the trees across the ravine two klicks away.

Kovan froze.

Backtracking, there it was again.

She magnified by eight and realized she was looking down her scope and straight into another.

Sniper to sniper.

Spartan to Spartan.

A slow smile grew on her face. Goddamn. She'd recognize that visor anywhere.

Kovan kept Bonita Stone in sight and raised a hand. Stone did the same, and then made a gesture to tell her to stay put. Kovan acknowledged, and stepped backward until hitting one of the massive boulders behind her. She removed her helmet and gulped in the fresh alpine air, pure relief washing over her so hard that her throat went a little tight and her eyes stung.

Stone was still alive. Miraculous, considering how many of her fellow Spartans had fallen to the Banished since they'd arrived in this hellhole.

It would take Stone an hour or two to traverse the gulf between them, so Kovan returned to check on the team before making her way back to the rendezvous point once more. For now, she kept Stone's reemergence to herself, partly out of habit—it was ingrained in her, as a member of Fireteam Shadow, to hold things close to her chest—but mostly because she wanted to debrief in private. The reunion with the others could come later.

Finally she heard the Spartan's noisy approach as she climbed onto the outcrop. They stared at each other for a good long moment, and then Stone removed her helmet.

Stone's dark eyes were filled with relief. A wide grin was parked on her face, and her head was shaking like she just couldn't believe what she was seeing. Beyond the welcome, though, Kovan didn't miss the gaunt quality to her skin, the shadows beneath her eyes, the busted lip and the blood crusted in her ear. Her dark hair had grown into her eyes, long enough to tuck it behind her ears. It made her look softer—an observation that, had Kovan voiced it aloud, would have gotten her a swift ass-kicking.

"Sure is good to see you again," Stone said.

Kovan cleared the lump in her throat. "Yeah. Same."

"And the others? Murphy, Dimik—"

"Everyone but Browning," Kovan interrupted. "He . . ." How could she even begin to explain?

But Stone seemed to understand her unspoken words. "You don't have to say it," she said gently. "Any word from Shadow?"

"Nothing. The Banished have signal jammers all over this fragment. My comms array and AI are fried thanks to a shock rifle hit. All I can manage is short-range comms with the team, and half the time can't connect. You?"

"Same. Long-range is completely out and so is my ID sensor. Sorel and Mako were in this sector last I heard. I managed to make contact a few times."

"How?"

"There's pieces of a crashed FOB in the mountains about forty kilometers from here," Stone told her. "Never had a chance to deploy before it was shot down, but there's a working comms satellite. Sorel and Mako found it and have been using it sparingly to reconnect with others. They've rigged it to broadcast a location ping by cycling through a digital signal chain. They leave debriefs at site for whoever shows up."

"Forty klicks is a long way for a signal like that to travel. I take it you've been on the move."

"Constantly."

Kovan knew something about that. They'd been on the move and had covered a lot of terrain themselves. "I've been in the dark since *Reverie*. Who else made it?"

"Vettel. He's out hunting down Griffin. Came across droppings from Jaide and Rosado as well, but no real data on their current status. We took a big loss. I'm not sure who made it out beyond that. If your comms are damaged, the others' might be too. . . . Where the hell have you been all this time?"

"On the run," Kovan answered. "Then hounding the Banished, doing the best we can, given the circumstances. The fractures and the mountains, everything is spread out and there's a lot of ground to cover . . . makes it slow work."

"Your armor looks like shit."

Kovan's brow rose. "Uh-huh. Speak for yourself."

"Your helmet's seen better days too. . . ." Stone studied the dent in the right side. "What—was that a gravity hammer to the side of the head?"

"Something like that. My density regulator is malfunctioning too," Kovan said reluctantly. The last thing she wanted was to place additional burdens on her teammate. But at the same time, a malfunction like this was a major liability to the boat crew and needed to be known. She couldn't tell them, but she could tell Stone. "It's why Browning ran out and . . ."

"Don't worry about it," Stone said knowingly. "We'll find you a new one, and I'll install it personally. We can't have the Stoic freezing up in the middle of a battle," she said with a smirk.

Kovan grabbed her helmet from beneath her arm and turned to lead the way back to camp. "Come on. The others will be happy to see you."

"Not as happy as you, though, right?" Stone clapped her on the shoulder. "Hey, come on . . . say it. You missed me. You know you're dying to. . . ."

Kovan responded with her typical snort and head shake. As if on cue, Stone let out a low chuckle. They'd settled right back into their usual camaraderie as though no time had passed at all.

Back at camp, the team gathered around Stone, their stunned and relieved faces mirroring what Kovan had felt . . . only on a more open scale. She leaned against one of the boulders and watched the reunion as Stone studied the group with a shocked expression.

"You look . . . different. You all look so different."

Kovan glanced around the group, trying to see them as if for the first time since *Reverie*. They had indeed changed. Longer hair, scruffy faces weathered by the elements; lean, hardened bodies; capable guerrilla fighters through and through.

How far they'd all come. And at such a heavy cost.

"Different as in"—Bender made a muscle with his bicep and slapped it—"*Holy shit, how the hell did this bad boy get here?*"

Kovan groaned and rolled her eyes.

"Glad to see some things haven't changed," Stone said with a laugh.

As talk turned to the recent Banished activity nearby, Kovan found a seat and settled in. "They're definitely heading up to the *Reverie* site," Stone said. "And one of those transports is from Escharum's personal fleet. Whether he's actually on it is anyone's guess, but . . ."

"If he is . . ." Kovan said.

A sudden quiet settled among them.

"If he is, we need to know," Murphy said. "And we need to take him out."

Her thoughts exactly.

CHAPTER 25

Lucas Browning stayed at the back of the Banished transport, making himself as invisible as possible. The Brute Itacus hadn't relayed anything at all when he'd taken Lucas from his cell in the Tower and dragged him outside across the tarmac to a Phantom dropship. He'd been shoved aboard the open side-bay door and then ushered to the back as it filled with other Brutes and Elites.

The Phantom kept its side doors open, which allowed the air to flow in and blow off the stink of Jiralhanae—a small but intensely welcome gift. As much as he wanted to know where he was going and why, after a cursory inspection he kept his mouth shut and his head down; after these past several weeks, he knew better. It was no longer fear, exactly—that had been systematically beaten out of him on the daily—it was the utter exhaustion that kept him compliant and constantly dulled any rising fear. He'd lost a good thirty pounds if not more, his body weak, his mind given to dizzy spells and emotional outbursts.

Today, though, his mental state became a little clearer just by virtue of it being different than all the other days he'd been held captive. He appeared to be the only prisoner on board, and was perhaps being transferred to another prison or about to be used for some other purpose. If they wanted him dead, it would already have happened by now. At least that's what he told himself.

The flight could've taken five minutes or twenty and he wouldn't have noticed. He'd stopped measuring things in time, as it only seemed to weigh heavily on him whenever he did.

Although it was too packed to see much during the trip, he did glimpse clouds and mountaintops the few times he lifted his head; and as the Banished craft began its descent, he noted the change in temperature from balmy to a crisp, arid cool.

The Elite contingent leapt out before the Phantom's embarking ramp touched the ground, followed by the Brutes as the craft settled into a low hover. Itacus's giant hand wrapped around Lucas's bicep and gave a jerk, lifting him onto his feet but thankfully not hard enough to dislocate his shoulder, or worse. During his captivity, he'd had the misfortune of witnessing the Brutes engaging with other human prisoners in a horrific game their captors called Tossers. The carnage and the screaming that ensued would haunt him until his dying day . . . which might be anytime now.

Stars danced in his field of vision, and he blinked rapidly to stave off the approaching dizziness as Itacus hauled him off the edge of the carriage and threw him to the ground like a rucksack. Pain erupted in his shoulder and hip and his head as it slapped onto the tarmac. Immediately warmth spread down the side of his face as he pushed himself up, gritting his teeth, not making a noise—they paid more attention when you made noise, that was for damn sure. He couldn't wipe the blood away because Itacus now had him by the neck, setting him back on his feet and pushing him along.

The Banished group that had amassed was the largest gathering he'd seen since *Reverie*—a crowd of Jiralhanae, Sangheili, Unggoy, Kig-Yar, all flowing toward one central location and drawing his eye up.

Lucas's heart dropped like a stone.

It was the *Mortal Reverie*.

The once-proud vessel rose above him, broken, blackened, haunting, but still doggedly there despite the newly created Banished outpost in her shadow. Slashes of red enemy war paint branded the outpost that now occupied the entire terrain along the portside of *Reverie*'s hull, filling him with rage and a deep, stinging grief. The sight forced him to revisit the terrible memories and sudden death, flashes in the dark, shrieks of pain, endless gunfire . . . Gavin.

His throat, nose, and eyes stung, but he was too dehydrated to produce a single tear—they just seemed stuck in his throat, choking him as anguish swelled his chest and pushed into his face until he felt the pressure to scream. Soon he was stumbling down a ramp and swept along a well-worn path that eventually led into one of the Banished outpost structures near *Reverie*'s stern. Within was a Banished command post with holographic displays and readouts, and more Banished staring strangely at him. He was ushered down a side corridor that bored deep into the mountain below *Reverie*—a location the UNSC forces previously occupying the frigate had, to his knowledge, never even seen.

Lucas dared not gawk or keep his head up too long if he

wanted to keep it intact, but at the end of the corridor they entered a large, dimly lit chamber littered with Banished excavation equipment. Here more Banished had gathered, and when they saw him, they parted to make way. He glanced nervously as dozens of eyes seemed to fall on him, following his progression farther into the chamber. His pulse kicked up a notch. The hairs on the back of his neck tingled as his gaze was drawn to the right side of the room and a strange yellow glow.

He tried to swallow, but couldn't. He tried to slow down, but failed to do that either. Itacus kept him moving with a hard poke in the shoulder.

Why did he feel so itchy all of a sudden, as if spiders were crawling over his skin?

Upright against the wall, a large rectangular device with a bizarre humanoid outline was lit with yellow pulsing light. Cables snaked out from the device and into Banished power generators and machines—technology that he'd witnessed previously being used to override Forerunner defense systems. Lucas's heartbeat seemed to change and pulse in time with the yellow light. A console sat in front of the device; off to the side, a massive Jiralhanae in red-and-gold combat armor turned slowly to gaze at him as he approached.

Instinctively, he knew. This was a figure of absolute authority. War Chief Escharum himself. Had to be. The Brute's skin was a weathered gray with deep furrows in his brow and along the ridges of his nose as though in a perpetual scowl. Wispy, light-gray eyebrows hung over small eyes of differing color—one opaque with a scar slashed from cheekbone to eyebrow and the other a menacing red. A pale beard hung from his chin. Another scar cut through the right side of his lips where a tusk should have been. His long mouth curved at the sight of Lucas, revealing a row of sharp teeth.

Lucas went light-headed and his steps grew sluggish as though he were walking through mud.

"War Chief," Itacus said from behind him. "Here is the human, as you requested."

"Bring him to the cylix." Escharum's voice vibrated the very air, going through Lucas like a drum and lighting every nerve.

He'd thought he was done feeling fear, but it rose swift and vibrant as Itacus led him straight to the towering war chief. Yet the massive Jiralhanae stepped aside, smirking as Itacus's immense leathery hand grabbed Lucas's wrist and tugged him toward the console and closer to the "cylix," as Escharum called it. Lucas glanced down at the console and then around at the assemblage, the alien faces looking back at him appearing oddly apprehensive. The sight was so strange he wondered if this was all just some terrible nightmare. Either way he'd never felt so helpless and alone in all his life.

Escharum gave a faint nod to Itacus. In a swift gesture, the Brute grabbed Lucas's hand and slapped it onto the cool, glassy surface of the console. The room seemed to hold its collective breath, but Lucas didn't know why or what was supposed to happen.

Suddenly the surface of the console became cold. Instinctively he tried to pull away, but the Brute held fast to his wrist, the bones starting to give. He wasn't sure what hurt more, the pain in his wrist or the increasingly freezing console, but it became so cold that it burned, burned until he bit so hard on his lip to keep from crying out that blood burst into his mouth and he blurted out, "Stop! Please *stop!*"

No one was even paying attention to him; they were all focused on the cylix, while on the console panel alien glyphs emerged. Light bled outward from the console and down into the cables that ran across the platform and up into the device, activating it.

The cylix shifted, alloy parts sliding out and folding away.

The thing was opening.

Horror coiled around his chest and his pulse beat wildly. For a moment he forgot about the cold freezing his palm. There was nothing in his training or education to identify what was being revealed.

The being within the device . . .

All Lucas could do was stare in awe.

It was remarkably tall with a lithe, mostly humanoid body, adorned with a large triangular headpiece. Nearly all of its form was covered in dark-burgundy armor with plates over its slim shoulders, forearms, hips, and thighs. Its torso was long and tubelike—more insectile than human. The same yellow light that had outlined the creature on the cylix began to glow from two circular insets in the armor, one in the breastplate and another in the center of the triangular headpiece, which curved around two widely spaced, closed eyes and a small mouth.

Its hands were bare, each revealing four long fingers tipped with claws.

As Lucas tried to pull away, the Brute held him still. But at least the cold was beginning to recede now that the cylix was open.

Apprehension lay thick in the chamber.

Several seconds passed, and for the briefest of moments, Lucas wondered if the creature was dead. But then the head moved from side to side, and its hands opened and closed.

Oh God. He swallowed, and couldn't seem to pull enough air into his lungs. Sweat dripped down the sides of his face.

The eyes popped open. Jet black and glassy. An unnerving, bifurcated mouth drew into a slow, sapient grin.

The being floated out of the device, then swept an imperious gaze around the chamber.

A slow, gritty female voice emerged from the violet-gray face. *"Who are you to gather before me?"*

Lucas wasn't sure how he understood her through his earpiece, but imagined that she spoke in some Forerunner language ONI had reverse-engineered.

Her gaze settled on Escharum.

"We are the Banished," the war chief answered, his words delivered with strength and precision. "We have set you free."

The emancipated creature tilted her head at him in mild momentary curiosity before returning her attention to her surroundings.

"Banished . . ." She dwelled on the term. *"I hesitate to believe you understand such a title's true meaning."*

"We know very well who we are." Escharum was firm but remained curious. "Now it is time we knew the same of you."

"I am the Harbinger," her voice rang out with utter superiority as she swept another glance around the chamber before settling once more on Escharum. *"All that you know shall be undone."*

He stared back, taking stock, and broke the silence with one simple word: *"Good."*

It echoed through Lucas with singular devastation. His legs went weak and he swayed, snatching his hand from Itacus's lax grip and cradling it to his chest, flexing fingers that ached; he hoped they weren't fractured or frostbitten.

His actions caused the Harbinger's gaze to snap to him. Ensnared like hapless prey, he froze, unable to look away.

Her head cocked with open curiosity; then a slow smile of recognition tugged at one corner of her mouth, the kind of smile that immediately turned the blood in his veins to ice.

"This one will be mine."

CHAPTER 26

The boat crew had arrived near the *Mortal Reverie* site the day before, making camp a good two klicks from the outpost in an area of sparse trees, uneven ground, and massive boulders that rose five to ten meters high. The location was excellent in terms of cover and vantage points.

Spartan Stone had used the time to complete recon of the area, putting the upgraded shield module she'd acquired to good use, while Spartan Kovan provided overwatch. The fact that the Banished had turned the *Reverie* into an outpost didn't surprise Stone at all. As a leader, Escharum was nothing if not practical, routinely repurposing UNSC and Forerunner sites to suit his needs, and if an opportunity also existed to demoralize his enemies, it was a solid bet that he'd take advantage of it.

The enemy had renamed the site Tremonius, after the Jiralhanae chieftain who led the assault against the *Reverie*, tossed most of the ship's supplies into the chasm, and deployed their prefabricated outpost structures around the far side of the broken

UNSC vessel, including a heavily fortified landing platform. Seeing the *Reverie* occupied by the enemy had sucker-punched her hard in the chest. For the briefest of moments, Stone was pulled back into those chaotic memories of battle on the other side of the frigate, the constant aim, fire, block, stab, kill, amid screams and munitions detonations . . .

The starboard side of *Reverie* was barely recognizable after the Banished assault. The frigate had been so severely battered by Banished mortar strikes that it had literally sunk into the mountainside, with all evidence of the previous conflict now lost under countless rockslides and ashen battleplate. The pass the Banished climbed to attack the UNSC's forces was now a tangle of charred trees, loose stone, and detritus—not even remotely traversable. The Banished had excavated new egress points below the mountain and were already using them to issue patrols.

It had been a harrowing fight, one she'd never forget, but she sure as hell wasn't ready to revisit it in her head. So she turned to what she did best—biding her time and playing the long game, using her skill set to figure out what Escharum wanted most. It was clear he wanted control of Zeta Halo, but the steps he was taking to achieve that goal . . . that's what she needed to find out. And once she did, Stone would do everything to stop him. Taking away his power, making him nothing . . . that was the kind of revenge she was looking forward to, the kind that would cut the deepest.

Over the course of the last twenty-four hours, as fog rolled in over the mountains and settled into the deep ring fracture that split the ridge in half, she'd meticulously recorded Banished movements around the outpost. The activity level remained abnormally high, the most Stone had seen since the *Reverie* ambush, and it was clear that something of significance had occurred within the last few days. Enemy talk was hushed and wary—even among the Grunts, which was *really* saying something.

And now there was no doubt the Banished were actively excavating and unearthing artifacts from a Forerunner facility below the *Reverie*. From her position sandwiched between the rocks far above the ship, Stone overheard critical intel and recorded footage of carts emerging from the Tremonius outpost, their strange contents of irregularly shaped alloy pieces and devices loaded onto transports that had set down on the landing platform. When a vehicle was fully loaded, its drives powered up and the enemy began boarding. Several Phantoms had already lifted off and were making their way south.

Just as she was about to duck down and prepare a transmission, her gaze lit on a dark-haired human in tattered clothing, barefoot and walking toward the last transport left on the platform. Her breath lodged in her throat as she magnified. Goose bumps skated up her arms. "Jesus," she whispered.

It was Browning. Lucas Browning.

A shadow of himself, however, his profile drowned in a beard and shaggy hair. He was so goddamn thin it made her chest give a painful squeeze. But it was him, all right. She'd recognize that fresh-out-of-med-school face anywhere, the same one that had gazed up at her with wonder when she pulled him out of the lifeboat.

According to the others, he'd run toward the Banished, drawing the enemy away from the rest of the crew—an act of either sheer bravery or utter foolishness—and by all accounts, he should be dead. How the hell he'd managed to stay alive all this time was nothing short of a miracle. Human captives, whether in the hands of the Covenant or the Banished, rarely lived long. Heart pounding, she watched him crawl onto a Phantom, its engine cold.

Stone bit hard on her bottom lip, forcing herself to stay still while everything inside her wanted to race down the rock formation and pull him out of harm's way. But the place was still overflowing with Banished. There was no way to infiltrate now, but there might be later once those other vessels made their way fully off-site.

Shaken, she sank back down between the rocks, took a deep breath, and focused. "Open a one-way transmission," she told Ouco, then reported: "Initial sweep of *Reverie* site is complete. The Banished outpost here . . . is more than a barracks. They're unearthing Forerunner tech from within this ring, including artifacts I've never seen before. But there's more. Over half the Banished detachment manning this post are peeling off to another excavation site, south of here. Orders from the war chief himself. A Forerunner facility called the Conservatory. Whatever it is, it's important enough to divert Escharum's sole focus.

"We need eyes on the Conservatory as soon as possible. I'd go myself, but I need a closer look at the artifacts here. All this time we've assumed that Zeta Halo was like the others. What if it's something more?"

She cut the transmission with that question ringing in her ears. Not if. *Is.* She was sure of it.

And now a massive detachment was preparing to depart for another part of the ring south of the outpost, which meant her message needed to find Sorel and Mako ASAP; she just hoped they were still in this sector and could intercept her encrypted signal.

As Banished ships began to lift off, Stone saw the Phantom was still cold.

Good. Hopefully it'd still be there when she returned. And if not, she had a pretty good idea of where it was going.

Reluctantly the Spartan moved away from her spot above the frigate and hiked a kilometer along the ridgeline before descending another kilometer toward camp, being mindful of Banished scouts—without her motion tracker, she had to do things old-school, and that meant taking her time and moving from one bit of cover to the next. But at least she knew the landscape pretty well since *Reverie* had been her base of operations before the attack.

Fog swirled around her feet as she made for higher ground to rendezvous with Kovan. Visibility was utter crap, but that also worked in her favor. Red and gray occasionally lit the heavy clouds high above as the whir of Banished vessels leaving the outpost filled the air.

As she entered a copse of evergreens clustered against a sheer cliff wall, the fog thinned. A twig snapped, the sound amplified in the quiet, while rustling among pine needles drew her gaze. She switched to thermal and saw a small flock of land birds pecking at the ground.

Kovan the Stoic was waiting for her as she cleared the woods.

After a quick debrief, the two Spartans headed down the trail toward camp. "You think they'll get it?" Kovan asked.

"There aren't that many signal jammers up here. Sorel and Mako weren't too far from my position when I found you, so let's hope it goes the distance. They'll have to carry on, find the Conservatory—whatever the hell that is—while I take a look beneath *Reverie*. Escharum wants total control over Zeta Halo, and my gut tells me he's on the hunt for something that will further that objective."

"Well, I know not to question your gut," Kovan said.

"There's one more thing. . . ."

Kovan paused on the trail and turned.

Stone wasn't sure how to say it, still shocked by what she'd seen. "I'm pretty sure I saw Browning."

Kovan ripped off her helmet, her eyes blazing. *What?*

"That's why I'm telling you now. If the others know, they'll want to do something stupid and the outpost is too fortified for them to handle."

Maybe telling Kovan was stupid too, because the Spartan started to pace, the wheels already turning. Her lips thinned and her eyes narrowed. It didn't take a genius to see how Kovan felt about the kid, especially after he'd saved her life.

"So you want me to lie to them."

"I don't like it any more than you do, but it's the right call for now. Our focus should be getting our guy out of Banished hands and not worrying about the others getting killed in the process."

Stone could see the moment Kovan agreed: the Spartan stopped pacing and let out a conceding sigh.

"It fits, right? Lucas being there," Stone went on. "The Banished are bringing up artifacts and they need humans to activate Forerunner technology."

"They have humans in their ranks."

"Yes, but I doubt few, if any, of those traitors have survived the Banished's anger over losing their homeworld. Serves them right. Besides, why risk loyal soldiers when you have prisoners? They're expendable. That's the smart play to make, especially if they don't know how a certain piece of tech would react upon activation."

"How sure are you?"

"It was him. Thinner. Weaker. But it *was* Browning. I watched him exit the outpost and board a transport. It didn't leave with the detachment and was sitting cold when I left."

Kovan ran a hand over her head. "So he's still there. Hell, now *I* want to do something stupid."

Stone grabbed Kovan's arm, but before she could say anything, Kovan returned the gesture and she wasn't gentle about it. "You don't understand what that kid did that night." Anyone else would only see Kovan's hard, ice-blue gaze and rigid jaw, but Stone saw straight to the pain and guilt. "None of us would be here. I mean it. *I* wouldn't be here."

Kovan shoved away and paced once more, suddenly stopping to stare out through the trees to the vague outline of the mountain range in the distance. "We're supposed to be the heroes, right? And that stupid, *stupid* kid ended up saving my life. Full stop. No question."

Stone still didn't have all the details about what went down, and she hadn't pressed Kovan about it. "Nina, I get how you feel. So . . . what are we going to do about it?"

Kovan donned her helmet. "Give me the full layout. Don't worry, I won't do anything dumb. At least, not if I can help it."

Standard recon procedure, Stone had already mapped the outpost and proceeded to share the intel with Kovan. There had been zero chance before when the Banished detachment was still around, but now there might be a very slim opportunity to get the medic to safety. And operating with such odds was kind of their thing.

"The transport is in a decent position," Stone said, "on a landing platform close to a supply depot and one of the barrier walls near the cliff. It's still heavily guarded, but if we approach cliff-side and go over the wall . . ."

"Not a word to the team. We'll wait for nightfall," was all Kovan said, before turning and heading back down the trail.

With nightfall came the wind. It thinned some of the heavy fog and pushed against Kovan and Stone as they picked their way down the ravine formed in *Reverie*'s wake when it first crashed into the mountain. Once they reached the edge of exposed ring fragment, they lowered themselves carefully down the jagged cliff and worked their way around the ring's substructure, well out of sight from the Banished outpost's perimeter.

High above them they could barely see the protruding titanium plating of *Mortal Reverie*'s bow, which hung over the deep fracture in the ring that cut back south toward their infiltration point. The cold winds coming up from the fracture pressed Kovan against the cliff face, making her way slow but steady—not her first choice of infiltration points, but a necessary one since her active camo was still on the fritz. Every small sound carried in this environment, but despite their size, the Spartans knew precisely how to use their suits and armor. They were ghosts. Shadows.

While Stone's faded-blue Mjolnir blended in perfectly with the gloomy night, Kovan would have to employ active camouflage once they reached the landing platform, which she did in short order, using the grooves between the linked sheets of alloy and the magnets in her boots to scale the wall, Stone right behind her.

Once there, she deployed active camo, her display showing the module was only operating with eighty percent efficiency. She threw a glance over her shoulder. "Ready?"

Stone's helmet dipped. "I'll have eyes on you the whole time." Then she slipped off to a well-covered scouting location near the bow of *Reverie*.

And without motion tracking, Kovan could use the second set of eyes. "Here we go." She moved carefully across the landing platform, tucking behind the supply depot, using her spotty thermal to locate any close targets—several near the central outpost and groups of Unggoy and Kig-Yar stationed at entry points across the site. The Phantom was still cold and dark, with a few Jiralhanae gathered near a fire about ten meters from the craft.

And there was one very faint thermal in the back of the transport.

She took her time edging around the supply depot, then moving behind weapons stations and supply crates until she was close enough to approach the Phantom and make a soft leap into its open carriage bay, settling her weight down like a feather in its darkened interior.

It was Browning all right, his form framed in the center of her HUD, trembling from the cold, still barefoot and wearing nothing but a threadbare flight suit two sizes too big. His knees were pulled to his chest, arms wrapped around them, head down and to the side.

His breathing pattern told her he wasn't sleeping.

Kovan crept right up to him and knelt. Perfectly still, perfectly quiet, she reached out and put a finger on his knee; the second he lifted his head, she put a hand over his mouth. His eyes were round over her hand, body stiff and poised.

The kid had been through hell. A quick bio scan told the tale of broken bones, torn ligaments and muscles, sleep deprivation, and dehydration, and the surface level wasn't much better.

His cheeks were sunken and shadowed with beard, making the facial bones prominent. She waited for him to realize who she was.

When he nodded his head in acknowledgment, she removed her hand. He stared at her for a long second and then broke down sobbing, eyes filling with tears and his entire body shaking.

Kovan took his arm, but he pressed back against the hull, fear flashing across his face. He lifted his wrists to show her what appeared to be shackles of some type, though they weren't attached to anything.

"If you take me out, I won't survive," he whispered.

"Explain."

"There's so much you don't know. She put these on me."

He wasn't making sense. "She who?"

"The Harbinger. The Banished . . . they brought her up out of the ring. They made me . . . wake her up." He grabbed her arm, still crying. "Kovan. She's *not* Banished, not Covenant or any alien species we know. She's not . . . anything good."

There was nothing in her database about anyone called the Harbinger. While she couldn't discount what he was saying, Browning also had all the earmarks of starvation-induced psychosis. "Where is this Harbinger now?"

"Already gone."

"Gone where?"

"I don't know."

"And these?" She indicated the shackles.

"She said she had a use for me. She said all that we know would be undone."

"Kovan, you've got two Brutes making rounds. They'll be coming up on your three o'clock," Stone's voice issued through her earpiece.

Kovan focused on the shackles and what she guessed was their linked sensor, a node she'd noticed attached to the hull, but Browning grabbed her again. *"Don't."* He was right, of course—there was no telling what would happen if she touched the sensor or attempted to destroy it. She was guessing the shackles would blow sky high. "Just go. Warn everyone. This is bigger than Escharum," he said fervently, trying to make her understand and believe it. "Or the Banished. Or anything. I know it sounds nuts, but I'm not crazy—"

Stone's tight voice crackled through her audio. *"Damn it, Nina, you're running out of time."*

Reaching into a small slot in her chest piece, Kovan withdrew several tiny recording transmitters and slipped them into Browning's flight suit pocket, then hastily attached a small tracking beacon at the base of his neck under his shoulder-length hair. "This is a tracking beacon. They won't be able to detect it. But toss it once you get to wherever they take you. I don't want them finding it on a physical search." If she left now, sight unseen, there'd be no reason for his captors to suspect he'd been bugged. Regardless, she knew she was putting him in danger, but if any part of what he was saying was true . . .

"Hide the transmitters. You can peel and stick them anywhere or on your skin. As soon as they attach to any surface, they start recording. Learn whatever you can about the Harbinger. Removing the transmitters initiates a signal ping that automatically links to any UNSC network or datapad in range, so just dump them on the ground or anywhere they can get out. They're designed to link back to any UNSC datapad transmitter."

Those transmitters wouldn't come back to her, but at least whatever intel Lucas recorded would hopefully be captured and saved by friendlies.

"Kovan! Ninety seconds!"

She ignored Stone, unable to make herself move, her augmented heart giving a painful squeeze as they stared at each other.

"I know," he said sadly, wiping his wet face against his forearm. "It's okay." He swallowed, lifting his chin, trying to convince them both. "It's okay." He drew in a shaky breath and released it with what was meant to be an encouraging smile. "Did . . . everyone else make it?" His voice trembled.

Goddamn this kid. With a curse she pulled off her helmet, determined to give him something human, something familiar and caring to see, because it could very well be the last time he saw the like.

Her throat went a little thick, but she managed a smile, hoping it comforted him somewhat. "Yeah. We all made it, thanks to you. We made it and we're together, even Stone."

That seemed to comfort him. His body relaxed and he let his head fall back against the hull, nodding, weeping.

"I have to go now, but I'll come find you, Doc," she promised. "I won't stop. You can count on it. And I always, *always* keep my promises."

With that, she donned her helmet, feeling like her heart was breaking in two, and disappeared once more into the shadows.

CHAPTER 27

Shortly before dawn, the Banished Phantom made its approach back to the Tower, back to hell. The thinning layer of fog hovering over the dark outline of the landscape below was illuminated by the thick band of red light surrounding the Tower's square apex. Not a beacon, exactly. More like a warning. And yet . . . Lucas wasn't afraid.

He swallowed the laugh that bubbled in his throat. Who knew that coming back to the Tower would give him more peace than he'd had in days? At least here, he knew what to expect—the daily routine, no matter how hard or painful, was better than the horrific uncertainty of the Harbinger or the anguish of watching his rescuer leave without him.

He wasn't sure which event had been worse.

Witnessing the Harbinger's awakening had left him shaken and confused, and he was still trying to make sense of it. But seeing Spartan Kovan had absolutely gutted him. He supposed if he had to choose, that one had been the harder of the two because it finally made him let go of any hope or expectation of being rescued.

Itacus must have been weary because, despite guaranteed abuse at any moment, the Brute barely paid him much attention as they debarked. His jailer hovered behind him like a hulking shadow, his breath visibly puffing in and out like a dragon in the cold air, as he nudged Lucas's shoulder with one large finger, prompting him across the courtyard and into the Tower's ground level.

They took the gravity lift to the first level, then climbed the ramp to the second level and proceeded along the corridor to his cellblock. While it was darkly lit by the red translucent energy barriers over each cell, Lucas didn't need any illumination to find his way; he could track it by the smell alone, a combination of old musky Brute, human body odor, and general rot. His steps were slow and shuffling as they stopped at his cell door. Itacus deactivated the barrier and Lucas walked in before the Brute could execute his customary shove.

The barrier returned, and he stood there in his small cube, unable to move.

They lived, at least.

The boat crew: Murphy, Dimik, Bender, Cam, Kovan, Stone . . . they'd all miraculously made it through the horror of the *Reverie* and were out there somewhere, surviving. He wondered how Cam's knee was doing, if Bender was still cracking jokes, if Murphy had picked up on those subtle looks Dimik sometimes cast his way.

His shoulders slumped. His head, too heavy to hold, bowed. Despair rose up and crashed over him in a suffocating wave.

After a time, he sank to his knees, the despair giving way to numbness.

And cold. Always so damn cold.

It sapped any strength he had, and while it was warmer here inside, he had no energy or muscle mass to regenerate or keep in the heat. He crawled to his favorite spot in the back corner where it was dark and next to the wall he shared with his neighbor; curling onto his side and pulling his knees into his chest, he finally gave in to the bone-deep exhaustion.

A cry woke him sometime later.

The noises of the day filtered in along with the dull light spilling down the corridor. His eyes were crusty, his throat sore and dry, making it hard to swallow. Everything in him wanted to sink back into sleep, but Lucas forced himself to sit up—knowing he was experiencing the effects of depression and starvation; that soon his organs would start shutting down due to the meager amount of food the Brutes provided.

He rolled to his hands and knees and stood slowly, using the wall for support, and waited until the dizziness faded. Then he made several deep inhales and exhales before stretching his limbs, engaging his body and circulation.

The flight suit he wore billowed around his thin frame. Threadbare fibers brushed against his thigh and suddenly he remembered the devices Kovan had put in his pocket. He slipped his hand inside.

Itacus hadn't bothered to check him; there'd been no reason to.

A zing of possibility went through him as Kovan's words swirled in his head. *Learn whatever you can about the Harbinger.* He might never see the Harbinger again or overhear talk about her, but he'd still try. Hell, he might never again leave the Tower in order to ditch the devices, but he could toss the transmitters down the central lift. The place wasn't exactly airtight after all, so it was worth a shot.

His gut gurgled and twisted intensely. His hand went to his stomach.

Inhale in, exhale out.

Hunger gnawed at his insides until he wanted to scream. He counted breaths until the urge passed, and tried like hell to avoid thinking about food. A few minutes later, Brute footsteps echoed along with the sound of dragging. It stopped just short of his cell.

Lucas listened until the footfalls retreated and the corridor grew quiet once more. He went to the corner and sat, leaning the side of his head against the wall separating him and the prisoner in the adjoining cell. "You there?"

When there was no reply, he tapped on the wall. "Hey. You still there?"

It was difficult to hear through the wall, but a faint rustling sound came, then a groan followed by several bouts of wet coughing. He knocked again. Eventually, there was a slow knock back. Lucas breathed a sigh of relief and let his head fall back against the wall.

"You've been gone." His neighbor's voice was deep and scratchy, winded, each word difficult to speak. Lucas could never see anything from his cell, but he could hear, and ever since he'd been at the Tower, the Brutes had taken the guy out religiously—and it wasn't for walks around the yard.

"Took a weekender to Azure Shoals," Lucas responded, closing his eyes and letting the image play in his mind. "Laid on the beach the whole time. Water was clear and blue. The sand warm . . ."

"Don't start talking about food or I'll call for the guards."

Damn, too bad. He'd been imagining a waiter crossing the sand with a fruity drink and a double moa burger.

"Where did you go?"

Lucas let out a harsh breath. *"Reverie."*

His neighbor was silent for a long moment before asking, "What for?"

Lucas was about to unload the entire story, but the telltale sound of the Brute guards returning interrupted his attempt and both of them went silent. Who knew what the enemy had in store for them now.

CHAPTER 28

Ever since Spartan Stone had made a loud enough distraction to draw the Brutes away from Kovan's rescue attempt at *Reverie*, the heat had stuck to her like glue in one form or another. She'd drawn attention, sure enough, allowing Kovan time to slip away, but they hadn't been able to rendezvous after that.

And worst of all, they hadn't been able to rescue Browning.

She'd eventually found cover in an obscure cavern beneath the outpost. At first it had appeared to be a natural part of the terrain—the mountainous cliff region was littered with such features—but she was beginning to think otherwise the farther she explored. A hundred meters in and the rock at her feet began to turn to alloy. She was either on top of a Forerunner site situated beneath the outpost or had found an entrance to it. Exactly what she'd been hoping for when she made her report to Sorel and Mako.

A combination of rock walls and dirt-strewn metal floor led up until cables and stacks of grav carts and excavation tools began to litter the way.

"Enemy ahead," Ouco said as four thermal figures appeared on Stone's display.

The corridor branched off into three directions, one of those leading into an adjacent rock-cut room where a group of Unggoy lingered.

It'd be so easy to pick them off. . . .

Today was their lucky day, however. She had no desire to bring the Banished to bear, not when she was close to finding out just what they were after here. A chamber ahead spilled red light into another branch of the corridor, drawing her eye. Bypassing the Grunts, Stone crept closer, glad that the bulk of the Banished presence had left the outpost; otherwise she never would have gotten this far. She slipped inside the excavated room, her gaze immediately drawn to a platform and the large rectangular device against the far wall, surrounded by the Banished cabling and a track system. An outline glowed on its surface, somewhat human in shape, but with long tapered arms and legs, a tubelike torso, and a triangular head. A life-sized glyph in the shape of a strange biped, but definitely unlike any Forerunner silhouette she'd ever seen. "Let's check the database," she said quietly.

Moving closer, she stepped over huge cables that snaked along the ground and past a Banished power juncture, to investigate the device from its side—at least it might give her a bit of cover if anyone entered the chamber. The glyph was embedded in a large, rectangular stasis field; it had all the earmarks, with bracing containment joists on the sides and an isolated power supply. She moved around to the front again and noted a reinforced energy barrier in what appeared to be the bed of the device. "Anything?" she asked Ouco.

"*Negative. While the technology is Forerunner, there's nothing else like it in the database.*"

"Well, we know one thing. Whatever was in here is gone." And she sincerely hoped that had been a long time ago and the Banished hadn't just liberated whatever was inside.

Stone returned to the Banished power juncture and looked for some kind of way to interface with it, but found nothing. Whatever Forerunner machine the Banished had linked to the juncture was long gone.

It was clear the Banished had brought the stasis device here from somewhere else. The chamber was recently excavated and the cabling and equipment were exclusively Banished. To learn more, she needed to find out where this thing had originated; with that thought, her lidar populated on-screen, revealing a lift extending down to a passage, which in turn led to an immense underground structure.

Slipping out of the chamber, she backtracked to the cavern's entrance. "Open a transmission. Short-range, encrypted signal to Spartan Kovan."

"*Ready,*" Ouco said.

A green light appeared on her HUD. "Hoping you're still in range to hear this, Kovan. There's a Forerunner facility beneath the *Reverie*. I found a way inside and am heading back in to get eyes on what the Banished are excavating. I'll touch base in a day or two." She started back inside, hoping her teammate was still within range to receive the message. Stone might be jumping the gun, but a chance to get in and out of the facility so easily might not come again.

Determined to see where this opportunity took her, she made her way to the freight elevator, using her thermal in place of her fried motion sensor to check for the all-clear before moving onto the large Banished-built lift. *"One moment, Spartan Stone,"* Ouco said, easily accessing the rudimentary control panel. *"I'm in. We're heading down now."*

"Nice work." The lift swiftly descended, depositing her in a dark room, revealed by the interior red lighting of the lift itself. Stacked against the nearest walls were containers, weapon crates, and excavation equipment. This had definitely been the Banished's staging area for their operation.

Stepping off the lift, however, it soon became clear that the room stretched out well beyond the elevator's platform into an even larger space, lined by ornate walls and majestic columns that had been heavily rigged with Banished equipment. The room was clearly Forerunner—grand in scale and design, yet remarkably detailed with delicate geometric etchings that were staggeringly precise. It seemed to have two access points, an arched door near the lift and an identical one past the columns on the other end.

She didn't know how long it'd take for the Banished above to realize the lift had activated, so she decided to move quickly and exited through the nearest doorway, which enigmatically opened on its own as she approached. She swiftly dropped down one side of a dual staircase, making her way to a corridor at the far end.

The passages in this space gleamed with smooth metallic walls, hard light illuminating her way in breaks along the walls and doorways. This corridor led a couple of hundred meters deeper underground before finally spilling her out onto a platform.

The view stole her breath. It was no wonder the Banished were scavenging the area. The space that greeted her was enormous and open, a sleek underground complex of gleaming gray alloy walls and cathedral-sized openings with bridges and monolithic columns and passageways, all softly illuminated by familiar blue light that ran through stylized geometric lines. The sheer size was astonishing, even more so because she knew—as her lidar and radar composite scans began to build a complete picture—that it was only a small part of what lay under the ground.

While the place was impossibly ancient, it appeared as if it had been built yesterday. Like a sleeping monster: not dead, just dormant. And waiting. The silence, in fact, was a little unnerving, if she was being honest.

A UNSC signal suddenly popped onto her display and then vanished.

"Did you see that, Ouco?" Stone asked.

"Yes. It was definitely a UNSC signal, but transmitting from somewhere deep in the ring."

"Just another reason to check out what's down here," she said.

It wasn't difficult to pick up the Banished's excavation trail— evidence of their work and passage littered the area. Burn marks, spent weapon rounds, discarded supply crates . . . She moved on, following the breadcrumbs for a while, seeing nothing but soaring chambers and colossal rooms, deep chasms, and hard-light bridges and platforms.

Her descent continued until the architecture began to change, and the structures divested themselves of their smooth silvery walls and geometric glyphs and lines to reveal something far more archaic and monolithic. It was clearly Forerunner, but different from the rest of the underground she'd seen so far. Rows of what appeared to be small stasis pods stretched across a vast open chamber, calling to memory the strange artifact she'd seen in the outpost above. She had Ouco transmit a brief message to Mako and Sorel. Maybe the Banished were after those things, maybe they were weapons of some kind? She wasn't sure. The other two Spartans needed to know, especially if they found their way to the Conservatory, whatever the hell that was.

The sound of something approaching made her cut the transmission short. There was a clattering noise in an adjacent space, followed quickly by a thrumming overhead. She looked around for several minutes but couldn't make visual contact with it. Whatever it was, it was gone. After picking her way through a few narrow corridors, she found herself back on the trail of the Banished's excavation group.

A long platform stretched across another vast opening, the depths pitch-black, save where her headlamp shone, and so deep that no other structures showed on her short-range scans. She felt tiny walking across it, but was drawn by the giant wall ahead of her with an arched nine-meter-tall doorway, and the gaping hole burned into its alloy, clearly the result of a focus beam. Wasn't hard to put the rest together. Judging from the size of the hole, the Banished had probably used a superheated plasma beam directed straight at the wall to burn its way through the alloy, creating an opening large enough for an excavation team to pass through. They couldn't access the door, so they'd created one for themselves.

Stone stepped through the hole—the edges still warm—to another wide pathway flanked by an arched access corridor on either side. The walkway stretched out for at least eighty meters, suspended over open space. Several Unggoy and Kig-Yar lay dead on the floor, along with a couple of abandoned Ghosts and one destroyed excavator beam emplacement, its mangled parts continuing to spark and smoke. Something had happened here, and it had happened *very* recently.

What could the Banished have possibly been fighting all the way down here?

Whatever enemy they'd encountered seemed to have vanished without a trace.

She followed the long pathway, which ended at a similar arched doorway as the one before; this one opened to another cathedral-like space. As she started across a hard-light bridge leading to the other side, the sound of subtle movements and whirring echoed in the pitch black above her.

"Picking up unknown contacts on thermal," Ouco said.

"What I wouldn't give for a working sensor," Stone ground out, slowly unshouldering the assault rifle pilfered days ago from a crashed drop pod and tipping her head to the darkness above. Without a motion sensor, it was difficult to pinpoint exactly what was out there and how many, but a switch to thermal imaging helped matters.

She almost ventured a hope that this was the UNSC signal that she spotted earlier, but any possibility of that was immediately quashed by the thermal reading.

"Yeah. I'd definitely say those were unknown. . . ."

Thermal showed fourteen small, lanky bodies, each with two elongated arms and what looked like four legs. Attached to each shoulder was some type of alien jetpack, and in their hands they held pulse carbines, needlers, and plasma pistols, weapons they must have taken from the dead Unggoy and Kig-Yar. "I think we can add intelligent to the list," she muttered, slowly turning, being careful not to point her weapon—at least, not yet.

They could have attacked at any time, but for now seemed content to shadow her, and she didn't plan on starting trouble as long as they stayed out of her way. Maybe this was what she had heard earlier in the middle of her message.

She made it across the bridge and continued following the pathway—which came to a dead end at a sheer wall with no console, no alternate path, and no options building on her scanner.

Since the trail had run cold, the Banished must have backtracked and continued through one of the access corridors near the head of the pathway—those were the only two divergent options.

As she retraced her steps across the light bridge, her new friends continued to shadow her from above; once she crossed the threshold of the arched doorway back into the area of engagement, they'd have to descend and come out of the darkness if they wanted to keep following. So far, they'd avoided showing themselves.

Through the doorway and making her way back past the Ghosts and the dead Banished, she heard the whirring sound again, louder and somehow angrier. She guessed they'd found an alternate route. Seemed they were finally making their move in the same place they'd fought the Banished. Damn it.

She hightailed it for the end of the pathway where the Banished had bored the hole into the wall, but put on the brakes when she heard her pursuers suddenly arrive at her position, the sound of multiple thrusters converging right behind her. Stone slid to a stop and glanced over her shoulder, still refusing to aim her weapon. She wasn't going to start this fight, and really hoped they wouldn't either, because she had only twenty rounds left in the AR's magazine, three frag grenades, and a total of sixteen rounds in the two M6 Magnums attached to her thighs, along with one full clip. She had no doubt she could take them out, but the smartest play was to be conservative if possible.

Overhead, the mysterious long-limbed creatures hovered, their jetpacks softly whirring and vents glowing. They watched her, unblinking round eyes framed by their armored helmets, but they didn't fire. Not yet, at least.

Slowly she backed toward the two arched access corridors on either side of the pathway, searching for any clue the Banished might've left, anything to show which direction they'd taken, but there was nothing. "Ouco, keep feeding me updated geometry scans."

"You got it."

Looked like she'd have to go with her gut and choose her own route. Keeping a ready hold on the AR, she took two steps back, then turned and ran. Needles suddenly hit the ground at her feet while bolts of plasma peppered the pathway, landing so close that heat warnings flashed on her display. She was nearly at the entrance to the right-hand corridor. A flurry of pulse carbine rounds struck close enough that the kinetic energy from the impact knocked her off her feet. Airborne, she tucked and rolled as she hit the ground and was up and heading straight into the corridor.

She ran as fast as she could for several meters, then stopped, turned, and aimed, waiting, heart pounding. After a long, tense moment, it became clear they didn't intend to follow in the closed space. Relieved, Stone straightened, shouldered her weapon, and kept going.

The corridor led downward, opening out to a series of enormous conduits, which descended into the darkness. Stone leapt onto one of the conduits and slid down, relying on her night vision to guide her. Eventually the conduit disappeared into a wall, forcing her to dig in her heels and jump to an alloy beam that stretched across a circular chasm lined with smooth alloy walls, building levels, and balconies.

"Contacts detected on thermal two levels below," Ouco said.

Stone knelt on the beam and scanned the platform beneath her.

Her gut never failed her. She'd found the Banished excavation team, and they were currently working their way into another part of the facility. Another portable excavation cannon had been positioned in front of a tall doorway, its plasma beam white-hot as it burned through alloy.

She used her visor to enhance the image, training her sights on a tall Elite adorned in a sleek black combat harness with red accents. What caught her eye was the fancy prosthetic left arm and mandibles—something she had never seen before. The warrior culture of the Sangheili abhorred weakness of any kind; they often preferred to die rather than cave in to medical treatment. That this Sangheili had chosen not only to survive but to cybernetically enhance himself made him a true outlier. The fact that he'd found a place with the Banished didn't surprise her. Atriox was known for welcoming all.

While she couldn't ID the warrior by his armor, the enormous black-haired Jiralhanae was another matter. The red power armor covering all but his head screamed Bloodstar—comprised of Spartan hunters and former Covenant special ops, the Bloodstars included the best of each individual species. Some of the best warriors the alliance had to offer. Atriox had wasted no time integrating the Bloodstars into the Banished's numbers, knowing full well that the Spartans were his greatest opposition.

Those two made things a lot more interesting and told Stone the ongoing excavation wasn't a run-of-the-mill salvage grab. They were clearly on the hunt for something significant.

The light from the superheated plasma beam ebbed as it

powered down, leaving behind a gaping hole surrounded by a ring of molten metal that dripped to the floor in small steaming piles. As soon as it was clear, the Elite motioned toward a war-skiff—a transport with one Brute gunner at the front, a Skirmisher driver at the rear, and between them an open frame. Another Brute standing near the skiff reached inside and hauled out a human female from within it. A civilian by the looks of her ragged clothes. She was in bad shape too, just skin and bones, and too weak to put up any kind of resistance.

The Sangheili warrior took her by the wrist and pulled her through the hole and into the room.

Visibility from this perspective was nil, so Stone crept across the beam and dropped quietly down a level to lie on her stomach and get an angled look into the room. Keeping her faceplate magnified and her recording on, she listened as they approached a console. From the curtailed view she had through the hole, the walls appeared to be in constant motion. Magnifying further, she saw streams of blue code by the thousands running down translucent screens.

The woman placed her hand on the console. It lit with all-too-familiar Forerunner blue. Once it was activated, the Sangheili bowed over the console. Eventually an area of code running down the screen appeared to slow while everything around it faded into the background. Simultaneously, in another section, the streams faded as another bit of data was brought to the forefront.

The Sangheili grabbed the woman once again and led her to the two outstanding streams of code. Stone watched, fascinated, as the woman reached up and actually plucked the first string of code as a physical thing; as it emerged, she took it to the second stream and pulled on it as well. The streams intersected as they were taken from the translucent wall and transformed into a small rectangular Forerunner device that fit into the palm of her hand. By the looks of it, the object was some kind of data node. It must have been capable of interfacing with a larger system to pull down information. Stone wondered what exactly that information might be, if it was important enough to draw the Banished into the deepest parts of Zeta Halo.

"Yes," the Sangheili said, taking the data node. "Escharum will be pleased."

"Good." The massive Jiralhanae stepped inside the room. "He'll need a contingency plan."

"Your loyalty is lacking as always, Gorian."

"He takes chances, Blademaster. Plays with old and unreliable things, creatures we know nothing about."

"All we need to know is that they bleed. And that is sufficient."

The Jiralhanae grabbed the Sangheili's right arm. "Do we, Jega? Do we know they bleed?"

The Blademaster jerked his arm free and held up the data node. "What does it matter? We now have the information we've sought: the ring's defensive systems, its capabilities and power— it all belongs to us now. With this, the Banished will grind the humans to dust and build a new world atop their ashes."

"As it should be," Gorian replied with a menacing growl, and Stone could see the raw fury in his profile. It was clear the Banished meant to make Zeta Halo their home, effectively taking back what Cortana had stolen from them—the ring wasn't just a strategic play for the Banished, they were going to rebuild Jiralhanae civilization on it, from the ground up. . . .

Stone knew there were only two options. Steal the data node or destroy it. And if it really did have access to Zeta Halo's defensive systems, it must also have the ring's present coordinates. This meant that stealing it was paramount. It might be the only way they could get a message back to the UNSC and request military aid of their own. Without that, no human would ever leave this ring, and the Banished would have won.

"Ouco," Stone said, "see if you can ID Jega: Sangheili blademaster, and Gorian: Jiralhanae Bloodstar."

The two warriors stepped back from the console. The woman turned to follow, but in a swift motion, Jega's energy sword manifested in his right hand, glowing red as he sliced through the woman's torso with ease before she even took a second step.

"Jega 'Rdomnai, Sangheili Blademaster, member of the Hand of Atriox. Gorian, Jiralhanae Bloodstar, clan affiliation: the Witch's Eye."

Heavy hitters the both of them, she thought as she watched Jega tuck the data node into his forearm brace and walk out without giving the dead woman a second glance. "Destroy the console."

At his command, the Brute who had retrieved the prisoner activated the excavator beam and it began spewing plasma through the hole and onto the console and vaporizing the body of the dead woman nearby.

Stone's gaze locked on Jega's arm brace. The Banished had come a long way and used a lot of resources to retrieve whatever information had been contained in that console.

Too bad it wouldn't be theirs for long.

There was no cavalry to call, no fireteam waiting in the wings; Spartan Bonita Stone was completely on her own. But from her point of view, the odds were pretty even. Gorian and Jega

'Rdomnai would give her a run for her money, of course, but the others . . . she wasn't worried. The strange flying creatures had turned the Banished excavation force into a small skeleton crew of three—the Skirmisher piloting the skiff, the Brute gunner, and a third Brute who had been controlling the excavation cannon— and those she could handle with ease.

There was no doubt that once the data node was handed off to Escharum, her chances of ever obtaining it were slim to none. Jega and the data were exposed *now*, and there might never be another opportunity like this.

Rubicon Protocol, she reminded herself.

Permission to act. Permission to execute with extreme prejudice. Whatever it takes.

The excavation force eventually made its way back up the long access corridor and onto the wide pathway. Stone kept her distance, using her active camo as she too reached the end of the corridor. Once she was within striking distance, she began formulating a plan of attack.

She'd be taking a risk—the damage her Mjolnir armor had sustained since arriving on Zeta Halo meant her energy shielding was nearly gone, though there was still some juice left in her upgraded shield module, and her camouflage might work long enough to achieve her objective . . . or it might fizzle out and make things a little more interesting. Either way, this was her moment to strike.

She lobbed a frag grenade at the excavation cannon's operator and then immediately another aimed at the war-skiff. As she hurried out of range, her alert showed active camo dropping to 65 percent. Stone ignored it, pulled her assault rifle, and set it to single fire to conserve ammo, as the grenades hit precisely where she wanted them to.

The force of the blast slid her back a few meters, but it blew the war-skiff into a tumble, violently crushing the vehicle's gunner. She ran headlong toward the Brute who was scrambling to ready the excavation cannon, but was far too slow. Stone planted her shoulder in his chest, lifting the Jiralhanae clean off the ground and over the ledge behind him. He wouldn't be a problem anymore.

Immediately, Gorian and Jega drew their weapons and turned to face her, the Sangheili activating a glowing red energy sword in his right hand and manifesting a wicked-looking dual-bladed short sword attached to his prosthetic arm.

The skiff pilot managed to right the vehicle and began squawking at the gunner who had fallen out to take the gun— but he wouldn't be getting up anytime soon. Once he noticed it, the pilot lifted a pulse carbine from the skiff's cockpit and fired a barrage of plasma bolts in her direction. One clean headshot with her AR, and the Kig-Yar was out of the game.

"Active camouflage at fifty-two percent," Ouco warned.

Damn it. She backed toward the corridor as Gorian and Jega moved in her direction. Suddenly the space between them was peppered with needler, plasma, and carbine rounds. The flying creatures were actually making themselves semi-useful. They hovered above the pathway like gnats, flitting back and forth and firing away.

Stone deactivated her active camo, saving what she had left.

Immediately Gorian fired on her position.

"Incoming," Ouco said.

"Yeah, I see it." Anger swept through her as it always did when she saw the enemy wielding a UNSC-issued weapon, in this case a Hydra—a gyroscopically stabilized, high-explosive micro-missile launcher. She dove out of its range, its blasts pummeling the corridor wall with a series of vicious explosions. Before she could get up, Gorian and Jega jumped on the abandoned Ghosts and tore through the burned-out hole in the doorway, leaving her to contend with the creatures.

"No, no, no," she ground out, seeing the data node getting away as she fired off a series of rounds at their contrails. Without hesitation, she stowed the rifle on her mag-clamp and withdrew both M6s, unloading into the hovering creatures as she bolted for the prone skiff. The excavator cannon had gone over the edge with the Brute, so she'd have to improvise. She ripped the vehicle's modular plasma cannon from its mount and then dove through the hole, rolling and firing through the opening.

As she ducked down, Stone saw the Ghosts receding.

No Jiralhanae or Sangheili warrior ever ran from a fight, and they especially didn't give up an opportunity to take down a Spartan. The fact that they'd fled only proved how important the data was to the Banished.

Risking a quick peek back through the hole revealed the creatures simply hovering above the pathway. For some reason, they didn't want to leave the area, which was fine by her. "Thank God," she whispered, and took off running after the Ghosts.

They were heading back the way she'd come, which meant Stone had to intercept them now instead of risking a fight near the lift where the Banished could swiftly increase their forces.

As they crossed the enormous cathedral-like space that had first taken her breath away, Stone took aim and fired the skiff's plasma cannon at the retreating vehicles. Red plasma bolts accelerated across the massive passage and struck one of the Ghosts, shredding one of its stabilizers until it exploded. The blast sent the Ghost veering sharply into the floor, throwing Gorian to the ground, as it continued to spin wildly before plunging into the depths beyond the platform.

The second Ghost stopped and spun around as Gorian rose from the floor. Stone held a deep grudge against these machines in general—those nimble little bastards had put a world of hurt on the marines she'd lost after the ring's fracture. Gritting her teeth, she fired a torrent of superheated plasma its way, but the distance allowed the Ghost to easily evade. Jega said something to Gorian, which made him stay back as the Elite suddenly gunned the vehicle, aiming right for her.

"That only makes you more of a target, hinge-head," she muttered, calmly taking aim.

The Sangheili's reactions were astonishingly quick and deft; he wielded the Ghost like a blade, weaving the vehicle through wave after wave of glowing red bolts, some coming within mere centimeters of the vehicle's hull. With zero cover to evade the Ghost's return fire, Stone realized that she'd have to rely on her enhanced reflexes and speed if she had any hope of stopping him. Launching from her position, she raced to meet the Ghost head-on, darting between its own channels of plasma fire.

As he came closer, Jega 'Rdomnai released the Ghost's controls and leapt off as its stabilizer caught the floor and it pinwheeled toward Stone, forcing her to the side. As he jumped onto the platform, the Sangheili's bloodblade and curved double-bladed short sword suddenly flared to life. The weapons cast a red glow over his black armor and made the amber color of his small eyes radiate. "It is over, demon," he intoned with a snarl that flexed his mandibles. "Darkness has found you."

His left prosthetic drew her attention. The data node rested in a small compartment on his mechanical forearm. She made a mental note to adjust her methods accordingly. Whatever happened to her, the data had to be retrieved.

As he stretched to his full height and prepared to attack, she rolled to the side of the platform and released another volley of plasma fire with the cannon. Before it reached him, Jega's form disappeared, engaging his active camo the moment she fired and slipping into the shadows around a series of columns. She continued firing in his direction, hoping one of the bolts hit him or at least disengaged the field of light that bent around him and made him invisible.

"See if you can track the thermal from his stealth generator," she told Ouco as she activated her own active camo.

"On it," Ouco said. *"Signal approaching! One o'clock!"*

The closer he came, the better she could make out his silhouette, which took on a clear distortion effect. With a remarkable burst of speed, he lunged at her, deactivating his stealth as he sliced the cannon barrel in two, his energy blade so hot it went through the metal with ease. Stone released what remained of the smoldering cannon, leapt back, and retrieved both M6s, firing as Jega unwaveringly continued his attack, flashing in and out of stealth, disappearing and reappearing to strike.

As her own energy shielding dropped by the second, Stone took cover behind Jega's overturned Ghost, reloading her last M6 magazine and focusing on depleting his shields with whatever she had left. Her odds weren't looking too great. Jega's speed and skill were extraordinary, unlike anything she had ever seen in a Sangheili. Without his shield, it might be a fair fight—but with it and the damage she'd sustained over the past several months, coming out of this unscathed was starting to look like wishful thinking.

If she could just steer clear of those blades long enough for his shielding to drop—

"*Behind you!*"

Stone ducked low and spun at Ouco's warning, instinctively throwing out her leg and hoping it connected. *Yes.* Jega appeared just as she swept his feet out from under him. Seizing the moment, she jumped on his torso and forced his arms down, using every ounce of strength she had until it felt like her muscles were about to explode. He roared, his mandibles snapping erratically as he attempted to thrust his energy blades toward her neck. Suddenly releasing the grip of her right hand, Stone slammed her fist into his prosthetic arm where it met his shoulder, momentarily stunning Jega and deactivating its twin energy blades. Struggling to keep him down with one hand, she tore the module with the data node free with the other, tightening her grip around it.

Before she could recover, he'd already gotten a leg under him and then a foot, shoving her off with a great bellow. Midair, Stone jammed the data node into the secondary port on her left forearm guard. "Ouco, copy and then corrupt the node. And do it quick. We don't have much time."

"*Copying now. Impact in two sec—*"

Stone slammed into the wall to the sound of her Mjolnir armor groaning and cracking. She slid down, landing on her feet, out of breath and shaky. An excruciating pain seared down her shoulder and back. Holding that Sangheili down and then landing that blow on his cybernetic arm must have torn her right arm and both shoulder muscles to shreds. And she was clean out of internal pain meds that would have automatically dispersed into her system.

Jega was now rising.

"Ouco . . ."

"Almost done."

Stone grabbed her last grenade and primed it, gritting her teeth against the pain and lobbing it at the approaching Sangheili. Then she quickly took aim with her M6 and used its second-to-last round to blow it just as the grenade reached him. The force blew Jega out into the deep chasm beyond the platform.

"Transfer complete," Ouco said.

As Stone released a relieved breath, the Ghost piloted by Gorian rammed straight into her torso, mercilessly pinning her against the wall. The force flattened her across its hull. A wave of warnings filled her Mjolnir's heads-up display showing a list of internal injuries that seemed to never end. The pain was so severe that Stone nearly passed out. Darkness at the corners of her vision began to creep inward and she felt herself begin to roll off the Ghost's crumpled front air dam. Reaching over the controls, Gorian grabbed her helmet in an iron-like vise and directed his Ghost across the platform and up the arched corridor leading to the lift. Evidently, the Bloodstar wasn't going to take any chances: rather than attempt to retrieve the data from Stone, he'd simply retrieve Stone. Whatever was left of her, at least.

That was a mistake.

Unable to reach her assault rifle, Stone had nothing to fight with now except her will. Taking hold of the Jiralhanae's arm with her right hand, she began pummeling Gorian with her left fist as he held tight to her helmet. The Bloodstar lifted her head and slammed it on the hull several times, trying to knock her unconscious. The trauma was so great that the display immediately blinked out and her visor began to crack. She scrambled to get better footing but couldn't achieve any traction on the Ghost's curved hull.

Without any words, Ouco released a reserve draft of adrenaline into Stone's bloodstream. The stimulant coursed through her system, giving her a final burst of strength.

Grabbing Gorian's wrist with both of hers, she used her core to twist onto her back, then pulled her legs into her chest, flipping herself over the Jiralhanae's head. A bolt of pain reverberated through her chest and arms, but she stamped it down and held on, allowing the Ghost's momentum to carry her to its back. In the process, she came down behind Gorian and, using what strength remained, she jerked the Bloodstar from the Ghost.

The two rolled for over ten meters before coming to a stop in the antechamber just outside of the lift area. A Brute captain hurried from the lift, mangler drawn. Beyond him still on the lift was a Brute Sniper, an Elite, and two Jackals. Her odds were starting to dwindle.

"Hectarius, no," Gorian growled.

The Bloodstar hadn't suddenly gone soft on her, she knew—he was simply denying the newcomer the right to a kill he'd worked so hard for.

Stone pushed sluggishly to her feet. Somewhere in the back of her mind, she knew things were not going to turn out the way she'd hoped. Only a few rounds left in her AR and no camo, her shoulders and arm screaming, but it had to be enough. She activated the enhanced shield module and immediately launched herself through the doorway past the captain and the lift full of reinforcements, darting across the larger area she'd seen when she first arrived, all the way to the door on the far side.

If she couldn't take the lift up, she'd need to find another way to the surface.

This door opened like all the others, leading to a short, narrow corridor and then a small antechamber with two parallel ramps that sloped down toward yet another door. But here there were four Grunts at the bottom of the ramps. *Great.*

She ran headlong into the first two with enough force to send their crumpled forms into the air. They hit the wall and bounced off in a slurry of blood and methane. Her continued momentum allowed her to land her fist into the third, lifting it off the ground with a cracking sound. The Unggoy's lifeless body dropped to the ground with a dull thud. The last Grunt turned tail and made a clumsy run for it, but she shoved her boot into its backpack, sending it careening toward the door with such speed that it splattered across the frame of the door, causing the closing mechanism to break and leaving the door frozen halfway ajar. She must've ruptured something in the creature, because the Grunt's body continued to spray blood all over the inside of the far corridor.

Plasma fire suddenly cracked against her enhanced shield, and she turned in one motion, retrieving her assault rifle from her back. She had little ammo left, and her armor's systems were failing rapidly. Pretty soon, the shield module wouldn't matter so much, as there'd be nothing left to power it.

This was it. All she had left.

Her assault rifle lit up the room, managing to take down the Brute Sniper and the Elite as they charged down the ramp on the right side. The rifle's magazine was spent by the time the two Jackals came in, their own weapons firing relentlessly. She dropped her AR and lunged at the first, yanking his firing arm toward her while her boot was firmly planted in his gut. With a loud snap, the Kig-Yar immediately stopped firing and went limp—broken spinal column, no doubt. She flung his body to the side of the room, where he fell to the floor in a heap.

The Brute captain—the one called Hectarius—filed in, barreling over and fatally crushing the remaining Jackal who had frozen up at the base of the ramp, terrified by what it had just witnessed. The Kig-Yar's crushed frame was kicked aside, coming to a stop by its friend. Before the Brute had time to attack, Stone was already slamming headlong into the captain. Hectarius was strong and well-armored, but Stone began punching the Jiralhanae's gut with a kind of unrelenting ferocity she didn't know she possessed. The beast reeled backward, falling heavy to the ground as his torso armor began to perforate and break off into pieces under the vicious blows. It was only a few seconds of punching his stomach dead-on before Stone knew she had won, letting go of the Brute as he crawled into a corner and began staring unbelieving at the mess Stone had made of his vital organs. He finally stopped moving and slumped over in a pool of blood.

Stone stood up, took a deep breath, and started toward—

"*Spartan Sto—!*" Ouco tried to warn.

Fire sliced through her spine, then her chest cavity, without warning. A gasp stuck in her throat as unimaginable pain exploded through her torso. A red glow lit on her front and the tip of an energy sword appeared in her field of vision as it pushed through her chest.

"Found you," Jega 'Rdomnai growled.

Instantaneously her wound was cauterized by the sword's heat, preventing body fluids and blood from moving through vessels, veins, and arteries, the force and energy causing mini-ruptures throughout her body.

As Jega pulled the energy sword slowly back out, he leaned in closer. "Does it hurt?" The pleasure in his voice echoed menacingly through her audio. "Take your last breath, Spartan, and behold your tomb."

Before she lost her wits, she removed the node from the secondary port in her forearm guard and cradled the now-corrupt data in a tight fist as Gorian approached from the doorway, a smug sneer on his face.

Blood bubbled up her throat and she coughed it out onto her faceplate as her knees gave out. She slumped to one side, her body coming to rest on the floor. She heard Ouco's voice in her ears but couldn't process the words.

Stone laughed, spurting up blood with the sound. Her hands fell limp, and her vision clouded with red. As she ebbed into unconsciousness, she felt no pain as footsteps approached and the data node was wrenched out of her hand.

"Nice try, Spartan," Jega said.

A massive hand gripped her arm and lifted, but Jega spoke again, sounding very far away. "Leave her. We must get this to Escharum immediately."

Elation swept through her. Her plan had worked. A wrench had been thrown into Escharum's grand scheme. And with that final thought, Bonita Stone let the blackness take her.

CHAPTER 29

Lucas Browning awoke with a start as the energy barrier de-activated and Itacus stepped into view with a sneer that pulled one side of his mouth away from a dirty tusk. "Get up, vermin. She wants to see you."

Immediately, Lucas's body tensed and fear gripped his chest—there was no way in hell he ever wanted to see *her* again. He scooted back into his corner, his pulse leaping wildly, as Itacus ducked into the room with a low chuckle rumbling in his throat and his dark eyes narrowed with satisfaction.

"Your fear is well-placed," he said, grabbing Lucas by the ankle, turning, and pulling him across the floor.

Lucas reached out with both hands for his corner, his safe spot, his only safe spot in this entire goddamn place, but it grew farther and farther away. He managed to grab the edge of the wall as they exited the cell, but that only got him a kick in the ribs. Pain shot through his side, making him scream. In the din, he heard his neighbor banging on his cell wall, sounding pissed and trying to taunt Itacus to take him instead, but the Brute just laughed and kept going.

Every bump and twist of his body radiated pain through his side, as did drawing in a deep breath. The symptoms didn't lie. No doubt one or two ribs were broken or cracked. Itacus couldn't care less, of course, and dragged Lucas by the ankle all the way down the corridor. At the head of the ramp leading to the first level, the Brute gave a great jerk and flung Lucas forward. He screamed again to the sound of the Brute's laughter, going airborne for a few seconds and then hitting the ramp midway.

Agony engulfed him. His eyes rolled into the back of his head and his stomach turned as he slid the rest of the way down the ramp, coming to a hard stop against a heavy gold-colored boot.

Its owner leaned over, contempt on his saurian face and ruffling his mandibles. The second Lucas saw Chak 'Lok, his fear spiked even more. Injuries be damned, he scurried back, his hand instinctively going to his side. No. No, that would draw attention. As much as he wanted to support and protect his ribcage, he let his hand fall to his lap and kept his eyes on the ramp. The vibration of Itacus's footsteps coming behind him made it that much harder to stay still, as each footfall sent aching stabs through his side.

Chak 'Lok picked him up by the neck. Lucas's feet dangled off the ground, making his neck, torso, and ribcage stretch, which in turn made his new injury unbearable. His breaths turned to pants as he tried not to vomit all over the warden. "You are not worthy of the honor she bestows upon you, worm," the Sangheili declared. With great disgust, he opened his hands and let Lucas drop.

And the pain just kept coming. . . . It was too much. A cold, clammy sweat broke out on his skin as he lay there gasping, the room starting to tilt.

"Bring him to the Phantom," Chak 'Lok ordered, and strode ahead of them.

Itacus yanked Lucas to his feet and shoved him forward. He felt drunk and disoriented, finally cradling his ribcage and limping across the ground level, following the Sangheili around the massive gravity lift in the center of the tower, then out onto the landing platform. He glanced up at a waiting Phantom, and somehow managed to climb aboard without passing out.

He had the shakes real bad and couldn't stop trembling no matter how much he tried to calm himself. He was too dazed to judge how much time had passed or even which direction they'd gone, but he was vaguely aware of landing and then being brought out into the largest, most intimidating and fortified outpost he'd seen so far.

The land mass here had split in two, revealing sheer cliffs of hexagonal Forerunner alloy. In the space between the two cliffs, a massive tower rose several meters from the ground—densely armored and heavily defended. Of the Banished's military structures he'd seen on Zeta Halo so far, there had been nothing quite like this one. Enormous supports extended from the top of the central tower to each cliffside, effectively anchoring all three structures together.

Daylight stung his vision, making him cast his eyes downward. What did looking matter, anyway? It was just another Banished outpost and another trip to shitsville, just like all the rest of the places he'd been to since landing on the ring. He stumbled. Itacus growled behind him, "Fall once more and I will make you bleed, human."

Lucas tuned him out. There were too many things happening at once, transports taking off, supply carts floating across their path, a group of raiders heading into another part of the building.

His heart raced erratically and he continually swallowed down the bile that kept rising to his throat. After heading across a large bridge, they entered the massive tower that seemed to rise impossibly high above him. Inside the central structure was a lift, and they rode this to the fourth level, debarked, and then passed two Brute guards stationed at the head of a clean, quiet corridor. The walk seemed to stretch, his vision growing fuzzy and turning the corridor into a tunnel whose walls began to close in, the two large beasts on either side of him seeming to grow even taller and wider and utterly suffocating. Fear of *her* had wound its way into his psyche and was slowly driving him insane. He didn't want to do this. Didn't want to see her again. Once was enough for a lifetime.

All sorts of crazy things went through his head—why she had sent for him, what she planned to do now . . . Tears stung his eyes and his breath came short. Of all the ways he'd thought he might die, this hadn't been one of them. He blinked back the tears, angry that the last thing he might ever see would be the Harbinger.

They stopped at a nondescript door. Chak 'Lok reached out and pressed the admission pad. The door slid open, but neither he nor Itacus moved.

Lucas's pulse was hammering fast now. He tried to swallow but couldn't. If they weren't moving, then the hell with it, neither was he. As he leaned to take a step back, Itacus grabbed his shoulder and shoved him forward into the room.

No!

Lucas stumbled inside with the Sangheili warden on his heels. The door slid closed, and immediately he wanted to run back, slap his hands on the metal and pound the door down with his bare fists, to shout until his lungs burst, but he was too terrified to make a sound. He simply sank to his knees, defeated.

"This is what you brought me?" Her voice snaked through the room, rough and silky, and making the hairs on the back of his neck stand. *"There is barely anything left."*

"He is yours to do with as you see fit," Chak 'Lok replied.

"Indeed he is."

She must have waved the warden away, because he heard the door open and Chak 'Lok's steps retreating. The door slid shut once more, and silence filled the room. Lucas stayed on his knees, shivering, head down, eyes squeezed tightly closed and wishing he could just disappear, just shrink away and evaporate into nothing.

"Were you treated unjustly in his tower, human?"

He didn't answer; he couldn't if he tried. Her powerful voice was like thousands of tiny insects crawling all over his skin. A soft whirring sound filtered through his fear, and her voice seemed to come from another spot in the room when she spoke again. *"We are not so different in this. I too know intimately of injustice. To be sentenced for crimes not your own."*

Wishing he were truly dead, Lucas bowed until his forehead met cold metal. "Please, I just want to—"

"Quiet," she snapped. *"I shall talk . . . and you shall listen."*

He stayed like that for several minutes, expecting her to begin talking, but she remained silent despite her words. Finally he lifted his head as a shadow crawled up the floor toward him. His eyes widened, and it felt as though all the blood drained out of his body.

The shadow withdrew and it grew quiet in the room once more until all he heard was his pulse thrumming through his eardrums. Finally, she spoke again.

"But to listen well, you must have all of your faculties. There is food and drink here on the table."

At the mere mention of food, his stomach clenched tightly and rumbled. Tentatively he looked up to see her figure, in profile, hovering at the only window in the room. Her triangular headdress turned slightly, revealing some of her bluish skin and pointed jaw. Her head dipped regally and one lithe arm, tipped by those long-clawed fingers, gestured to the table.

His eyes grew round. Instantly his mouth salivated. The table was full of food.

Jesus. He started to sweat and wondered if he was hallucinating.

He was pretty sure he was going to die, but damn, if what he was seeing was real, then at least he'd die with a full belly. Screw her. Screw the Brutes. And screw this entire goddamn ring.

His legs trembled as he held his side and pushed excruciatingly slowly to his feet. He shuffled forward, wary of her watching him, but drawn to the contents of the tabletop. Metal plates piled high with steaming shredded meat. Several types of fruit, though he couldn't identify any of it. Didn't matter. His nostrils flared as he picked up a chunk of perfectly cooked meat with his fingers and shoved it slowly into his mouth. It reminded Lucas of venison. He tried, he really tried to take it slow, but as soon as the savory taste hit his tongue, he lost all decorum, all train of thought, his brain shifting to survival mode.

And the water. Dear God. There was a metal pitcher and a cup already full, and it slid down his throat like a dream, fresh and cool and blessedly clean, washing all that glorious food straight into his stomach. It had been so long since he'd had anything like this.

He was only halfway into the feast when her voice pierced the air. *"That is enough,"* she said.

He hadn't even flinched at her words. Just obeyed like the dog he apparently was. He felt like he'd run a marathon. His breath came fast, his entire body buzzing. He wanted more, but her presence so close and so dominating quelled his desire. Facing her, he saw that her eyes weren't black as he'd originally thought but a reddish purple, and the thick bones along her jawline were more like flaps than bone and they moved when she spoke.

"*Now,*" she said promptly. "*Let us begin.*"

CHAPTER 30

Zeta Halo
April 27, 2560
Day 137

urphy was getting damn tired of the runaround Spartan Kovan was giving him—runaround, silent treatment, whatever you wanted to call it, it was all the same to him. He stormed out of camp and up the trailhead, refusing to back down or let her walk away from him. "Goddamn it, Kovan, stop!"

She paused finally, glancing over her shoulder, that irritating, inscrutable helmet staring down at him. Murphy didn't slow, just stepped onto the rocks next to her and grabbed her chest plate, leaning in to look directly into eyes he couldn't see. "Either you're part of this team or you're not. There are no secrets anymore, no intel you have to protect. . . . All the protocols are gone . . . so what the hell aren't you saying?!"

Slowly her head tipped down. Somewhere in the back of his mind, he knew he was on very thin ice, but emotion had overridden self-preservation. And in this case, it was warranted; there was no way he was backing down.

Several moments passed. Murphy heard the others come up the trail, stopping a few meters away and whispering.

"Shit."

"You ever see Murphy get mad?"

"Never. You?"

"Nope."

Kovan's hands curled around his wrists and squeezed. She could have crushed them to dust without much effort, but that wasn't where this was going. At least, he hoped not. She removed his hands from her armor and then stepped back, taking off her helmet and tucking it beneath her arm. The cold stare from those glacial blue eyes went straight through Murphy like an arctic wind. He actually felt a small shiver and had to give Nina Kovan her due—she could certainly be intimidating as hell. Her mouth was set in a grim line and just a faint pink of anger had come to her pale cheeks. Good. She was just as pissed off as he was.

"Don't ever do that again," she said, each word carefully measured.

He opened his mouth to argue, but stopped, drawing in a steady breath, trying to reason with her. "It's been days. Stone's still not back and you're not exactly being forthcoming."

When Kovan had returned alone from their nighttime recon sweep of *Mortal Reverie*, Stone staying behind to monitor the site had seemed like no big deal. The boat crew had been busy anyway, prepping for an exhausting and tricky nighttime supply run to a wide ledge jutting out from the chasm four hundred meters below the *Reverie*. The ledge had caught some of the "human refuse" the Banished had tossed over the cliff as they cleaned out the UNSC frigate. In the trash, mostly consisting of personal effects, they'd recovered twenty-two scattered MREs, a couple of thirty-six-round box magazines, two spare flight suits, an energy bayonet and sound dampener for an MA5D assault rifle, and a few canisters of biofoam.

When they'd returned and Stone still hadn't showed, Kovan's response had been "It's need to know," which was all kinds of bullshit. "Need to know," "eyes only," "above your pay grade"—none of it mattered anymore. And out here, on their own, being privy to such clandestine knowledge might actually keep them alive for another day.

"If something's going on up there . . ." He dragged a hand through his now-chin-length hair. "If she's hurt . . ."

Kovan frowned. "No. She's not hurt."

The team drew closer and gathered on the rocks, ready to listen, staring at Kovan expectantly. The pressure was on. Everyone was tired of being put off. They were ready to make tracks into new territory, but Kovan was keeping a tight lid on when that might happen and refused to give them an update on Stone's sitrep.

"If she's not hurt, then what's her status?" Dimik asked, sitting cross-legged.

Finally Kovan let out a martyred breath. "The Banished have been excavating beneath the *Reverie*, bringing up Forerunner artifacts. Two nights ago, we went"—she rolled her eyes and let out a curse in her native tongue—"to rescue Browning."

Murphy's mind blanked.

Oh, he heard what she said; it hit him like a slap in the face. The others started talking at once, but he was too shocked to say anything other than "Browning is alive." Emotion squeezed his chest, making him too afraid to believe it, and, man, he wanted desperately to believe it. He lifted his gaze to Kovan's. "Browning is alive."

The talk abruptly stopped.

Kovan held his gaze for a long moment, then said, "Stone saw him during her initial recon sweep. He was being used to activate

Forerunner technology. I didn't say anything be—"

"This is bullshit." Bender pushed off the rock he'd been leaning against, a deep scowl darkening his face. "Because you didn't want us to, what, do something stupid, is that it?"

"That's it exactly," she replied.

The anger and disappointment on Bender's face was something none of them had ever seen from him when it came to Kovan. His mouth twisted wryly. "So much for trusting your team. Or maybe we were never really a team to you?" Not waiting for an answer, he cursed under his breath and marched back down the trail to camp.

"Goddamn it. Bender, wait!" Dimik jumped off her perch and ran after him.

Cam crossed his arms over his chest and parked a shrewd eye on Kovan. "So . . . you and Stone went back to rescue him and only you came back." He paused. "Are they both dead now?"

"Not that I'm aware. I was unable to extract Browning, but I did see him and talk to him. Stone and I were separated and she ended up finding an entrance beneath the outpost. Her last message to me said she was venturing in to see what the Banished have been excavating. That was the last I heard."

"And Lucas?" Murphy asked.

"Taken away on a Banished Phantom. To where, I don't know. I gave him a tracking beacon, just haven't caught the signal yet."

"And that's where you've been—reconning the outpost."

"Yes, and trying to figure out where he went, what the Banished are up to, and waiting to pick up Stone's signal as well."

Murphy allowed himself a long minute to digest the news. He understood why she'd kept it to herself. She was too proud to come right out and admit she cared, that she'd done it to protect them, to keep them from going into a situation too big for the four of them to walk away from. Hard to fault her for that—yet Bender was absolutely right too.

They weren't idiots; they'd cut their teeth out here, earned their stripes, and more importantly earned each other's trust. They'd learned the hard way how to keep cool heads, be patient, and not get themselves killed. She should have trusted them with the information.

So yeah, it stung.

Annoyed, he scratched his head and then tried to put the irritation behind him. "Come on," he said, "let's pack up camp. We might not know where Lucas is, but we know where Stone went. We'll start there." He walked away. She could join him or not.

The boat crew moved single-file along a winding path of loose gravel and massive gray boulders. Spartan Kovan led the way, followed by Dimik, Cam, and Bender, while Murphy brought up the rear. He gave a quick check behind him, the darkness and fog revealing nothing, before tugging his makeshift scarf to his chin.

The air had grown colder and damper the closer they came to the *Mortal Reverie* and the chasm she overlooked. It was the kind of air that carried sound with ease, so they took things slow and stayed frosty. This time they weren't approaching the crashed ship from the starboard side as they'd done once upon a time, back when *Reverie* was controlled by friendly forces, but had taken a southern path through the large wake it created when it crash-landed. The wake spilled out along the edge of the ring fragment, leading to a lower track that allowed them to come up below the massive frigate and on the far side of the Banished's outpost structures.

Kovan told him the Banished had rechristened the crash site as Outpost Tremonius, named after the ruthless Jiralhanae commander who had led the retaliation force against *Reverie* months ago. It made Murphy's stomach turn and awakened some primal desire in him to fight to the bitter end just to take it back. The vessel's stern loomed over the outpost from this angle, held tight in the cliff rocks, the sky above her a haze of yellow and red from the auxiliary lights the Banished had installed, which lit the prefabricated buildings that wrapped around *Reverie*'s midsection cargo bay. Murphy didn't know how much of the ship was still accessible after the battle, but it didn't seem like the Banished cared about utilizing the ship at all.

The line ahead of him slowed, bringing them shoulder to shoulder as they edged around a rock face and came to a stop. They were at the very end of the ring fragment, the substructure visible just below their position. The surrounding area was comprised of loose detritus and charred tree trunks, where the frigate's crash had churned up the side of the mountain, spilling rock and ship parts off the edge of the ring fragment. Even months later, it continued to collapse in places.

"This is it," Kovan whispered.

According to the Spartan's debrief, "it" was the cavern that Stone had found near the outpost, which would lead them up into the outpost and then down into the Banished's excavation efforts below the *Reverie*. Given the constant stream of loose soil and rockslides above the entrance, it was remarkable that Stone had even found it. In a few weeks or months, Murphy wondered if the opening would be accessible at all.

"Eyes and ears," she reminded them, and went silent, motioning for them to follow.

No one knew what they were walking into. After months of sustained damage, Kovan's integrated systems were pretty much shot. She had no motion sensors, no lidar, no thermal, no AI. But the outpost had been relatively quiet since the large detachment of Banished troops had left the site. Quiet was good. Understaffed was even better; one could only hope . . .

Murphy kept a ready hold on his assault rifle as the crew made their way inside. The air was pungent with the scent of damp rock. The cavern walls, ceiling, and floor were natural formations and showed no signs of occupation until Kovan knelt suddenly, staring at the ground, then indicating the tracks she'd found. Her nod and gesture to move on told him that they were indeed on Stone's trail.

A hundred meters in, the ground thinned in places, revealing alloy beneath, and eventually they intersected another dark passageway. Banished lighting bathed the way ahead in red, and their support buttresses lined the interior wall of stone. They cut their lights as supplies, crates, excavation tools, grav carts, and discarded refuse began to narrow the passage.

Coming upon the first chamber brought the first sign of the enemy: the nasally pitch of a Grunt.

Kovan turned and motioned for them to stay put as she eased up to the chamber, peeked inside, and continued past to get a better idea of which way to go. A minute or two ticked by before she returned and they picked up the pace. As they passed the chamber, Murphy got a quick look inside at a Grunt reclining back on his methane tank, talking in his sleep.

It was a good sign.

They encountered more excavation equipment and crates, piled up or in some cases tossed casually to the side. The lack of guards and the state of the discarded equipment made Murphy wonder if the Banished had halted their efforts not just for the night, but more long-term. As they passed through a Banished doorway into a barely lit corridor, Murphy's gaze snagged on the far end of the chamber, where a rectangular panel hung upright and some kind of glowing yellow inlay traced out the shape of a triangular-headed figure.

A shiver skated up his arms and pricked the back of his neck. Whatever it was gave off a bad vibe, and he was grateful to be moving along to a separate corridor leading to the supply elevator up ahead. If Stone had been hunting for what the Banished were trying to dig up, then this was the place she'd come.

The line stopped, and Murphy crouched behind a stack of weapons crates. The lift sat just a few meters away like some gaping mouth oozing Banished light. Two Brute guards in leather armor sat dozing at the intersection of the corridors. While these Jiralhanae were low in rank among their own kind, they were still seven hundred kilos of destruction, capable of ripping apart a human with their bare hands.

Still, Murphy and his crew had learned a thing or two in the last few months.

Kovan leaned forward, indicating to him that she'd take the one on the left while they should go for the one on the right. And above all, they had to do it quietly. Murphy nodded, let his rucksack slip to the ground, and then retrieved the energy bayonet they'd salvaged earlier as Bender unsheathed his precious combat knife. Cam and Dimik followed suit with their own blades.

It was delicate business, killing such a massive creature quietly.

But they'd done it before in a tight spot, and they could do it again.

Since they'd been lucky enough to come upon the guards as they slept on the job, Murphy gave the crew the two-one-one signal with his fingers, code for the takedown tactic they'd use: Cam and Dimik at the legs, Murphy at the gut, and Bender at the throat. The key was striking in unison and with Kovan in order to keep their targets from calling in reinforcements.

As Murphy waited for her signal, Kovan removed a sleek Jiralhanae combat knife she'd taken from the body of a Stalker a few weeks back. She turned her head and he was met with those two gold-colored eye lenses as she gave him the three-second countdown signal.

She started the count: *one . . . two . . .* On three, they moved, Kovan edging her way around the wall to come up beside the Brute on the left; Murphy and Bender made a direct approach to the other as Cam went to its right side and Dimik to its left.

Closer they crept, easing each footfall down as quietly as possible until Murphy was near enough to the sleeping Brute that he could smell charred, sour meat on the alien's breath.

A quick glance showed Kovan lifting the wildly serrated blade, roughly the size of a human arm, which the Jiralhanae had used to cut through hide and bone.

After a quick nod between them Murphy dove for the Brute's stomach, stabbing the tip of the energy bayonet against the leather covering his gut, then activated it as the enemy jerked, eyes flying open. Murphy forced the bayonet straight up through the Jiralhanae's chest cavity as Bender cut his throat, sending a spray of wine-colored blood over his hand and arm. At the same time, Cam and Dimik cut the tendons behind his knees. They'd learned to cover their asses—if the larger wounds didn't stop the Brute, taking out his mobility would sure help.

The Jiralhanae never had a chance to scream. And Kovan had overtaken her target just as quickly, her knife nearly decapitating the guard. She shoved the body to the ground, stepped over it, and then faced the lift. "Good work," she whispered as they gathered around.

Cam leaned into the lift and gazed through the grated floor. "Looks quiet down there."

"Using this thing might draw too much attention," Dimik said, looking back along the dark passageway to where the Grunt still slept in the nearby chamber.

"We can take it down and then deactivate its control panel from the other end," Kovan said. "If anyone does hear, it'll take them a while to get it started again."

Murphy retrieved his rucksack and was first onto the lift. "What are you guys waiting for? Let's go."

Surprisingly the lift was quieter than they'd anticipated; he'd be surprised if the sleeping Grunt heard a thing. But just to be safe, as soon as they hit bottom, Kovan, Bender, and Dimik were out with weapons drawn, as he and Cam took care of the panel—nothing fancy, just a little rewiring job to keep the Banished off their backs.

They'd been delivered into a relatively small staging area that led to a larger room beyond. The space was pitch dark except for the abrasive red light coming from the lift, which shone against the nearest wall, where there was more excavation equipment, crates, and containers. As they emerged from the lift and his eyes began to adjust, Murphy immediately recognized the space as Forerunner. And it was extraordinary to take in.

During their time on Zeta Halo, he'd seen countless Forerunner structures, towers, and pylons that stretched up from the surface of the ring with incredible size and majesty, but he'd been inside only a handful of them. None of those could match what they were witnessing now: the level of detail and the geometric precision . . . it was staggering to behold. The room was a dozen or so meters high, with large columns, dividing structures, and an elevated walkway that seemed to run around the perimeter. There were doorways leading out of the space on both ends of the room.

Which one were they supposed to take? Trusting Kovan's instincts, Murphy let her make the call and they ended up heading across the entire room to the far side.

They stayed silent moving toward the door; everyone seemed to be taking in the impressive architecture while keeping their eyes open for Banished soldiers. The enemy's equipment and cabling snaked all over the place, which told Murphy that their assault on *Reverie* wasn't just vindictive or strategic—they were looking for something within the ring. The door opened automatically into a blue-lit short corridor, and then yet another door.

On the other side two Grunts fiddled with a Banished crate in the corner. When the door suddenly opened, it startled them, but they had no time to respond. Murphy plunged his bayonet into the nearest one's gut, and Kovan quickly broke the other's neck before he could even raise his weapon.

Very carefully, the boat crew fanned out into the next room. Two low, sloping ramps went down from the landing to a long rectangular area, which seemed to lead into another chamber. Kovan and Dimik took the right ramp while he, Bender, and Cam took the left. The room was filled with Banished machines, cables, and . . . dead bodies?

A handful of dead Banished soldiers were scattered across the floor at the base of the ramps, blood and weapons fire on the walls and floor indicating that it had been the site of a pretty intense battle. There was a slew of Banished equipment cluttering the floor among the bodies, and the smell of spent weapons was still fresh. Whatever had happened here, it was very recent.

"Shit. Murph . . ." Bender nudged his shoulder, gesturing to his right.

Murphy followed his gaze and saw the legs first, and the familiar faded-blue Mjolnir armor. . . .

Heart sinking, he hurried down the ramp. It was Spartan Stone all right, slumped against the base between the ramps, legs splayed, head hanging to one side, a vertical burn in the center of her chest armor. He knelt just as Kovan slid down beside him, bumping him out of the way, calling Stone's name and shaking her by the shoulders.

No one in the boat crew spoke. They collectively stood there, digesting the reality, trying to process the fact that Bonita Stone— one of the mightiest Spartans they'd ever known, who'd saved their lives time and again—was just sitting there dead on the ground.

A string of curses rolled through his mind, and his heart tightened until pain radiated through his chest. Without Stone, he wouldn't have made it out of that crashed lifeboat. She could easily have bypassed them to engage the Banished, but she hadn't, and then she'd led them through hostile territory until they'd reached the *Mortal Reverie*. And even then she'd looked out for them, helping them escape the utter chaos of that event.

After a long time, Kovan leaned forward and gently retrieved the VISR data chip from Stone's helmet, then slipped the small device into her own neural interface.

"What's she doing?" Dimik asked quietly.

"Accessing Stone's log, probably."

Cam sat on the ramp, shaking his head. "I can't believe she's gone."

After everything they'd been through. All the hardships and losses. It didn't seem fair. It *wasn't* fair. Zeta Halo was proving to be a great equalizer.

Murphy knew what it was like to lose friends, good outstanding comrades, to war—so many of them over the years that he'd stopped counting. But Spartans didn't fall as easily and often stayed together for many years. He wanted to believe he understood what Kovan was feeling—at least that way he'd know what to say or do to help—but in the end he knew the mind of a Spartan, the way they viewed the job, their fireteam, was way more complicated than he could possibly imagine.

"She was a badass through and through" was all Bender could say after a while.

"Were they together for a long time, her and Kovan?" Dimik asked.

"Since before *Infinity* was commissioned."

Kovan removed her own helmet and sat back on her heels, staring at Spartan Stone's lifeless form. Her head bowed, her pale hair falling to obscure her profile. All he could think about was the deep sadness and grief that she must be feeling.

"Ten years," Kovan finally said. "We met on the reconnaissance starship *Relentless Watch* before joining the SPARTAN-IV program. Recon was hardwired into her DNA from the beginning." She removed the chip from her interface and stared at it in the palm of her hand. "And straight on to the end."

The metal groan of the lift in the room beyond made them

all jump. Murphy scrambled to his feet and rushed back into the staging area to see the lift rising in fits and starts.

"They're manually pulling it back up!" he called, returning as Kovan stood and donned her helmet. Once the Banished finished hauling the lift car back up, they could manually lower the lift from the top or even just cut through its floor and drop through the lift shaft.

Murphy could see that the crew wasn't sure what to do about Stone—he wasn't either. No one wanted to leave her. Hell, they were still absorbing the shock of suddenly finding her. But the Banished weren't going to wait around for them to grieve. They had to leave now if they wanted to create any sort of distance between them and the enemy.

It was up to Kovan, but the way Murphy saw it, there was very little choice. While Kovan could carry the body and its accompanying armor, doing so would slow them down considerably, and with the Banished hot on their heels, that decision could jeopardize the entire crew. And Stone wouldn't want that.

With a grim expression, Kovan straightened, unshouldered her rifle, and motioned for the boat crew to file out. Evidently, she knew from the data chip where Stone had been and where they needed to go next if they wanted to evade the Banished at the top of the lift. It had to be breaking her heart to leave, knowing this hellhole would be Stone's final resting place, but she stood there, shoulders straight, ready to do the right thing. As he walked by her side, he dipped his head in acknowledgment and understanding. She took the lead and they hightailed it through the next chamber. And the next. And the next.

Hours had passed in a blur since Murphy and the boat crew had successfully evaded the enemy, traversing a maze of interior passageways, chambers, and open cavities threaded with immense support beams, girders, conduits, and pillars. At first it was a scramble just to get away from the Banished staging area, but when it became clear they'd lost their tail, the group had slowed to a steady, manageable walk. Now that Murphy had time to really look at his surroundings again, he couldn't help but be amazed. If the first room was impressive, what they were seeing now took his breath away. Walls soared dozens of meters high. Pathways seemed as wide as starships. Glyphs and geometric lines decorated surfaces of smooth alloy untarnished by time, while hard light illuminated some of the lines in a familiar Forerunner blue.

He had expected it to be big—the Forerunners did everything on a divine scale—but this was beyond imagining. The size was astonishing, and it truly felt as though they were walking in the shadows of ancient gods, through corridors and chambers meant for titans. Apart from the occasional rumble of what sounded like a distant thunderstorm, a hush lay over the area, like a place in waiting, where at any minute the Forerunners might suddenly reappear from eons past and continue where they'd left off.

And there was Stone, lurking in the back of his mind, his grief at her death on hold as they'd fled from the Banished, Kovan leading them on a dizzying path as though she knew exactly where to go.

Occasionally they came across evidence of Banished excavations: plasma burns through metal, slag on the floor, broken consoles, and empty chambers. Who knew what things the enemy had uncovered, what additional advantages they'd gotten out of their endeavors.

The team was exploring a set of chambers that surrounded a central chasm, the depth of which was lost in the utter darkness below. "As if we didn't have enough to worry about," Bender said irritably, nudging a severed piece of cable out of the way, "now they're lining their pockets with Forerunner tech."

"Bastards don't let up, do they?" Cam muttered. "They just think the ring and everything in it belongs to them."

The agitated mood encompassed the crew, Stone's death hanging heavy over them all.

"We'll set up camp here," Kovan said, ignoring their conversation as she picked a spot against the wall.

Murphy dropped his rucksack and walked over to Kovan. "Where are we going, exactly? I know we can't go back the way we came, but we've been on the move for a while now. Should we be trying to find a way to the surface?"

"After we see what Stone was doing down here." She removed her helmet and looked at him with weary eyes.

"You're retracing her steps." He'd assumed as much, but wished Kovan would clue him in on what was on Stone's data chip, how she'd died, who had killed her. . . . It still didn't seem real, like some anomalous blip on a radar screen, seen, but not understood. He wanted to know what had happened, to make a plan, take action, do something, anything, to make it feel as though he could at least honor her memory. But until Kovan shared, his hands were tied. And the last thing he wanted to do right now was push her. How could he?

Murphy let it go and sat down, using his bag as a backrest. Dimik handed out water rations, and Bender MREs. They ate in silence, casting concerned glances Kovan's way as she rested, back against the wall, one leg pulled up and eyes closed.

Eventually he grew drowsy and fell into a deep, troubled sleep, so far down that he didn't even wake on his own. Instead a very bright light flashed across his eyelids, causing him to flinch. The flinch led to a curse and Murphy jerked awake and instinctively reached for the rifle lying next to him. A quick glance showed Cam, Dimik, Bender, and Kovan all sitting upright against the wall, their faces bathed in light as a hovering, round, metallic orb canted its eye over each one of them.

"Uh, what are we looking at?" Bender asked quietly.

"Stay calm," Kovan said. "Hands off the weapons."

The orb floated above the chasm. Sure as hell looked like the briefs he'd seen of a Forerunner AI, also known as a monitor—spherical in shape, usually with silver alloy, though this one's finish appeared dulled and weathered. Hard blue light glowed within a round lens that acted as a central eye, and the orb's sides bulged slightly outward. It moved closer until it was hovering just above eye level in front of them. Without warning, a transparent blue beam shot from its lens, scanning Spartan Kovan from top to bottom.

Kovan remained still, but Murphy thought the others might be growing antsy and concerned. The "eye" moved on to Bender. He went ramrod straight. "Uh . . . what the hell is happening?"

"*I am scanning you,*" the monitor answered in an impertinent female voice, moving in front of each team member in turn before going back to hover in front of Kovan. Murphy quietly let out the breath he hadn't realized he'd been holding.

"*Greetings, Reclaimers. I am Submonitor 091 Adjutant Veridity. However, you may call me Veridity.*" She released an exaggerated sigh, her eye turning up as though lost in thought. "*The past always repeats itself. Cycle after cycle . . .*"

Kovan stepped forward. "I'm Spartan Nina Kovan of the—"

"I scanned your rudimentary software. I know who you are."

Undaunted, Kovan replied, "As a submonitor, you're not the true monitor of this installation?"

"Oh, if I were the monitor!" she said brightly, flying in a big, looping circle, then coming back to a hover, her voice turning somewhat dark and excited. *"The Banished would be dead. All dead. Done. Done. Dead as dead. That's how dead they would be. But, alas, I am but one submonitor among many. And a friend to any Banished enemy. That would be you!"*

The submonitor was obviously a bit eccentric or unhinged, but Murphy was too curious not to push for more information. "Who is in control of the ring?" Her eye shifted his way. "Is it the monitor . . . or Cortana—?"

"Pfft!" she said, offended. *"That horrible name. . . . Good thing she is dead too. She thought she could take control . . . such trouble she caused, moving and damaging our installation. Such trouble . . ."*

Murphy had wondered as much, and it was good to finally have confirmation. "So the monitor is still in control, then?"

Veridity went very still, her blue gaze locking on him for a long moment. *"Well . . ."* She began swinging from side to side, then brightened: *"Oh, happy day! You will set her free and restore our access! You are Reclaimers, after all."*

A term Murphy knew well. He'd heard it many times during debriefs after *Infinity*'s mission to Requiem back in '58. The Forerunners had intended for humanity to be their inheritors, calling them Reclaimers and giving them the means to access their technology.

"What do you mean, set her free?" Kovan asked.

"When Cortana arrived at our installation, she sequestered our monitor, Despondent Pyre, in the Conservatory and limited

her communication with the ring's defense network. The other submonitors and I have been maintaining systems in her absence, but we have been unable to release the hold placed over Pyre or to access the defense network on her behalf.

"This Conservatory," Kovan said thoughtfully, "does it have access to the ring's communications network?"

"Normally, yes . . . But without Pyre some system functions have been limited."

"Kovan, what are you thinking?" Murphy asked.

"Stone followed the Banished to some kind of information center and saw them remove data from its data stream."

"This is what brought me to investigate," Veridity said. *"The Banished stole two sylloge nodes from one of our local data hubs. These hubs are scattered throughout the ring and are part of our Conspectus network, which oversees the entire historical record of Installation 07 from its inception to the present."*

"And a sylloge node; what is that, exactly?" Dimik asked.

"A collection of data regarding the installation—it could be as trivial as the ring's status and coordinates or as significant as control-keys to its defensive systems. I have reason to believe the Banished have accessed both of these."

"According to Stone's video feed," Kovan said, "they were after data that gave them control of the ring's defensive systems. They want to use Zeta Halo as a new homeworld, replacing what Cortana took from them, but one with infinitely more strategic capabilities and firepower."

Bender groaned as the reality of her words sank in. "If the Banished now have access to the ring's defenses, that pretty much means game over, right?"

"Calm yourself, human," Veridity commanded. *"The Banished*

will find deciphering the data rather challenging. Security protocols protect the data housed in the Conspectus network, and sylloge nodes pulled from the network stream must be decrypted via ports in our Cartographer facilities or in the Conservatory."

"I don't think we need to worry about them deciphering anything," Kovan said. "Stone fought to steal the data from the Banished. Once she had it, she made a copy and her AI corrupted the original. Whatever the Banished have is useless now."

"Wait a minute. Does this mean we actually have the ring's coordinates?" Murphy asked, although he was pretty sure everyone else was thinking the same thing. The defensive systems of any UNSC space station included a full suite of astrogation data as part of its strategic capabilities, so there was no way Zeta Halo didn't have likewise. And if they had that data, it meant they might be able to relay their location to the UNSC and call in reinforcements to turn the tide. They'd only need a way to broadcast the coordinates back to UNSC space.

"*Of course,*" Veridity said. "*If the Spartan does indeed have the data the Banished removed from the network.*"

Unbelievable. So that's how Stone had died—preventing the Banished from ever using the data. Murphy ran a hand down his face and sighed heavily. Stone had single-handedly bought them all one hell of a reprieve. And now they were in possession of the ring's coordinates in space.

"*Nevertheless, Banished forces have already arrived at the Conservatory,*" Veridity said gravely. "*It is only a matter of time before they discover what Spartan Stone did to their data. They might seek to extract the proper information and authority rights directly from Despondent Pyre and take full control of the ring. Though . . . it will take them a very long time to enter the Conservatory and even longer to find Pyre's cradle, if ever. That's the beauty of its design. Shall we?"* She started off along the pathway around the chasm humming; when no one followed, she circled back, keen to move them along.

If the Banished were already at this Conservatory, already at the threshold of getting to Zeta Halo's monitor, time wasn't on their side. And if War Chief Escharum somehow gained access to the ring's defensive systems, like Bender said, it'd be game over. Here and across the galaxy.

But now they had the coordinates and they had Veridity. If they somehow gained the support of the ring's monitor and she helped them decrypt the data and contact the UNSC, then the game changed. Humanity and Zeta Halo's defenses working together . . . If that were to happen, yeah, they could absolutely turn the tide and defeat the Banished presence here once and for all. Just the possibility set a tiny kernel of hope burning in Murphy's chest.

CHAPTER 31

Reaching the Conspectus hub using the map that ONI AR operative Kate Stalling had provided had been a matter of trial and error. Orienting himself to land formations spread over an expanse of thousands of acres, some that were no longer relevant due to the fracturing of the Halo ring and subsequent remedial shifts, had proved frustrating and at times seemed impossible—as did finding his way around or across deep fractures in the ring itself. All of these challenges had taken Horvath additional weeks to navigate while deep in Banished territory, which meant taking the opportunity to cause a little trouble whenever possible.

It made for a very long hunt.

Many times, the echo of gunfire reverberated across the canyons and valleys, and he knew he wasn't alone, that the UNSC was still out there, persevering. Those times were the hardest. He yearned to rejoin the fight, but preventing the Banished from obtaining the intel Stalling had mentioned was far more important and urgent than his longing for camaraderie.

When he found the high-altitude lake after a day's climb, Horvath knew he was on the right path. It was situated amid sparse conifers and tucked into a rocky slope. A cracked umber-colored crust lay over most of the lake's surface. The cracks were circular, similar to the concentric wave patterns of rocks thrown into water. From the cracks oozed a pitch-colored substance, making the lake look like a puzzle broken apart. Stalling had written *hard lake*, and while there was no water he could see, there was a thin shoreline of pebbles. Horvath made his way there, broke a nearby branch from a tree and stuck it into one of the cracks. It came back covered in an oily black sludge.

He tossed the stick and contemplated his next move as his AI created a grid of the lake on his HUD.

"It appears the lake is made up of a tar-like substance and the oils within the tar have evaporated and dried, likely over thousands of years, to create the surface crust. Some of it is quite solid."

The area marked by Stalling was near the center of the lake, but no matter how hard he looked, all he could make out was a smudge while everything around it was clear.

"Try deep-scanning that area again," he said.

"I am unable to get a proper reading," Fi responded. *"This may be indicative of Forerunner stealth technology."*

Forerunners were known to have employed stealth technology over important sites, using machines called bafflers or dazzlers, both of which distorted an area viewed from ground and air. If that was the case, then he must be on the right track.

"Can you find me a path across?" A path that would support nearly six hundred kilos of armored Spartan might not be an easy feat.

"I can, but prolonged weight will disturb the viscosity of the

crust." Elfie measured depth through the crust layer and found him a connected way toward the hazy lake center. *"Once you begin, walk quickly,"* she told him. *"Do not stop or you'll sink."*

Horvath drew in a deep breath, studied the path on his HUD, and walked along the shoreline until he found the starting point laid out on his display. The first step onto the crust produced a loud crack. Instinctively he slowed and made to step back. *"Go!"* Elfie shouted in his ears. He started forward. *"But don't run!"*

"Okay, okay." Careful wasn't exactly his strong suit—he was more a barge-in-and-destroy-shit kind of guy—but he concentrated on moving as swiftly and as lightly as possible, every step along the meandering path crunching and cracking the layer like a bear walking across thin ice.

The idea of the tar beneath his feet permanently entangling him kept him going forward, but also instilled some concern. The distorted area lay ahead, and then what? He might have no other choice but to stop. His apprehension grew. Of all the crazy things he'd done . . . And here he was putting his faith in a crudely drawn map created by an ONI operative who might or might not have been in her right mind at the time.

Too late to stop now or reconsider his decision; Horvath pressed on, passing over the circular patterns, following the most solid route until he entered the haze.

The cracking stopped and the telltale sound of his armored boots on metal rang out instead. With a huge breath of relief, he saw he was through the distortion and standing on a flat seven-sided surface the same color as the pitch—black, but somewhat translucent, suggesting there was depth beneath the platform— but he didn't have time to enjoy his success as a hazy white field erupted around the perimeter of the black surface.

"You are being scanned," Fi told him. The platform suddenly dropped without warning, knocking him off balance as it plummeted straight down into the lake, zooming past intermittent circles of blue light. At this high rate of speed, he should be off his feet, but the field seemed to act as some kind of protective bubble. It was like dropping through an ejection tube, without the drop pod.

Eight hundred meters in mere seconds.

The elevator platform came to a swift but controlled stop. He withdrew the salvaged pulse carbine he'd taken off the body of a Sangheili mercenary and referred to his display. No threats or friendlies in range on his thermal. The field evaporated and the platform went dormant.

He stepped off into a vast underground facility with dark-gray alloy walls that soared from the depths below and into the darkness above. There were walls on three sides of him and the shaft, leaving only one direction to go, along a long suspended pathway over nothing but open space, lit by hard light coming from channels in the path. Elfie was only able to build a small fraction of their location simply because the space was so large.

"I guess we're going this way," he muttered, starting across the bridge and feeling a little apprehensive.

He was going on faith now. The lake had been the last marker on the agent's map. All he knew now was that somewhere in the enormous underbelly of the fractured Halo ring was a hub where one could access the Conspectus network.

Simple, right?

But Horvath stayed on the path seemingly laid out for him. He'd walked for a few hours, stopping occasionally to rest, before thermal picked up an eye-shaped anomaly far in the distance. Eventually the pathway ended on a large platform extending over yet more open space. All around him, a curved multilevel facility rose from the depths and extended beyond his ability to view. The "eye" he'd been heading toward was actually the edges of a plasma burn through a massive arched doorway.

Avoiding the cooling slag pooled on the floor, he stepped through the hole and into a long chamber about ten meters high, with translucent screens streaming data. If he looked closely, he could see there wasn't just one layer of data filling a screen but several, one behind another going back farther than his eye could see. A console had once stood in the center of the room, but was now nothing but a melted pool of metal and bits of circuitry.

"Is there any way to access the data?" he asked Elfie.

"Without console access and permission protocols initiated, there is no way to retrieve the data."

"Damn it." He moved around the room, inspecting the data streams, but unable to access them. Disappointment settled on his shoulders. There had to be something he could do.

"I'm . . . I'm picking up a Spartan signature," Elfie announced suddenly.

Horvath froze, unsure he'd heard her correctly.

"Five human signatures in all." Fi wasn't given to exhibiting strong emotion, but there was a trace of excitement in her tone.

Like a bucket of cold water, the news stole his breath. "Okay. Show me."

Through the blueprint that populated on his display, he watched as five beautiful green signals appeared two levels above him, tracking almost out of range. Leaping through the hole, he took off down the path materializing on his HUD.

Adrenaline coursed through his veins as he scaled up balcony levels, leapfrogging from one to the next, then crossed a massive conduit cable to an access corridor that delivered him onto another long pathway.

His heart pounded out of sheer, unadulterated hope and complete desperation to catch up to them before they disappeared altogether.

Gaining on the targets, he sprinted down a wide pathway and up a ramp, hauling ass across a massive corridor to a hard-light bridge over an open cavity where he finally caught a visual of them at the other end of the long span.

The Spartan on his HUD should have picked up his signal, yet they kept moving. He came to a halt and shouted across the open space at the top of his lungs: *"STOP!"*

The word reverberated through the cavernous space, carrying and echoing until it faded into the unknown. The group paused and turned around. Somewhat light-headed, out of breath, and stunned, Horvath jogged across the bridge.

The Spartan separated from the group.

Jungle camo. Cradling a STORMFALL helmet and a BR75 service rifle. Pale hair, strong bone structure, perpetual frown . . . Nina Kovan. Fireteam Shadow. The Stoic. Sniper extraordinaire.

Jesus Christ.

Panting, Horvath ripped off his helmet. A deep throaty laugh skated past his lips, and once it started, he couldn't seem to stop.

She took a few more steps forward, her brow furrowing deeply as if she couldn't quite believe what she was seeing. Her eyes actually went glassy, and for a moment he saw the presence of deep, deep grief. His laughter eased, and he gathered his emotions, running a hand down his face, and letting out a loud, shaking sigh. Finally, after all this time . . .

"Well, I knew one day you'd lose it, Horvath, but didn't know I'd be the lucky one to witness it." And there was that typical sardonic style, a wry smile pulling one corner of her mouth. He'd never seen her hair below her ears before, and now it hung long and straight to her shoulders. Had it been that much time? "Where the hell have you been?"

"Ah . . ." He stumbled over a response, still trying to get hold of himself. His eyes were a little glassy too, but he didn't care. "You wouldn't believe me if I told you." He stared at her for another long second. "Goddamn, it is good to see you, Kovan. Really good. Your armor looks like shit, by the way."

She surprised him with a laugh and moved in for a brief hug and a slap on the back. "Have you actually seen yourself lately?"

He stepped back and glanced down. He'd been through one destructive event after another and could only image the picture he presented. Four others then approached; three men and one woman gave him the unimpressed once-over—hardened, weathered, war-bred faces eyeing him carefully. A rough-hewn group by the look of them, they had a no-bullshit aura and were loaded down with as much ammo and weapons as each could carry and wore a random collection of combat gear. The barrel of a rocket launcher peeked over the woman's shoulder and her vest was chock-full of ordnance, grenades, and explosives.

The oldest guy of the bunch narrowed his gaze. His shaggy sun-streaked hair was tied back and laugh lines curved around the weathered, tanned skin of his eyes. Those pale eyes seemed very familiar, but the beard obscured the bottom half of his face.

Recognition suddenly flashed through the man's gaze and his

mouth dropped open. "Horvath?"

Oh, he *definitely* knew that voice. "Shit. Murphy, is that you . . . ?"

Lieutenant and all-around kick-ass Pelican pilot TJ Murphy burst out laughing and walked right up to Horvath and slapped the Spartan a couple of times on the chest plate. "Jesus, man. It's good to see you."

To witness his sincerity and the raw joy in his expression made Horvath feel lighter and more unburdened than he had in weeks. A thought suddenly occurred to him as he remembered that Mayday call he'd picked up the second day on Zeta Halo. "Wait. Is this your group from the lifeboat?"

"Yeah." He moved aside to introduce the crew. "Robin Dimik and Isaiah Cameron. And Kovan picked up Bender here on day one."

The guy gave him a light nod. "Erik Bender," he said by way of introduction.

Horvath dipped his head in greeting, noting the guy had the look of an ODST, a big, capable-looking soldier who seemed at home in his skin—they all did—as he stood there with an assault rifle hanging against his front, both hands resting casually on top of the stock.

"Cameron," Horvath said, shifting his gaze to the young man. "Bridge comms, right?"

"Used to be. You can call me Cam," he replied easily.

"And the medic . . . Browning? The one I was talking to on comms?" He hadn't forgotten the promise he'd made to the man from his homeworld.

A somber curtain seemed to fall over their expressions.

Horvath's heart sank. "Ah, hell." The news stung. He wanted so desperately to have kept his oath. "I'm sorry."

"He's not dead," Dimik said, insulted.

"He was taken by the Banished," Kovan explained a little more kindly. "They used him to activate Forerunner tech."

Horvath wasn't sure how to respond to that. Being taken by the Banished . . . the kid was on borrowed time if not already gone.

"You humans are very slow. You must really make an effort to keep up," an annoyed female voice echoed from the other side of the bridge, approaching fast.

Horvath moved back and lifted a hand to his shoulder to grab his rifle, but noticed no one else seemed alarmed as a spherical Forerunner machine swept across the bridge. It stopped above them, pointing its blue eye from person to person. It then lit on Horvath and proceeded to scan him from bottom to top.

"This is Veridity," Kovan said.

"Submonitor 91 Adjutant Veridity," she introduced herself. *"We really must not delay."*

This day was full of surprises. He moved closer to Kovan. "Wanna give me the sitrep?"

"We're following her to a place called the Conservatory. C'mon, I'll fill you in as we go. We should be making camp soon."

He fell in step beside Kovan as the submonitor led them on, but before he asked for more intel, there was something more pressing that he needed to know. "I've been out of the loop and alone since day two, was separated from Fireteam Intrepid during the explosion that tore the ring apart. Have you made contact with my team?"

"No," she said, shaking her head. "And none of us have heard anything from *Infinity* since we made landfall."

"Wait," Cam said from behind him. "You've been alone since day two?"

"That's right."

"So . . . we're the first humans you've seen in months . . . ?" Murphy pondered that surprising revelation.

Horvath nodded and cast a glance over his shoulder. "After the ring split apart, I ended up on a small ring fragment that had flipped upside down. Was stuck there with a Bloodstar Brute."

Dimik winced. "A *Bloodstar* Brute? How'd you make it back?"

"We reprogrammed a damaged sentinel and used its impulse drive to fly back to one of the larger fragments."

"Hold up," Bender said, stopping. "You're telling us you and a *Bloodstar Brute* reprogrammed a sentinel and you used it to fly through *open space*?"

They'd all now halted and were staring at him with varying expressions of disbelief. It was just wild enough a tale to ring true.

Kovan snorted. "Show-off." And kept walking.

As they continued, Cam asked, "How the hell did you get a Brute to cooperate rather than tear you to pieces?"

"He didn't have a choice. Neither of us did. The gravity and atmosphere on the fragment were failing. It was either we worked together or died together."

"Surprised he didn't choose the latter anyway," Murphy said.

"Oh, he tried a few times, believe me. Gorian—"

Kovan whirled on him so quickly that he nearly bumped into her as she gripped the edges of his chest plate. "*Gorian?*" This close, he saw clearly the history in her eyes, the pain and fury.

"I . . . take it you know him," he responded evenly.

She frowned and finally let go, turning away and starting off again.

Horvath let it lie. They'd make camp at some point, and then he hoped he'd have all his questions answered.

CHAPTER 32

Conservatory
Zeta Halo
May 3, 2560
Day 143

The boat crew made camp in the shadow of a massive power conduit that ran along a wide avenue. Cam tossed MREs while Dimik handed everyone a water ration and an energy bar. Murphy, though, couldn't stop staring at Horvath. The passage of time was written plainly on the Spartan's face. Months of living on the ring, fighting, surviving . . . Wavy dark-brown hair hung long enough that it was tied behind the Spartan's neck. A beard covered the lower part of his face. Horvath was already a big, burly, good-natured troublemaker—the kind you wanted at your back—but now his gruff appearance made him into an even larger presence.

Kovan was in the process of relaying the events on the Halo ring before and after the explosion, and the state of the UNSC presence as she knew it, all things they'd heard or seen themselves plenty of times before.

"And so you've heard nothing about Captain Lasky, Palmer . . . the Chief?" Horvath asked.

"No. And it's been mostly quiet since what happened at the *Reverie*."

"*Mortal Reverie?*"

"You don't know?"

"Trust me when I say I've been offline and out on my own."

"She crash-landed mostly intact, served as a rally point for a while, had a number of fireteams operating out of the site. Eventually, things fell into place for us to make a move against the Banished, and Griffin, Sarkar, Panago, and Malik drew straws to assassinate Escharum. But the mission failed. Griffin was apparently the only survivor . . . managed to get word to us that the Banished were mustering a force to retaliate against *Reverie* . . ." Her voice dropped and she was quiet for a long time before she offered a half-hearted shrug. "We were outnumbered a hundred to one. It was . . ."

"A bloodbath," Bender muttered.

"Vettel made it," Kovan said. "Sorel and Mako too. Stone made contact with them for a little while, said they were trying to find out more about the ring repairing itself, and Vettel, he struck out to look for Griffin."

It might have happened some time ago, but the memories of those two days were fresh in Murphy's mind. The last thing he wanted to hear was a recap of the details concerning that awful night, which already haunted him enough as it was. As he tore into a chunk of the bland energy bar, he changed the subject. "How did you end up on our tail?"

The monitor, Veridity, moved closer, hovering just beyond Kovan's shoulder, apparently curious to hear Horvath's side of things as well.

Horvath nudged hair out of his eyes as he gathered his

thoughts, letting out a small laugh as if unsure where to start. "Well . . . when I was marooned on that fragment and found Gorian, he was trapped inside a Phantom with a Brute captain and a couple of pilots—all dead. Their ship was carrying excavation tools and crates of stone artifacts that we haven't seen in our databases before. They seemed to hold some importance to the Banished, so I stole the flight data recorder, and once I made it back from the fragment, retraced its path to find out where they'd been excavating and what they've been looking for."

"And did you?" Bender asked him.

"Not exactly. I found what seemed to be ancient ruins and a dying ONI operative, Kate Stalling. She was part of asset recovery."

Dimik glanced around the group. "Am I the only one who doesn't know what asset recovery is?"

"ONI runs an asset recovery division," Kovan answered. "Operatives are pulled from special ops across the military and trained to hunt down high-value assets. That often includes Forerunner artifacts and technology."

"They're some of the best survivalists and trackers in the business," Horvath said. As he stared off into the darkness, it was clear to Murphy that the memories of finding the ONI operative weighed on his mind. "Gorian and a Sangheili blademaster, Jega 'Rdomnai—they left her in a bad way.. . ." He ran a hand down his beard. "Never seen anyone hang in there in that state . . . said she'd been on the ring since before the Banished arrived, hunting intel on the same artifacts the Banished have been excavating. I think she must have uncovered evidence, something that made her think there's more to Zeta Halo than we know. She left a crude map, said they'd go to some kind of data hub next, which I think I found, but—"

"They got there first," Kovan finished for him. "Jega and Gorian. Stone's recon took her to the same data hub and she saw them access a control panel and then retrieve two data streams. They were after the ring's defensive systems."

As expected, Horvath had the same stunned reaction they'd all had upon the news. Kovan brought him up to date on how they met Veridity, what the data nodes were, and how Stone had managed to steal it from Jega 'Rdomnai and Gorian.

"So this data," Horvath said, taking it all in, "it's not just local defenses . . . it includes the ring's current status and coordinates. Information that the folks back home would be able to use to locate Zeta Halo and send reinforcements here."

"That's right," Kovan said. "We'd just need a way to relay it. Some kind of—"

"*Supraluminal communications array?*" Veridity spoke up. "*We can do that from any beacon tower. We only need access to them, something I can procure from the installation's monitor—Despondent Pyre.*"

"So that's it," Horvath said with a weighty sigh. "If we can bring the full weight of the UNSC here, we could kick the Banished off this ring for good."

Kovan nodded. "And for what it's worth, I think your ONI operative was right. There is more to this ring than we know— more threats than the Banished alone. During recon, Stone ran into some strange flying creatures that were attacking both her and the Banished. They actually took weapons from the Banished and were using them on anything that got too close."

"Hold on," Horvath said. "You're telling me that there's another intelligent species on Zeta Halo—and they're taking down Banished and then using their weapons?"

"That's what she saw. Maybe something they ran into down here during their excavations? When I found Browning, he told me that the Banished used him to open a stasis pod Escharum had brought up from beneath the *Reverie*."

Instantly Murphy remembered the strange outline in the rectangular panel he'd seen in the chamber at the outpost.

"According to his story, it's intelligent," Kovan continued. "Called itself the Harbinger—he said it was different from anything we've seen before. And when she woke, she told Escharum that 'everything we know will be undone.' And he was on board with that. Their goals seem to align somehow."

"What the hell, Kovan?" Dimik said, leaning forward, elbows on her knees. "You said he was being used to unlock Forerunner tech. When were you going to mention the part about him waking up a whole new species?"

Murphy completely sympathized. It came as a shock to him as well. They'd had this conversation before about keeping secrets; but he guessed that, as a Spartan, Kovan was used to keeping her intel close to the chest—it had been ingrained in her, part of her life and duty for such a long time.

"I saw no need to mention it until it's officially confirmed. All I had was Browning's account until now, and—"

"And that wasn't enough?" Cam asked in that quiet way of his—not confrontational, just straightforward. "It's Browning. Like he's going to make something like that up?"

"No . . ." Kovan replied easily, not getting rattled by the group's reactions. The stubborn tilt to her chin told Murphy that there was much more to the story, and if he'd learned anything about this Spartan, it was that she always had a reason. "He . . . wasn't in good condition. . . ."

"Ah, hell," Dimik murmured, dragging a hand through her hair and leaning back.

It was a nice way of saying he'd been tortured by the Banished and likely not in his right mind, which meant Kovan had to question how reliable a witness he'd been.

Horvath broke the gulf of silence growing among the team. "You mentioned Stone's recon and how she got the data back," he said to Kovan, "but where is she now?"

A steely curtain seemed to slide over Kovan's features. No one moved or knew if they should speak up.

"Here," Kovan answered after a long moment. "This will help." She tossed Horvath a data chip from her secondary port. "I transferred this from Stone's armor."

Frowning, he grabbed his helmet, slipped it on, and then inserted the chip into his neural port.

After some time, Horvath removed his helmet and the data chip, handing it back to Kovan, eyes a bit red and looking angry and shaken. "And they're headed to the Conservatory now, Jega and Gorian."

She nodded.

"Good," he ground out, barely containing the fury in his tone. Then he eyed the submonitor for a long moment. "And you—what do you get out of all this?"

At first, Veridity didn't reply, and Murphy wondered if she was even listening, but then her central eye snapped to Horvath. *"The same as you, Spartan. We need to release the monitor, Despondent Pyre, and expel the Banished from this installation."*

"And the Harbinger?"

"I do not have access to any records of her kind. I only learned of her through the activities of the Banished. I know nothing of her loyalties or plans."

"We'll assume she's hostile until we know otherwise," he said. "Once we get to the Conservatory, the goal is twofold then. Free Despondent Pyre and send a message to the UNSC with the ring's coordinates."

"No," Kovan corrected. "The goal is threefold." She stared at Horvath intently. "Eliminate Gorian and Jega 'Rdomnai."

And they'd do whatever they could to see it through. They all would. Rubicon Protocol.

"All right then. Those are solid goals," Murphy said at last. "With Veridity's help, we'll be able to finish what Stone started."

CHAPTER 33

Lucas slumped against the wall as tears tracked down his dirty face. His body shook uncontrollably and his chest burned as though all of his pain and exhaustion and fear and hyperawareness had been gathered around his heart like dry tinder and set ablaze. Nightmares plagued his sleep—the kind where he failed to escape, unable to work the latch to an unlocked door or running in place when the path to freedom was clear. Waking or sleeping, there was no safe place, nowhere to rest where he wasn't on alert or overwhelmed. The logical part of his brain rarely won out over the survival part. But there were times when he knew he was losing it, knew extreme PTSD had a grip on him and he needed to try to take whatever steps possible to help himself cope.

Knowing and doing, however, were two entirely different things, too far apart to bring together, and with every moment spent in Banished captivity or in the presence of the Harbinger, the distance grew greater.

He was past the point of recovery, of tending to his own

damaged mind and body. He no longer had the strength to mentally work his way through.

"I can't do this anymore." His lips barely moved, the words coming like a whispered prayer, over and over. He ran both trembling hands down his wet face. "I can't go back there again. I can't do it." The volume rose until he was shouting. "Can't do it. *Can't do it. Can't do it!*"

"Deep breaths, Lucas." His neighbor's voice echoed through their shared wall. "You can handle it. Just focus, all right? Inhale. Exhale. That's all you have to do right now. In. Out . . ."

Lucas grabbed on to that dependable voice like a lifeline. *Breathe in. Breathe out.*

Eventually his heart rate slowed and his insides no longer felt bloated with pressure. Now there was just a hollow void that quickly filled with hopelessness. "This is it," he said, letting his head fall against the wall at his back. He stared through bleary eyes at the ceiling. "This is what it's all come to. All twenty-five years, growing up, going to school, studying my ass off in nursing college . . . just to end up here."

He laughed, shaking his head at how ridiculous it had all turned out, despite his best efforts. "Not sure holding on is worth it anymore, you know? It all seems pointless." Because the end would be the same, regardless. There was no help coming, no one to breach the Tower and be the hero, and it was getting harder and harder to slog through each miserable day.

"Hey, come on. It's not over yet. Hang in there. Every day we survive is another day closer to getting out of here."

"How do you figure?" Every day here was a day closer to the end, in Lucas's opinion. "How can you stay so positive?" His neighbor had been the warden's favorite torture subject ever since

Lucas had been interred in the Tower. He wasn't sure how the guy had managed to stay alive this long. He was pretty sure Chak 'Lok kept healing him and bringing him back from the brink of death, just so he could torment the man anew.

How can you stay so positive? wasn't exactly a fair question. His neighbor made an effort to help him hang on when, in reality, the guy had to be even more miserable than Lucas could imagine. He had to know their chances of ever getting out of the Tower alive were slim to none.

"A situation can change on a dime," the man said at length. "You never know who could burst through that door. Trust me on that."

When he spoke in such a way, with unflinching conviction and experience, it stirred Lucas's curiosity. "You ever going to tell me your name?"

"I told you—"

"Yeah, I know," he replied, sighing, "it's better for me to not know. The less I know, the safer I am." Lucas had news for him . . . no one was safe. Not here. Not in the Tower. Not even out there.

His neighbor grew quiet for a long moment, and Lucas heard some shuffling as though the man was trying to get comfortable and simply couldn't.

"You doing okay over there?" he asked.

"Seen better days."

The answer was clearly pained. "What are they doing to you?" Lucas asked quietly.

After a few moments, his neighbor said: "Seeing how much to push before things break." He gave a short, sarcastic laugh. "Not sure how much more I have left to break. . . . Have to admit, this isn't exactly how I thought I'd end up, either."

"You want me to throw your words back at you?" Lucas said with a weary smile.

"I'd rather you not. Whatever worth I have to them is ebbing away. . . . But you've got an ace up your sleeve. They're keeping you alive for some reason. So you have value."

"If you say so."

If his neighbor was favored by the warden, then Lucas was favored by the Harbinger. And he couldn't help but wonder when his value would start slipping.

He'd spent time with her again today. Was that twice this week? He wasn't sure, couldn't access the clarity of mind he needed to be sure. It was all starting to blend together, his time with her always fuzzy and ringed with uncertainty. And while their meeting this time had felt surprisingly normal—he ate, she spoke—something unsettling stirred within him, something dark and twisted.

Maybe if he talked it out, he could figure out what was wrong. . . . He wanted to tell his friend about the encounters with the Harbinger, about what was happening to him—but for some reason he hadn't been able to. Even now as he opened his mouth to replay the conversation, the words on his tongue did not match the ones in his mind. "Two . . . four—" Stunned, he froze. *What the hell?* He tried again. "Two . . . four—" Panicked, he slapped a hand over his mouth, his blood pressure rising. "Oh God. What— what the hell did she do to me . . . ?"

"You okay, buddy?"

"No. I . . . don't know what's wrong with me. I'm trying to tell you what happened to me, but I can't . . . get the words out. It's like something in my head is preventing me."

"Try again."

Slowly, Lucas let his hand fall and tried again. Numbers—that's all that he could form inside his mind.

He covered his mouth again, stifling an alarmed cry.

"Try to talk about something else. Anything else."

Fear gripped Lucas's throat. What if nothing came out? Like a switch had been hit, and that was it?

He swallowed down the massive lump in his throat and forced himself to speak. "My name is Lucas Browning . . . I was born on Alluvion . . . I'm a combat medic for the UNSC Marine Corps . . ." Relief crashed over him that the numbers didn't come out again.

"Okay, so you can still talk. You just can't recount what happened to you. Sounds like they don't want you revealing your interactions to anyone. Better to stay on the safe side, then, and keep it to yourself for right now."

Lucas had been using Kovan's transmitters to record every time he was taken to the House of Reckoning to see the Harbinger. She never seemed to suspect anything. He'd been dropping the devices near the tarmac afterward, hoping they'd be carried by the wind and jettison a signal to a UNSC receiver somewhere on the ring. Even if he couldn't reveal the conversations himself, those recordings had to be worth something.

"How is this even possible?" Lucas openly wondered. "What's happened to me?"

"Don't let it weigh on you right now. You're not with them. You're here . . . and I'm with you," his neighbor responded thoughtfully. "We'll get through this together . . ."

Lucas believed him, and in the moment that was enough.

CHAPTER 34

The closer they came to the Conservatory, the more Kovan imagined Jega 'Rdomnai's demise. As macabre as it was, she'd replayed Bonita Stone's death several times, studying the blademaster's movements and techniques, looking for patterns and weaknesses. Kovan was well aware that, with her damaged armor, she was the weaker opponent, so when they met in battle, she couldn't afford to make a mistake.

Ahead, Submonitor Veridity's blue glow guided them to a sheer wall that stretched solid in all directions with no end in sight. The alloy was dark gray and inset with a deep geometric pattern centering on a stylized arched door cut with hard-light panels that cast the alloy in a glossy shade of blue. The arched outline of the door repeated, expanding outward.

Veridity paused in front of the arch, her optical lens shooting a beam that moved from the bottom of the path and up the tall doorway. The metal and light folded back and disappeared, allowing them entry. Once everyone had crossed the threshold, the submonitor scanned again and the door solidified once more. *"We are now inside the Conservatory complex."*

"And the Banished?" Kovan asked as Spartan Horvath came up beside her.

"They have gathered at an exposed part of the facility's exterior." The AI's tone was amused. *"There is a large number of them and they are establishing a fortified position. They will not find a door and will be forced to create one of their own. That will take some time."*

"You don't seem too concerned," Horvath commented.

"The Conservatory is a labyrinth that will keep the Banished occupied for the time being—it is specifically designed to confuse those who enter without invitation. They may never find Pyre's Cradle."

"Then we'll just have to deal with them later," Kovan said, gritting her teeth.

Veridity then turned 180 degrees and moved forward. As they fell into step behind her, Horvath brushed shoulders with Kovan. "You sure your crew is up for that?"

Kovan glanced back, understanding what he was saying. Once they completed their mission with Zeta Halo's monitor, Despondent Pyre, Jega and Gorian remained as imminent threats. And despite the heavy Banished presence gathered outside the Conservatory, neither Spartan was going to pass up the opportunity to take the bastards down. "They're free to do what they want, but they'll have our backs regardless."

"You seem certain of that."

There was no good way to explain it, what they'd been through together and the bond they'd formed . . . at this point, Kovan could no more walk away from them than they from her.

The Conservatory was indeed a maze, though the word didn't

quite do the enormity of it justice. It was dark and sleek and lit with subtle blue light. Weaving through massive levels were countless ramps, bridges, corridors, chambers with walls that streamed blue code . . . and they were seeing just a fraction of its size as Veridity took them on the direct route.

In less than an hour they made it to the Cradle, a large chamber with a pyramidal structure in the center with a flat, rounded top, accessible from the floor by a broad ramp. Atop it was a plinth console and in the very middle hovering above it was, presumably, Despondent Pyre. The monitor had a gleaming dark-gray casing, its dulled-out optical lens canted down and lit with just a hint of green. It seemed quiet and peaceful, as though in a state of hibernation. Several submonitors hovered around the perimeter, also seemingly in a state of rest.

As Kovan proceeded up the ramp, Veridity stopped her near the top. *"Cortana sequestered them within an energy barrier that I and my fellow submonitors have been unable to deactivate. Reclaimers, however, might bring an entirely different result."*

"Kovan," Horvath said, alerting her to a long console at the base of the Cradle. She gestured for him to attempt access—his AI was in a much better state than hers to begin the process of breaking the hold over the monitors.

As Murphy and crew moved slowly around the room to get a good look at their surroundings, Veridity hovered at the top of the Cradle, just outside of the barrier.

"Good ole Reclaimer access for the win," Horvath said, looking up from the console as a golden energy barrier shimmered into visibility and then faded into nothing.

Veridity flew right up to Despondent Pyre and shouted, *"Wake up!"*

The crew shared a bewildered look as Kovan motioned them toward the ramp. When Pyre didn't wake, Veridity began moving erratically around the silent monitor before facing it once more and shooting a bright-blue beam straight into Pyre's lens; again, nothing happened. Frustrated, Veridity backed off with a loud huff.

"She does this sometimes," the submonitor said after pulling herself together.

"Does what, exactly?" Kovan asked, noticing the other monitors were still in a state of dormancy.

"Falls into despair. She is old and weighed down by the past. Always contemplating Forerunner decisions and their consequences . . ." She turned her attention back to Pyre.

"This usually works." Veridity flew forward, ramming Pyre with her carapace and knocking the monitor back a meter.

Pyre simply floated back to her original position, though more green seemed to bleed into her lens, and she roused slightly. *"Ah, Submonitor Adjutant Veridity . . ."* a rather proper-sounding female voice issued from the carapace. *"Please join us in our contemplation."*

Pyre's light began to dim again and Veridity hurried to prevent it, shouting, *"Reclaimers are here!"*

"Oh?" Pyre's eye cast slowly around, finally landing on the humans standing in the chamber, gazing up at her.

Kovan immediately expected a scan—typical of a monitor— but Pyre's interest faded on a sigh. *"Irrelevant,"* she said tiredly.

"Irrelevant?!" Veridity was apoplectic, her blue light shifting to red. *"The Banished continue to desecrate our installation! Our duty must be to conserve the ring, to protect its biomes, its wildlife, the Monument; it is all under our care! Entire sections have already been lost! It's time to wake up!"*

This didn't seem to be going as smoothly as the submonitor had hoped, and Veridity was losing herself in her own outrage. Horvath joined Kovan on the top of the Cradle, the boat crew waiting anxiously at the foot of the structure. "What now?" he asked.

"We need them. I say let it play out a little bit before we intervene. . . ." Monitors were tricky, from what she knew, and anything uttered would surely be heard. It was better to stay quiet for now and let them work it out. She cast a glance Horvath's way as he dipped his head. If things didn't turn around soon, then more drastic measures would have to be taken.

"We have survived this long by being discreet and patient," Pyre told Veridity. *"Eventually anything that lands here either leaves or dies. That has been the way of things for so long. Let them war on the surface. This installation will repair itself. In another hundred years, they will have been forgotten . . . and we will still be here."*

"Then give me full access to the communications network," Veridity snapped.

Pyre regarded the submonitor. *"Why would you need such a thing?"*

"Why do you care?"

"No. Permission is denied."

"What do you mean, no?" Veridity asked incredulously. *"The Banished have obtained access to the ring's local defenses from the Conspectus network. They have no plans to leave! And . . ."* she said, in what seemed to be a hushed tone, *"they have awakened the Harbinger! How can you allow—"*

Despondent Pyre went very still, silently regarding Veridity. *"So the Harbinger is free."*

"The Banished brought her cylix to the surface and used a human prisoner to release her," Kovan said. "They seem to be working together."

A golden beam suddenly shot out from Pyre's central eye and scanned Kovan and Horvath before enveloping the submonitors, releasing them from their imposed contemplation. Apparently it hadn't been voluntary. Pyre swept toward them, appearing to communicate orders. Almost instantaneously they flew from the Cradle and dispersed in different directions.

Pyre returned to hover above the central apex of the Cradle. *"The Harbinger must be stopped at all costs."*

"Give me access to the beacon towers," Veridity implored. *"Allow the humans to call for reinforcements. We must rid our installation of the Harbinger and the Banished."*

"It seems that we have lost control of the energy beacons," Pyre revealed. *"An unfortunate result of the human ancilla's actions. However, a security override may bring one of them back online. One moment . . ."*

Kovan removed Stone's data chip, intending to give it to the monitor for decryption. On it was everything Stone had copied from the stolen data streams—everything they needed to get UNSC reinforcements to the ring.

"Keep it," Pyre said. From detached to determined, it was like night and day, the change in the monitor. But Kovan certainly wasn't going to complain about it or the dismissive tone—after all, she could relate. There were times when intense focus took over and all the inconsequential things were simply brushed aside without much thought to the delivery method. They were so close to reaching their goal it didn't matter how the monitor was behaving, just as long as she acted.

"Override sequence is complete," Pyre said as the plinth came to life. A port extended and from it emerged a sleek two-toned data key, one half alloy, the other hard light. *"You must insert the key*

into the central plinth within the beacon tower. Once the security override sequence is complete, adaptation protocols will instruct the beacon to send a supraluminal message into human-occupied space with Installation 07's current galactic coordinates and the site's pertinent data."

"Excellent!" Veridity exclaimed as Kovan took the key from the port. "Come, Reclaimer friends, I will lead you from the Conservatory and to the nearest beacon!"

Horvath started down the ramp; as Kovan followed, she paused and looked over her shoulder, giving Pyre a nod of thanks, which the monitor returned.

As they joined the boat crew, Veridity was already making her way to the chamber exit. "Not you, Veridity," Pyre said.

"But—"

Pyre's lens brightened and a yellow beam shot out, seizing hold of the submonitor. "We have work to do."

Horvath spun. While he still cradled his rifle versus taking aim, his stance was ready to shift at a moment's notice. "She's our quick ticket out of here."

Otherwise it might take them days or weeks or even months, if Veridity was to be believed, to find their way out of the labyrinth.

"The Reclaimer is right!" Veridity cried out, struggling and managing to break free. "I am their only way out of the Conservatory!"

Kovan's HUD lit up as unintelligible code was dumped into her internal software system, and a path out of the Conservatory built on her display.

"Those directions will lead you safely out of the facility," Pyre said. "If what Veridity has said about the Harbinger is true, I cannot expend any of the installation's executor staff to assist you."

Pyre turned away as Veridity was pulled back to the Cradle and the door to the chamber slid open—a pretty clear get-out warning. And while the crew was looking a little baffled by these events, they ultimately knew the rest of their journey could be finished without the aid of the submonitor. Given what just happened, it would have to be.

"We have everything we need," Kovan said. "Move out."

CHAPTER 35

Murphy kept pace behind Kovan as she led the way out of the Conservatory. The path apparently laid out by the monitor took them to a four-meter-wide translocation pad. As soon as Kovan stepped onto the bright surface, a holographic console appeared.

"Can you activate it?" Horvath asked.

Since the pad was level with the floor and barely discernible, Murphy had to grab Bender's arm and drag him within the perimeter. "Hurry up. Stay on the pad," he said, motioning to the floor as Cam and Dimik gathered close.

"Pyre provided the correct symbols," Kovan answered as shining Forerunner hieroglyphics appeared over the console. She pressed a sequence of the glyphs, and a compressed slipspace field generated around them.

"What the—" Cam's eyes widened as the translucent field of energy activated.

"Hold on to your lunch, kids—it's about to get dicey," Horvath announced.

Ah. This was going to be a bi—

Vertigo sucker-punched Murphy in the gut as he gripped Bender tightly, squeezing his eyes closed and gritting his teeth, every muscle in his body going taut.

It was over in an instant, the miniature slipspace field delivering them to another pad on Zeta Halo's translocation grid. Fresh air filled Murphy's lungs as he opened his eyes and viewed a rocky outcrop about a kilometer or two from what he guessed was the exterior of the Conservatory. That was all Murphy saw before his gut wound up tight and then let loose the contents of his stomach; he dropped to one knee and puked out energy bar.

"Ugh. Goddamn . . ." Panting, he swiped an arm over his mouth and looked up to see Kovan standing at the precipice of the overlook. Horvath was bent over groaning. Dimik sat flat on her ass, green around the gills and dazed, and Cam had fared no better, while Bender was looking at everyone with a frown on his face, oblivious to their pain. "What the hell is wrong with everyone?" he asked.

"Adverse effects of translocation," Horvath ground out, turning his head Bender's way. "I see you're one of those annoying people not affected. . . ."

Bender grinned smartly.

"We've got a problem," Kovan interrupted, unshouldering her rifle. "Everyone get down."

The beacon lay just ahead, and it was occupied by Banished.

While the topography worked to their advantage, they took heed, hurrying off the pad and sliding a few meters down the outcrop to find cover behind the rocks. The beacon tower soared above the trees on an elevated platform like a sleek, etched sword blade glinting in the fading light of day. They had seen several of these towers during their time on Zeta Halo, but they were almost always populated by Banished, being used as a makeshift garrisons or lookout towers. The structure would intermittently launch a brilliant surge of blue energy from its center, disappearing somewhere in the sky above. The boat crew had usually given them a wide berth.

From their position, they could easily continue down the stony slope, cross the meadow, and enter the beacon with minimal visibility. But the site was well-defended and near enough to the Conservatory that any visual contact would lead to a very loud skirmish, and that had the potential to alert the enemy and bring reinforcements to bear in minutes.

Murphy could even hear the sounds, carrying across the distance, of the Banished forces building up a heavily fortified site in order to bore their way into the Conservatory. There had to be hundreds of them. "Well, this is going to be interesting," he said. "If we draw too much attention, we'll be outnumbered and outgunned on one hell of a scale."

"We'll have to be quick about it, then," Horvath said, all his focus on the beacon and the guards surrounding it.

"I'm counting the odds at about six to one—what about you?" Dimik asked him.

"Ten Grunts and eight Jackals on approach. Guessing the same on the other side. Two Elites near that entry there . . . and who knows how many inside."

"We need a closer look," Kovan said.

They double-timed it away from the translocation pad, heading into the trees and large boulders that peppered the alpine landscape behind the exposed outcrop, making their way full circle until they were back on the wooded hillside facing the beacon again. *That meadow is going to be an issue*, Murphy thought as he hunkered down by a boulder; Cam settled beside him. "Why the hell is it we're always outnumbered?" the ensign said as Dimik and Bender joined them.

"C'mon, now, if we were evenly matched, it just wouldn't be fair." Bender grinned. "Or fun." He spat on the ground to his left and checked the chamber in his assault rifle. "That ride left a weird taste in my mouth."

Murphy rolled his eyes at this. "I feel for you, man, I really do."

Bender chuckled as Dimik rooted through her vest and rucksack. "I've got eight MX-10 mini-bricks left . . . and enough grenades to make some yummy plasma sandwiches." Dimik was fond of mixing explosives, in this case sticking plasma grenades between two mini-bricks, the end result *extremely* powerful.

Horvath ducked down after checking out the opposition. "I like your style."

She broke into an easy, disarming smile. "Just wait and see what I can do if I ever get my hands on a blow pack and a spike grenade."

"As soon as things get hot here," Kovan broke in, "the Banished force from the Conservatory will hear the commotion and send reinforcements. Could be both aerial and ground. They'll come right up that pass." She gestured behind them to the wooded ravine a short distance on their left. "Dimik, you and Cam place the charges through that area—when the Banished fill it up, blow the whole thing to hell."

"I like your style too," Horvath commented under his breath, amused.

"You like anything that involves chaos," she replied.

He shrugged. "The bigger, the better. I'll clear the beacon approach. That should give you enough distraction to get inside and access the main controls. Murphy, Bender, you make your way as close to her position as possible. Once she activates the controls, she'll be a target. . . ."

"On it," Bender said. "We'll have her back."

"Here, you're gonna need this. . . ." Dimik passed Horvath her spare assault rifle, an MA5K she'd picked up in the wreckage field of a UNSC lifeboat. "It's got sixteen rounds left, and here's thirty more," she said, passing him a spare magazine. "Don't go crazy."

Murphy hid his smile. She had no idea that Horvath's suit was equipped with state-of-the-art gun control software and as soon as he touched the rifle, all relevant information would be fed instantly to his display. He felt a little pride in her words, though. In the beginning of their training, he'd constantly had to remind them to avoid fully automatic firing options to conserve ammo. In this environment, ammo was like gold; it had to be used precisely and sparingly.

"Got it," Horvath said, reaching across them to take the offerings.

Murphy had every confidence that Horvath could handle the Grunts and Jackals; it was the massive Banished force at the Conservatory that worried him. "Let's get this done quick," he said, then turned to Dimik and Cam. "How long do you need to set up?"

"Give us twenty minutes."

They'd faced the enemy countless times since crashing on Zeta Halo, and he hoped it had prepared them. Murphy's gaze passed over each face. Cam, Dimik, Bender . . . they'd become more to him than just friends and colleagues. They were family now. He'd looked out for them, taught them, yelled at them, and laughed and cried with them. The things they'd been through together had been extraordinary. And now the three of them were facing some pretty steep odds for the slightest chance that they might turn the tide. In all their time here, it was the best opportunity to do something bigger, something more than just being a thorn in the enemy's side.

"We all know what's at stake," Murphy said, shoving down the emotions and getting his game face on, "and we might never get another chance like this, so let's make it count." He jerked his head. "Go on, then."

"Roger that, Lieutenant." Cam gave him and Bender a quick rifle bump before he and Dimik set off, disappearing into the tree line.

"Murphy, Bender," Kovan said. "Let's get into position."

They headed out in the same direction, sticking low to the rocks as they made their way around the perimeter of the beacon, working their way closer. When Horvath started lighting things up, they'd make a run for the interior.

Twenty minutes later, Horvath sighted through the MA5K, Dimik's words echoing in his head as he targeted the methane tank of a Grunt chatting animatedly with four others around a portable shield unit at his ten o'clock. There were four similar units stationed in front of the beacon tower, and two plasma cannons with two groups of Jackals lurking closer to the structure. He played through his firing scenario one more time, and then said, "Look lively, folks," into the short-range comms link Kovan had given to him.

The armor-piercing round cracked through the calm air, lighting up the Grunt's methane tank. Immediately, the Spartan shifted aim across the units. One o'clock. Eight o'clock. Four o'clock. Four additional tanks blew in the blink of an eye and eliminated more than half of the Grunts. The Jackals dispersed, two jumping on the cannons while the others engaged their point defense gauntlets—energy shields fixed to their arms—and waited for the battle to come to them. Horvath shouldered the rifle, withdrew his M6, and sprinted to the first shield unit, taking out the Grunt behind it with three decisive head shots.

"Let's go!" Kovan darted from the rocks.

To keep up with her, Murphy ran as fast as his legs would carry him to the tower's base, flattening his back against it as Bender joined him. The Jackals in front were pulled toward Spartan Horvath's position, allowing them to ease quietly to the console at the left of the door. As soon as Kovan accessed the console and the door slid open, they slipped inside and hurried down a long corridor that led beneath the beacon. The corridor split at its end, turning hard to the left and right, both winding back in the opposite direction. Two Elites were stationed right at the center of the juncture, red-armored enforcers by the look of them.

Murphy's pulse beat wildly, adrenaline kicking in as he opened fire on the enforcers with the others, tagging one in the gut several times until its shield buckled and it dropped, before the other rolled into the left corridor. Quickly, he lobbed a grenade down after it, the explosion lighting the enemy's shields.

"Shit. It's gone stealth!" Bender yelled, eyeing the disappearing enforcer while biting the tip off a smoke canister and tossing it down the left corridor. The split path meant that any number of Banished could be on either side, waiting for them to turn the corner.

"Taking the left," Kovan said, turning hard down the corridor and disappearing into the smoke to meet whatever lay within. Murphy and Bender hung right, weapons raised and ready to fire.

In the corridor were two more Elites, already firing pulse carbines as soon as they came into view. Their shields flickered, showing that they'd absorbed a good bit of damage from Murphy's grenade and were probably disoriented. Bender took one down quickly with a headshot as Murphy dove next to the dead Sangheili enforcer, taking its mangler and firing a round from the floor. The hot tungsten spike buried itself into the remaining Elite's red harness and sent him off his feet and slamming into the wall.

Murphy sighted the right corridor, making sure it was clear, and then turned back toward the left where Kovan had disappeared. A flurry of weapon fire illuminated the smoke in the corridor, followed by the sound of two large bodies crumpling to the ground.

Kovan's voice cracked through comms. *I'm in and at the central plinth.*

He had no idea what would happen when she inserted the key and the beacon began to activate—nothing outwardly obvious, if they were lucky, but they had to assume the worst.

"Hurry," Murphy said, pushing to his feet and running toward Kovan's location from the left corridor. As they passed underneath the tower's base, vibrant blue energy roiled at the center of the beacon, no doubt the origin of the surges the beacon launched into the sky. The corridor eventually led into another circular chamber with a cathedral-type ceiling cut through with supports and spokes that rose in the center.

Kovan was already at the plinth, staring up as a holographic interface manifested. Golden code written in Forerunner symbols began flowing across the translucent background. Recognizing that the Banished could easily follow them down, Murphy motioned for Bender to take up position and guard the right side while he took the left. Just then a sudden surge of energy ran through the facility, collecting in its central chamber, where a conflagration of blue began churning in a violent circular pattern. A deep groaning sound began to shake the entire structure.

"Get ready," Murphy said. "There's no way anyone could have missed that."

"We must hold this area until the sequence completes and the message is sent," Kovan said.

"Got it," Bender replied.

Footsteps echoed down both corridors. "We've got more coming," Murphy said, taking aim. As soon as the first Banished soldier appeared, he started shooting. He had no idea how many there were, but he did know that as far as positions went, his own team was at an extreme disadvantage. On the flip side, they did have a Spartan in their corner and Bender was just crazy enough to help pull this off.

Murphy tossed a frag while Bender followed suit. When the dust cleared, the smoke swirled oddly. Damn it. Another Elite in stealth. And where there was one, there were probably more. He opened his mouth to warn Kovan, but was suddenly gripped by the neck from behind, lifted into the air, and thrown down the corridor. Bastard must have crept up on him before he threw the grenade.

Murphy landed hard on his back, the wind knocked out of him, his rifle clattering somewhere nearby. Instinctively he rolled, seeing Kovan block an Elite's attack while the sound of Bender's weapon echoed over the din.

An energy sword came out of the smoke, arcing down. Murphy scrambled out of the way, rolling onto his back and withdrawing his M6, firing, then ran toward Kovan's position.

"I'm out of ammo!" Bender shouted.

Murphy swiped a plasma rifle off the ground and winged it across the floor. "Incoming!"

Bender turned and snatched it, firing down the corridor.

Seeing that he was down to an M6, Kovan tossed her assault rifle to Murphy as she switched to her blade and Sidekick. The Elite she fought suddenly disappeared as the energy roiling in the central chamber began to pulse and compress.

From the left corridor, red plasma bolts streaked through the air, just missing the console. Shit. He saw it all clearly. The next round might hit the console. If they failed, then everything they'd done, everything they'd been through, would have been for nothing. Bender knelt, firing continuously down the corridor until a plasma round slammed into his chest plate and sent him tumbling back. The plasma ate through the plating as Bender frantically tried to pull his armor off before it went clear through to his skin.

Kovan had made it back to the console and was protecting it with her body, scanning the corridor where the stealth Elite had disappeared. Murphy then saw the other Elite appear in Bender's former position, taking aim with his pulse carbine, his small eyes narrowing behind his red helmet. He wouldn't miss the console this time. Murphy got to his feet and ran, leaping as high as he could as the pulse carbine pumped out a barrage of bolts.

Superheated plasma slammed into his lower chest, flipping him backward as the energy above the chamber compressed into a single shining pale-violet beam before it shot up the central power shaft at blinding speed. Pain stole his breath as he hit the floor. He gasped for air, but none came.

Kovan's form appeared in his field of vision as she leapt over him and fired relentlessly into the Elite's face until it fell dead to the floor.

They'd done it. The message had been sent. That was all that mattered.

Tears clouded Murphy's eyes as his insides burned, the smell of flesh and the acrid tang of plasma filling his nose. His back screamed as he felt the plasma eat through his spine, and after that, all he felt was very numb and very cold, so cold he shook all over.

Or was that the floor shaking?

Yes. Dimik's explosions—he could hear them.

As Bender slid down next to him and Kovan knelt by his side, Murphy's lips twisted into a smile and his body relaxed—he was so damn tired of fighting . . . so tired of pretending he didn't miss home, that he wanted desperately to go back.

To autumn in Lexington, the chilly air, the crisp scent of apples and fallen leaves. He remembered it well. Running up the hill behind his house with a bucket of paper airplanes . . .

CHAPTER 36

Horvath didn't have a visual yet, but he tracked Cam and Dimik through his display as they hauled ass toward the beacon after detonating the pass. *"Aerial contact,"* Elfie warned as a couple of Banshees streaked overhead, laying down plasma fire. Immediately he finished off the last Jackal with a vicious twist to its thin avian neck, relieved it of its forearm shield and plasma pistol, and then ran for the mounted plasma cannon.

He grabbed both firing mechanisms, standing behind the cannon and taking aim, unloading on the Banshees as they tracked overhead, taking one out while the other banked and flew out of sight. A Phantom appeared next, a kilometer away, coming in low over the treetops. It slowed to a hover near the overlook that housed the translocation pad. A hulking shadow stood in its open bay door. Horvath's body went completely still.

A Brute in red Bloodstar armor jumped from the Phantom and landed on the flat rock, the sound carrying and ringing through the Spartan like a bell. The Jiralhanae straightened to his full height, a brute shot hanging loose in his grip and extra ammo on a sling across his chest.

Gorian.

The murderous alien's deep, slow laughter echoed across the open space as he stared down the slope toward the beacon.

Should've killed him when I had the chance. . . .

"Spartan Horvath, you are in no condition to face that Brute again," Fi warned.

Since when had that ever stopped him? Besides, he didn't have a choice. It was either fight or surrender. And he sure as hell wasn't surrendering.

Horvath turned as Bender and Kovan exited the beacon without Murphy. He knew instantly by the pale, grim expression on Bender's face that the lieutenant hadn't made it. It was a loss that stung, but there was no time to dwell on it as Kovan tossed him a pulse carbine. "Go. We'll hold them off," she said. They were in a no-win situation—Gorian bearing down on them, the Banished making their way around the detonated pass, aerial support at their beck and call. "No mercy."

Horvath nodded. "No mercy." They'd done what they'd set out to do—shot a warning message through the debris-littered space around Zeta Halo and out somewhere into the galaxy. The rest—taking out as many Banished as they could, with as much prejudice as they could—was gravy.

He shouldered the rifle and strapped on the dead Jackal's energy shield. Bender tossed him the hilt of an energy sword, taken from some unlucky Sangheili inside the beacon, he guessed. Horvath caught it and stuck it to his mag-clamp, dipping his head in thanks, then jogged across the edge of the meadow and up the rocky slope to meet the Brute one final time.

"Spartan Horvath, you are not—"

"Can it, Fi," he said, slowing to a walk halfway up the slope, removing all thoughts and emotions and focusing solely on the fight ahead.

The Bloodstar stared at Horvath as he approached, a wicked smile growing on his face. "You," said Gorian approvingly.

"Yeah, me. Still breathing."

"Not for much longer, pup. You have lived only to meet the true might of my fists." The Brute's lips drew back, revealing his fangs and more of his tusks. "Are you finally ready to die now?"

"And here I thought we had a good thing going."

Horvath kept his distance, grateful for the sloping terrain and the rocks. He had to play this smart; with his armor in its present condition, one hit from Gorian's brute shot—a handheld weapon that could fire four powerful explosives every three seconds—and it'd be game over. The weapon wasn't known for its great aim, so he'd use that to his advantage, along with the environment, and his all-around superior intellect. Gorian would no doubt put all of his focus on one thing—killing the Spartan—while Horvath would think smarter.

Baby steps.

Horvath aimed the carbine and rapidly fired pulse after pulse, targeting the Brute's armor and forcing the shielding to recoil and overload.

What ensued was a cat-and-mouse game as each brute shot grenade slammed into rock and exploded way too close for comfort. A few times Horvath went airborne, but was up and running, dodging and firing on the Bloodstar armor.

But he was running out of places to hide.

Kovan watched as a Terror Wraith emerged from the debris-clouded pass, hovering low over the ground, its menacing eight-bladed front bearing down on Cam and Dimik as they raced toward the beacon. Kovan swung around the mounted cannon that Horvath had vacated and fired at the single pilot, but the Wraith was well-armored and its gravity propulsion engine was nimble. Dimik and Cam separated as Banished infantry emerged from the trees around the pass.

A Thrasher missile shot up from the growing Banished force surging up the pass. "Missile incoming!" she shouted into the comms as Cam veered left, the first Wraith still on his tail. "Bender, the Wraith!" she yelled into the comms as she aimed the mounted cannon to the sky and began firing, hoping to hit the missile before it struck.

A horrified shout echoed in her earpiece. Kovan turned to see Cam across the field, his body prone behind the retreating Wraith as Bender ran out into the open, firing a plasma pistol he'd picked up from one of the Jackal corpses. He launched himself onto the vehicle, wedging the pistol into a narrow breach in its armor, and fired close-range at the pilot.

One of Kovan's shots streaked into the missile as it descended, igniting it over their heads, the massive concussive shock shoving her and everything else to the ground.

Kovan lay still for a few seconds, stunned, lines skating along her HUD. Debris pinged her armor as she pushed up and took stock, immediately seeing Dimik facedown and unmoving on the edge of the field.

Bender was on the ground next to the Wraith, struggling to rise to his hands and knees. Kovan ran to him. "Bender!"

"I'm good. . . ."

She hurried behind the Wraith to Cam's location. She knew he was dead before she got close, but she grabbed him by the back of the collar and dragged him toward the facility, laying him behind one of the energy shields. When Kovan turned to get Dimik, she was gone. Still alive, at least. Before she could search, a plasma mortar struck the ground nearby, driving her back toward the beacon as three Jackal squads and a band of Elite mercenaries led by Jega 'Rdomnai surged from the pass.

By Horvath's count, Gorian had three shots left. One hit the rock in front of the Spartan before he had a chance to dive, sending him off his feet and slamming into a nearby boulder, breaking it apart. He lay bent on the ground, trying to catch his breath and make his body move. He lifted his head as gravel tumbled down the slope, and the sounds of Gorian's footsteps grew louder.

As he went to roll to his feet, his gaze collided with . . . Dimik? What the hell was she doing here?

She was crouched behind the rocks along the tree line. Blood was smeared on the right side of her face and arm, and her skin was ashen, eyes wide with shock. Slowly she held up a spike grenade. Hope shot like lightning through Horvath's veins as she reached out on her hands and knees and laid the explosive device on the stone.

Suddenly she whipped her head around as though she heard something behind her, took one last look at him, and fled.

Spurred by her courage, Horvath forced himself up and ran a blazing path down and then around and in between rocks, coming back up the other side of the slope and circling around Gorian. The Brute noticed and merely laughed, heading back toward the top of the slope. "Tired yet, pup?" he called out, his voice dripping with arrogance.

As Horvath reached the overlook, the brute shot sang out, forcing him to dive onto his belly as the projectile flew overhead. His hand snaked out and he grabbed the handle of the spike grenade, surging up and running across the flat rock, drawing Gorian to fire again. The Brute just missed him.

Horvath leapt off the overlook, the last grenade from the brute shot passing below his armpit as he twisted his body in midair and flung the spike grenade toward Gorian's feet. The grenade struck the rock almost between his legs, instantly arming on impact.

The grenade exploded as Horvath hit the slope and rolled. It wouldn't be enough to kill the Jiralhanae, but the Brute's shields would pay the price, and a few errant shards might do some well-deserved damage. At least now they would be on a level playing field.

As soon as he found his footing, he was up and running back up to the overlook, only to glimpse Dimik pinned down behind a tree. His display showed two Jackals trying to flank her position. With extreme speed, he pulled the carbine, aimed for the head, and fired two consecutive bursts at each Kig-Yar. They dropped as Horvath tossed the hot, unvented carbine, intending to take the enemies' weapons, but at that moment, Gorian reached the overlook.

Horvath turned as the Brute charged. The energy sword that Bender had tossed to him earlier was still magnetically attached to his Mjolnir. He grabbed the hilt as the Brute's massive shoulder drove into his gut, lifting him high. Horvath punched the hilt into the side of Gorian's ribcage and fired it up. The blade slid easily through bone and tissue and organ and came out the opposite side of the ribcage.

"Your mistake was letting me live," Horvath ground out as the Brute's momentum slammed him down onto the translocation pad. He knew his opponent was dead when the Jiralhanae released a long, audible breath and settled about seven hundred kilograms of dead weight on top of him. Barely able to catch his breath, and pinned against the translocation pad, Horvath had a clear view to the beacon and of Dimik scrambling down the slope to join Spartan Kovan and Bender. His heart sank as a round from approaching enemy forces slammed into her shoulder. She fell and rolled as Bender ran to her aid.

While his lungs burned and his strength was waning, he shoved at the massive Brute corpse as a hum went through his body.

"Spartan Horvath, the translocation pad is—" Disbelief flew through him as he scrambled to free himself while a slipspace field materialized around him.

"No, no, no! *Goddamn it!*" he bellowed, furious, but it was already too late. He was swept away from the battlefield.

CHAPTER 37

Lucas sank into the back corner of the gravity lift, hiding behind Itacus and Chak 'Lok as the lift rose to the fourth level to deposit them into the care of a waiting Sangheili guard. The guard was always there, minding the way to the Harbinger's quarters. As soon as Itacus's massive hand hauled him up and pushed him out, Lucas's panic reached an all-time high. His entire body rattled and his legs gave out, leaving him trembling limp on the floor.

"How long has the human been this way, Chak?" the Elite asked.

"A matter of days," Chak 'Lok replied. "It seems their feeble minds cannot contain the power of her words."

"Closed space . . . off-limits . . ." Lucas found himself saying involuntarily. "Still there . . . they were still there . . . the only ones . . ."

"You should feel honored, human," Chak 'Lok said. "The truth has apparently set you free."

"Price paid . . . sentence given . . . we never knew . . . so old . . . so far . . ." He couldn't stop the words, the rambling, the shaking. . . .

"Bring him to her chambers. She has more to tell him, if his mind can last. . . ."

Lucas flinched. Then he smiled as Itacus grabbed his arm and jerked him up. They sounded so stupid. If only they knew. . . . Their ridiculous, stupid babble coming out of their stupid alien mouths compared so very little to *her*. Laughter bubbled up his dry throat, but it never made it past his vocal cords because they were already in use—always repeating.

Repeating.

He couldn't stop himself.

That which should not be forgotten.

Had to remember it. Had to.

Always.

Or else.

Price paid. Price paid. Price paid. Never knew. Never knew . . .

His feet barely touched the ground as he was moved forward. Like a ghost, he was, moving down the corridor, going on The Walk. Always the same—fifty-six steps. That's all it took. Fifty-six steps to hell.

Hell wasn't in some faraway, abstract place, or in another religiously defined dimension. It was right here, on this ancient construct. On Zeta Halo. Right down the hall.

Only fifty-six steps away. That's it. Simple.

He laughed.

And then he cried.

The laughter always brought the sour tang of tears to the back of his throat and a dry, dehydrated burn to his eyes. Every time he laughed, the sane part of him knew he was losing his mind.

At twenty steps, the fear began like clockwork, and he started to struggle.

Always at twenty. Not one step before. Not one step after.

No turning back. No turning back now.

Down the corridor and they were at the door. Just like that. Simple, see? Not far at all.

The door slid open. He was released and poked in the back hard enough to make him stumble inside. The door slid closed in a sweeping, sinister whisper that announced his arrival.

The Banished were never allowed inside during their time together.

Just him. And her.

The Harbinger.

That hideous . . . *thing* had worked her way into his brain with her silky words, gently poking and prodding until he caved and let them in, to burrow inside of him, all the way in, nestled down deep. Those words . . . and the terrible tale. Never forget the terrible tale. Each word spoken, every syllable uttered, was a prick, a bloodletting, until Lucas was bloated and choking on words, until they spilled out of his mouth as numbers. . . .

"Four, two . . . four . . . one . . . zero. Zero . . . two, two . . . one . . . four . . ."

The Harbinger was there by the window. Always by the window. Her lifeless black gaze bored into him, shiny like two polished stones, assessing, judging, calculating. Was she proud of him? Pleased, even?

"Do you see why this must be done?" Her attention shifted to the door beyond which Itacus and the warden waited. Oh, she didn't like them; he understood that much. *"These primitives, these . . . Banished."*

He didn't like them either.

Oh God, she was coming closer.

"We both have watched our worlds crumble under the instruments of Forerunner arrogance." He trembled so hard, his teeth vibrated together. She hovered so close, he could reach out and touch her— not that he'd ever . . . *"Your kind were once their rivals,"* she said thoughtfully. *"A long time ago."*

With a sigh, she moved away and he let loose a shaky breath.

"You were spared. Forgiven. A luxury not afforded to us. To those they could not control. Humanity was the culmination of their final plan.

"But plans change. . . ."

Her long pause made him look up, and he instantly regretted it because she was once again in front of him, smiling with a certainty that brought a chill to his bones. *"We are returning."*

CHAPTER 38

They'd arrived on the ledge poised above a deep gorge four days ago. Warm wind blew in from the far valley where a large storm cell churned slowly, green lightning flashing from deep inside the gray mass. Kovan's heavily damaged helmet and Mjolnir armor plates lay in a heap beside her.

"Jesus Christ," Bender grunted, wincing as he and Dimik hefted her backplate out of its emergency release attachment.

"Just lift it out of its lock and ease it down," Kovan instructed, sitting on a low rock as they stood behind her. "And then I can reach around and grab it."

"You do realize it weighs a million kilos," Dimik said as she and Bender lifted in unison. "And I'm working with one good arm here. . . ."

A click indicated the Mjolnir plate had freed from the dented lock. "You got it."

The two huffed and strained behind her, letting the plate down slowly and awkwardly until Kovan could twist her body and grab it, using her enhanced strength to help ease it the rest of the way to the ground. They had spent the better part of these four days mending wounds and repairing equipment, her armor easily being the most damaged and most challenging to rectify. Some of her plating could be removed and reconfigured in the field to accommodate for the damage it had taken, but the sheer weight of each piece and the complexity of the process was a severe limitation without the right equipment.

"Thanks," she said, watching Dimik limp toward a downed tree and sit down wearily on its trunk. She seemed to be doing better—after the battle at the beacon tower, Kovan had treated the plasma wound to her shoulder and a few other superficial wounds with biofoam. Bender, still standing behind Kovan, was nursing a nasty stab wound to his side, a broken nose, and a couple of cracked ribs.

She often though about the day they'd sent the message. Despondent Pyre's key had caused the beacon to function as a supraluminal communications array. Their message to humanity had been sent. But she didn't like to dwell on Murphy having to die in order to see it through. Didn't like to remember Cam dead on the ground, or looking up from the battle to see dozens of Banished closing in on the three of them, or Horvath and Gorian going down on the translocation grid, and not knowing which one had won that fight or where Horvath had ended up.

All she knew was that as soon as Horvath vanished, a thrasher missile obliterated the translocation pad and a large portion of the outcrop, turning it into rubble and eliminating any possibility of returning in the future to access the pad and find out just where on the ring Horvath had been deposited.

Kovan had kept firing and swinging for as long as her body had been able. When all her ammunition was gone, when her armor began to fail, when there didn't seem to be any hope left, she still fought. And that bastard Jega 'Rdomnai just watching it all as he directed his forces toward the beacon. She knew in that moment the crushing feeling of defeat, of not being able to avenge Stone or protect what was left of the boat crew.

Until the submonitor, that small orb of gray alloy and blue light, came barreling up the pass, focus beam raging from her lens, and everything faded away into black. . . .

Veridity had somehow escaped Pyre's reach and come to their aid, right when everything was closing in around them. She had miraculously retrieved and delivered them . . . well, somewhere on the ring. Where, exactly, Kovan didn't yet know.

"Here, eat this." An energy bar appeared overhead, dangling in front of her face. Kovan took it as Bender came around and eased himself into a stiff leaning position against the rocks. She could relate to his pained expression. She was broken and bruised and feeling every ounce of the pain that came with her injuries. But none of it mattered. She would heal, her augmentations giving her that advantage at least. Recovery for her companions, however, would take far longer.

"You think she'll ever come back?" Dimik asked, watching the storm start to roll across the green valley.

"Who, Veridity? I don't know." Right now, the submonitor was probably back in the Cradle, arguing with Despondent Pyre about what their next move should be. Or she was out there going rogue, helping to thwart the Banished just like they'd been doing from day one. And, Kovan hoped, would soon do again.

"Are we going to be able to put you back together?" Bender asked, referencing the black tech garb that all Spartans wore beneath their Mjolnir and the ultra-dense plates spread out across the ground.

"Yeah. It won't be easy, but we'll manage. We have to."

"You think it worked? The message?" Bender asked, turning his face into the summery wind blowing in from the storm.

Kovan drew in a deep breath and released it, pondering the question. They'd sent it, had sacrificed so very much to do so, but the rest was up to chance. The message might travel straight through human-occupied space and out the other side, never having pinged a single relay grid or been picked up by a friendly colony or allied civilization. It all might have been for nothing.

But she had to believe that someone, somewhere, would receive it. And she just prayed they knew what to do with it. Without that, there was a good chance they'd never get off this ring alive.

"Whatever the case," Kovan said, massaging the tendons in her sore wrist, "we should focus on surviving, healing, getting our bearings."

"And then what?" Dimik asked.

One possibility she'd been thinking about for days stood out. "There's still another one of us out there from the boat crew, alive."

Both heads turned sharply in her direction. "Lucas."

Kovan nodded. There was only one place the Banished kept long-term prisoners. . . . "What do you say we liberate the Tower?"

A slow, slightly maniacal smile spread across Bender's face. "I knew there was a reason I liked you, Kovan."

"Yeah . . ." Dimik's eyes grew glassy and utterly resolute. "Yeah. We're in."

All in, like always.

CHAPTER 39

leven days had passed since the translocation pad tossed Horvath along with Gorian's dead body onto the exposed snow-swept side of a partially collapsed mountain facility, somewhere very far away from the beacon. As soon as he had extricated himself, Horvath stood over the Jiralhanae, thinking of ONI agent Kate Stalling, and then placed his boot on the body and shoved it off the edge and out into the thin mountain air. He'd watched the Brute drop through layers of puffy clouds before disappearing.

Good riddance, finally. If only it had happened sooner.

As Horvath straightened, the world had stretched and tipped, and he'd slumped back onto the ground to the sound of Elfie listing his injuries.

"Broken ribs, plasma burns to your back, left hand, and elbow . . ."

And then he'd fallen into unconsciousness.

Without his Mjolnir armor and physical augmentation, he would surely have died of exposure, lying half-comatose—mostly from exhaustion—for a day before he came to again. Since then it had taken him nearly a week to slowly navigate the broken, snowy peaks, and then a few more days to descend the edge of the mountainside. Finding the crash site was something of a surprise, a shuttle from *Infinity* by the looks of it, which had slammed into the slope, leaving no survivors. But there was a week's worth of water and rations, and weapons.

He'd slept for two hours in the shadow of the burnt fuselage, then ate one of the MREs simply labeled SANDWICH—a tasteless slab of meat between two thin pieces of bread but better than nothing—eyeing the expansive view from his lofty perch.

Below was a high-altitude plateau, cold, windswept, and barren. There'd be no cover there, but the bit of camouflage canopy he'd found in the wreckage would come in handy to keep wrapped around his shoulders, something to sink under should he need to.

There were times he started to feel claustrophobic, very brief thoughts of wanting to get out of his failing armor before things completely shut down and he became trapped.

Those dark thoughts seemed to evaporate as soon as they appeared, but it did leave him wondering and worried. The last thing he needed was to start getting inside his own head and giving those whispering, lingering ideations more attention.

He had to focus on the job at hand—rejoining the fight, finding his team, finding . . . hell, anyone. There *had* to be other survivors somewhere beyond this section of the ring, beyond the Banished outposts. If he made it across the barren plateau and up over the next mountain pass, he was sure there was something on the other side—he'd seen a few Banished aircraft far in the distance over the last few days going that way, enough to feel certain.

He tipped his head to the whitewashed sky, scratching the skin through his beard with the tip of his combat knife. As snow flurries fell and the cold wind whipped at his dark hair and flapped the canopy behind him, he wondered how far their desperate message had to soar, how many star systems separated them from humanity and the UNSC.

For a long moment he studied the view, scanning, planning his route . . . then drew in a deep breath and started his daily transmission on another time-cycling channel that he hoped would evade enemy notice.

"To any UNSC personnel in range . . . This is Spartan Tomas Horvath, Fireteam Intrepid. And I appear to be . . . alone." Once again. What else was new? "I am heading up-spin, beyond the reach of the Banished, to search for survivors. For my fireteam. I don't know what else to do. The silence on UNSC channels is not encouraging . . . but I will be listening. Watching. Surviving."

He liked to think that somewhere on Zeta Halo, Intrepid, Commander Palmer, Captain Lasky, and a massive number of Spartans and marines were currently grinding the Banished into the ground . . . that they knew about the existence of the Harbinger and that Escharum was close to finding the monitor of the ring. . . . *Infinity* had been full of crewmembers and held the largest division of Spartans on record, including Blue Team and the living legend himself, the Master Chief. If there was anyone who could turn the tide, it was Sierra-117.

Horvath opened his channel again, on the smallest chance it might be heard. "Chief, if you can hear this . . ." he said. "We need you. Now more than ever."

With that, he rose, stowed his supplies into the salvaged rucksack, and tied the canopy over his shoulders. He leaned down, grabbed his helmet, and slid it over his head, pausing to gaze at the landscape spread out below him, his own plea echoing in his head and tightening his chest.

We need you. Now more than ever.

ACKNOWLEDGMENTS

Many thanks to the following: 343 Industries and the RUBICON team: Jeremy Patenaude, Tiffany O'Brien, Jeff Easterling, and Alex Wakeford—always a pleasure working through the manuscript's evolution, and chatting about all things *Halo* and beyond; the art department and Will Cameron for another magnificent cover; my family for always having my back and doing what's needed so I can focus on work; the fans and readers—much love for the readership and support; and finally the entire team at Simon & Schuster, copy-editor Joal Hetherington, and my stellar editor, Ed Schlesinger, who helps move mountains, sticks with me through some very questionable drafts, and always makes me a better writer.

ABOUT THE AUTHOR

KELLY GAY is the critically acclaimed author of the Charlie Madigan urban fantasy series. She is a multipublished author with works translated into several different languages. She is a two-time RITA nominee, an ARRA nominee, a Goodreads Choice Award finalist, and a SIBA Book Prize Long List finalist. Kelly is also the recipient of a North Carolina Arts Council fellowship grant in literature. Within the *Halo* universe, she has authored the widely lauded novels *Halo: Point of Light* and *Halo: Renegades*, the novella *Halo: Smoke and Shadow*, and the short story "Into the Fire," featured in *Halo: Fractures*. She can be found online at kellygay.com.

2 IN 1

HALO
INFINITE

MEGACONSTRUX.COM

*Instructions included for main model only. Other build(s) can be found at **megaconstrux.com**. Most models can be built one at a time.

 XBOX

343
INDUSTRIES

HAL⊘
GEAR SHOP

GEAR.XBOX.COM/HALO

For more fantastic fiction, author events,
exclusive excerpts, competitions, limited editions and more

VISIT OUR WEBSITE
titanbooks.com

LIKE US ON FACEBOOK
facebook.com/titanbooks

FOLLOW US ON TWITTER AND INSTAGRAM
@TitanBooks

EMAIL US
readerfeedback@titanemail.com